Masquerade

Mallory Kane
Kate McKeever
JK Ensley
Leanne Tyler
Donna Wright
Felita Daniels

CONTENTS

Lexie's

Journey

Lyn Sie,
Love you bunches!
Enjoy Lexie's journey.
Kate McKeever

Kate McKeever

Lexie frowned and shut the door of the old manor house she'd been hired to rehab, and spoke into her cell phone. "I'm sure I can design the house to keep its integrity and still meet your needs, Mrs. Marshall."

Her client interrupted, outlining the changes she wanted made to the hundred plus year old manor house, complete with stainless steel appliances, fixtures and skylights galore. Lexie sighed. When the project concluded she'd have a house with an 1850's shell and twenty-first century interior. The opportunity for advancement in her job in restoration design, in addition to the opportunity to visit Ireland on her employer's tab, had seemed perfect. "So much for that," she muttered and turned to walk off some of her frustration.

Why didn't the client value the history permeating the property?

Her sturdy boots sank into the mud and moist peat as she veered into the wooded area surrounding the house. Her mood lightened and she entered the moss lined trees.

Soon the green enveloped her and she drew in a quick breath. All around grew trees, along with low bushes and the odd mushroom. Moss covered fallen trees and ivy crept up trunks of ancient growth, adding to the many hues of verdant green.

If only she could have seen what the trees looked like in another time. A time when the old manor house would have been treasured for the beautiful house it was. How had it looked without a hundred and fifty years of wear? And could she complete the job of tearing out the very soul of the house and replacing it with pale and sterile technology?

Lexie turned to look as a small flash caught her attention, expecting a rabbit or squirrel. Instead she spied a smallish man darting around a tree. Not a fairy or wood nymph. Where the fairies of her imagination were willowy and wore filmy dresses or tan hide pants, this little man wore a suit of green, blending in with the flora. Or at least until you glanced at his head, full of reddish gold hair and a bushy beard. A dwarf? No, she idled, a leprechaun. "Where is your pot of gold, my man?" she murmured.

"Ye'll never find it, English.ye never will." He snickered and trotted off.

How had he heard her? Shaking her head at her folly, she hurried after him, breaking into a trot. She dodged the swollen tree roots and bushes around her, making her way into the darkening wood. Determined to turn around and head back to the gravel road and her rental car, she stumbled and fell, landing on something soft and pliable, and also extremely rank.

"Let me go! Let me go and ye'll be granted three wishes." The bundle cried.

Lexie stood and helped the small red bearded man to stand. "Sorry. I didn't mean to fall over you. Are you all right?"

"Aye." He glared at her. "Yer wishes. Let me have 'em."

"Wishes?"

"Aye. I'll not give up me pot of gold. Ye have to use the wishes." He grumbled, straightened his olive green tunic then stamped his leather clad feet. "I'll have them now."

This was fun. "Ok, I want the lady who wants to change the house I'm working on to be happy with my design."

He nodded and squinched his eyes shut for a moment.

"Done," he muttered. "Next."

Lexie's phone burped a text, and she started to pull it from her pocket then hesitated at the little man's frown.

Her thoughts on the faded furnishings in the manor house, she murmured, "I wish I could see the house when it was first built."

He grinned, showing his pointed teeth, which appeared to be that of a predator rather than a human. Narrowing her eyes, she leaned forward to examine him more closely, only to find his image blurring. Lexie tried to straighten, but found herself falling faster. She felt her head strike something sharp, and then she knew no more.

"Lass? Are you all right?"

Lexie heard the lilt in the man's voice and smiled inwardly. Irish men, yum. She'd wake up in a few minutes, after her headache eased. She started to roll over in bed then realized her mattress felt hard. And rocky. She grimaced as she came awake, lurched into a sitting position, and moaned at the sharp pain ramming through her temple. What had she been doing the night before? And how was she in the middle of the woods? Not good.

Finally, she focused her vision, and seeing the man crouched down before her, leaned backwards and almost fell over.

He splayed his hands out in front of him. "I'll not harm ye, lass. I just wanted to see if your cut looked bad."

She eyed him warily for a moment then looked around the woods. She'd been chasing, no, talking to a little man earlier. Where had he disappeared to?

"Are you lost?" This definitely wasn't the little, red-haired man she'd been talking to. This man looked the epitome of an Irish hunk. Dark brown hair drooped over his forehead under a slouch cap, and he wore a tweedy looking jacket and pants with a collarless shirt.

"No, I don't think so. Maybe."

"You have a bad gash on your temple, lass. Here." He handed her a cotton cloth, clean, but not a pristine white.

She eyed it a second before pressing it to her temple. Another sharp pain shot through her head, and she closed her eyes against the nausea welling up in her stomach.

When Lexie opened her eyes, she noticed several things looked out of place. Even the air smelled different. Fresher.

"Are you ill?" The man's voice sounded calm and lilting, almost as if he were trying to calm a nervous animal.

She glanced up at him around the cotton she still held to her temple.

"Other than a headache, I think I'm fine. I need to go to the bed and breakfast and change. Could you point me in the right direction?" She smiled hopefully.

"Bed and breakfast?" His brows furrowed in a perplexed frown.

"The Entwhistle B&B." She saw the continued confusion and tried to clarify. "The bed and breakfast? It's in Thornton, near the manor house." She waved a hand in what she hoped was the general direction. Where was the lane to the house?

"You're staying with the vicar?" He pressed.

Lexie started to stand. "No, the—" Whoa. Everything spun in circles, and Lexie automatically reached out to steady herself. He enveloped her hand in his own larger, warmer one. She closed her eyes again and tried to quell the urge to throw up. After a couple of minutes, she opened her eyes and tried to stand again, this time successfully. "I'm staying in a house owned by the Entwhistles, of Thornton. It's near the manor house."

"I know of Mr. Thornton, the vicar of the village yon." The man gestured down the small road they stood beside. One she hadn't seen in her run after the little guy. Hey, the little guy! Maybe he could help clear things up.

"Thank you for helping me. Where is the little man?" She glanced around.

"'Little man?"

"He's about this tall." She held her hand at just above her waist. "And has red hair and a red beard. A little man with a red beard." A giggled escaped. She wouldn't be describing this anywhere but in the British Isles.

"You must mean Finnegan. I saw him walking down the road just before I found you. Did he do this?" he gestured at her head.

'No, but I was talking with him earlier." Her hand went to her bare throat and she gasped. "Where did he go? Does he live around here?" She glanced around, wobbled on her feet, and would have fallen had he not caught her arm and steadied her.

"You need to rest a bit, Lass." He glanced around him. "Allow me to walk with you to the castle. You can sit for awhile."

Lexie eyed him and the woods around her. "Castle?"

"It's beyond those trees." He explained with a nod in the opposite direction. "I'm heading that way myself."

"You live there?" She breathed in and started walking, concentrating on managing the slight rise of the hill. The man trod slowly beside her, and she noted his attention seemed divided between her and their surroundings, as if scanning for something, or someone. The mysterious Finnegan, perhaps?

"No, I'm going to repair the house lift, which Finn is responsible for, as well."

She sighed, "I didn't know the castle even inhabited anymore."

"The Kilmartins have lived in the castle for as long as I can remember and before, according to the local folklore. Mr. Kilmartin's father, grandfather and beyond have passed the land down for generations. And cared for the folk around and about."

"You're an engineer?" She concentrated on putting one foot in front of another. The air around her seemed to sparkle and was a little fuzzy around the edges. Or, was it her headache causing the glitter in the air?

"No, just a tinkerer." He breathed a sigh as they stepped up onto the gravel road. A bulging canvas pack lay at the edge of the lane. He shouldered it and stopped mid-motion. "You all right, lass?"

"Tinkerer? That's an odd term. No one uses it anymore, you know?" She gazed at the lane, with the horses and odd carriages that puffed steam as they trundled along. Huh, she noted and wavered on her feet. Did a head injury cause hallucinations?

Eying her, the man waved down one of the horse drawn carts. After a token hesitation, she complied and allowed his assistance to climb into a cart laden with fragrant, but scratchy, hay. He nodded to the cart driver and began to walk beside. "Ye'll be able to rest once you're at the castle, lass."

"Thanks, and you can call me Lexie."

He smiled, and ignoring the arch look the farmer sent him, responded. "I'm Derick, Derick Coyle."

As they neared the castle, Derick remarked on Lexie's pallor. "You're still pale, lass. You'll need to rest a bit before returning to the vicar's place."

Lexie started to correct him but gave up. How many times had she tried to explain where she was staying? Was he a bit dim? Or maybe it was her. That was it. She'd not recovered consciousness back there. She was still sleeping and having a wild dream. Dream on, girl. It wasn't awful, but she'd rather not feel like she'd been hit by a truck while dreaming.

When the farmer pulled around to the rear of the castle, Derick helped her from the cart then ushered her into a door.

A woman dressed in an ankle length black dress stood inside a plain hallway. "What's this, Mr. Coyle?"

"She fell and struck her head. I found her near the road leading here." Derick frowned at the woman. "I started to take her around front, but she looked like she needed immediate attention."

Mrs. O'Brien studied Lexie a moment before indicating a room to the right. "Take her into the kitchen. Mrs. Wolcott will see to her."

Mrs. Wolcott, apparently the cook or chef, looked at Lexie and asked her a few questions. The woman huffed as if she wasn't satisfied with either the answers or Lexie's looks. "She's only addled from the fall, Mr. Coyle. And look at her clothes! She's out of her wits. I'll see to her. Go about your business."

He stepped back, clearly relieved to be rid of her. Lexie tolerated the cold rag the woman used to attend her cut, wishing he'd stay on.

He and the little red-haired man were her only connections to sanity. He left the room with another woman, this one in a plain brown dress with a voluminous apron tied around her waist. After several minutes, Lexie managed to assure the cook she was fine, if not suffering a bit from a headache. Mrs. Wolcott nodded sagely and ordered her a strong cup of tea with sugar. "That'll help set you to rights, my girl. Then we'll see about returning you to the vicar."

"But I don't...." Lexie gave up. What was it with them trying to foist her off on a minister?

Derick returned to the kitchen, took the seat opposite, and soon they both had a cup of tea and a plate of scones and cookies thrust in front of them. "I'm trying a new recipe. You might as well taste them and tell me what you think."

Lexie smiled at Derick and bit into a tart with currants and something that tasted like a tangy jelly inside. "Yum. It's wonderful. What is it?"

"Have ye not tasted quince jelly before?" The cook looked at her with a suspicious eye.

"No, but it's very good." Lexie answered and took another bite.

"Cook is the best baker in ten miles." Derick praised the woman and bit into another treat.

"Well, lass. Are you feeling up to traveling back to the vicar's?" The cook noticed the empty tea cup and obviously wanted Lexie out of her hair. Lexie nodded but clarified. "I'm not staying at the vicar's house. I'm staying at the Entwhistle's."

Cook eyed her and then cast a sad look at Derick. "She doesn't know where she's from—"

"I do know, but it's not from around here, apparently." She rubbed her forehead. Okay, start at the manor house and work from there. She cast a desperate glance toward Derick. "Isn't there a house beyond the woods?"

He shook his head, "Only the village beyond. Perhaps that is what you're speaking of."

She shook her head, "No. It's a three story house, old but stately. Beautiful. It has some orangey-red vine blooming all over." Her voice broke. "It's there, I promise." She gestured toward the woods and beyond.

"The sea and cliffs are that direction, no houses or 'bed and breakfast,' as you call it." Derick looked pained to tell her.

Lexie sighed then rubbed her forehead. "I can show you, if you'll take me there."

Derick glanced at cook, then again at Lexie. "You don't look in any shape to be traveling over three miles in a cart, lass."

"Right you are, Mr. Coyle." The cook focused on Lexie. "Let's find you a place to stay tonight, lass and tomorrow you can return to wherever it is you're staying. Were you traveling here for the festivities, by chance?" The cook looked hopeful, as if she were solving a puzzle.

"Festivities? No. I was here on a job assignment." Lexie stared at the empty plate before her.

"Work? So you came to work here?" Cook pressed.

"Not here, but at the manor house." Her headache, which had been receding, flared to life again and Lexie winced. Cook, seeing her pain, reassured her.

"You rest easy, lass. We'll clear this up. In the meantime, we'll take care of your head and find a bed for you." She turned her attention to Derick, "Didn't the master call for you, Tinkerer?"

"That he did. I'll be on my way. Miss Lexie." Derick nodded his head toward Lexie and spun on his heel to exit the room, his backpack bouncing slightly on his back.

Lexie watched as the only connection to what she hoped was her sanity strode from the room and sighed. So much for counting on anyone but her own devices. She wasn't a damsel in distress, no matter how the surroundings influenced her. She winced as the older woman patted her head again with a cloth soaked in strong vinegar. "Thanks, I think I'm okay."

Cook frowned and then laid the cloth on the table. "You're a friend of the tinkerer?"

"No, we just met." She started to explain but quickly gave up. Whether this was a historic park chock full of role players or a figment of her imagination, it seemed clear she didn't belong. "He helped me when I fell."

"Well, you'll be good to steer clear of him, I say. He's a good lad, but full of ideas. A moving staircase, indeed. It's always breaking down, so what's the use of it all," Cook grumbled and turned to toss the cloth into a basket sitting against a wall. "Well, if you're better, we'll get you situated. I can call a boy to collect your luggage."

"My luggage? I don't have any." Lexie stood, steadying herself with a hand on the rough work table. A glance around the room confirmed her idea. "I didn't have any reservations but I'd love to take a look around the park."

"Well, if you've not been invited, I daresay Mrs. O'Brien should be notified." Cook looked over Lexie's shoulder and gestured toward a young girl dressed in plain cotton dress who scurried away. "We'll see to your missing bags directly."

The woman Derick had indicated as the housekeeper entered the kitchen, stared at Lexie for a moment, and then gestured for Lexie to follow her. "I'll find a room for you lass, if you don't mind a plain one for now. A guest room will be prepared for you as soon as possible,"

Lexie followed her to a staircase at the end of the hallway. The housekeeper started climbing, saying over her shoulder, "Mr. Coyle, I trust you'll have the stairs repaired in time for the guests' arrival?"

Lexie leaned over the edge of the stairs and spied Derick, shoulder deep in the edge of the staircase. "I will, Mrs. O'Brien. Assuming Finn doesn't find more honey to pour in the works."

"We'll keep a weather eye for him, sir." Mrs. O'Brien continued to climb, her next sentence floating back to Lexie. "He's a menace, that man."

"Derick?" Lexie frowned at the housekeeper, a bit irritated. He'd done nothing but help her.

"The leprechaun." Mrs. O'Brien returned and stopped at a landing for Lexie to catch up to her. "He doesn't like the tinkerer and his gadgets."

"So he mucks them up?"

"Exactly. I only wish he'd wait until after the masquerade ball. Having a moving staircase would be very convenient for us all." They ascended another floor and then stepped out into a large, tastefully decorated hall. Lexie followed the older woman down the corridor to a door and inside a large bedroom with a sitting area at the end of the room. A bed, reminiscent of a sleigh bed with curlicues and made of a dark wood rested in the center of the room with small tables and lamps on each side of it. The room, with its heavy draperies on the windows and portraits on either side of a blazing fireplace, should look overpowering but the white walls and vastness of the room kept it from being frumpy. If this was one of the plainer rooms, what did a suite look like? And how much would one night in this place cost her?

Mrs. O'Brien glanced around the room, examining the orderliness of it all and then turned to Lexie. "Will this suffice, miss?"

Lexie swallowed, "Yes, but you heard that I'm not attending the ball, right?"

"Yes. We'll figure out everything tomorrow. But for now, you're to stay here. I'll have a change of clothing brought up for you, as you haven't your own to change into." That was said with a slight grimace at the state of Lexie's outfit, then, "As well as a tray for the evening. Do you require anything else?"

"No, thank you." She just wanted to sleep now, Lexie thought. Tomorrow, when she woke, she'd be in her own rented bed in the B and B and could fly home as soon as possible. She'd even turn down the manor house assignment. Ireland clearly sent her imagination too far into fantasy.

Lexie woke several days later to the sound of a light knock on her door. She sat up in the bed and shoved her hair out of her eyes. "Come in."

A small girl slipped into the room from the door. "Sorry, Miss. I meant to have this to you earlier." The girl carried a steaming pitcher in towel wrapped hands and had a couple other towels draped over her arms.

She watched as the girl poured hot water into a basin sitting at the edge of the room, near a paneled divider. "Thanks, Jennie."

With a small curtsey, Jennie scurried from the room. Lexie grimaced as her bare feet hit the wooden floor but cast a grateful look toward the fireplace, where a healthy flame rose. She'd slept through stoking the fire that morning.

Lexie quickly used the convenience behind the divider then washed, quickly stripping and then donning the bloomers and cotton shift laid out for her. She'd learned not to dally, as the maid assigned to her tended to rush in without waiting for a response to her knock. Sure enough, Flora hustled in, ready to torture Lexie into her new wardrobe.

Ten minutes later, Lexie found herself bound up in the corset, followed by a hoop thing she'd never be able to get out of and, finally a skirt and blouse. Short thick hose were cinched with garters above her knees and stiff short boots with square toes pinched her feet. Her hair was pulled into a small bun at the back of her neck, neat and tucked. All in all, she looked like a proper Victorian lady. "Thank you Flora."

"You're very welcome, miss. Mrs. Kilmartin said for me to tell you she'll be waiting in her saloon, miss, when you've dressed and eaten."

Lexie nodded and hurried out of the room to the small breakfast room. Her hostess for the last few, rather unsettling, days hadn't asked for explanations, only offered her and her husband's hospitality. Lexie nibbled on a scone and waved away an offer of porridge. How had she ended up like this? Her numerous walks around the castle grounds and beyond had yielded nothing more than blisters from her odd shoes, freckles the maid seemed to think were worse than chicken pox, and frustration.

She knew she wasn't mad, she remembered her life, Darn it. She remembered falling and hitting her head, remembered the little red haired man she'd followed in the woods. Remembered the stately but worn mansion she'd been hired to refurbish. So where were all of those things? And how had she ended up in Victorian Ireland, complete with steam powered coaches, a couple who were unearthly handsome, and no way in sight to return to her time?

She shook off her melancholy and went to meet Mrs. Kilmartin. She knocked lightly on the saloon door and, at the soft entreaty, opened the door.

Mrs. Elsbeth Kilmartin sat gracefully on a long brocade bench. She patted the seat beside her and Lexie joined her, taking care not to upset her hoops and expose her ankles, or more.

"Have you been on your daily walk, my dear?" Mrs. Kilmartin smiled and patted Lexie's hand.

"Not yet. I've covered all of the area around my fall, as well as the space where the village lies."

"And no evidence of the portal?" Mrs. Kilmartin stood and stepped to the fireplace, where she retrieved a small box from the mantle.

"No, nor the house I stayed in." Lexie eyed the slim red haired woman who'd taken her in without a qualm. "What is the portal, exactly? I know you've told me that's how I arrived; that Finn must have opened a time link. But how? Why? And more importantly, how am I to return?"

Elsbeth Kilmartin sat opposite Lexie in an upholstered chair, her back ramrod straight. Lexie knew from hard lessons it was the corset with the great posture, not necessarily her hostess. "As to what, you have explained it well. It's a link from your time to ours. As to why, I suspect you said something or did something that made Finn want to impose a prank on you. He has a rather malicious nature, I'm afraid."

"And how do I return to my own time?" Lexie hoped her impatience didn't show but was afraid it ran through her sentence. Living in 1854 was a strain, but not as much as she supposed it could be. Surprisingly, she'd enjoyed most of the changes, including spending time with the house's inhabitants, both above and below stairs. Not to mention the tinkerer, Derick. As always, Mrs. Kilmartin didn't have an answer for her, only a vague shrug and smile.

She took her daily walk, again trying to find either the portal, which she hoped would shimmer or something to alert her, or the little man Finnegan. Elsbeth described him as a leprechaun but Lexie wouldn't admit that such existed. After all, she was stretching every imaginative bone in her body to admit she was in 1854 rather than 2017. If she had to admit magical creatures existed, she might tip over the edge.

She'd just entered the exterior walls of the castle when Derick Coyle approached her.

"Miss Franks, how do you fare this fine morning?"

"I'm fine, Mr. Coyle. And you?"

His smile dimmed a bit and he gestured toward the house, "Finn has struck again, I'm afraid. I'm off to repair the lifting box, elevator, as you called it."

"Finn? Is he here?" Lexie wanted to get her hands on the little monster long enough to find out how he'd planted her here.

Derick shook his head, "I haven't seen him, but apparently he's found the salt supply and poured it into the elevator cogs. I'll have to clean them completely before it can be made moveable again." Derick fell into step alongside Lexie. They spent the next few minutes talking about the improvements he'd been able to make to the castle, including the moveable staircase in the servants' hall, the elevator and a musical machine he hoped would be ready for the ball the next day.

"I've asked Mr. Kilmartin to have it watched. If Finn mucks with it, it will never be ready."

"Why does he mess with your machines? They only make work easier." Lexie glanced at Derick, glad of the excuse to spend more time with him. Victorian values hindered flirting.

"I think he hates anything that interferes with magic. He doesn't like the steam conveyances Mr. Watt has invented but the grooms keep a close eye on Mr. Kilmartin's coaches. And will do so for the guests' as well, I'd say."

"So, you're his target?"

He nodded grimly then turned a slight smile toward her. "But I'll prevail. And if my music machine is successful, I may find more customers than just Mr. Kilmartin."

She returned his smile, "I'm sure you will. Is that your hope? To expand your tinkering business?"

"No, to become more. To become a master clocksmith." His eyes shone with excitement and he led her to a small bench at the opening of a hedge maze. Lexie sat and he stood before her, dropping his ever-present pack to the ground with a clank. She listened as he outlined other machines he wanted to build, fantastical clockwork robots she was pretty certain had never existed outside of television and print. Had she also been dropped into another realm? Minutes passed with no sounds besides the buzz of bees in the flowers bordering the maze, a faint snip of hedge trimmers and Derick's rich baritone.

A man exited the hedge with a canvas bag full of yew trimmings. Derick colored slightly and turned to Lexie. "My apologies, Miss Franks. I do get carried away with my work."

She laughed, "I don't mind, Der— Mr. Coyle. You see, I have some mechanical inclinations myself." She held her hand up at his widened eyes, "Not as advanced as you, merely an interest."

"You wouldn't want to look at the elevator with me, would you?"

"I would," she replied. And if Finn popped up to sabotage the thing, she'd be there to nab him.

They veered away from the main entrance as Derick mentioned he never entered that way when working. Lexie frowned at the weird dichotomy that existed in this time. He'd been to dinner the night before and had been met with courtesy by both the Kilmartins, had even drank brandy after dinner with Mr. Kilmartin while she stewed in the parlor alongside the missus. Now, just because he wore suspenders, no tie and carried a knapsack, he had to enter through the servants' entrance?

At the rear of the building she came to a halt and stared.

In the field behind the castle several men tugged on taut ropes leading into the sky. At the other end of the strands floated a large balloon, enmeshed in a net of knots and what looked like twine from her perspective but had to be wrist sized cords. Clambering over and amongst the netting were small boys and girls with balloons strapped on their backs.

"Ah, the guests have started arriving," Derick said as he stopped alongside her and peered at the balloon.

"Are those kids?"

"Aye. They're rigging boys, and girls, I suppose." He gestured toward the floating kids, "They fasten the top anchors to the balloon. The ground men secure the bottom anchors. It's more effective than securing from the basket."

Lexie stared, aghast at the size of the kids. None could be over ten years old. She held her breath at the sight of one boy who gave a whoop when he released the ropes and started dropping slowly toward the ground. Another kid grabbed him and gathered him in to a lower point of the balloon where he got to work, his laughter drifting down to her.

"I guess it's fun for them, huh?"

Derick nodded, "I wanted to be a rigging boy, but I was too old when the floaters started in force." He smiled at her, "I have to settle for riding in them on occasion."

She shifted her gaze down the length of the ropes and found a little man with red hair and beard with a knife in his hand. He was sawing at the rope just above an anchor pounded into the ground. A small boy had both hands wrapped around the tether worked to fasten his end of the anchor, oblivious to Finn. Clearly, the kid had problems controlling the rope and Lexie swallowed a yell as the leprechaun severed the rope, sending the little boy up into the air and away from the balloon, powered by a gust of wind. Screams and yells ensued, men running to grab the end of the rope and the boy, white and pale, grappling to hold on to the cord.

"Finn?" Lexie raced after the little man, followed closely by Derick. Just as her hand wrapped around his forearm, he whirled around to face her. "You'll not catch me again. And you'll not get your last wish if you can't catch me!" In a flash of red he twirled around as if to run away but stepped into nothingness, disappearing.

Lexie blinked at the now empty space Finn had occupied only an instant before. The clamor of the people running to catch the little boy at the end of the rope above her soon interrupted her shock and she joined in the chase. She breathed a sigh of relief when a burly man ran ahead, climbed on the roof of a shed, and plucked the boy from the rope. All around her, descriptions of Finn's demise drifted. Lexie couldn't blame any of the men. "How can one little man be so mean?"

"Because he hates anything that isn't magic," Derick said.

"Magic? You believe in magic?"

"Did you catch Finnegan? Here," Derick gestured. "Did you catch him?"

Lexie thought of the flash of red and then nothing as the little creep disappeared. "No."

"And I wager he didn't just run away," Derick waved at one of the workers, and then turned to walk toward the castle, Lexie beside him.

"No."

"Magic. Even if you don't want to believe it, sometimes there's no other explanation."

"So, he doesn't like you because you make things that don't rely on magic?"

"And things that may replace his magic." Derick shook his head. "As if I could make something disappear, or fly."

"Did you do that?" Lexie pointed at the floating balloon.

"Not the craft, but the smaller floaters the small ones wear. It helps to curtail injury if they have the balloons attached."

"Why allow children to do such dangerous work anyway?"

"No one lets them. Most of the small workers are orphans. If they don't work, they don't eat. So they find jobs no one else wants, or can, do. Taking care of the ropework on the balloon takes small hands and light bodies."

"And you helped by inventing the balloons they wear on their backs?"

He nodded. "Even if they fall, it slows the fall enough to lessen the damage, unless there's a gust of wind, like before. It's not a solution to the bigger problem, though."

Lexie's heart swelled. "But it is a solution for the time being."

He half smiled. "For the time being."

They approached the castle before Lexie asked him the question that had been bothering her since the night before. "Last night. Were you already invited to dinner?"

"Yes. The Kilmartins invite me on a fairly regular basis. I think Mr. Kilmartin is trying to make a gentleman of me."

"And how do you feel about it?"

He shrugged. "I'll never be more than a tinkerer in most folks' eyes."

"I didn't ask that. I asked how you felt about Mr. Kilmartins helping you."

His gaze turned toward the sea and the vastness beyond, as if trying to see his own future. "I want to be more than I am, but how can I when I can't even defeat a little man intent on destroying me?" Lexie followed him to the servant's hall.

"I want to check on the moving staircase first. Mr. Burke won't admit it, but he has problems with the stairs and with the ball coming up, he's overworking as usual. I don't want Finn to muck the thing up again." Derick opened the door and motioned her ahead of him. They found the stairs in working order, with servants cranking a huge handle then stepping on the bottom step to be slowly, but efficiently, taken up a level to the main dining hall. Lexie asked Derick if he was planning on installing the mechanism on more levels.

"If I can keep a certain little green rat out of the workings," he shot back.

"May I help?" She wanted to find Finn. It was the only reason she had the urge to be near Derick. The only reason, she told herself.

He eyed her dress, ivory with pale green flowers embroidered on the bodice. "I don't think you're dressed to assist."

She twisted her mouth into a grimace. She loved the dress and Elsbeth had been wonderful about supplying her with a temporary wardrobe. She held a finger up, "Wait right here."

A few minutes later she emerged with a white maid's apron covering her from bodice to hem. She smiled triumphantly at his shocked gaze. "Now, I can help."

He shook his head slightly and led the way up the moveable staircase.

They ascended to the dining hall level and made their way to the elevator. Derick soon had the cogs out and wiped off. Lexie watched as his hands flew in his own brand of magic.

Their next stop was the vast ballroom. They used a servant's entrance, a door when, once closed, blended into the pale tan wooden panels lining the wall of the vast room. Intricate gold molding framed the tan panels and the huge windows easily ten feet tall. The Rococo design should have been too much. Too many curlicues of gold, too much painted ceiling, too much majestic stairs. But this room, Lexie thought, seeing this room in all its overwhelming glory, made the weird time slip she'd suffered worth the trouble.

Her eyes and mind on the fantastic architecture, Lexie blocked Derick's entrance into the room. She apologized and moved out of the way.

"No worries, I had the same reaction the first time." Derick smiled and headed toward a dais and the metal contraption arrayed on it. He removed a large canvas sheet and spread it on the gleaming wooden floor in front of the dais. "Ready to get to work, Assistant Frank?"

"Ready. What exactly are we working on?" She enjoyed seeing this playful side of him.

Derick gestured toward the metal conglomeration. "We need to make sure the orchesthrall is synchronized."

"Orchesthrall?" She glanced around. There were no musicians and only a few things that resembled instruments. Upon closer inspection, she made out a violinish-looking instrument, a harp-like object, and what looked like a tubular upside-down octopus, as well as other items she'd never be able to name, all connected by wood and cogs. She walked around the contraption, trailing her hand over the curves of brass pipes and plucking a few strings along the way, and came to a halt near the only truly identifiable item, a harpsichord. "You're tuning it?"

"I'm synchronizing the mechanical instruments so they all play the same song in the same tempo and at the same time." He opened a small door at the rear of the harpsichord. Inside lay a metal tube pierced with tiny protrusions over the surface. Derick removed the tube and carefully placed it on the harpsichord's surface. He wedged the huge wrench inside the doorway and, instead of cranking it in a huge movement, barely twitched his hand. He peered inside and then inserted his hand and muttered under his breath.

Lexie watched as Derick twisted his body into a pretzel trying to reach something inside the small opening of the piano. She leaned close for a look and then tapped him on the shoulder. "Can I help?"

He glanced at her and then her hands. With a sharp gesture he had her move closer. "See that series of toggles?" he asked and pointed inside the opening.

Lexie bent over and looked into the dimly lit space. What she wouldn't give for a flashlight. She narrowed her eyes and counted eight tiny toggles. "Eight of them?" she said without looking away.

"Yes. Each toggle has four positions. The first toggle needs to be toggled down three levels." As she worked, Lexie tried not to curse when a slight shift of her hand resulted in the previous toggle being pushed out of place. It took a quarter of an hour to get the sequence right, and when she finished, Lexie realized her back had been in one position for the entire time. She smothered a groan at the stiffness and turned to Derick. "All done."

"Done with one instrument. We have twelve more to go." He grinned at her widened eyes. "No worries, not all of the mare so difficult to reach." He replaced the tube and walked toward the octopus.

"What was the tube?" Lexie asked as she followed him.

"Have ye never heard a music box?" He opened a compartment on the head of the octopus and removed a larger tube.

"Sure."

"But you've never seen the inside, have you?" He lay on his stomach and reached inside, his gaze on his hand.

"No."

"The tube is pierced with a stylus in a manner that the little metal spikes cause bands of metal to move. Hence the song."

"And the instruments will all play the same song?"

"The instruments will play the same song, and I've had a metalist musician make forty of the songs. All for the different instruments. He's truly a wonder."

"Did he make all this?" Starting to realize how truly intricate the setup had to be.

"No, I did." He didn't brag. In fact, he tilted his head critically and eyed the octopus instrument with a wry expression. "I'm not a musician, so I needed someone assist with it. But I think it will serve."

"You've not tried it yet?"

"Oh, aye, I've tried it. That's why we have to synchronize each instrument today. When we're finished, we'll give it a whirl, eh?" He flashed a grin at her and she found herself returning his smile.

They worked all morning on the task, stopping only when a kitchen maid bade them come to the downstairs dining hall and have a bit of lunch. After eating a hearty stew and bread Lexie and Derick returned to the ballroom and the rest of the instruments. As she worked alongside the tall, dark haired Irishman, Lexie realized his genius. He'd taken cogs, wheels, clockwork and other mechanical elements and paired them with the delicacy of string and petal. He'd even managed to make the band self-perpetuating, with one instrument's pressure, percussion or vibrations powering the next instrument. Over a dozen instruments, all powered by one person winding a large key and pushing a lever. What else had he invented, she wondered.

"Do you work at the castle full time?"

"No, I've only had the luck to work for the master and his lady this year." He leaned back from the last instrument, a stringed barrel, and sighed. "If only I can deep all of the mechanicals working…."

Lexie frowned, "If?"

"I've been a tinkerer all my life, just as my father before me. I've spent my life fixing others' possessions."

Lexie gestured at the self-perpetuating band. "This isn't someone else's, even if they own it."

"Oh, the master and his lady don't own the orchesthrall, not yet, anyway. I've a chance to show them the machine, along with the mechanical server and the automated lift. They've bought the lift outright, but the others are for display for now."

"And they'll work." Lexie asserted and he grinned.

"I think they will, assuming Finn stays away from them. If they work, I'll no longer be a simple tinkerer. I'll be a mechanical deviser."

She nodded and with a start, realized they were finished with their task. He stood and stared at her, still seated beside the barrel. "Well, want to try it?"

The large key, the bow the size of a dinner plate, lay at the back of the metal platform on which the instruments rested. Lexie looked at Derick, then the key. "May I turn it?"

"Give it a try," he directed.

She took hold of the key with both hands. One crank, two. On the third try she couldn't push it into a third rotation.

Derick took over and rotated it several more times and stood away from the key.

"Won't it go too fast?" Lexie asked as he reached for the lever to start the band instruments.

"No. I've added a drag to keep it from starting and exerting too much force then rapid descent." He pulled her away from the lever to a safe distance, "You never know." He gave her a mischievous wink.

A low thrum filled the air around her, and she straightened. The octopus hummed low and sent vibrations through her. Another note flowed from the violinish-looking instrument, and more instruments blended seamlessly in. Lexie stood in awe as she watched mechanical arms strum, and wooden finger-like levers plunked the harpsichord keys. She'd have to listen to music for hours to take in all of the movements of the orchestra, but she loved the graceful flow of music from the instruments.

While she listened, entranced, Derick prowled around the platform, inspecting his treasure. At the end of the song the band came to a halt and Lexie frowned, "I thought they were self-perpetuating."

"They are, but it takes a minute or two for the mechanism to switch the cylinders. This gives the dancers a chance to rest or seek refreshment."

The harpsichord began a trill of notes. Another song, another chance to watch the mechanical orchestra. That is, until Derick strode to a stop in front of her. "Will you do me the honor of this dance?"

"Wha—"

"Dance. You can dance, can't you?"

Lexie giggled, "Not the kind of dancing you do, probably. But, I do know how to waltz." Thank God for childhood dance lessons.

He held his hand out to her, and she stepped into his embrace. After a slight stumble, their steps began to smooth until they glided around the huge dance floor, covering no more than a fourth of the area. Lexie smiled up at Derick, aware of the flutters of attraction in her stomach.

"I didn't lie, you know, when I said I wasn't from here."

He didn't respond for a moment, then his eyes warmed and he nodded. "I know."

"You believed me when I said I lived in a bed and breakfast in town? And that there was a manor house in the field?" She shook her head, "I wouldn't believe me."

"I believe you are not from here." He spun her in a perfect circle and somehow, she was closer in his embrace. "I know you are separate from this place and that saddens me."

The jitters in her stomach threatened to rise into her throat and she smiled mistily at him. "Why?"

"Because it means you are not going to stay here, that you will leave before we can become better acquainted. That's why we're working together, after all."

She didn't respond because she couldn't. She so wanted to go home, to sleep a full night on a real mattress. To sit at her drafting table and computer and design a house.

They danced the song through and then stopped in the middle of the floor, staring at each other. Lexie wondered at the light in Derick's eye, a gleam that told her he was attracted to her as well. She opened her mouth to say something when a great crash reverberated through the room.

They sprang apart and turned to see Finn prancing about with a wrench almost as large as he. He approached the orchesthrall, and Derick muttered a curse and ran toward the leprechaun. Lexie tucked up her dress and sprinted around in another direction, hoping to head the little demon off when he changed directions. Sure enough, when Finn saw Derick gaining on him, he veered away from his goal of the octopus horn to the harpsichord and Lexie sprang in front of him. "Don't you dare, you little monster."

"Och, ye calling me names, lass. Not a way to soften me up for that third wish." Finn sneered.

Lexie bunched her hands into fists. "The only way to soften you up is with a rolling pin, you little creep. That little boy could have fallen to his death out there."

"But he didn't. His da took care of him, didn't he?"

"But you didn't know that when you cut the rope," She shot back and took a step toward him, heedless of the wrench. His ways weren't full-on attack. He snuck in to do his dirty work.

"Run away, Finn. Go find someone else to torment." Derick stepped toward Finn from the other direction and the little man's sneer faded to almost concern. "And give Lexie her third wish."

"Never," Finn barked. "I'll not see her tarnish me house. Never!"

And then he vanished in a flash of green and red, the wrench crashing to the floor.

Lexie huffed a sigh then turned to Derick. "What did that mean? He'd not have me tarnish his house? Does he think the castle is his house?"

"Can't be," Derick picked up the wrench and examined the floor for dents or scratches. "If he did, he'd want you away from it, wouldn't he? If he thinks you're a danger to it."

"So, it's another house? The manor house?" Lexie sat on the edge of the dais and thought. She'd first encountered the leprechaun in the woods as she walked, frustrated that she'd have to change the whole nature of the manor house for a client. Had he heard her conversation with Mrs. Marshall?

"I think I've figured it out." She muttered and faced Derick. "I have to find Finn and explain."

"Explain what?" Derick pressed.

Lexie ignored the question for the moment. "How well do the Kilmartins know Finn and his habits?"

Derick looked at her for a minute then nodded. "Let's go find Mrs. Kilmartin."

It took them almost an hour before they found Elsbeth Kilmartin in one of her gardens, this one an herb garden. She wore a light blue dress today and looked almost as otherworldly as her guests from the night before. She laid down her basket of herbs and shears upon seeing them, and they all sat on several benches resting in a sunlit alcove. Lexie and Derick filled her in on Finn's appearance and his accusation.

Elsbeth studied Lexie. "Would you? Tarnish the house, I mean?"

"If it's the manor house, and if I fulfilled my contract for the clients. But I'd almost decided not to take the job," Lexie protested when she saw the disappointment in both Elsbeth's and Derick's faces. "I felt it would change the nature of the house. And it would."

"So, he has a point." Derick's voice wasn't accusatory or scathing, but Lexie felt burned all the same.

"He has a point," she agreed then looked at Elsbeth. "What I need to do is explain to him that I won't take the job. And even if I don't take it, the Marshall's will find someone who will do it for them. They have that kind of money." She finished on a sigh.

"If you could talk to Finn what would you say?" Elsbeth pressed.

"I'd tell him I'll try to keep the house from being changed. That

I'll find a way to stop the renovation." How she'd do it Lexie didn't know, but if it got her home, she'd do it.

Elsbeth's gaze drove into her, as if trying to divine the truth. Endless moments later she nodded. "I cannot contact him, but I know someone who can. Keep working on the inventions, and I will work on my assignment."

Derick wanted to check all of his inventions, seeing as how Finn had been on the premises. Sure enough, a jar of honey was open and slowly leaking into the works of the moving staircase and they spent a couple hours cleaning and re-greasing the gears. Then they checked the moveable lift, which reminded Lexie of the pneumatic tube thingies her bank's drive through had. It even felt like being in an open tube when they tried the elevator, though, with its filigree metal structure, it resembled a bird cage more than a pneumatic tube. She felt the slight tug on her eardrums as the vacuum sent them up three floors and to the small workroom Derick had on premises. He showed her the elaborate locking mechanism that he hoped kept Finn out of his newer inventions. "It has so far, anyway," he said as they entered the messy, yet oddly organized room.

Lexie laughed at the small owl that greeted them. Made of clockwork and wire, its eyes small eyeglasses, it tilted its head and whooed at them in greeting. Derick flashed a boyish grin when she complimented him on the small creature. "I've had several versions of him. He's Hoot three, and my favorite."

"What did you do to one and two?" Lexie asked as she petted the metal head of the little bird, grinning as it lowered its faceted eyelids to half-mast.

"They're at my house, keep me company at home. And Three keeps me company and on my toes while I'm here." He nodded toward Three's feet, which perched on a large clock. Just as the clock struck, the owl hooted four times, and Lexie broke into a chuckle. "A who-who clock!"

Derick grinned and showed her his other inventions, most in parts all over the worktable. He had a steam tea kettle that could be hooked up to a large water tank for parties and larger occasions, a small round serving device that, once supplied with schematics of a room, could roam the room with a serving tray atop its flat surface, and lastly, a security alarm he was working on to attach to his inventions. "I'd not planned on using this, but with Finn and his shenanigans, I suppose it's necessary."

Lexie nodded, "What happens if you start distributing your inventions to other households?"

Derick shrugged. "There's only one Finn, but as you know, he can do a lot of damage."

"That he can," she said and studied a blueprint he'd drawn for something that resembled a giant fan inside a balloon. A dirigible? And would it fly? She thought about what he'd said earlier and the thought occurred to her. In Finn's mind, Derick was stealing his magic. When she shared this thought, Derick waved it away. "No, my contraptions are made of metal, not pulled from the air around us."

"But does Finn understand that? In our minds, everything is based on science. The science of steam, of metal working against metal or rubber. But for Finn, it must look like magic. Like the kids with the balloons on their backs. For him, you're stealing his magic." She felt a thrill of realization that, with that one piece of information, she might be able to help Derick.

Over the next couple of days, Lexie and Derick worked on maintaining his current inventions and, in their spare time, on his serving cart. He hoped to have it up and running, at least in the servant's hall, his training ground, by the huge masquerade ball the Kilmartins were hosting. As the day approached, the servants became either giddy with excitement or snarly with anxiety. Lexie fast learned to steer clear of Mrs. O'Brien as she stalked through the halls on her way to inspect yet another bedroom. On the other hand, if she skulked near the kitchen during the day, Lexie was sure to get a taste of something luscious Cook was prepping for the ball. Derick engineered a cooling box that didn't have to be replenished with ice by harnessing a nearby spring and pumping it through the ice house and then into the main kitchen, saving steps and days' of work for the kitchen staff. Lexie wasn't sure, but she thought if Finn attempted anything on that contrivance, he'd end up in a stew, for sure.

She managed to get on Cook's nice list as well when she fixed a steam cooker with a length of rubber from one of the delivery boy's bicycle tires. Cook made her a rice pudding in return, and Lexie had to ask Jennie to pull her corset in tighter the next day.

Each day they searched for Finn, and each day, he didn't show. Even when Derick displayed the now finished serving barrel, the leprechaun didn't show to pour vinegar in the works or unscrew the wheels from the assembly. And nothing else had been touched either. "What do you think is happening?" she asked Derick as they watched the little flat topped barrel whirl around the servant's dining hall as it delivered sausages to the table.

"Either the person Mrs. Kilmartin was going to contact Finn has scared him, or he's resting up for the ball." Derick sounded grumpy. "He'd have a much larger audience for his tricks that night."

Lexie winced. And Derick would lose any hope of expanding his business. She had to find Finn and talk to him on her own.

They left the servants with the serving barrel and headed upstairs. "Are you staying for dinner?" Lexie asked as they rode up the moving staircase. Derick shook his head.

"I'll not be back until the night of the ball, unless Finn jumps into action." He glanced at her as they stepped off the stairs at the landing leading to the main hallway. "Are you going to be in fancy dress?"

Lexie shook her head. "I'll be helping you, remember? With the orchestra and the displays."

He tilted his head and looked at her with a half-smile. "Pity. I'd like to see you in a party dress." He nodded at her and turned to descend the stairs at a run, not bothering to reverse the direction of the movement.

Lexie stood and stared after him, and wondered at the longing in his eyes. And why did she suddenly want to dress up like Cleopatra to impress him? She shook her head at her fancy and opened the servants' door to climb another flight of stairs, these festooned with wooden curlicues and graceful spindles, to her room.

Dinner on this night was busy. Apparently in her absence during the day, several couples had arrived to spend the night. Tomorrow, the ball would be all anyone would think of. Except her. She had to find Finn.

Finding Elsbeth alone in the parlor after dinner, she asked if her hostess had had any luck with her search for Finn. Elsbeth grimaced. "I haven't. I've contacted everyone I know to contact, but he's in the wind it seems. What did you say to him the last time you saw him?"

"Nothing. I told you everything that happened."

"Maybe he feels he exposed himself too much when he

mentioned the house," Elsbeth posed then smiled at Lexie. "Are you unhappy here, dear? I'd hoped you would find something to keep you here with us."

Lexie smiled back. "I do like it here, but do I belong? Wouldn't it be wrong to stay here?" Why was Elsbeth even asking the question, Lexie wondered. And when had the thought of leaving here resulted in a pang in her heart?

"Sometimes life presents opportunities that shouldn't happen. It did for Devlin and me when we were younger. We took the opportunities presented and have been satisfied with our choice." Elsbeth clasped Lexie's hand in both of hers. "Don't forgo a chance for happiness when it's presented, just because it isn't the happiness you expected." She squeezed Lexie's hand briefly before releasing it. A tall, thin woman approached them and the moment for confidences had passed.

Lexie excused herself as soon as manners permitted. She'd changed into her nightgown and released Jennie from her duties before she let her mind replay the conversation she'd had with Elsbeth. Did she want to stay here, in this time? Why? Oh, she knew why, or rather who tempted her to remain. She admired Derick more than any man she'd ever known, and they hadn't even been on a date. Hadn't kissed, yet she knew in her heart she didn't want to leave him. Didn't want to leave this time.

Still she needed to find Finn, to show him Derick wasn't stealing anything. If only she knew where the little weasel was hiding.

After a restless night filled with dreams of fairies, Lexie rose to unusual noises on the grounds. She glanced out her window and into the interior courtyard. Instead of the usual orderly movements of servants, moving from one part of the house to another, new faces and uniforms of various colors, obviously visitors' servants bustled about. Trunks, masts with flags? Huh? Something for the ball, perhaps. And in amongst the hubbub stood a little man with red hair and a red beard, laughing as he tripped a baggage carrier.

Lexie drew in a sharp breath and retreated from the window before Finn spied her. Just as she did, Jennie came into the room, neat and orderly in her plain frock and apron, carrying Lexie's bath water.

"Jennie, I have a favor to ask of you."

In five minutes, she sidled out the door dressed in Jennie's maid uniform. The skirt was a bit short, granted, but it fit otherwise. She tucked a loose strand of hair into the maid's cap ignoring the girl's pleas to 'Take care to avoid Mrs. O'Brien or she'll have my job.'

Lexie ran to the closest servant's door, slid through, and down the stairs and out of the door leading to the courtyard.

Finn pranced around, darting out of reach of everyone, and generally causing an uproar as overturned trunks and flattened hat boxes littered the courtyard. Lexie kept to the edges, sliding along the walls until she stood directly behind the little man. She leaned forward, grabbed his tunic, and whispered, "Gotcha!"

Finn squealed like a little girl when he realized she had a firm hold on his clothes. He glared at her. "I won't give ye me gold."

"I don't want your stinking gold, little man. I just want to talk to you."

"No one wants to talk to Finn Finnegan. Only want something of him." The leprechaun sneered and folded his arms. Lexie saw several men marching toward him, and she reached around the smelly little man, grasping him around the middle, and hauled him to her. "He's mine for a few minutes. You can have him later."

The foremost man raised his eyebrows. "I can wager he's not a good kisser, lass. Ye'd be wanting someone taller, I think."

Lexie grinned at him. "Undoubtedly. But I need to talk to him on important business. At least it'll give you a chance to clean up around here," she nodded toward the mess of now muddy clothing littering the ground.

The men reluctantly turned back to the job at hand, and Lexie lowered the grumbling Finn to the ground, making sure she had a firm grasp on the material of his shirt. "Now, we need to talk about Derick Coyle."

"What about him? And why aren't you asking to go home?"

"I'll get around to that. Derick isn't stealing your magic." She knelt down to be on the leprechaun's level. "He isn't. He's just manipulating metal enough that it looks like magic. Your magic is still much stronger."

"Of course it is," Finn mumbled, his brows covering his beady little eyes. But Lexie could still tell he doubted her.

"If I show you how things work, how Derick manipulates things, will you leave him alone?" She pressed.

Finn was silent for a minute then narrowed his eyes, "And what's in it for you?"

"Nothing. I've just had enough of cleaning the moving stairway every day." She wouldn't admit to the little man she wanted Derick to be happy. Anything that smacked of sentiment wouldn't go over well, she figured.

"And if I stop meddling with the tinkerer, what do I get in return?" Finn rubbed his hands together.

"I don't have any gold to give you," Lexie searched her mind, but she had nothing to bargain with in this time.

"If you forfeit your last wish, and do it aloud, the wish will turn to gold." Finn wheedled.

"Forfeit my last wish?" And not go home again.

"Aye."

"If I go home, I was going to--. Never mind. How long do I have to decide?"

"You were going to what? What?" Finn asked, his eyes gleaming darkly.

"It wasn't important." Lexie took a breath and repeated her question. "How long do I have to decide about the last wish?"

"Until tomorrow night, at the ball. I'll be the one dressed as a wee man." Finn laughed and twisted out of her hold then vanished.

Lexie walked the castle grounds that day and the next. She walked inside the vast castle, exploring the rooms and thinking. Then she walked the exterior grounds, bypassing the hedge maze and the party goers trying to find their way out. She nodded to guests arrayed in their finest day dresses and fawn pants and waistcoats. Where once she'd have stared and wondered at the folly of wearing multiple petticoats and corsets, now she barely noticed the tightness of her own clothing. Instead, she thought of Derick and tried to swallow past the knot in her throat at the thought of leaving him. But he hadn't given her any indication she should stay, other than an odd remark now and then. So, what should she do?

Her stroll took her the garden where she'd often encountered Elsbeth with Derick. Smells of rosemary and sage greeted her as she entered the small enclosure, and she found the benches in the sun and sank onto one. As she closed her eyes and lifted her face to the sun she heard footsteps. "You've escaped as well, I see," Elsbeth smiled and twirled a sprig of lavender before handing it to Lexie and sitting beside her.

"I've been walking," Lexie began then stopped at Elsbeth's chuckle.

"I've seen you. You've walked from Galway to here and back again over the last two days. What troubles you, my friend?"

Lexie told her of her conversation with Finn. Elsbeth didn't question her or try to convince her either way during the conversation. Instead, she looked out into the small garden and listened. Lexie fell silent after her spiel and waited. And waited. Finally, after what seemed an eternity, Elsbeth turned her gaze on Lexie. "I made a promise to someone many years ago that I would love him and stay with him, no matter how costly it would be. Though there have been difficulties along the way, I've never regretted that decision. You must make a decision as well, Lexie. But to make it, you need to talk to Derick. And remember, whatever decision you make will be final. Either you will sever your ties to the future, or to the man you know here and now. And no matter how much we talk about it, you can't make the decision here."

Lexie nodded, "I know." She sighed and stood with the lavender in her hand. "Do you know where he is?"

Elsbeth smiled in her serene way and pointed toward the house. "In the ballroom, tinkering with his mechanical orchestra." Lexie turned to leave but stopped and looked at Elsbeth when she called to her. "Do you know what lavender gives us?"

"No."

"Serenity. May your decision be met with serenity, my dear."

The benediction seeped into her, calming Lexie as she strode toward the ballroom and Derick. She twirled the lavender in her hand, eliciting its fragrance with each spin of her fingers. At the grand double door, she smoothed her dress, tucked the lavender into the comb in her hair, and opened the door.

Derick stood in front of the orchestra, his hands on his hips. Lexie walked toward him. "Problems?"

He spun and looked at her, surprise in his eyes. "I thought you'd be joining in the festivities."

"Nah, I'm not a party kind of girl." She came to a stop next to him and, her courage failing her, looked at the machine. "Is it ready to go?"

"It is. I've checked all of the mechanisms, ordered the tubes in the sequence of songs the Kilmartins want, even shined up everything. It's as ready as it can be."

"Good. It'll be a smash, I know it will." At his look of confusion, she explained, "A huge success."

"I hope so," Derick said then turned to her. "Did you want something?"

Lexie nodded and knotted her hands together. Where'd she put that lavender? It'd give her something to do. "I wanted to ask you a question."

Derick led her to the dais where he gestured for her to sit. She did and he lowered himself on the raised platform beside her. His intent gaze didn't help anything so she watched her hands instead. "I saw Finn earlier."

"You did?" He frowned, "Why are you still here, then?"

Great. That didn't sound as if he wanted her to stay, but she needed to know, so Lexie plowed ahead. "He gave me a choice. Of staying or going, I mean."

"And?" Derick leaned over his knees, his hands folded together but his face turned toward her.

"I told him I needed to think about it."

"I see."

"I need to know how you feel about it," Lexie choked out, astounded at her timidity. She'd faced down executives in her time, had thrown old boyfriends out of her apartment without a qualm. Yet, here she was, terrified of what this man would say.

"About you leaving here, never to be able to return?" He pressed.

She leapt to her feet, unable to remain still and began to pace. "Yes. Would you care either way?"

Derick stood slowly and put his hands in his pants pockets. He stared at her, then at the floor beneath them, silent and still. Lexie had made two circuits of the small circle she trod when his hand shot out to stop her.

"I'd care." He stepped closer, his feet brushed the hem of her dress, and he rested his forehead against hers. "I know it's selfish of me, but I'd care a great deal if you left me." He kissed her forehead and the tip of her nose. "And I'd care even more if you stayed." Then his lips closed over hers, warm and firm. Lexie leaned into the kiss, her hands still knotted together. Thrills of heat coursed through her veins, warming her from within.

Derick eased back and stared down at her, his hands covering her clasped ones. "Would you stay? Here, with me? I don't know what the future holds for me, but I want to share it, share everything with you."

She nodded, and her eyes filled with tears. "I'll stay. You may have to explain things, teach me things, but I'll stay."

He smiled. "I'll be happy to teach you anything you need to know, my love."

Jennie stared at Lexie, a wide smile on her gamine face. "You look a picture, Miss. Lovely."

Lexie smoothed her hand over the black wig with the elaborate head dress and grinned back at the maid. "Thanks. I hope this contraption stays on my head though."

The rearing snake coiled around the wig on her head but as the wig was only pinned on, Lexie had a vision of the snake, wig and all toppling off her head before Derick could even see her. "I was lucky Mrs. Kilmartin had the costume for me to borrow."

"Och, the Lady has a whole room of them, miss. Keeps them for occasions such as this." Jennie swept up some laundry and walked to the door before turning toward Lexie. "Will you be needing anything else, miss?"

"No, thanks Jennie. You've been wonderful." Lexie stared at her reflection one more time before turning to go downstairs to the ball. She'd given Derick hints that she'd be someone different tonight, but she still wanted to surprise him with the Cleopatra look.

She'd reached the bottom of the stairs and turned to go into the ballroom when she heard him. "Well, young lass. Have ye decided?"

Finn emerged from the shadows with a prancing strut. He'd cleaned up for the ball, after a fashion anyway. His unruly hair had been slicked down with what she hoped was water and he sported an emerald green tunic and leggings. He held a hat in his hand, the band of which glittered gold. Lexie took a breath to respond when she saw Derick out of the corner of her eye. He'd seen Finn and was hurrying toward them. Finn saw him as well and wheeling around, confronted Derick. "Well, well, it's the tinkerer. Did she tell ye? That she's thinking of forfeiting her last wish?"

Derick came to stand next to Lexie. He didn't touch her but she could feel his heat through the costume. "She did. Is that why you're here?"

"You mean am I here to muck up your machines?" Finn sneered. "Nay, I'm here to complete a business transaction."

"Business?" Derick looked from Finn to Lexie.

"He'll get gold if I forfeit the wish," she explained.

"And ye'll get me off your back," added Finn.

"Off my back?" Derick studied the leprechaun then turned his attention back to Lexie. "What does he mean, Lexie?"

"Nothing," Lexie said and extended her hand to Finn.

Derick blocked the two hands before they could link. "What business?"

"If she forfeits the wish, I do get me gold. And you and your machines will be left to do your machines in peace. At least in peace from me. Machines such as that will never succeed." Finn finished in disgust.

"You made a bargain for me?" Derick asked Lexie.

"No, I just explained about his magic and your machines. The difference in them." She saw the distrust in Derick's eyes. Why was he upset about this? "I only explained to him."

"And made a deal with him, even though you know how much I despise him." Derick shot back.

Lexie stared at him. She didn't know what to say, or how to defend herself. What had she done wrong?

Finn looked from one to the other and chortled. "Oh, it's nice when things come together. Young lass, you have until the end of the ball to find me and tell me your decision. If you don't then I'll disappear, you'll be here for good, and I won't have to keep my word about the machines. Hah!"

She didn't notice him disappear, but Lexie definitely noticed when Derick turned and walked away from her.

She made it to her room without crying. She even made it through removing the costume and putting on her own clothes. The tears burned her throat and the back of her eyes as she ventured downstairs, ignoring the stares she got from guests. Finally, she encountered Burke, whose frown did something nothing else had. It cut through her misery. "You can't enter the ballroom with those, Miss Frank." He pointed toward her khakis with an imperious finger.

"I have to find someone, Mr. Burke."

"That may be, but you cannot enter in such attire," he reiterated.

"What if I have something over it?" She said, eying a guest wearing a voluminous robe.

"Perhaps, if it appropriately conceals your current state of dress."

"Give me a minute." She swiveled around and went in search of Mrs. O'Brien. Minutes later, wearing a midnight-colored velvet cloak, hood down, she re-encountered Burke "Good enough?"

"As long as it remains in place." He said with a slight twinkle in his eyes.

Lexie almost felt like herself as she scanned the room looking for Elsbeth. She hoped she'd be able to avoid Derick, and since he'd be behind the orchesthrall, that should be simple enough. But she owed it to her friend to inform her of her decision before locating Finn.

Elsbeth was in a knot of people, ordinary and some who seemed not of this world. Costumed guests glided around the dance floor, but all Lexie registered were swirls of color. Her attention was on saying farewell to Elsbeth and finding Finn, in that order.

Elsbeth took one look toward Lexie and excused herself from the conversation. Taking Lexie's hand she pulled her to a relatively quiet corner. "What happened?"

"Derick found out about the deal I was making with Finn and exploded." Lexie swiped an errant tear from her cheek. She couldn't start crying now. If she did, she'd never stop.

"He got angry?" Elsbeth frowned.

Lexie nodded. "He hates Finn, mainly because Finn doesn't really care who he hurts when he does his pranks. I didn't realize how much Derick hated him though. Apparently, any deal, even one that benefits him, is too much contact with Finn."

Elsbeth's frown deepened. "That idiot. Let me talk to him."

Lexie shook her head. "No. I just want to go home right now. I need to find Finn." She leaned in and kissed Elsbeth on the cheek, just beside the mask the pretty woman sported. "Thank you for everything."

She fled before her tears began and made it to the other side of the room, ignoring Elsbeth's call. There were only a couple of people who noticed, and their attention was soon taken by the sound of the harpsichord beginning a new song. The song she'd danced with Derick to.

Lexie frantically glanced around the room. She had to find Finn and get out of here. Was it him in the knot of trees? No, someone held a red reticule. Lexie groaned. She'd never find him in this mass of people.

"Ye looking for me, lass?" He spoke from behind her, his voice calm and assured. Lexie turned to face Finn and nodded, too unsure of her voice to speak. He gestured for her to follow him, and they exited through one of the servant's doors on the edge of the dance floor. As she followed the little man, Lexie chanced a glance in a mirrored panel beside the door. Her face, blotchy and pale, looked stricken, like she'd lost everything. And maybe she had. But she could make sure the manor house kept its integrity. Somehow she'd insure that.

Finn turned to face her in the gloom of the hallway. Lexie took a deep breath and held out her hand. Finn grinned as he took her hand in his smaller one, dry and rough as if he spent his time counting rough coins. Lexie breathed in again and began, "I wish—"

"Stop!" the door swung open and Derick stepped through, followed by Elsbeth. Both were breathing hard, and Derick swept his hand down, breaking contact between Lexie and Finn.

"I need to talk to you, Finn." He said, stepping in front of Lexie.

"What about, tinkerer?" Finn sneered at Derick, and Lexie touched Derick's arm in automatic support.

"Did you make a deal with Lexie?"

"Or were you convinced by her?" Elsbeth interrupted. "Did she convince you that Derick is no threat to your magic?"

Finn eyed Elsbeth narrowly before answering. "What does it matter? The girl was going to make a business deal with me."

"But would you have ceased interfering with Mr. Coyle's inventions, either way?" Elsbeth pressed, and Lexie caught her breath.

The leprechaun eyed her hostess with a glitter of anger in his eyes, and Lexie saw the truth. "You were quitting either way, weren't you? Whether I forfeited my wish or not?"

"If he doesn't weaken my magic, what does it matter? The machines are too easy. There's little fun in them, they don't' bleat complaints or bleed." Finn scoffed and Lexie's hand tightened on Derick's arm as she felt him tense toward the leprechaun.

"So, if she wishes to return home?" Derick ground out and Lexie's heart sank.

"She'll go."

"And if she chooses to stay? Forfeits her wish?"

"She stays." Finn bit out.

"And you get more gold for your pot," Lexie said, her mind whirling.

"Aye," Finn grinned, sure of himself again.

Lexie looked at Derick, then at Elsbeth, and remembered her friend's caution. This decision would make all the difference in her world and would be final.

She held her hand out to Finn again, but kept her other hand on Derick's sleeve. "I wish..." Lexie looked at Derick and finished her sentence, "To stay here."

Finn shouted, "Tisn't fair! You made a deal."

"I made a deal with a cheat. You were never going to bother him anyway."

"And now I am!" Finn raged, "I'll muck up everything he makes from now on, you see. I'll do it." The little man raged and ranted, stomping his feet and shouting until a firm voice halted him.

"Finnegan, halt."

Finn shut up mid shout and raised wide eyes to the being who had joined them silently. "What are you doing here?"

"I was invited, Finn. Unlike yourself."

"But I don't need invitations, I'm a leprechaun."

"A leprechaun who has gone beyond the measure of his powers, I think. You will leave this man and this woman be for the remainder of their mortal lives. Do you understand me?"

Finn nodded, his eyes wide again, this time with what Lexie identified as fear. She turned to look at the being who held such sway over the leprechaun. The man, tall and craggy looking, appeared no more threatening than Devlin Kilmartin, yet there was a steady, ancient power even she could sense in him.

"Finn, you've outstayed your welcome here. Leave."

Finn disappeared in a poof of red and green and Lexie sighed, slumping into Derick's side in relief. He wrapped his arm around her and addressed the tall man dressed in brown and green. "My thanks, sir. I'll not ask for particulars as to your relationship with Finn, but my thanks."

"No need for thanks, Mr. Coyle. Keep up the good work, but remember. The earth is but one, do not desecrate it."

The tall man turned and, with a nod toward Lexie and Elsbeth, opened the door to the ballroom and disappeared.

"Who was that green man?" Lexie quipped then chuckled. "I have a feeling I'll be telling a lot of jokes no one gets."

Derick released her waist and took her hand in his. "I'm sorry I let my temper get the better of me. It almost cost me you, Lexie."

"Yes, it did. All because you wouldn't let me explain," she said, not quite ready to forgive him yet.

He smiled slightly, "What do I have to do for your forgiveness?"

Lexie eyed the ceiling a moment then smiled at him. "Play me the song we danced to again?"

He grinned, "Only if you agree to marry me."

She nodded and accepted the firm, warm kiss she'd been so ready to lose.

Lyn Su —
Much Love!

Liam's Secret

Donna Wright

Donna Wright

Liam McDonnell hurried down the busy street—his thoughts like an ocean taking him under the waves, spinning him mercilessly through an undercurrent of elation and fear. Claire. Her name alone moved him, effortlessly stirred his heart and caused a fever in his soul.

Just one more block to go and—A raspy voice behind him stopped him in his tracks.

"McDonnell, I see you there."

Liam slowly turned. He had never been a fan of leprechauns. He'd seen some of their handiwork. Not something he enjoyed. "Finnegan." He paused and narrowed his gaze. "What are you doing in town? Don't you normally stay in the country, counting your gold and finding malicious ways to destroy others' lives?"

The little man cocked his head to the side and studied Liam. "You will never forget that day, will you? Do you realize how long ago it has been? Why don't you just let it go? Or, perhaps…you enjoy the soothing relief of that bitter poison."

"What poison?"

"The poison you greedily harbor within your heart. You must know…holding a grudge is like ever imbibing a noxious tonic. Let it go, McDonnell. Quit drinking it." The small man paused a moment, then changed the subject. "As I am certain you are aware…The Kilmartin's Annual Masquerade Ball is almost here. Thus, my visit to town. I came to buy appropriate gifts for my host and hostess. We must always mind our manners, McDonnell—social responsibilities and all."

"They are not your host and hostess, Finn. One must receive an invitation to be considered a guest, and I know you did not. You're up to something. I can see it in your beady, little eyes."

"Is that so?" Finn smiled a sort of crooked little smile. "And might I ask what brings you to town? Hmm? A pretty gal, perhaps?"

Liam hesitated. "A bit of business. None of which is yours." He half smiled as he tipped his hat. "Good day, Finn."

Finn yelled after him, "Now, now there. Don't take things so hard, McDonnell. It's not like anyone died, you know."

Liam spun around. "Miss Gray had to be treated with my blood, Finnegan. Mine. When she found out about me, when she learned the truth…she never saw me again." He purposefully pointed his cane at the little man. "Never again interfere in my life, Finn, or you may regret it."

Liam continued down the street without waiting for the other man's answer. Today, he had an appointment with Claire's father. A formality really, but as Finn pointed out, social niceties needed to be observed.

Claire's father expected, no insisted, on those niceties. Mr. O'Connor still preferred old world traditions, and the man would want to know, to hear the words of how Liam would love Claire forever. No matter what it took, he would convince Mr. O'Connor of his utter devotion to Claire. Per custom, the man would hear him out, bluster a bit, and in the end, give them his blessing.

Liam smiled to himself. And after the gala on Friday night, he thought, I will give up my immortal life…for her. For the woman I want to grow old with.

For two centuries, Liam had waited for this perfect life. He dreamt about this life, longed for it.

Taking a deep breath, he lifted the brass knocker. Three quick, yet purposeful, knocks rang dully beyond the thick wooden door. He waited, his heart drumming louder than the summons he had just sent forth.

The footman quietly opened the door and ushered Liam into the library, and Liam glanced around at the massive amount of books the O'Connor's owned. Ancient tomes filled every shelf and littered one corner of the ornate coffee table. He admired people who bettered themselves through the written word. From the Bible to Shakespeare, all of the great literary works graced this enormous room. His gaze went to the flowered sofa, and he envisioned Claire at rest, reading her favorite sonnet.

A smile played across his lips at the thought of her in his library, reading his varied and large collection. He looked forward to all the precious little things their coming happiness would entail.

Quietly reading together. He slowly closed his eyes as his smile widened. *What a peaceful little heaven that would be.*

Claire's father ambled into the room, and Liam bowed to the man.

"Please, Mr. McDonnell." The man motioned with a slight wave of his hand. "Have a seat."

"If it's all the same, sir, I wish to stand. I have come here for an important reason."

The older gentleman sighed heavily. "Yes...I feared so."

"I'm sorry?" Liam narrowed his gaze slightly, no longer smiling. "I don't quite understand your meaning. Is something amiss?"

"It is you who must say the words."

"Very well, then." Liam squared his shoulders. "I've come to ask for Miss O'Connor's hand in marriage." He slowly released the breath he'd been holding. "But you know that, don't you?" A statement, not a question.

"Please, son, sit down."

They each took a seat opposite the large fire place, and although Liam noticed the portraits and various sculptures lining the carved mantel, he paid them little attention. His mind and heart raced. Raced with dread. Raced with the bitter unknown.

"I hate to turn you down, Mr. McDonnell." Claire's father firmly held Liam's narrowing gaze. "You are a fine young man. Any other father would be pleased to have you as a son-in-law."

"But, not you."

"I do not refuse you because you are less than what I want for my daughter, no. I must refuse you because...there are certain situations, a set of *rules* for my family which I must abide. I appreciate your regard for her. I do. Alas, I must say no."

Liam stood. "And does Miss O'Connor feel the same way?"

"She will not go against her duty, sir. She will do as she knows she must."

"Then we have nothing left to say to each other."

"Yes, we do." He stood. "Mr. McDonnell, I am asking you as one gentleman to another, do not try to see her again."

Liam boiled inside. "I will leave that to Claire, Mr. O'Connor."

"My father is right, Mr. McDonnell."

Claire. Somehow, she'd walked into the room undetected and stood before him. Her chin quivered, and her striking blue eyes glistened with tears that contrasted the firm set of her shoulders.

"I fear he speaks the truth. I..." Her gaze fell to the floor, and after a moment she spoke again, her voice strained. "I cannot see you again."

Her father lowered his head and stepped aside and Claire continued. "I should never have imposed upon you as I have, Mr. McDonnell. I regret the grief my attention has caused you. I hope someday you will be able to forgive me."

Her words tore through his heart. He swallowed hard, and forced his voice not to crack. "Forgiveness? You play with my feelings as if they were a game of chance. You know I love you, and you deny me. Yet you speak of forgiveness?"

He waited for her to say the words he wanted to hear, to say that she couldn't live without him. That she needed him as he needed her. To tell her father how she loved him and only him and must break with the family tradition. But, it never came.

She simply stood there and stared at the floor.

"So, this is all you have to say? And you expect forgiveness? I will not now, nor ever, give you hope of ever finding it from me."

Liam raced from the room and burst out onto the street. His thundering heart had trouble keeping up with his racing mind. It echoed in his ears like the maddened wails of the hopeless damned. He had gone two full blocks before he slowed his pace and steadied his harried thoughts. He quickly glanced around and the fates no one seemed to notice his departure. In fact, there were very few on the street at the moment. He didn't break his stride as he stepped into the next alleyway, and vanished—leaving this pain-filled place for the very last time.

Claire climbed into the carriage with her lady's' maid and settled in for the few hours' journey to the Kilmartin's castle while her father stood on the steps of their home. A sad smile clouded his noble face, put there by her actions. He knew her heart and asked her to leave early because of Liam McDonnell. He didn't want them to see each other again for fear of her refusing family duty to run away with Liam.

The lap blanket didn't stop the shiver from crawling over her skin. She'd almost forgotten she could shiver, but the look on Liam's handsome face the moment he vowed he would never forgive her brought them on. She believed him. Believed every hurtful word that spewed from his trembling lips.

This was *her* fault, and she would do the right thing by him. Liam held her heart and she truly did only wish him happiness. She gently touched her red handkerchief to the corner of her eye. For that reason, she would leave him to a real life. Not the cold heartless one she offered.

The tears rolled down her cheeks as she thought and rethought every individual scene, every move that had led to this very moment. They had immediately formed an attachment. Their thoughts, their humor all that they believed, feared and appreciated were the same.

She lingered on the first time they met over six months ago. The day had been fine and the fall day stunning. Claire and Merry Rose put up their parasols and walked to the corner where the bakery's fragrance left them in need of one of their famously delicious iced cakes. Then, they had found a bench where they could enjoy their goodies.

Two handsome men stopped to speak, each tipping their hats.

"Miss Merry!" the blond spoke, "I see you could not waste this sunshine."

"Nor could my dear friend," Merry said through a smile.

The ladies stood and inclined their heads as the men bowed accordingly.

"Please Mr. Banwell…" Merry motioned to her companion. "Allow me to introduce Miss Claire O'Connor."

"Of the Alder House O'Connor's?" Mr. Banwell asked.

"Yes." Claire nodded and extended her hand.

"I met your father at my club. We spoke an entire evening of good Port and the best courses and gardens in Ireland. I must say, I enjoyed my evening well. It is very nice to meet you."

"And you as well, good sir," Claire answered.

"Please allow me, Miss Rose and Miss O'Connor, to introduce my friend who is just returned from France. Mr. Liam McDonnell."

Mr. McDonnell took her proffered hand and lightly kissed it. "Miss O'Connor."

It took only that single, chivalrous moment in time to enslave her to his dark good looks and azure blue eyes.

A sudden carriage jolt brought Claire's mind back to the present. She dabbed her handkerchief to her eyes once more and silently settled in for the rest of the ride.

Claire was surprised that Elsbeth Kilmartin herself greeted her on the steps of the castle.

The footman helped Claire from the carriage, and as she walked toward Elsbeth, the woman came toward the carriage. The women met partway, and Elsbeth took Claire in her arms. Claire's tears fell freely and Elsbeth held her.

"Let us go into the house and away from the prying eyes of the servants."

Inside, Claire and Elsbeth sat in the setting room beside the lady's chambers.

"You must tell me everything." The gentle sound of pouring tea caused Elsbeth to glance toward her maid who curtseyed and left them to talk.

Claire sniffed as she glanced towards the retreating woman. "I suppose by morning's end, they will all be gossiping about me."

"No, my maid is as silent as the grave."

"Elsbeth, you cannot ever understand what I have done. Liam…he is the most handsome and kind man. And, I have ruined him, knowing my—"

"Shush, child! I am more than convinced you would never purposefully hurt someone."

"Knowing my family obligation, I should never have allowed his affections to grow."

"You did know better, my dear. Alas, your heart did not. Tell me about this man."

"Liam McDonnell. He is the owner of Birmingham Place. It is a lovely home on the edge of town. He also has an estate not far from here. You may know him?"

"I do. He is a fine man." Her thoughtful expression puzzled Claire.

"Do you know why I am here this early?"

"Of course, my dear."

"Yes, I'm certain Father already sent you a glow-message." She paused and thought about how such a little thing like a glow-message with its magical light appearing in the shape of a scroll, would have enchanted her Liam. And she imagined the surprise and delight of his seeing the scroll open to look like a glittering written page, which when once read, floated away like dust moats in a ray of sunshine. But he was her Liam no longer, and without him, her world was now devoid of any sweet surprises or delights.

A little sigh escaped her lips. "What did Father say?"

With a gentle touch on Claire's arm, Elsbeth leaned forward. "That you were hurt and needed to be here with me."

"I should have—"

"Do not chide yourself. At one time or another, we all can say that we should have, or could have, done something differently. But, we didn't. The past cannot be altered, and we must go forward from the present. Even we can't go back, Claire. We can only move forward. And, for now circumstances dictate you assist me with the preparations for the ball."

Claire stared blankly out the large window—thankful for the brief respite Elsbeth had granted her, yet still anxious about the coming evening. Her mind played dangerously upon things it shouldn't. Things concerning Liam…her family…her secret. Yes, she was young. Yet, she knew bitterness and regret, especially regret, would make for a long and empty life.

The little corgi the Kilmartins owned took a seat on the window sill next to her.

"You want to sit with me?" Claire scratched the happy pup behind the ears. "We'll watch all the magical people arrive and settle in at the party. Then the mortals will also find a place, but such a thing will be much more boring to watch."

A slight twinkle in the waning light caused her to finally focus on the odd parade now approaching the Castle Amhrán Oiche. Her heartbreak did not keep Claire from wondering with awe at the elaborate arrival of many of the Kilmartin's honored guests as she gazed over the beautiful lawn and estate.

A tiny smile tugged at her full lips as she leaned forward and lightly pressed her hands against the beveled glass. "I've never seen a carriage quiet like that one before. Who could it be, Mucha?" She stroked the dog. "The Lord of the Night?" She nearly chuckled. "Such opulence and obvious wealth. The pampered occupants apparently have no qualms with showing their worth, do they?"

Mucha snorted, but offered no other answer as Claire continued to rub her back.

The gilded black carriage came to a gentle stop. The sculpted silver-work shone like a celestial beacon. Countless silver tassels ornamented the canopy atop the carriage, surrounded the scalloped bottom, and completely embellished the finely-suited driver's seat. They swayed and sparkled and played like flickering magic in the glorious rays of the setting sun.

"Obvious royalty," she mumbled. "Yet...apparently unafraid. Riding about in such grandiose luxury caught more than just a few envious eyes, to be sure. The creature inside is either extremely strong...or extremely vain and foolhardy. Highwaymen would pluck that gem in a heartbeat. If they could."

When the footman reached for the glimmering door handle, curiosity caused Claire to flip the latch and gently push open the large window.

She inhaled deeply. "Pine cones...flowering moss...and all things green." She smiled. "Elves—arrogant and haughty...and with every reason to be so."

Her refined sense of smell was her most treasured gift. It defined her memories—good and bad. Each and every core moment of her life was engulfed with a particular, emotion-producing scent. Cherry blossoms, from a childhood visit to the exotic East. The spiced tea her great aunt's sweater always reeked of. Chocolate-dipped marzipan...her very first kiss. Claire smiled.

When the Vale King stepped from the exquisitely adorned black carriage and reached back to help his wife exit as well, Claire's smile only grew.

"Called it...Elves. Nearly untouchable creatures. So pure. So divine." She thought of childhood holidays spent with her father's friend in the Summer Lands and the sweet spring nectar. "So delicious." She glanced down at the dog. "I wonder if the Pixies will fly in all at once as they did last year. The Queen the brightest of them all."

As if on cue, they appeared as a stream of fireflies dancing through the dusk sky and in through a small window on the second floor.

"The Pixie Queen appears to be wearing blue this year." Claire half frowned. "I rather enjoyed her green from last year…but that blue is amazing as well."

An approaching chariot raced down the dirt road and left a cloud of dust in its wake. When it got closer, she realized a huge lion, its fiery mane flowing in the wind, drew the magnificent, gold chariot.

"Oh my!" Claire held her breath. "Is it?" She gasped. "It is! The Egyptian Dragon Prince! But…Elsbeth didn't think they would be represented this year." She leaned even further out the window and gazed intently at the tall, darkly tanned gentleman. "Oh…my…" His handsome features pulled a deep breath from within her. "Perhaps, he could be the cure for what is ailing me."

A large, dog-shaped golden headdress and loin cloth were his only adornments, and black tattoos covered his glistening body. Claire had no idea what they meant, she only wondered how far under the cloth they led.

Shadows played over the grounds as airships pushed gently through the crowds. "Clever contraptions…but obnoxious and gauche." She sighed. "Time moves on, I suppose. Dirigibles are only the beginning, I fear. Humans envy wings to the point of madness."

Gray smoke belched from the large ballooned craft as it came to a soft rest in a nearby field, and Claire scrunched up her delicate nose. "Nasty things. Nasty smells." She gently closed the window. "Advancement in such things will bring epic death. Mark my words."

She held her red, silk handkerchief to her nose and inhaled the sweet scent of blood lilies, before tucking it safely back within her cuff. "There we go. Much better, now."

Claire spared another tiny moment of curiosity at the continuing parade outside the elegantly draped window, before turning toward the elaborate spiral staircase.

"Best join the gala," she whispered to Mucha, and each step help steady her nerves as she made her descent. "The ball awaits. Let us hope it's filled with magic."

Liam landed softly in the shadow of the Wishing Tree and vanished his wings. A longing to wrap a ribbon around one of its ancient branches washed over him, but without Claire's ribbon alongside his….

He looked toward the ballroom and changed his appearance to his more human form in order to blend in with the other guests. One of the advantages of being a Deliberate. A class of vampire turned more by magical means rather than by blood alone. He still needed blood to survive, usually from animals, but not as much as the bloodborn, and he had the same advantages as the bloodborn; charisma, the gift of flight, immortality. But until Claire, he'd never realized how lonely forever could be.

Deliberates possessed advantages the bloodborn did not, though. The ability to walk in sunlight and the gift of choice. With Claire by his side, he'd planned to give up the magic, become human again, and spend the rest of his life making her happy.

Now? Perhaps he'd leave Ireland altogether and travel to Nice. A *Deliberate* community thrived there. In a way, Nice was his birthplace. Where he'd accepted the magic, drank his first blood, and first looked upon the world as a vampire.

Long strides carried him to the castle entrance, and he flowed with the river of bodies entering the castle. At the landing, he stopped and handed his invitation to the butler. The man gave him a stern look and pointed to Liam's face.

"Oh, yes, sorry." Liam glanced around to make sure no one happened to be looking his way, touched his finger to his forehead, trailed it down to his chin, and his mask appeared in its wake. "Better now?"

The man nodded, turned toward the ballroom, and bellowed. "Gladiator."

Liam moved on and scanned the partygoers for Claire's enchanting tresses. The crowd engulfed him. In his mood, he almost wished them all away. And, although he could, he didn't dare.

He joined the line to speak to the host and hostess. Elsbeth, one of the most intuitive women he had ever had the pleasure to know, raised a single brow. "She is here."

"I will not do either of us the injustice of asking of whom you speak. So, I will thank you for the information."

She lightly touched his shoulder. "Do not be ill at ease. Things like this oft have a way of working themselves out."

They shared a smile and Liam nodded before moving on.

Claire moved quietly in all the noise, taking note of the beautiful decor that never failed to leave her breathless. The castle's beauty was complimented all the more by the evening's elegantly dressed guests. The many colorful dresses and silken fineries appeared to glow all about her—jeweled masks and vibrant feathers highlighting each exquisite costume.

She turned her thoughts from the growing crowd back to Liam. If only...

Mrs. Byrne, a friend of her father's, dressed in a lovely black gown, her feathered mask adorned with red jewels, stopped Claire as she wandered through the crowd. "My dear Miss Claire, I almost didn't know you. What a lovely ice queen you make. Are you well this evening?"

"I am. Thank you."

"I saw that nice young man of yours speaking with Mr. Kilmartin. Dressed as a gladiator! Such a gentleman, that one. You are an extraordinarily lucky young woman."

Claire's heart flipped in her chest and she nearly gasped. "I didn't realize Mr. McDonnell was here tonight. We are not..." Her voice trailed off then. She didn't want to give more fodder for the gossips.

But Mrs. Byrne leaned in, appearing concerned. "I am sorry, dear girl. Perhaps there can be a repair."

"No, Ma'am." Claire found a spot on the rug to study. "But, thank you for your kind words."

"Perhaps you think not. But, your gladiator is walking this way," Mrs. Byrne whispered, and quickly disappearing into the crowd.

Before Claire could disappear as well, Mr. McDonnell stood before her.

"Good Evening, Claire."

She inclined her head and dared look him in the eye. "Mr. McDonnell."

"I am happy to see you."

"I find that surprising. You were quite unhappy with me, only a few days ago."

His gaze dropped. "I still am."

Dare she say his name lest he hear the crack in her voice and her true feelings for him? She swallowed. "Liam, I have not the words to express how utterly sorry I am. Please forgive me. I should never have allowed our banter to become more."

"Did you always know our fate, Claire? That we could never be together?"

Tears pooled in her eyes, yet she refused to let them fall. "I am ashamed to say the truth of it."

"Your deceit makes this all the more unthinkable. If you had not known, I could possibly forgive your actions."

She nodded. "I do not blame you for your feelings, sir. I just hope that someday...someday you will find it in your heart to forgive me."

"I will always love you, Claire. Forever. Do you comprehend the depth of it? If so, perhaps you can perceive the torment of such an unrelenting desire. But forgive you? After forever and a day, I may find the grace to forgive you."

Each angry step as he walked away echoed in her broken heart. Yes, she knew the truth of forever, and knew she would feel the sharp sting of his words for the entirety of it.

And love him still.

But on this night of celebration, she vowed to let no one see the tears behind the mask. She no longer had the luxury to mourn her dreams. Lifting her chin, she pasted a smile on her face and scanned the crowd for her father.

Liam strode through the crowd and went straight to the refreshment tables behind a magical veil that kept them hidden from humans. Other magical folk had their own tables, and he usually enjoyed sampling the Elven or dragon fare, but tonight, the novelty didn't interest him. He craved blood. He chose a bold, red bloodwine. The blood, human, and sweet like honey on his tongue, was provided by a sect of Kith He didn't particularly agree with their practice of providing blood for vampires, but at the moment, he appreciated it. The drink sated his yearning and strengthened his resolve to dismiss Claire from his thoughts.

"Dear Liam, is it you?"

The feminine voice falling upon his ears immediately caught his attention. "Suzette?"

The slender woman dressed in a red gown and jeweled red mask moved in and gave him a long, sensuous hug. Even behind the veil, her behavior broke social convention.

"I heard you were back in Ireland." She smiled sweetly and twirled her fingers in his hair. "But I never *dreamed* we would see each other again."

He wished her mask did not cover so much of her face, as he couldn't properly read her expression. "I do not plan to stay for much longer."

"Is that so?" She finally released him, but kept a hand on his hip. "Well, my plans are not settled as of yet, either. I am free—ready to come and go as I please."

Her touch did nothing to stir him, and he gently removed her hand. "May I get you a drink?"

A mischievous smile played across her face. "I'll have what you're having."

He poured the drink and handed it to her.

Suzette took a sip of the wine. "A fine vintage." She held the glass up in a toast. "So, why are you leaving Ireland, Liam?"

"I think I may return to Nice."

"Ahh… Spoken with the tone of a man whose heart has been broken."

They strolled away from the table and allowed other guests their turn.

Two steps outside of the veil, and the bright fairy lights in the ballroom made him squint. "Would it be rude for me to tell you to stay out of my business?"

"We have known each other for over a century. Nothing we say can be considered rude." She once again sipped her wine. "So, is the lovely lady here this evening?"

Liam stopped and drank the rest of his wine in one draw.

"Oh, she is! What fun!" Suzette searched the crowd. "Which one is she? Who has stolen the heart of my Liam?"

"I was never *your* Liam."

She took him by the elbow and turned him to face her. "When you offered me wine over a hundred years ago, you became mine and I became yours. You have run from me since then, yes, but I always seem to find you. And, do you know why?"

"Because I have terrible luck?"

"Aside from that." She smiled. "It's because we are bound together by the blood. Your blood. But, here is a word of knowledge for you." Before she could finish a small man dressed all in green suddenly appeared.

"I hope you are having a good time, McDonnell. I found your friend here…" He motioned towards Suzette. "… and brought her to the party."

Liam stepped toward him. "Another reason to find you utterly detestable."

"Step back, vampire. I have more magic than you, and have no qualms about using it, celebration or no."

"Now, now." Suzette moved to stand between them. "We do not need to come to blows, gentlemen." She turned and faced Liam. "The truth is I was not looking for you and didn't know you'd planned on attending."

Of all the nights in the world that Suzette Perry-Jones decided to make an appearance in his life, it had to be *this* night. His emotions raw. His thoughts jumbled. Liam accepted her explanation, but refused to remain in her company any longer. With no more flourish than the flickering of a candle, he disapparated to the other end of the ballroom.

Devlin Kilmartin smacked him on the back the moment he became visible again. "Do you play Enslin, Liam?"

"No, not in a very long time, Devlin." He narrowed his gaze. "Don't tell me you have a game going this evening?" He needed a quiet place to collect himself, and a card game might just be the answer.

"As a matter of fact, there is a game going on in the upstairs sitting room as we speak." Devlin must have sensed his hesitation. "Very few people are there, Liam. Perhaps the respite you need from the crowd."

"I would very much like to play."

Devlin motioned to a servant who led Liam to the room where four tables were set out. People—both men and women—watched in anticipation. The exquisitely painted cards held the fantastical likeness of rare and magical creatures, each having a particular power level and appropriate ability. Enslin was a complicated, strategic, battlefield sort of game. Only the magical dared play. The cards were infused with power—bewitched by the Pixies. No one touched them. Not even the dealer.

One of the games ended not long after Liam entered the room. A gentleman he had never seen before called out, "Pixie fire!" signaling a winner. One of the four players at the table slid his chair back and stood, an indication of his bad luck. He left the table with a look of disgust.

Liam sat in the empty chair. "May I be dealt-in on this game?"

"Of course you may. We are in need of a fourth."

The sweet feminine voice came from an iridescent being…a Pixie.

Only the Kilmartins could manage a Pixie actually attending their gala, Liam thought.

The cards gracefully floated through the air, five dealt to each person. The Pixie swooped down to the middle of the table. "Your cards." The small creature snapped her fingers and the cards at each place flipped so the holder could see them.

Liam reached into his pocket, threw a few bills on the table, and nodded at the card to be tossed to the middle of the table. "The Request." He named the highest card with which to start.

The next person mimicked his motions. "The Answer."

The third person also made the needed moves. "Daronna." The game's version of cupid. One of the highest cards in the deck.

The lady to Liam's left rolled her eyes. "Really? Daronna…this early in the game?" She huffed and motioned toward her desired card. The only card with the ability to cover Daronna, but usually played later in the game. "Fulamel."

The Pixie flew around the four of them. "Call the game! Call the game!"

"Pixie Fire!" the woman shouted.

The Pixie allowed all the cards to fall face down upon the table.

"If you had Fulamel, why were you so angry he played Daronna?" Liam asked.

"I would like the game to have lasted longer than a single round, for my money." She lifted a hand and a glass of wine appeared.

The Pixie swooped in and hovered in front of Liam. "Your next card, sir." She snapped her fingers. The card turned upside down on the table.

Liam nearly groaned aloud when he saw the brightly-painted picture of Lucinda—the game's version of love.

"This card is for you, Liam." The Pixie tilted her head to the side. "Your love is here with you, sir. The cards do not lie. Embrace that knowledge."

It seemed no matter where he went, he couldn't escape being

bombarded with heartache.

The Pixie continued, "Look for the red, good sir. And know this… It may not be what you expect."

She flew away then, leaving the table minus a dealer. The surrounding players quietly left, one by one. Liam only sighed.

Claire wandered through the party in search of entertainment. She moved around the room, studying the lighting, the colorful costumes, and the many smiling faces. And, despite her unhappy state, managed to smile in return.

"Miss O'Connor?"

Claire turned to find a small man dressed all in green. "Yes? I am Miss O'Connor. Do I know you, sir?"

He only reached her chest in height and his countenance held something mischievous. "Not personally, no." He smiled a crooked sort of smile. "Alas, we do have mutual friends. The Kilmartins speak rather highly of you."

"Oh, well…thank you for your kind words." She smiled politely. "And may I have the pleasure of knowing to whom I speak?"

"Finn Finnegan, at your service." He removed the funny pointy hat showing full head of bright red hair and bowed low. "I have known the Kilmartins longer than either of us wish to admit."

The funny little man seemed harmless enough, so she returned his smile and offered a slight bow. His mask appeared quite real, and Claire wondered how long it had taken him to fashion it.

Unless, he is…

"I have to wonder, lass, why are you not dancing and laughing like the other young ladies?"

She wasn't about to tell him the truth concerning her broken heart, it was far too intimate a conversation to confide in a completely new acquaintance. "Well…I haven't found anything that makes me want to dance or laugh. Honestly, at this point, I could leave right now and be content."

"Is that so?" He reached into his pocket. "Then, shall we find something to bring you laughter?" He leveled his hand in front of her and blew some type of dust in her direction.

She spattered. "What is this?"

The room began to spin around her. The little green man weaved in and out of her line of sight.

"Now, my dear…tell Finn which man hurt you so."

Inhaling the dust left her more than just a bit off kilter. "I never said that. What makes you think someone hurt me? What have…? What have you done to me?"

"Shamrock dust." He chuckled. "It will make you happy. Even when you do not wish to be."

A fit of giggles left Claire's mouth before she even knew she had laughed. She didn't like the fact she couldn't seem to stop the laughter, even though she found nothing funny about the situation at all.

"Now tell me, lass. Who is he? Name the man. Is it…Liam McDonnell?"

"It is." She tried to cover her mouth, halting any more unwilling words their escape. "It is indeed Liam McDonnell who weighs down my heart and my smile."

"I knew it!" He turned to walk away.

"Hey! Little man! I told you what you wanted." She giggled again. "Don't leave me like this! Come back here right now and undo what you have done."

Finn tugged on his right ear. "You'll feel better in a moment." Then without another word, he disappeared.

"Blasted leprechaun!" Claire fell to her knees, wrinkling the silver-blue gown she wore.

"Madame!" A tall man gently took her hand and helped her to her feet. She remembered him from earlier today. His golden coat covered the tattooed body, but she recognized him even in her present state.

She nearly gasped. The Dragon Prince. Claire stood and looked up at him, smiling even though she tried not to. The ridiculously handsome man's brown eyes—more like that of a cat than a person—mesmerized her.

"What happened?" he asked, his arms still clasping her elbows as he steadied her.

"Finn Finnegan is what happened." She softly cleared her throat. "Shamrock dust."

"I see. The man continued to hold onto her, not withdrawing.

She glanced up and down his glittering costume, noting that he had added a robe of gold over the loin cloth. It covered him from his shoulders down to his ankles, and his mask gleamed golden in the candlelight.

Pity, she thought. "It's like a truth serum—shamrock dust."

His deep voice pulled her gaze back to meet his. "Did you tell the vile creature what it was he wanted?"

"I did." She barely nodded. "Only because I was afraid. For just a few moments, the dust made me panic."

"As well it will." His perfect jawline hardened. "Last year, he sprayed me with the disgusting powder as well. Fear not. As soon as he can be caught, I will have him removed from the castle."

"Is he really a leprechaun?"

The Dragon Prince narrowed his sparkling gaze. "You know of the magical?

She nodded. "I do."

"I see…" He studied her a moment more. "Yes, Finn is a real leprechaun. And a malicious one at that."

"Aren't they all?"

"Not like this one, I fear." He helped her to one of the tables where she had a glass of wine and pulled herself together.

"He will not be happy if we meet again," she promised. Then once again, she took a moment to study her champion. "If you don't mind me saying your… English is sheer perfection."

"No, it's not." He smiled softly. "What you hear is but a ruse. I have an enchantment around me. You hear me in English, yes. Yet, I hear your voice in my native tongue."

"That's remarkable."

He bowed low. "I apologize. I have not properly introduced myself. I am Prince Omar Ali of the Draco *Pantage*."

"*Pantage?*"

"In our special language, it would be your word for heritage, family or parentage. All words do not translate well, I fear."

"And, I am Claire O'Connor of Aldon House."

"It is very nice to meet you, Miss O'Connor."

"The pleasure is all mine, Prince Omar."

A tinkling glass bell rang out around them. The lovely Elsbeth Kilmartin stood in the middle of the dance floor, patiently waiting until her guests fell silent.

"We have prepared some extra special entertainment for you throughout this evening." The elegant woman smiled. "For the more adventurous among you, there will be games within the hedge maze out back. For those of you who choose to remain indoors, a schedule has been prepared for the various events available to you as well." She motioned towards her son and the table he was standing next to. "My husband will be seeing to the more spirited among you, while Stefan and I do our best to keep the rest of you on your excited little toes."

A collective chuckle caused their host to pause and smile.

"Now… for those of you willing to brave the chill, Devlin awaits you through the garden door. For my inside guests, we will resume once the crowds have cleared."

"I must go now. I have promised to…" The Prince's voice trailed off.

Claire knew he was afraid to speak of magic in her presence. "I watched you race last year." She glanced up to him and smiled. "You were amazing. Will you race tonight?"

"Without a doubt." He extended her his arm. "Would you do the honor of accompanying me outside to watch?"

Her eyes widened slightly as she accepted his proffered arm. "The honor would be all mine."

Liam moved toward the outside of the castle amongst the throng of other magical peoples. The guests who ventured out into the cool night went in all directions. Some toward the hedge maze, some to other games, and some to the special place on the estate where only the magical could enter.

He spotted a flounce of silver and refused to hope, but there Claire stood with her hand looped around the arm of the Dragon Prince. Liam stopped dead in his tracks. Not because of jealousy—not entirely—he didn't have the presence to think of that annoying emotion at the moment. No, at this second…he tried to balance his time with hers. Why was she here, at this particular spot? And did she have the ability, or did she have the ability, to see what it was this man now led her to…to an area of the party where only the magical were allowed.

How is this so? Claire?

Liam continued to walk, an ambling stride so as not to draw their attention, and followed the couple down to a large field set up with benches and flags. The benches were for spectators, and the flags to mark the track as markers for those running the race.

Pixies floated on the air above him as they spread their luminescent dust. Their queen then cast a spell to light all the dust as it floated. It did not fall, nor burn away, but hovered over the crowd and lit the event. The Enslin game used this same magic as a call for the win—Pixie Fire. With the track well lit, the pixie's announced the beginning of the race by Frier song.

Five people lined up at the beginning of the race as Liam found a spot to sit several benches behind Claire.

The runners readied themselves.

"I am not sure I understand." The tall elegant woman masked as a black cat looked toward Liam as she spoke. "I have never seen a Shifter Race before. My husband is inside playing Enslin and I thought I would entertain myself with this particular bit of excitement. Yet, I fear I do not understand the rules."

"Then, Madam, allow me to be your guide. To whom do I have the pleasure of speaking?"

"Lady Alcott, of Hamilton Park."

He bowed. "Lady Alcott, it's a pleasure to make your acquaintance. I am Liam McDonnell of Birmingham Place."

She gave a shallow bow, as well, the green feathers on her mask swaying with the movement.

"The tall Egyptian man is Prince Omar of the Draco heritage. I won't tell you how they shift. For a first-time onlooker, it is the fun bit."

She smiled in response to his comment. "And the beautiful woman of dark skin?" She motioned to one of the racers. "Her ensemble is amazing, is it not?"

"I must agree." Liam nodded slightly. "That is Luanna Serene Shazier—an African Corna."

"Truly?" Lady Alcott's eyes widened. "I have never met a Corna before. I know her change will be a lioness. I hope I can meet her after the race. I must compliment her colorful choice of dressing. So lovely…"

Liam smiled. "You will not be disappointed with her acquaintance. She is quite charming."

"Have you any idea how large the Luanna is over which she resides?"

"The largest in all of Africa. It is why she is here, to represent the entire continent."

"Absolutely fascinating."

"Yes, she is."

"The man in the top hat? He is quite the gentleman, is he not?"

"I wouldn't say that, Lady Alcott. That is Griffin Naughton."

"No! I do not believe it!"

Obviously, Lady Alcott knew of Naughton, the werewolf pack leader of London.

"Yes." Liam nodded. "He has done a lot of good for the wolves of England and for the safety of the populace."

"I am in agreement, sir. Are you also familiar with the Scotsman in his flowing kilt and the cowboy in that rather large hat?"

"Not personally, no. The kilted gentleman is a guest at Woodhull Bury, I believe. And, the cowboy, as you call him, is staying at Caldecott Priory. I am not certain of their names. I only know they are here specifically for the race."

The horn sounded then and the running began.

For the first ten paces, by rule, each runner kept his human form, but after that…the event looked more like an animal stampede than a footrace. The man in the top hat shifted into a werewolf—teeth bared, enormous paws thundering against the ground. The woman, Serene Shazier, transformed into a beautiful sleek lioness. The kilted Scotsman seemed to almost disappear, as his form took on that of a soaring falcon. The unnamed cowboy's shift was smooth and effortless, and another wolf now ran in stride with the others. Ahh…But it was Claire's Egyptian Prince who shined as the star of the show. He became a Dragon—thirty feet in length, flying as close to the ground as was the falcon.

Liam's attention turned back to Claire as she cheered her new friend, oblivious to his presence. Even in her golden jeweled mask, Liam knew Claire's eyes would be bright with her enthusiasm. She cheered loudly when the first turn of the race went to the Dragon. Yet, her shoulders slumped when the lioness sped ahead for a few seconds. When the wolf, a newcomer to the yearly gala, outran them all on the second turn, a hush fell over the crowd. Out of the last turn, the falcon made his play. Then, the werewolf took the lead. But in the end, if only by mere seconds, Claire's Dragon friend crossed the finish line and was proclaimed the victor.

"Excuse me." Liam bowed again to Lady Alcott and left her side. He pushed his way through the elated crowd, to Claire, and taking her by the elbow, moved her away from the race and toward the hedge maze. To his surprise, she didn't pull away from him.

Once away from the crowd he stopped. "I do not mean to manhandle you, my dear."

"I know. You would never hurt me, Liam. I am aware of that."

"I didn't know you were magical. Or you knew of magic."

"Nor did you tell me the same."

They walked slowly and deliberately toward the maze.

"Claire, protocol does not allow me to ask."

"No, it's quite rude for one to ask another's magic."

He stopped and made her face him. "Why have we been connected for so long and you have not told me anything?"

Her gaze captured his. "Could I not ask the same of you?"

"Yes. I suppose you could. But, if we knew these things about each other, maybe it would allow us our lives together." He took her hand. "The life we wish to share."

She lowered her gaze. "I cannot imagine what you must be. Perhaps a shifter or a wizard. But my magic is considered dark, and I am afraid you would never be able to accept it. More than that, it is not compatible with other magics, and it is not possible for us to be together."

She gently pulled her hand from his. "It is of no consequence. Neither my magic, nor yours, would not be advantageous to our situation."

"Claire? Come here." Her father arrived with a dark scowl marking his features.

"Papa, this is all quite innocent. We are only talking."

"Come here," he spoke through gritted teeth.

She huffed and obeyed.

Liam took a step forward. "Mr. O'Connor, we were only talking."

"Mr. McDonnell. I have asked you to leave my daughter alone. You have not." He pointed his cane at Liam. "I am not going to tell you again."

He turned on his heel, his hand on her elbow, and led her away from Liam.

Claire walked with her father in a slow amble. She did not speak. It would do no good.

Finally, her father broke the silence between them. "I told you all you needed to know."

"Yes, Papa."

"And, you have disobeyed."

"Not really."

"Young lady, you are not going to pull out your usual sweet and loving logic, as I like to call it, and win me to your side. This is a direct order from your father and protector: you are not to be seen with McDonnell again. Have I made myself clear?"

She stopped and looked up at him. Never had she seen him so serious. "I cannot make such a promise, Papa. He is an attendee here and there is always the chance we will see each other—"

"Stop!" His eyes grew red, his skin sallow. "You will not speak with him again."

Her father had never shown his true self to her in the past. Until this moment, Claire had never been afraid of this kind man. But, it had all changed now.

"Yes, Papa. I understand."

Her father changed back to his human features and strode away from her in anger.

She found her breath, but the recovery wasn't complete, and she wondered if it ever would be.

Liam found himself at an unveiled refreshment table drinking human whiskey. Not quite as potent as the spring nectar the elves provided, but he yearned for the burn of the human drink and not the sweetness of the nectar.

Prince Omar stood walked up beside him and poured a good amount of whiskey into a glass.

All Liam thought about was the way Claire had looked toward this man after his win.

The Prince downed his drink as if it were water. "I saw you leave the race with Miss O'Connor. Perhaps, you may know where I can find her?"

Liam cocked his head to one side. "She and her father left me outside. Have you met her father, Mr. O'Connor of Aldon House?"

"Do you know her well?"

"You could say that."

"She did not share with me what allows her to know those of us who were in the race?"

"You mean her magic? She did not share her magic with you?" He poured another shot and threw it back. "I cannot help you. She never shared it with me, and it would be vulgar to ask."

"Have you known her long?"

Liam kept searching the crowed for her. "Quite some time. We... I asked her to marry me."

"Then allow me to apologize. She never said."

"No, she would not. It is not a topic of pleasant conversation."

The Prince raised his glass. "But the lovely lady owns your heart, it is obvious."

He threw back another shot as he saw a beautiful woman dressed in red approach. His heart dropped. This was not what he wanted for his life, but he remembered the Pixie's words to look for red.

"Prince Omar, have you met Suzette Perry-Jones?"

The two nodded and the Prince prepared a drink for Suzette. They talked animatedly as Liam tried to focus on the people around them in the hopes of finding Claire. Perhaps, if he found her without the escort of her father, he could whisk her into one of the curtained alcoves where he could tell her the truth.

The Prince and Suzette chose to dance, leaving Liam alone at the table. The whiskey started to take its toll, and he moved to another table behind the veil. Juice laced with blood was the remedy he needed to counter the effects of the alcohol. It would dissipate the alcohol in his system. He didn't want to be drunk if Claire did return to the party.

He turned around to find Finn there. "Dear Lord! Why are you here and what the hell do you want?"

"Claire O'Connor is here tonight. Did her father find her? He stopped and asked me if I'd seen her."

"You. I should have known."

"He told me that he wanted to be sure she was safe. How can you blame a Da who wants to protect his child? His only little girl, at that?"

"You have interfered in my life for the last time." As Liam reached out for him, the little man disappeared.

"Son of a—" Liam marched out of the house and onto the grounds, his mind a whirr of anger.

Mrs. Alcott approached Liam. "Mr. McDonnell! Are you playing *Montone* tonight?"

He drew a breath and smiled. "I am not. I do not have a partner."

"Oh, how sad. You know, I saw a lovely young woman, just over there, who is at a loss for a partner as well. Perhaps you could fill the void?"

As she moved to his side, Liam saw the woman was Claire.

He needed to talk to her. What a perfect chance to do so without interruption. "Yes. I believe I would like to play."

"I thought I might be able to convince you of your importance to tonight's game."

He smoothly walked to where Claire stood. She already had the scroll in her hand. "Let us hurry."

He pulled his watch from his pocket and announced the time to Mrs. Alcott. "The time is nine fifty-seven."

"You will have one hour to find your way back to me. Your scroll will help guide you," she replied.

They walked into the enchanted part of the maze for their game. The hedge stood at least eight feet tall and covered a large portion of the lawn. For *Montone*, a witch enchanted certain hedges so they grew and moved according to the time it took for players to answer their riddles and the accuracy of those answers. Others and non-magical folk, played a similar game where they were tasked with being the first to the center of the maze. The magic of keeping the two games separate but together in the same maze astounded Liam, and not for the first time, wondered how the Kilmartins came to such knowledge.

Claire waited several steps before she spoke. "I am glad you joined me." Even though the scroll was lit, much like a glow message, the light did little to dispel the darkness around them. "I still will not speak about the magic, but this will be a chance for us to say goodbye."

"If that is what you wish."

They found their way to the first light. The lovely sorceress, her robes flowing in the breeze along with her blonde hair, smiled and lit the area around her like a lamp. "Welcome to the *Montone*! I am Alia and your first riddle is this: The more you take, the more you leave behind."

The two looked at each other and then back to the Sorceress.

"My mind is not on simple riddles, my dear."

The bright woman gave them no hint. "Your time is important. I must mark your scroll when you answer."

"We need to speak, Claire. This is unimportant."

Alia rose from the ground, her robes and her hair seemed to inflate and grow. She filled their view. "You are on the right path." Her voice echoed in their ears. "Without your steps in this maze tonight, you will not find your destiny."

As she returned to her previous manner, the couple stared at each other.

"We are here for a reason, Liam. We must do as Alia asks. Now think."

"Fine, what do we leave behind and not before us?"

"The question is the more you take the more you leave behind."

Liam couldn't think of something such as this at this moment. He shrugged. "My dear—"

"Oh, I know!" Claire found the answer. "Footsteps!"

"Very good!" Alia held out her hand. "Allow me to mark your scroll."

Claire placed the parchment into Alia's open hand, and Alia waved her hand over the scroll. It opened, and with a twinkle, the sorceress marked the time, and handed it back to Claire.

"Now, my dears, please hurry. The maze moves and grows behind you, but the next couple follows closely."

They obeyed the order and moved quickly toward the next stop.

"Claire, please do not play this infernal game. Talk to me."

She stopped and looked at him in the whispers of light still visible from the sorceress. "Liam, this game tonight, I believe it will lead us on the path to be together. I do not know how, but Alia knew something, and although she could not say it, she led me to think that we must continue the game to be together."

In the dim light, he could not see her eyes, but he could feel her strength and more, her love.

"Then, please my dear, let us continue."

They moved toward another bright area in the maze. When they came to it, several pixies rested on the leaves of the hedge. They began to twirl in the air and their voices joined in the night: "Tonight we see the stars above, the earth below. Do you know what we are? If you do, then you may go.*"

The pixies moved above them, then each found a place in the sky in which to hover.

Liam studied the beautiful lights for a long moment. "Do you have any idea what they are doing?"

Claire also gazed upon them. "They almost look like the stars."

Liam studied their placement. "Yes, yes. They have formed the constellation Andromeda."

The fairies sang out and returned to their positions on the hedge. One of them reached forward with her tiny hand, making their scroll fly into mid-air and marking it, as per the game. "Follow the game, my dears. An obstacle has been removed. Your destiny will come at the end. Now you must hurry!"

They moved forward, the scroll lighting their way and leading them where they needed to go.

"You are right, my dear. This game will end with our unity. I am sure of it, now." They stopped and Liam took her in his arms. "I love you, my dear."

"And, I you."

Before their lips could meet, they saw a light ahead.

"We should hurry. The faster we get there the faster we can be together."

When they found themselves near the next light, there was a small fence that blocked their way. A little mound of dirt lay next to it.

They looked first at the fence, then to the dirt, then to each other several times, unsure if the barrier contained a riddle, or if they should simply climb over the fence and continue on their path. As Liam prepared to help Clair over the fence, the dirt fell away and a small rock troll eyed them. She looked first to Claire, then to Liam. "Liam McDonnell, as I live and breathe!"

"Mirach? I did not know you would be here." He leaned down to greet her. Rock trolls were tiny creatures, not over two feet tall made of what appeared to be smooth stones, although their skin was not as hard as their appearance would have one believe.

"Who is this lovely young woman?"

"May I present Claire O'Connor of Alder House? My dear, this is Mirach. A very good friend of my family."

Clair bowed her head. "It is nice to meet you, Mirach."

"Liam, she is lovely. I hope you will keep this one?"

"That is my intent."

Mirach then held her breath and began to grow. When she reached around ten feet tall, she spoke in a deep, almost masculine, voice. "You wish to be together, but the magic keeps you apart. This is no longer the game, but life. You must share your gifts before it is too late." With that, Mirach let loose a deep breath and once again became the small creature they had first found.

"Now, go children. Become who you are meant to be."

Without waiting for their scroll to be marked, they all but ran from Mirach to find a quiet place off the path of the game. The hedges rustled and moved, and surrounded them in darkness. The scroll ceased to provide any light, as its enchantment only worked if the players remained on the path of the game.

Before either of them could speak, however, Finn Finnegan appeared, lit well by his own magic. "I see you two have found each other." He floated in front of them, a smirk on his face.

Liam balled his fists. "I will not tolerate this, Finn! I will see you thrown out on your arse for interfering where you do not belong!"

"Oh, but you will see so much more."

At that moment not only did their masks disappear, but Liam knew he was no longer in human form, and for a long moment, he could not move at all.

Claire's face filled with awe and what he perceived as fear.

When he could move again, he disappeared himself long enough to spread his wings and leave the area and Claire. Possibly forever.

Claire could not believe what she had witnessed. Her mouth still open, she turned to look at Finn. "So, you thought to plant fear in my heart with this revelation?"

She threw her head back and laughed until tears ran down her face.

"This is wrong." Finn landed beside her. "Why do you laugh?"

"I have a question, Mr. Finnegan. What is his *Min*?"

"His *Min*?"

"You understand me, little man." She reached out and grabbed his ear. "Now, tell me his *Min.* You know what I'm asking. What type of vampire is he?" She tugged hard on his ear.

"Ouch! He's a *Deliberate.*"

"A *Deliberate*? Very magical. The French group that can give up the magic at will."

"And, he didn't tell you, dearie. He kept the secret from you."

"And I held my secrets close as well. You're attempt to discredit him in my heart has failed. You are the most pathetic Leprechaun in the world."

She took a few steps and realized that he followed. Turning around, she put her hand out toward him. Finn flew to the hedge, his back against it. "Let the next couple find you here. Perhaps you can grant them a wish or two!"

With that she raised her hands and flew above the hedge, unseen by the party goers.

Liam returned to the party out of necessity. He was there for a reason. He promised the Deliberate he would carry their gift to the Kilmartins. He could not leave and never had he felt this imprisoned.

And, there was Suzette in that red dress.

"Where have you been?" She fawned on him.

"I have been...It doesn't matter." No longer caring what anyone saw, he raised a hand and received a glass of wine. Throwing it back, he received another.

Suzette's beautiful features changed to concern. "Are you well, Liam?"

"I am not. I don't want to hurt you."

"You never have. I tease you and even mock you, but the truth is I can be, or not be, what I am. I love my life. I should be thanking you."

"Then why are you here?"

"The Leprechaun told me I would be part of a joke. I only came for fun." She looked away. "I should go. My presence here has only caused you pain, and honestly, I do not want to distress you."

She kissed him on the cheek and then, looked over his shoulder.

"The Dragon Prince will be here in a moment. He is taking me to Egypt tomorrow. Did you know his chariot, lion and all, can fly?"

"I travelled to Egypt a few years ago. I think you will love it."

The Prince found them. "Did you tell your friend you will be accompanying me home?"

"I did." She looped her arm inside the Prince's. "I believe we shall have a very good time."

They bowed to Liam and made their way through the throng of people.

Before he strode to the bar, Liam realized something. The Pixie was wrong. But, Pixies are never wrong. How could the Pixie have chosen red? There has been no red except Suzette's dress. He gazed across the room. No, Suzette could not be his destiny, as she was at this moment making promises with her eyes to the Prince.

He felt a presence behind him and found Claire.

"Follow me." She led him by the hand to a small, curtained alcove off the grand ball room. With a flick of her hand, the torch flamed to life.

This did not surprise him, as he had learned she contained magic.

"You left before I could speak to you."

He tried to be stoic, and since his mask had reappeared, it was easier. "You know now, I am a vampire. I suppose you could now tell me of your magic?"

"You are *Deliberate*, are you not?"

"I am."

"You planned to ask me to marry you."

"True. I would have given up my magic to spend my life with you. Now you know."

"I have spoken to my father. He would like to meet with you, now that we know."

"What do you mean?"

She smiled, took his hand as if to kiss it. But, instead, she turned it, bit into his wrist, and drank of the red blood flowing out. He immediately changed to his true form, as did Claire.

A vampire!

Her lovely soft features went sallow and her eyes turned red. She continued to bite, then pulled away and looked up at him. "You are absolutely delicious."

The sensuality of her act coursed through him. "And, my blood holds my magic. You now have powers you did not have before."

He pulled her against him, and the two of them drifted slowly into the air, kissing, biting, and holding each other.

"I have spoken to Papa. He will allow us to marry now that he knows it will not ruin your life."

Liam's opinion of her father changed. The man only wanted to protect Liam from a life of vampirism.

"And what is your *Min*?"

"We are Avior. Distant cousins of the Deliberate, though over the centuries, we lost the ability to surrender our immortality. In most other ways, we are able to live as humans. We require more blood, but my family prefers the blood infused into human food and drink. And we can walk in daylight, though it is uncomfortable."

"You have given me a miracle, yet while my blood can enhance your magic, it does not have the power to return the choice of mortality to you. I feel I have given you nothing in return."

"Oh, Liam. You give me your love, and it is far more precious to me than any magic. And someday, you will give me children born of such unconditional love."

"Children?" He swallowed hard. "How is this possible?"

She laughed. "Surely, I don't need to explain how babies are made, Liam McDonnell. We'll have dozens! Like the Deliberate, we are not bound barren by the darkness."

His heart soared. "Marry me. Here. Tonight."

"Yes. Yes. A thousand times, yes." She gave him a frisky, little bite on his neck, and whispered, "And I'll be wanting the honeymoon straight away."

Loli's Dilemma

J.K. Ensley

A forgotten little jar, discarded and then lost within a yet-to-be-discovered corner of the ancient castle. When Loli picked it up, the protective clay crumbled away revealing the rolled up parchment within. She blew the dust from her palms and carefully stretched out the aged paper… a crackling bit of history containing only these words—deliberately etched in blackest ink—*Carpe noctem. Mutare fata.*

"Seize the night. Change your destiny."

She flipped the tiny note over. Nothing.

Loli read the strangely prophetic words again.

She had discovered the message's secret hiding place quite by chance. A single bottle of the first batch of Spring Nectar, that's all she was after, but the quiet scratching coming from the other side of the wine rack drew her attention. Thinking it must be Bidley the House Elf, sorting out the various libations needed for this coming evening's affair, the curious Princess took a quick peek around the corner. What she saw changed her previous assumption. When Loli screeched, the busy little rat in the corner had scampered away. Upon closer inspection of the tiny intruder's digging, the all-too-curious Faerie had discovered the small hole in the wall down next to the floor… with just the tiniest bit of pale blue now exposed.

"Here now. What's this?" She brushed the moldy dirt back and tapped her fingernail against the strange blue discovery. "Are you a tiny hidden treasure?" Loli giggled as she turned back to make sure she was still alone. "Let's see what we've found, shall we?"

One swift kick with her boot heel had felled the ancient mortar and wholly revealed the clay jar within.

"Well, now… Who left *you* here?"

Whether caused by her semi-violent removal, or simply by age alone, the clay had promptly disintegrated in her tiny hands.

"Seize the night, huh?" She shrugged and snatched up a bottle of Spring Nectar sent over by the Summer King for tonight's festivities. "Seems appropriate enough. I'll seize the night alright… change my fate once and for all."

"Ye down there, Mistress?"

Loli quickly crammed the small parchment into her pocket. "I'm right here, Moll. No need to shout."

"I've been looking for ye all over. Yer bath is drawn, Milady, readied by the fire." The maid gasped. "Aye, now! How'd ye get so filthy?"

"Crawling about upon the floor."

"Wha— Mistress Loli!"

"What's the big deal, Moll? Isn't the time when you're about to get in a bath the perfect time to be dirty? Stop squawking and gawking and come along."

"But what brought ye down here tae this moldy old cellar in the first place, Mistress?"

Loli held up the sparkling golden liquid. "Spring Nectar."

"Aye. But it's for the Ball, Lass."

"Am I not an invited guest of said Ball?"

"Aye. Of course ye are, Mistress. But—"

"Then I am precisely one of the guests this delicious little libation was sent over for. Am I not?"

"I suppose so, aye."

"And tell me, Moll. What goes better with a relaxing warm bath than a few glasses of Faerie wine?"

"A *few* glasses?" The maid shook her head. "Best be careful with that stuff, Mistress. It'll knock ye for a loop afore ye even know it."

"I'm not a child, Moll." Loli rolled her eyes. "This isn't my first Ball, nor is it my first bottle of Springtime's enchantment. If I am to handle those vile creatures I'm expected to dance with this evening, a bit of Nectar will do me no harm at all."

"If ye say so, Mistress." The blushing servant looked away. "The Goblins are nae all bad, Milady. Least nae the ones I've run across."

"They are too all bad, Moll. You and I obviously run in different circles. Have you ever had to dine with a Goblin?"

The girl shook her head.

"Dreadful." Loli grimaced. "The smell *alone* just about does me in." She visibly shivered. "Their clothes reek of the bogs, Moll. Trust me. They're disgusting. There's nothing but filth to be found amongst the Goblins... smelly, arrogant, unpolished filth. They haven't even any semblance of manners. Absolutely horrid creatures—the lot of them."

"If ye say so, Mistress."

Loli glanced back toward the darkened corner, and lightly touched her pocket where the hidden secret was safely tucked away. *Change your fate, Loli girl. Tonight.*

"Ye okay there, Mistress?"

The Princess slowly focused back on the furrowed brow of her worried maid. She smiled.

"Right as the rain, Moll. Come on then." She started up the narrow stone stairway. "We've a party to get ready for."

As the two women made their exit, a tiny man dressed all in green stepped from the shadows. He smiled to himself, almost chuckling aloud, as he watched the Faerie Princess and her mysterious hidden note, disappear from view.

When her maid carried the chest in and popped the domed lid, Loli groaned. "Must I be a swan, *again?*"

"Per yer father's request, aye, Mistress, ye do. It's only just arrived." Moll smiled as she lightly ran her fingertips across the luxurious fabric. "The needlework is stunning… masterful. Yer father has impeccable taste, he does."

Loli peeked up over the edge of the large brass tub. "Did he at least request a different color this time?"

Moll held up the costume and smiled. "As white as freshly fallen snow. Appropriate, I should say."

"Ugh…" Loli sank back down into the cooling water. "The same as the last four years."

"Nae true, Milady. Look at this." Moll held up the matching cape. "Nae a gaudy feather in sight, this time. Seems they're stitched upon the silk, and all in gold." She smiled "Now, ye'll nae have tae worry aboot sneezing or constantly spitting the flyaway bits oot of yer mouth all evening."

"How will I ever manage to contain such joy?" Loli grumbled under her breath. "Hey… What costume is Izzy wearing?"

"Izzy?"

"Isabell Birch, the Elf maid who occupies the room across the hall."

"Aye. Well… I dunnae quite know for sure, Mistress. I wasnae told tae attend tae Lady Birch."

"I didn't imply that you were her attendant, Moll. I simply thought perhaps the servants might gather together and gossip at the end of the day. That's all."

"Perhaps they do. I'm nae sure." Moll shrugged. "Me? I'm normally too tired tae do much more than sleep. By the time darkness comes tae visit, I'm way passed spent, Milady."

"You? But you're still so young."

"Aye, but age isn't always an indicator of stamina."

"Of course it is, silly." Loli stepped out of the tub. "If not age, then what?"

"Station in life, I suppose. It's nae easy, mind ye—taking care of the Winter King's favorite daughter."

"Favorite? Bah!" She plopped down in front of the large beveled mirror. "If I am his favorite, why does he keep trying to push me off on those hideous Goblins? Why can't he just let me choose my own mate?"

"That's the way of things, Princess. In exchange for a life of luxury and ease, ye play yer part by joining with a rival clan, or a strained ally, or a volatile Goblin horde." She laid the elegant dress across the bed. "Would ye rather yer father chose ye a husband from one of the wee Dwarf Princes? Oh… how aboot those delightful Druids tae the north? Would ye like tae bear children for one of those inked-up chanting Priests?"

"Bite your tongue, Moll."

The maid chuckled. "Aside from the Elves, the Goblins are a rather good fit for the Fae. At least they're nae diminutive and gnarled… or all covered in scales."

Both women shivered then.

"I don't know, Moll." Loli slowly ran the brush through her starlight-colored hair. "I suppose you're right. I mean… I *do* have it easy, I guess. At least physically. I don't have to wash linens, or clean fish, or dig in the garden. While you're hanging out the sheets, I get to arrange flowers and mix up sweet perfumes."

Moll turned to look at her mistress when the Princess's words softened.

"But my blessed royal life also means I don't truly get to be *me*." She sighed. "I envy Bryndle more than he could possibly know."

"Yer brother?"

Loli nodded. "Going about seeing the world, drinking in its pleasures and mysteries. I begged to go with him when last he left. Father wouldn't hear of it."

"Aye, and that's because Bryndle isnae on a jolly holiday, Mistress. He leads yer father's royal legion—vanquishing enemies, settling skirmishes, protecting our borders."

"I know. Isn't he amazing?" She furrowed her brows then. "Yet... he gets to have all the fun and adventure."

Moll smiled to herself.

"He's the defining scale by which I measure all other men, Moll. You know that, right?"

"Aye, Mistress. I know."

Loli smiled softly. "Bryndle Frost—handsome, charming, playful, gallant. I love him almost as much as I do Father."

"Aye, that be the truth of it. And the lad treasures ye as well... dotes on ye, taught ye things the King wouldnae allow, had he known of it."

"Yeah." Loli's smile slowly faded.

"How long has it been now, Mistress?"

"Three years this past autumn," she barely whispered. "I miss him so much." Loli bit her bottom lip to keep from crying. "He's the brightest light in our dreary winter world."

"Aye. He's definitely an angel, that one." Moll smiled softly. "But he's done ye a grave disservice, Milady."

"Bryndle? How so?"

"He has set the bar too high, Mistress. There's nae an Elf, or a Faerie, alive who could surpass yer brother. Nae in *yer* eyes."

Loli smiled at her own pale reflection in the looking glass. "It's true, Moll. Every word of it. His is a pedestal no one else can reach."

"Aye, and how's such a thing fair tae the rest of the world, Milady?"

The Princess glanced toward the other woman in the mirror.

"Goblin or nae, there'll nae be a man tae ever satisfy ye. All because of yer *glorious* Bryndle."

Loli giggled. "You're so silly, Moll."

"Aye. Silly, but honest."

"Prince Bryndle..." Loli sighed. "...out there having all the fun, while I'm locked up within my ivory tower."

"Sounds torturous for ye, Lass."

Loli didn't miss the smirk turning up the other woman's thin lips.

"It is, Moll. I never get to do anything exciting. I never got to fly off with the other Faeries during the solstice celebrations. I didn't get to make my own friends, choose my own clothes, or even pick what I wanted to eat for dinner. I may be a pampered little Princess in your eyes, but I will never know what it's like to fall head over heels in love—tummy full of butterflies and stars in your eyes. That's a luxury you take for granted, but is forever denied me." She sighed. "Yes... I envy my big brother. My life may be easy, looking at it from your point of view, Moll, but the truth of the matter is...I'm nothing more than a beautifully painted pawn. A gilded game piece set atop an elaborate chess board, *forced* to make the moves my master demands."

Moll gently took the brush from the Princess's trembling hands. "It's nae *all* bad, is it, Mistress?"

Loli smiled softly. "How can I say, Moll? It's all I know—good *or* bad."

"Aye." The maid nodded. "It's true. We each have our own place in this world, and nae by our own choosing."

"Yes. I'm afraid we do." Loli scooped some rose-scented lotion up with her fingertips. "I wasn't meaning to get all whiney, Moll. Truly, I wasn't. I know your life is harder than mine. It's just..."

"The grass is always greener on the other side?"

Loli smiled. "Something like that, yes."

"Princess Loli... are you decent?"

She spun towards the door when she heard the distinguished voice coming from the other side. "Yes, Father. You may enter."

Moll didn't say a word as she curtsied, lowered her head, and hurried out of the room.

The King walked over to the window and stared silently out at the waning day.

"There is an enviable peace about this place," he half whispered. "Lord and Lady Kilmartin rule over a particularly ethereal slice of this mortal realm. I enjoy our time here each year. It brings a sense of calm to my oft harried mind." He sighed and turned to face his youngest daughter. "Loli, angel of my life, speak to me the truth of your heart."

"My... my heart?"

He nodded. "There are many ears and eyes within every castle. This one is no different. The rumors of your displeasure with me have followed us from the Winter Realm into the mortal one."

"I am not displeased with you, Father. Who would speak such lies?"

"Displeased with my appointment for you, my child."

"Appointment?"

"Choice of date for this evening's Ball."

"Oh… that."

"Why are you angry with my pairing, little one? I am your loving and devoted father. Have I ever brought you pain? Intentionally or nae."

"No, Father. Of course not. Never."

"And why is it you feel I would start *now*?"

She blushed and looked away.

"I would ask nothing of you that I would not, and have not, asked of myself. Alliances and treaties are instrumental to the survival of any realm. Our snowy home is no different. Our people know peace because *we* ensure such a thing. It is our job, our responsibility, and our royal duty. Alas, I would forego said peace for my precious daughter's sake. If I felt a mate from the Goblin horde would bring you any harm whatsoever, I would draw my blade and violently cease our fragile talks."

"No, Father. Please. I would never ask such a thing."

He smiled softly. "Nor would I ask such a thing of you, my dear. Trust me in this. You are my first priority. Never forget that."

"Of course, Father."

The King smiled again, gently kissed the top of her bowed head, and quietly left the room.

Loli held the crystal decanter upside down until the very last golden drop of Spring Nectar begrudgingly released the lip and silently plopped into her waiting glass.

A soft rapping brought her attention to the door.

"Enter," she half sang. "It isn't bolted."

The Princess's eyes widened when the door opened.

"Izzy! Come in. Come in."

The elegant Elf woman bowed slightly and politely stepped inside.

"I see you started celebrating a bit early."

Loli giggled before offering the half-empty glass to her lovely Elven friend. "Have a little nip, Iz. It's absolutely... sublime."

Isabell chuckled. "If only to save you from yourself." She tipped up the elaborately etched glass and emptied it. "Mmm... Sublime indeed. The Summer King has outdone himself this year, again."

"Yes, again. Ahh... To be Princess of the Summer Lands. No heavy coats. No need for woolen stockings. No fuzzy, thick boots dragging in muck from outdoors."

"No relief from the buzzing insects. No warm spiced cider. No crackling fires, nor making snow angels."

"I never said it was *perfect*." Loli plopped down across her bed. "But a little change every now and then is good for the soul. Don't you think?"

"I wouldn't change a thing about my life." Isabell sat down beside her. "My father is an honorable man—First Knight to the Vale King. He loves me, dotes on me, taught me to use a bow when I was only three years old." She smiled. "I don't get to do *everything* I want, no... but I'm thankful for the blessed life I've been given."

Loli threw her arms around the other woman. "Oh, why couldn't I have been born an Elf?"

"Why can't you just like being who you are?"

"Huh?" The tipsy Princess sat up. "What do you mean?"

"I *mean*... why not enjoy the blessings all around you, Loli? Instead of always dreaming about being someone else or going some other place, why don't you just open your eyes to the glory you have obviously ignored?" She motioned towards the empty bottle of Nectar. "This is all about your Goblin date, right?" She sighed. "Our fathers pick our mates. So what? Our mothers went through the same things and they are happy enough. Wouldn't you agree?"

"Yes, but *they* were wed to their own kind. Even *you* get to be with another Elf. Maybe not a River Elf, but at least a Wood Elf, or an Earth Elf. I am not so lucky."

Isabell smiled and patted her friend's knee. "Look at your plight as an amazing new adventure. Yes, I will one day marry an Elf, but what will change for me? I will still lead an Elven life, whether it's down by the waters or up in the trees. Nothing much will change for me. But *you*... you get to start a brand new life in a completely different world. What could be more amazing than that?"

"Finding love on my own."

"Pffts. A fool's dream, at best."

"You are not the *first* person to call me a fool."

The two women shared a soft laugh.

"You're right, though." Loli glanced out toward the waning sun. "We are lucky. Our elevated station—while not earned, per se—provides us with many luxuries others will never know."

"Yes." Isabell smiled. "This is my first stay here at Castle Amhrán Oiche. You?"

"Fourth." Loli held up as many fingers. "The Kilmartins are exceptionally gracious."

"Well, your father *is* the Winter King, after all."

Loli only nodded slowly, her mind and gaze was still on the world outside her darkening window.

Isabell stood. "So… what are you going as?"

"Another swan." Loli sighed. "My father is nothing if not consistent and predictable." She turned toward the Elf woman. "What's your costume?"

"I am a peacock."

"Of course you are."

They were still laughing when Moll returned.

"Aye, Lasses, the carriages are already arriving—guests piling oot in droves. Ye maids better get a move on afore ye lose the good light." She pulled the curtains back wider. "Come on, Mistress. Hop up for me. Yer hair wasnae the only thing wanting decoration. Ye need tae get yer clothes on as well."

"Moll, the slave-driving Scot." Loli sighed and stood, folding her wings down between her shoulder blades as she held out her arms. "Very well. Make me look like a human for the night. Cover me in feathers and let's get this thing over with."

Isabell chuckled as she turned to go. "I'd try to always keep some of the Summer King's Nectar on hand if I were you, Moll. The alcoholic kiss of spring makes her *much* easier to handle."

"Ye look lovely, Mistress. As human as any other lass. There'll nae be a one of them able tae ootshine ye."

"Too bad they can't tell it's me under this mask." Loli turned sideways and examined her profile in the looking glass. "I've got to hand it to you, Moll… you can work some special kind of magic, that's for sure. It almost makes me excited to attend this ridiculous celebration."

A sharp rap at the door sent the blushing maid scurrying over to answer it.

"Are you ready, dear daughter?" The Winter King stepped into the room. He gasped. "Loli… you are enchanting, little one. As beautiful as your mother." He gently took her by the hands. "You take my breath away, lovely Princess."

She curtsied politely and smiled. "Gratitude, Father. Your taste in costumes is impeccable, as always."

"Nonsense. Such finery only gilds your rare beauty." He turned toward the waiting servant girl. "Run along, Moll, and make certain the sconces are all lit. Ridley sometimes gets excited and forgets his tasks. I assured Stefan we would see this wing of the castle was taken care of. His parents have their hands full this evening, as you can well imagine. Be a dear and walk the halls in this area."

Moll curtsied and left without saying a word. The King turned back to Loli and extended his elbow.

"If you would grace me with the honor, my dear."

"The honor is all mine, Father." She took his proffered arm, but halted just as they reached the door. "Oh, I need a moment."

Loli ran back to her dressing table, snatched up the tiny scroll she had found in the cellar, and secretly tucked it within her bodice.

"Everything well, little one?"

"Yes, Father. Just remembered a little good luck charm I recently stumbled across."

"There is no need for such as that." He smiled when she rejoined him. "Your unique radiance is all the luck any being could possibly need."

"You are prejudiced in my regard, Your Grace."

"And what father wouldn't be? You are the star in my crown, dear one. Tell me. Are you feeling better about this evening?"

"Yes, Father. Your wise counsel always erases any worry I may have dreamed up."

"I am ever proud of you, little one."

When they started down the elegant staircase, the King squeezed her hand in the bend of his arm. Loli looked up to his handsome profile.

"There is someone special attending this evening's gathering who is extremely eager to meet you, Princess."

"Is that so?" She tried to keep from grumbling, but the edge in her voice was hard to miss.

"Yes, it *is* so." He squeezed her hand again. "He is dressed in crimson—head to toe. When you see this man, make every effort to speak with him. He is anxious to share a dance with you."

"As you wish, Father. When I see the devil dressed in red, I will do as you say."

The King chuckled. "Yes... more like your mother with each passing day."

Loli smiled then, unable to hide her swelling pride.

He gently patted her hand before placing a light kiss on her wrist. "Have fun this evening, my dear, and do not forget the precious gift our hosts will require of you at the evening's close."

She nodded. "I will not forget my duty, Father."

He smiled. "My beautiful little Loli... nights like this are oft filled with magic. Keep your lovely eyes open, Princess. I do not wish you to miss a moment of it."

"Yes, Father. I promise to have fun."

The King kissed her cheek, and made his way toward their waiting hosts. The guest's official arrival had not been announced, seeing as how this was a masquerade ball and all identities were to remain secret, but the Winter Faerie King needed no introduction. The ruling monarchs would each show up dressed in elaborate fineries, yes, but were not *required* to don masks. Loli's handsome father was one such guest. He chose to let his stunning Fae features be the only needed compliment to his divine wardrobe.

Loli's growing pride swelled all the more as she watched her beloved father royally greet their honored hosts, then she quickly scanned the gathering crowd for the red-decked demon the King had only just mentioned. Sighing happily to find her evening was still *crimson-free* for the moment, the Princess ducked behind a marble pillar and eagerly sought out a tray of that delicious Spring Nectar. The droll server didn't even bat a lash when she swiped *two* goblets as he passed by.

"Hitting it hard a little early, I see."

Loli nearly spit the sparkling golden wine out when the stranger spoke. She coughed a couple of times before regaining her composure.

"Excuse me?"

"Or perhaps I was wrong." The black-cloaked man stepped closer. "I assumed both goblets were for you. Could I have been mistaken? Your bold choice with that particularly potent libation seems to prove my initial error." He smiled softly. "Was I wrong, Lady Swan? Did you retrieve some wine for your date as well?"

"You weren't wrong." She downed the first drink and placed the empty goblet on the table behind her, then smiled and tipped the second chalice towards him. "They are *both* for me. Good day to you, sir."

"It would be a better day if you chose to remain in my company."

"As flattered as I am by your gallant request, I fear my dance card is all booked up."

"Not even a single moment to spare?"

"I'm afraid not. Sincerest apologies." She smiled politely before turning to go. "May your evening be laced with magic, Lord Black."

The man chuckled as she walked away, already sipping on her next Spring Nectar.

"Hello there, Lady Peacock." Loli giggled. "Spotted any pointy-eared suitors yet?"

Isabell turned toward her tipsy friend. "Already back in the Nectar, I see. Really, Loli. You'll be making a complete fool of yourself before the sun's even good and set." She grabbed the goblet just as the Princess made to take another sip, and downed the whole of it. "Ugh… And I'm going to be right there with you if I keep trying to save you from yourself."

"I don't have any other idea how I am to get through this night, Izzy. I'm at a loss and open for suggestions."

"First suggestion… step away from that golden Faerie swill you're far too fond of. Now, what do you mean? —getting through the night."

"That Goblin I was telling you about earlier…"

"Yes?"

"Father said he would be dressed in red from head to toe. Told me the vile man couldn't *wait* to meet me. Oh… and he would demand a dance as well."

"And you believe you can handle the situation better by getting drunk right off the bat?"

"No. It's just... liquid courage, I guess."

"Well that *courage* will soon be dripping from your chin—staining the front of your lovely gown. My second suggestion for you, dearest Loli... Throwing-up all over *any* man, even a Goblin, will probably make a *memorable* first impression, but not a good one. Stay away from the wine. Plus—if you would rather look at it *this* way—being inebriated, even slightly, will make it all the easier for your *filthy* Goblin to take advantage of you. If you keep pouring that sweet Nectar down your throat, it'll wash all your fight away." Isabell sighed and took her friend by the arm. "Come on then, Loli girl. Let's get you some air."

When the Elf pushed the door open to the large patio, the Princess stumbled on outside.

"Lady Peacock, there's someone here who would like a word with you, if you please."

"Yes, Mr. Kilmartin. I'll be right there." She turned back to Loli. "Psst... Hey... I'll be out in a minute. Stay right there. Promise?"

The woozy Faerie only nodded her head, before deeply inhaling the cool night air.

"Already trying to escape, lovely Swan?"

Loli caught the faint sent of honeysuckles a heartbeat before she heard the smooth, deep voice coming from behind.

Mr. Dark Cloak, Wine Warden. She smiled, but didn't turn to face the man. "Not *escaping*, really. I just needed some fresh air. That's all."

"Is your date aware that you're out here in the dark, all alone?"

"I've yet to meet my *date*. He'll be a hard one to miss, though."

"Oh? And why is that?"

"I have been told he is dressed like a cock's comb—red from floor to ceiling."

"Floor to ceiling, huh?" He chuckled softly. "Is he a giant? Or just an overly-sized Troll?"

"Pffts. Worse than either, I fear. He is a Goblin. A smelly, old, mannerless Goblin."

"And why would a divine creature such as yourself be tied to a filthy Goblin?"

"Why indeed?" She sighed. "Alas, it is my father's wishes."

"And do you *always* do what your father wishes?"

"I usually throw a fit—stomp around and pout for a few days. Yet... I eventually come around, yes."

"And why is that?"

"Because my father is a great man—kind, noble, caring. He would never put me in harm's way... never ask me to do something that wasn't in my best interest."

"He sounds like a noble man indeed."

"He is." She paused. "The more I think on it the more I am coming to realize... perhaps this isn't such a *bad* thing after all. My father loves me. I trust him in all things. Whomever he has chosen as my potential husband... the man can't be *all* bad, no matter his race. Father wouldn't allow it." She smiled softly. "If a Goblin is his choice, there must be a deeper reason for our match. Father would never *sell off* his daughter for politics sake."

That fragrant aroma of wild honeysuckles grew stronger, completely surrounded her. Loli started to turn, but then sensed the man was standing directly behind her. She froze.

"Are you happy, lovely lady?"

The heat from his sweet breath, the vibration of his deep voice, the feel of his presence—so very close, yet not touching. She nearly swooned.

"Wha... What did you say?" She took in another clearing breath of crisp air.

"Happy... I asked if you were happy."

"I am well taken care of, and beyond blessed."

"That's not the same thing." He gently touched the single curl softly framing her face. "Are you happy?"

She spun to face him then, nearly stumbling in the process. The stranger caught her, steadied her, then carefully released her.

Loli swallowed hard. His scent, the warmth of his touch—far too intoxicating for her current inebriated state.

She cleared her throat. "Thank you, but... I've got this."

"Oh?" The black-cloaked stranger smiled. "You don't *look* like you've got this."

"What are you talking about? Pffts." She held out her arms. "Are you kidding me? This is my *I've got this* outfit. Couldn't you tell?"

He bit his lips together, then chuckled. Loli joined him.

"Tipsy White Swan, would you like to stroll with me down by the water?"

"Hmm... Well, as long as we stay upon the path, within the torchlight, *and* within sight of the castle guards... then yes, I would love a stroll with you."

"As you wish, Milady."

When he extended his elbow, she smiled and accepted.

"I am honored."

"As well you should be, Milord."

The man chuckled again as he tenderly patted her captive hand.

Loli glanced up to his strong profile. "You have a striking, regal-looking jawline, mystery man in black."

"It pleases me that you think so."

"Does it?"

"Greatly, yes."

She tilted her head slightly, trying to sneak a tiny peek under the edge of his mask. "Are you handsome under there… or is your costume the lesser of two great evils?"

He smiled with only one corner of his mouth. "Appearance is relative, I suppose. You may find me hideous… or not. I do not yet know your tastes, Milady."

"True. There's no accounting for it—individual tastes."

"Agreed. Yet… does it truly matter to you? —my looks."

"I suppose not, no. As long as you behave as a *proper* gentleman, I care not what that pale mask of yours now hides." She quickly stepped in front of him then and took in the whole of his costume. "Tell me. Who are you, good sir?"

"Ah, ah, ah, Milady. *This* night is to be filled with secrets, is it not?"

"Father said it was to be filled with magic."

"Yes, and the rarest magic is the secret kind."

"Pffts." She fell back in step beside him. "I didn't mean, *who* are you in the daylight. I meant…" She gently squeezed his arm. "Who are you supposed to be *tonight?*"

"Ahh… I see." He glanced down at her from the corner of his eye. "I am a Phantom, Milady. Can you not tell?"

Loli stopped just as they walked beneath the next torch. "The water is lovely, is it not?" She smiled and closed her eyes. "I love the way it sounds, especially at night. The gentle movement of it… the soft, lapping whispers it makes. It brings calm to the night. Calm, comfort… peace."

The man turned to face her as she spoke. When next she opened her eyes, Loli was met with the stranger's captivating gaze. She almost gasped.

"Are… Are your eyes… purple?"

He smiled softly. "They are lavender, yes."

"Wow… They are truly beautiful." Without thought, she touched the side of his smooth face. "And I bet they're even *more* stunning in the daylight."

"I have been told that, yes." He placed his hand over hers at his cheek. "But never by one quite so fair."

"Oh, apologies." She quickly jerked her hand away. "I didn't mean to—"

"Think nothing of it, Milady."

She blushed. "Are you here alone, Phantom? Did you come to the Ball by yourself?"

"I did, yes."

"Are you hoping to meet someone special tonight?"

"That was my plan." He smiled. "Is that not why we are *all* gathered here this evening?"

"Well, that's not really what I was asking. What I meant was… do you *know* who it is you are supposed to meet tonight? Did you come with a particular someone special in mind? And would that someone… would she happen to be an Elf, perhaps?"

"No, my curious little angelic Swan, I am not here to meet an Elf. Yet I am curious as to why you would think that."

"Never mind." She paused a moment. "Well, if not an Elf, then… who?"

"I am not entirely certain myself. Not just yet. Soon, perhaps." He smiled. "I trust this night to hold her secrets until the time is ripe. Now… come." He turned back toward the stone patio, spinning her around with him. "Your excessive intake has apparently dulled you to this chill." He adjusted her cape, making sure her arms were covered. "Besides, we mustn't stray *too* far, Milady. Your eager red giant might take our chance encounter the wrong way."

"Would that he did," she half mumbled. "No… I didn't mean that. If Father *had* to choose a Goblin for me, I'm certain he picked the least-gross, less-smelly one of the bunch."

He chuckled. "You don't seem to think very highly of the Goblin race, Milady."

"Well, I guess I don't really know them that well." She shrugged. "The last time we visited their realm, I was only a little girl. Still… I will never forget it."

"What stuck in your memory, Lady Swan? What turned the Goblins foul in your eyes?"

"…The smell." Loli visibly shivered. "The smell of that rancid old bog bordering their village."

"How old were you then?"

"Five… maybe six. Still a small girl. I wasn't yet old enough to ride my own horse. Not *that* far, anyway."

"Ahh… Just after the last clan war then."

She nodded. "There were dead things everywhere—horses, sheep, Faeries, Ogres… and Goblins. It was awful."

"Yes, it was. I remember those days well."

"Who could forget them?" She sighed and glanced off into the distance. "When we finally made it through their enormous black gate… the stench only seemed to grow. There were some children we rode passed—playing with a dirty old ball, in dirty old clothes, with their filth-covered dirty old dog. One of them waved to me. I remember it scared me so badly, I began to cry. Father pulled me back against his chest and covered my eyes."

"Your father truly is a kind man… sheltering you from all the ugliness of this world."

"Sheltering is right." She paused. "He has never placed *severe* restraints upon me. Still, I was never allowed to venture too far from home."

"It's because he loves you so much."

"I suppose so. Yet… it doesn't always *feel* that way."

"Love makes us *feel* many different ways. That's the beauty and the magic of it."

"I suppose…"

He chuckled softly. "You have only ever felt familial love, am I right?"

"And what's *that* supposed to mean?"

"Nothing bad, Lady Swan. I only meant that your experience with love comes from your ties with your family."

"Yes, I guess that's true enough. I haven't really had the chance to get close to many others."

"So your only opinion of other races comes from your jaded memories of when you were a child?"

"No. I'm not a hermit. I don't *visit* much, no, but I have entertained people from all over. We're constantly having guests from this place or that—going to parties and feasts and balls."

"Balls… like the one you are hiding from right now?"

"I'm not *hiding*."

"Oh? Aren't you?"

"No. I just needed some air. That's all."

"Because you were busy tossing back Spring Nectar, two goblets at a time?"

"No." She lowered her head. "Mostly because I stole into the cellar earlier today and snuck a bottle—polished it off during my bath this afternoon."

"A whole bottle?"

She nodded.

"Pffts. You truly *were* dreading this gathering, huh?"

"Not really dreading the gathering… just the ugly Goblin my father wants me to meet."

"How do you know he's ugly? Have you seen him before?"

"No. It only stands to reason, though."

"What does? That's he's ugly simply because he's a Goblin? Have you had many Goblins over for dinner?"

"Eeww. No."

"Then how is it you know so much about them? Because of that war-torn visit from your childhood?"

"That… and the Masquerade Ball here at the castle every year."

"You mean… your father has chosen you a Goblin date for every ball that you've attended?"

"No. Only *this* one. But Goblins show up every year—eating with their bare fingers, kicking off their smelly shoes, laughing too loudly and being unspeakably rude to the staff."

"I see." He smiled. "You mean, at the end of the night when too much wine has been had by all?"

She shrugged.

"The same direction *you* were headed but a few moments ago?"

"Hey, now. No matter how inebriated I may get, I'm not going to belch, howl like a beast, then grab some poor servant girl and pull her onto my lap."

He chuckled softly. "Fair enough."

They walked a moment in silence.

"So you don't think Goblins are *physically* ugly, only that they act that way."

"I'm not sure. It's true I cannot recall properly how they actually *looked*—seeing as how I was mostly hiding within my father's cape the whole of our visit. And you can't really count the times at the Balls." She pointed to her own mask. "Faces pretty much stay a secret."

"Yes, I suppose that's true. So what you're saying is… you don't like ugly *acting* people."

"Exactly."

"Then you would be fine with a man's poor looks, as long as he treated you with gentlemanly respect."

"And others as well, yes."

"So as long as he is beautiful on the inside…"

"We should get on quite nicely, yes."

"I see. Well, here we are, Milady. Back, safe and sound. You feeling better? Ready to rejoin the party?"

"In a minute. You go on ahead."

"And leave you out here in the cold… all alone, in the dark?"

"Pffts. I'm not afraid of the dark, dear Phantom."

"Perhaps you should be. What if your red-clad Goblin suitor is lurking just beyond the torchlight? What if you step one foot further into the night, and he snatches you away forever?"

The man chuckled when her eyes grew wide with his words.

Loli squirmed and grimaced, then reached inside the top of her bodice.

"What is it you are doing, little Swan?" He furrowed his brow and stepped toward her. "Is something wrong?"

She pulled out the tiny scroll she'd hidden away earlier. "It was scratching me… getting itchy."

"What've you got there, Maiden?" He took the parchment and carefully unrolled it. "Seize the night… Change your fate." He looked back up and met her gaze. "What's this mean?"

"I'm not sure. I found it hidden behind some crumbling mortar when I filched the Nectar from the cellar earlier today. I took it as a sign."

"A sign?"

She nodded. "I took it as a sign that I could use *this* night to change my destiny—kept it as a good-luck charm."

"How do you plan on changing your destiny?"

She shrugged. "I'm not really sure that I should. Not anymore. I don't want to disappoint my father."

"You think your destiny is to marry this red Goblin he picked out for you?"

"Yes. No. I don't know. My fate is in my father's hands. There's nothing new about that. And... he has never been wrong before."

"Never?"

She shook her head. "Not to *my* knowledge."

The Phantom smiled. "Very well then... come on." He grabbed her hand. "Let's go check out your fated Goblin man."

Loli pulled back against his tug. "No. I'm not ready."

"If not now, when? The night is wasting and there's dancing to be done. Am I right?"

"You go on. Find *your* magic. You don't have to babysit *me*. I mean... thanks for taking care of me so far, but..."

"But... you've got this now?"

She smiled. "Yes, Lord Phantom. I've got this now."

"Good." He bowed toward her. "It was my honor to be of assistance, Milady. Now, I must go and find the future keeper of my heart."

She giggled. "Good luck to you."

"And you as well, Lady Swan."

"Loli!" Isabell grabbed her hand and pulled her off to the side. "Where did you get to? I was worried sick."

"When? What are you talking about?"

"I told you to wait right outside the door. When I came back, you were nowhere to be found. You had me on the verge of tears."

"I'm sorry, Iz. I guess I was a little tipsier than I thought."

"Ugh... My stomach's hurting just thinking about what your father would have done, had I told him."

"Told him what, Izzy? I did what you said—waited."

"You did no such thing."

"Yes. I did. Then this man asked me to go for a stroll down by the water. So, I went. And I'm glad I did, Iz. It really helped to clear my head."

"What?" Isabell grabbed her shoulders and squeezed. "You went off alone with some stranger?"

"I—"

"Did he molest you? Did he try anything?" She glanced around the hall. "Where's your father? He should be aware of this."

"No, Izzy. Calm down. The man was a complete gentleman. Trust me. He even worried that my arms might get cold—didn't have a clue I was a Winter Fae."

"Did he touch you, Loli?"

"Only to tighten my cloak. That's all."

Isabell sighed heavily and leaned back against the wall. "Thank the stars." She looked back to her friend and narrowed her gaze. "Never. Do. That. Again."

"Okay, Iz."

"Promise."

"I promise. I promise."

The relieved Elf sighed again.

"Hey… While you were searching for me, did you come across the man all dressed in red?"

"Your Goblin date?" Isabell shook her head. "Oh, there was a couple with black and red patches on their costumes."

"No. No. Completely red—head to toe."

"I know, Loli, but I haven't seen anyone like that."

The frustrated Princess sighed and rubbed her forehead.

"Still anxious about your Goblin, huh?"

"He isn't *my* Goblin."

"Well, you know what I mean. The Goblin's the one in red, right?"

"I don't know of anyone else Father would possibly think to mention to me—intentionally describe." She frowned and looked away. "It *must* be the Goblin."

"Hey… Loli…" Isabell gently touched her arm. "I know this whole thing is hard right now, but it'll get easier. Promise. Meeting new people is always nerve-racking, *especially* if that person is a potential suitor." She smiled softly. "Why not give the poor man the benefit of the doubt? Tell me. Do you truly plan on defying your father in this?"

"…No."

"Then why make things harder for yourself and for the red-dressed stranger as well? If you already know you'll eventually give in, quit being so difficult. Besides, if you are rude to the man and hurt his feelings as soon as you meet… that'll just end up creating another huge obstacle you'll have to overcome. There'll be plenty enough challenges as it is. New relationships are like that."

"I know you're right, Izzy, and I'm trying to sort it all out. Believe me."

A tinkling glass bell rang out around them. The lovely Elsbeth Kilmartin was standing in the middle of the dance floor, patiently waiting until her guests fell silent.

"We have prepared some extra special entertainment for you throughout this evening." The elegant woman smiled. "For the more adventurous among you, there will be games within the hedge maze out back. For those of you who choose to remain indoors, a schedule has been prepared for the various events available to you as well." She motioned towards her son and the table he was standing next to. "My husband will be seeing to the more *spirited* among you, while Stefan and I do our best to keep the rest of you on your excited little toes."

A collective chuckle caused their host to pause and smile.

"Now… for those of you willing to brave the chill, Devlin awaits you through *that* door. For my inside guests, we will resume once the crowds have cleared."

"What do you say?" Isabell's green eyes sparkled. "Want to risk a game within the maze?"

Loli smiled. "Just try and stop me."

"Everyone clear on the rules then?" Mr. Kilmartin waited for any objections. "Very well. Find each item on your list and make it through the maze. Couples count as a single player. Winner gets to open the chest and claim their prize, only once the requirements have been properly met. Ready? And… begin."

When they entered the maze, Isabell went left and Loli went right—both giggling all the way. The excited Faerie stopped under the first torch and rechecked her list.

"A heart-shaped pebble… Three blue leaves… One fluffy ball, and a platter of cheese. Platter of cheese?" She glanced around. "In a hedge maze?" She growled under her breath. "How's that even possible? *Or* sanitary?"

Later, when Isabell finally stumbled upon her, Loli was lying back across a stone bench—in the very center of the maze—popping cubes of cheese into her mouth off the platter atop her belly. The Elf woman stared for a moment, then burst out laughing.

"What in the world are you doing?"

"Looking for a fluffy ball," Loli said, not even turning to face her friend.

"Oh? Really? Pffts. Looks to me like you're stuffing your face. Where'd you get the cheese, anyway?"

Loli pointed off to her right, then popped another cube in her mouth and sat up. "Want some?"

The Elf joined her on the bench. "How are you doing so far?"

Loli opened her left hand to reveal a tiny heart-shaped pebble and three crumpled blue leaves atop her palm. "How about you?"

"I've got two more items to go." The Elf unfolded her list. "A purple coin, and a… call to dinner. Whatever *that* means."

"A bell." Loli swallowed another bite. "It means a bell. I haven't seen one of those, but the purple coin is about twenty paces from the entrance."

"Thanks!" Isabell giggled and stood. "You giving up?"

"There is no fuzzy ball. Trust me. I've searched high and low and everywhere else in-between." She flicked a small yellow cube at her friend. "This cheese is probably better than the grand prize, anyway. Go on. Grab your coin and find that bell. *One* of us needs to be the winner."

Isabell laughed and disappeared back through the bushes.

Almost as soon as her friend had vanished, Loli sensed something was amiss. She quickly looked to both sides before realizing that it was her—her mask was gone. She hurriedly scanned the surrounding ground, but could find no trace of the ornate white covering she had just been wearing. Within the next heartbeat she heard various screams and yelps popping up from all over the maze.

What's going on here? Loli peeked around the tall shrubbery. *That man is unmasked as well, and oy… does he ever need one.* She giggled, then walked back to her stone seat and picked up the silver platter. "Well, looks like things are going to get a little more interesting around here." She took another bite. *I'll just hang out until the smoke settles a bit.*

It didn't take long. Before she even had the chance to enjoy being disguise-free, her mask suddenly reappeared. She sighed.

"Hope they find the trickster… and make him do more than sweat. Strip him nude and lock him outside."

She chuckled to herself at the visual play-by-play her words conjured, then popped another cube into her smiling mouth. Suddenly, she was surrounded by the sweet smell of honeysuckles.

"Can you spare a morsel for a starving man?"

"Nope." Loli finished chewing. "*This* is my consolation prize."

"Cheese? You'll settle for a plate of cheese?"

"Not a plate… a platter."

"Pffts." The Phantom laughed softly before sitting down beside her. "A draft blew across my face just a few minutes ago. Were you thusly unveiled?"

"Yep." She held up a cube of cheese in front of his still-speaking lips, but didn't actually turn to look at him. "Too bad you missed it."

The man paused a moment—his wide lavender gaze fixed upon her dainty fingers—then slowly leaned toward her waiting hand.

"Bite me and I'll slap you."

He smiled, then gently closed his lips around her fingertips. Loli didn't respond, except to offer him another bite. The Phantom didn't hesitate the second time.

"Find all of your items?" she said while chewing.

"I'm not playing."

He lifted one of the small cubes and gently touched it to her lips. Loli immediately opened her mouth and let him feed her. The Phantom smiled.

"Did you find all of *your* items?"

"If I had, I'd be opening the chest right now, wouldn't I? Not sitting here in the dark… foundering on bits of delicious cheese."

"What all do you lack?"

"A fuzzy ball. Seen one?"

"No." He picked up her paper. "Got the stone and the leaves?"

She opened her hand via response.

The Phantom glanced toward the hedge when he heard a tiny noise.

"It's just a rabbit." Loli gave the man another bite. "We've been sharing in my bountiful blessing. Haven't we, little guy?"

When she tossed the bunny another treat, the tiny creature grabbed it, then slipped back under the hedge.

The Phantom leaned over and touched his shoulder to Loli's. "What about *that?*" He pointed toward the retreating rabbit. "Look like a fuzzy ball to you?"

Loli's eyes widened. She almost dumped the remaining cheese when she jumped up and went after the creature. The Phantom gave chase as well. They went from one side of the bush to the other—ducking and diving and trying to catch hold of the scared little thing. When the Faerie ran to get more cheese for bait, she turned back around to find the smiling Phantom—wiggling bunny in hand.

"How did you—"

"Grab your other items. Hurry up. We've still got to make it to the end of the maze."

They were both giggling like a couple of school children when they burst through the only exit, loot in hand.

Devlin checked their crumpled list, then furrowed his brow. "I could have sworn that platter was nearly full when I hid it."

Loli patted her tummy. "And it was truly delicious."

Their gracious host smiled with one corner of his mouth before making a sweeping gesture towards the large chest. "Claim your prize, Milord... Milady. It was well earned."

Mr. Kilmartin then rang the large brass bell signaling the game's end.

Loli hurriedly popped the latch on the chest and gasped. She clapped her hands together and hopped up and down.

"What is it?" The Phantom peered inside. "No way."

The Faerie Princess squealed happily as she pulled out a bottle of glowing golden liquid.

"You won a whole case?"

"Two, actually," Devlin added. "Twelve bottles in all."

Loli giggled again—beaming smile spread impossibly wide.

"Lady Swan..." The Phantom placed his hands atop her shoulders, slowly ceasing her delighted bouncing. "Promise me you will not open them this evening. Not even the one you now hold."

She tilted her head to the side and almost frowned.

"No need to fret, Milady. They're yours. You've got them." He glanced back to the chest. "Twelve whole bottles." He met her pale blue gaze. "Just promise me you will save them for another day. They'll keep just fine. You know that. Please don't go back to the way you were when first we met. I'll worry too much... if you don't promise me this."

She chewed on her bottom lip, but didn't answer.

"Perhaps the lady would like them delivered to her room," Devlin said softly.

"You're staying *here*?" The Phantom furrowed his brows.

Loli nodded. "For a couple of nights."

Their host leaned closer. "There they will be safe and sound, Milady... patiently awaiting your enjoyment on another day."

When Devlin snapped his fingers, a tall servant approached.

"No need, Mr. Kilmartin." The Phantom lifted up her treasured prize. "I'll take care of our lovely little Swan."

"As you wish," Devlin said, waving the nearing man off.

"Lead the way, Mistress Swan."

Loli giggled again. The Phantom couldn't help but smile as he followed the bouncing woman back towards the castle.

"Here we are." Loli whispered to the door and the latch popped. "Just set them right inside. Anywhere will do."

He placed the cases up against the wall and looked around. "Wow... How did you manage to rank *this*?"

"My father has the pull. Not me."

"Who's your father?"

She wagged her finger at him. "Secrets, Phantom. Remember?"

The man chuckled as he made his way to the window. "I bet this view is *stunning* during the day."

"A more ethereal dawn you will never greet."

He turned back towards her and cocked a single brow.

She shrugged. "Well. It doesn't get a *whole* lot better. That's for sure. Watching the sun glint off the water as the boats go by... it is breathtaking."

"Know what else is breathtaking?"

Loli furrowed her brow as the man neared. "What?"

"Your glowing smile."

She felt her cheeks start to burn.

"You are the perfect mixture of child-like wonder... and a grown-up lust for adventure. I am in awe of you, little Swan. Wholly captivated."

Loli swallowed hard. "Gratitude, Lord Phantom. I kind of like your company as well—comfortable, yet exciting."

"Is that so?" He exited into the hallway and waited for her. "You do not *act* captivated when I am near. More like... bored."

"I'm not *bored*." She closed up the room. "Just... resigned, I guess."

"Resigned to be with your mysterious red Goblin?"

She nodded. "...Yes. What other choice do I have?"

When the Phantom moved closer, Loli backed up until the door halted her retreat.

"Have you never fantasized about falling in love? —floating through space, oblivious to all else. Have you never dreamed of meeting that *one* special person who lights up your world... starts a fire within your soul?"

"Every single day," she barely whispered.

When the cloaked man moved so close that only their clothes were separating them, Loli looked up and met his brilliant gaze. There, beneath the lit sconce by her door, the Phantom's lavender eyes sparkled like the rarest of gems. The butterflies she had always dreamt of burst to life within her.

"I have a confession to make," he whispered.

"Wha-what is it?"

"You haven't left my sight since the moment you came gliding down that grand staircase. I haven't just been stumbling upon you, Lady Swan. I have patiently waited for each precious moment to present itself—the glorious bits of time I could be near you."

Loli opened her mouth, but no words came out.

"When you told me the story of your fated Goblin... I shrank a little inside. I have watched the doors—scanned every darkened corner—trying to catch a glimpse of the man I *wish* I could be... yours."

"Phantom, I—"

He leaned down and inhaled deeply, pulling in the delicate scent of her starlight hair. He smiled. Loli's breath caught.

"When you blankly offered me that tiny cube of cheese, I was surprised you could not hear the fierce pounding in my chest. *I* could hear it—echoing loudly throughout the maze."

"I'm sorry. I didn't—"

He lightly ran the tip of his sharp nose across her brow. Loli gasped, reflexively grasping his contoured sides, clutching tightly to his firm waist. The man nearly growled.

"Lady Swan… if given only the tiniest of chances, I would worship you every moment of every day. Never would you know loneliness. Never would I let tears stain your lovely pale cheeks. My devotion to you would be unparalleled, unmatched by *any* man. Your smile would be my sustenance—your joy, my feast." He gently rested his forehead against hers. "Lovely angel in white… with my sworn vow still lingering in the heated air about us… If I ask it, would you deny your father?"

Loli tried to catch her breath. "Your whispered words are the sweetest I have ever heard. Alas, Lord Phantom, my future is no longer mine to give." She tightened her grip when she felt him stiffen within her embrace. "Your feelings are precious to me. And… I will not lie and say that I do not share in them. I am tempted, Milord."

"Lovely Swan…"

She gasped when he cupped her chin, tilting her face up as he forced her to meet his captivating gaze.

"Phantom, I… I…"

Her heart started racing uncontrollably. She could have sworn her breath caught, but her chest continued to heave.

"Go on, Milady," he whispered against her trembling lips.

"No matter how badly…"

"…Yes?"

His sweet breath was nearly her undoing. Those warring butterflies filled her tummy so fast they raced up her throat, threatened to gush forth all over the suddenly sensual man.

"I cannot crush the one I have been promised to," she quickly said, before her will was wholly stolen. "If my father invited a man—even a Goblin—to come here tonight with the promise of nothing more than a single dance… I would not break his noble vow."

"Why not, dear Swan, when I have vowed so much more than just a single dance?"

Tears burned the backs of her eyes. "Because… I know how devastated *I* would be. If I came here with the promise of meeting a man like you— no. If I came here with the promise of meeting *you*, only to have you deny me once we had met—or worse, *hide* from me— I could not bear the pain of that devastation. I will not, not even for the thing I have always longed for, do that to another living being. I pray my soul never turns *that* dark."

"And what of your good-luck charm—the prophetic little note

you found in the cellar? Do you no longer see it as a sign? Tell me true. Do you no longer want to change your fate, Lady Swan?"

"I do, but… not like this. Not by doing harm unto another."

"But I thought you *hated* Goblins."

Tears began to leak down behind her snowy mask. "Like you said… those are jaded judgments from my childhood memories. How can I find fault with a man I have never met?"

"Shhh…" He tenderly kissed the top of her head, pausing there for several long heartbeats. "It is as you say, Milady," he whispered. "If that is your wish, I pray you let me help you in it."

Loli tried to smile as she reached for his flowing raven locks. "Are you real… or did I wish you here?"

"Well, the night *is* full of magic. Isn't that what your father said?"

She barely nodded.

"If that is true, I fear all the wishing was on my part." He closed his eyes and smiled. "Your gentle touch steals my will, lovely Swan."

"I'm sorry. It's just… your hair is so beautiful. If you were mine, I'd scarce be able to keep my fingers from this glorious mane. I would brush it, braid it, and weave buttercups and morning bells all through it."

He opened his eyes then and smiled down at her, a sparkle lighting up his enchanting lavender gaze. "You would gild my manhood by making me go about with flowers in my hair?"

"I fear I would be minus the will to stop. Would you be ever cross with me?"

"Never, Milady." He tenderly fondled the starlight curl hanging down by her cheek. "If my love wished me crowned all about with tiny petals, I would wear the lovely work of your dainty hands with pride."

"If only," she barely whispered.

"Yes, Milady… if only." The Phantom took her trembling hands in his. "Come, Mistress Swan. If we remain but a moment longer, I will most certainly lose what little strength yet remains me. Let our precious friendship remain as it was before we ascended in that gilded lift— before that metal door opened and released our fragile hearts down this darkened hallway." He gently tugged and she hesitantly followed.

Loli sniffed. "Yes, Phantom. Let us remain as we once were."

"I swore you would know no tears," he half whispered, then smiled back at her. "Hurry up, Milady. The Belle of the Ball shouldn't keep her Red Romeo waiting all night."

Loli sniffed again and half chuckled.

"Let us find your Goblin Prince together, Lady Swan."

"What makes you think he's a Prince?"

"If *I* had a daughter as remarkable as you, I wouldn't promise her to anyone less."

When the bell rang to signify the start of the next game, Isabell found Loli standing stark still—staring at the table lined with various drinks.

"Hey... Time to head back out to the maze. You coming?"

Loli didn't respond.

"Swan Princess, I'm talking to you."

Still, Loli didn't turn to face her friend until the worried Elf grabbed her arm.

"Hey... You okay?"

"Oh. Umm... Yeah, Izzy. I'm fine."

"You don't *look* fine. What happened?"

"Nothing." She turned back towards the wine-filled goblets. "I think I'll sit this one out. I don't feel much like maze-running right now."

Isabell turned from her friend's haunting profile and scanned the room. When she caught sight of the Winter King deep in conversation with another royal, the Elf sighed inside.

"Want to dance then?"

Isabell grabbed her hand and tugged. Loli half smiled.

"With who? You?"

"Of course with me. I'm bored. If you don't want to go play outside, let's mingle around the dance floor."

Loli glanced back towards the swaying partygoers. Not a red mask to be found. She shrugged. "Okay. If that's what you want... sure. I'll dance with you."

"And what about me?"

The Faerie Princess swallowed hard when she heard that deliciously deep voice coming from behind her. She took a filling breath and painted on her best fake smile before turning to face the Phantom.

"*I'm* not the one who's bored. My lovely Peacock friend here is the one with antsy feet."

Isabell and the Phantom glanced towards each other, but neither spoke.

"The music is quite lovely. Enjoy yourselves. Now, if you will excuse me… I fancy a bit of air."

As Loli turned to leave, Isabell grabbed her arm. "Perhaps your father could do with a little air as well."

The Princess quickly glanced toward the King, then sweetly smiled. "I wouldn't dream of taking him away from his friends. He is in his element at the moment. Fretting over a stroll with me would only throw him off his noble game."

"Then let's play a game of our own." The Phantom gently took each woman by the small of the back and guided them towards the door. "I fear we've missed this current bout of craziness, but a whole new scheduled jaunt through the maze should begin soon enough. What do you say, Lady Peacock? Wouldn't you agree that your snowy little friend would fare better with company, than all on her lonesome?"

When Isabell opened her mouth to answer, Loli cut her off.

"I'm not lonesome. I'm not a child. And I certainly don't feel like playing another stupid game."

"Why not, honey?" Isabell took her hand. "Tell me what happened. I won't stop harassing you until you do."

Loli sighed and squeezed her eyes shut, trying to fight back her coming tears. "I'm just so torn, Izzy. My heart and my mind are at war. All I want to do is drink myself into a stupor and wake with the dawn."

When she began speaking, the Phantom stepped away, leaving the two women to their much needed privacy.

"Tell me what happened, Loli."

"Iz… I found my butterflies."

"…What?"

Loli smiled and wiped her cheeks. "My heart was beating so fast, I actually felt it pushing against the inside of my bodice. It felt like it wanted to be free, Izzy—fly out of my chest and soar straight up to the heavens."

"…You fell in love." The Elf pulled her into a comforting hug. "I'm so happy for you, Loli girl. I *knew* your dreams would come true one day. I just knew it." She pulled back and smiled down at the sniffing Faerie. "Was it your Goblin? Where is he? I want to meet him. Does your father know?"

"It wasn't the Goblin." Loli shook her head and looked away. "I haven't even *seen* the man in red, much less *met* him."

"Wait. Then… who gave you butterflies?"

"A stranger." A tiny smile turned up the corners of her mouth then. "It came completely out of nowhere. I was blindsided, Iz. We spent some time together—he even helped me win the scavenger hunt. We were fast friends almost from the get-go."

Isabell wrapped her arm around her friend and tenderly rubbed her shoulder.

"I never *dreamed* he felt… like he felt. I only thought he enjoyed teasing me about my Goblin dilemma. But when he confessed the truth of his heart… I wanted nothing more than to tell him I felt the very same way. Well… I didn't—didn't *feel* that way. At least… I didn't realize I did. Not until his whispered words nearly did me in. Ugh…" She wiped her cheeks again. "It all happened so naturally, so… out of the blue. I didn't know what to say." She turned back to face the Elf. "I'd been so caught up in my fears—in finding and then hiding from the red Goblin—I hadn't noticed what was *really* going on inside me. Not until just a little while ago."

"…What are you going to do, Loli?"

Her silent tears returned. "Exactly what I'm supposed to do. You already know that." She sighed. "I'd just like to get it over with now. I wish this crimson-masked stranger would finally appear. Teetering on the brink like this… it's maddening. I want the Goblin to show up now, or just that somehow the Ball would come to a screeching end. I want to go to bed, Izzy—cry myself to sleep and wake up like none of this ever happened. Moll was right… I was a fool for dreaming about falling in love."

"Love isn't foolish, Loli. It can be confusing, even dis-combobulating at times… but it is never foolish." She squeezed the Princess's shoulders. "You finally found your butterflies."

"Yeah… I saw stars as well. Lavender stars."

Isabell smiled softly. "No matter what happens from here on out, no one can steal that memory from you. Lock it away, Loli. Never forget how you felt—how *love* felt."

The bell chimed to signal the end of the current game.

"Want to go back inside? I won't even make you dance."

Loli snorted out a chuckle. "Sure… Playing—and snotting and fretting and wishing—isn't what I need to be doing right now, anyway. I have a suitor to prepare for. Our initial introduction… he should see me smiling, not frowning."

"I agree." The Elf nodded as they stepped back into the castle. "Besides, you'll probably need to save some of those tears for later."

"Wow, Iz. That makes me feel *so* much better."

The Elf only chuckled.

The Winter King smiled as his swan-draped daughter approached. "Hello, my dear." He kissed her forehead. "Enjoying your evening?"

"I've yet to stumble across the crimson stranger you wanted me to dance with."

"No worries, little one. He must have been delayed. That's all. Yet, his absence shouldn't rob you of your fun."

"There's nothing else I really wish to do."

"Nonsense, my child. The Kilmartins are famous for making things happen when you least expect it. Have you joined in any of their games?"

"One. I won."

"You did? What was the prize?"

She smiled. "Twelve bottles of Spring Nectar."

When her father frowned, the man at his side smiled and leaned forward. Loli's eyes widened when she realized it was the Summer King himself.

"Best prize of the night, Princess. Trust me. If you only won a single game, *that* should have been the one."

Her father sort of nudged the other man backwards. "Careful, my child. This carefree King and his vile brew have been the fall of many a good Fae. Best pass the bottles out amongst your friends. No one needs *that* much Spring Nectar."

The Summer King only laughed at her father's warning. "Let the girl live a little, you cold-hearted goat. She is young. She is beautiful. She elegantly wears the noblest title in your kingdom. This poor child deserves to leave the snow and dance in the sun for a change. Come, my dear." He reached his hand out toward her. "I would be honored if you allowed this old man to sweep you along to the music. Dance with me, Princess. Enjoy a bit of the glories of summer."

"She will do no such thing." The Winter King snorted and grumbled at his sunny counterpart. "Take a good look at this vile man, Loli. Take a look at what his glorious *Nectar* can turn you into. He is King of the Summer Fae, yet he now laughs like a foul-bred Ogre peasant."

"Ahh, yes." The Summer King chuckled. "Heavy is the head that dons a crown as glorious as mine."

When her father only growled at the man again, Loli covered her mouth and giggled.

"May I have this dance, Milady?"

When the Princess heard that familiar deep voice right behind her, she sucked in a quick breath and strangled on air.

"What happened, my child?" The King softly patted her back, concern furrowing his noble brow.

"Noth... Nothing, Your Grace." She coughed again. "I was just startled. That's all."

"Would you like a drink?" The Summer King offered her his goblet, but her father gently pushed it away.

"My apologies."

When the black-cloaked Phantom spoke, the Winter King glanced toward him.

"I fear I am the sole cause of this lovely Swan's current distress. I surprised her with my sudden request, it seems. Please, forgive me."

"No forgiveness needed, my good man." The Winter King inclined his head. "You're exactly what this enchanting woman needs. Yes, please... take her to the dance floor and keep her there as long as she will allow. Her fair presence is far too gentle for the likes of these foul men I am forced to spend my evening with."

"But, Fath—"

"Run along, child. This fine young man's is the company you need to be keeping right now. Not mine."

When the Woodland King of the Elven folk motioned for another tray of wine to be brought over, Loli's father all but pushed her into the Phantom's waiting arms.

"Shall we, Milady?" he whispered close to her ear.

Loli didn't answer. Couldn't. She felt as if she were being led through a hazy dream—a field of smiling couples and haunting melodies. When he took her by the waist and pulled her to him, Loli's heart leapt up into her throat.

"I didn't mean to catch you off guard earlier, Lady Swan." He smiled. "But I'm thrilled to know the sound of my voice chokes you up."

"You didn't *choke me up.*"

"Didn't I?" He sort of shrugged. "Perhaps I misread your reaction."

"Or perhaps it was just wishful thinking on your part."

"Oh, trust me. It was *definitely* wishful thinking on my part."

She blushed. "What do you think you're doing, anyway?"

"I think I'm helping you obey your father... Princess."

Loli's eyes widened. The Phantom chuckled.

"I'd say there are scarce few guests who do not know who the Winter King of the Fae is." He spun her around and tightened his embrace. "I'm sorry I spoiled your secret, lovely angel. Take comfort in the fact I still do not know the true beauty of your face. You were right when you said your father was protective. While his royal face is widely known and recognized... I know of no one who can properly describe *your* glorious features."

"Then how do you know they are glorious?"

"My dreams have never let me down before."

"You've *dreamt* of me, huh?"

He spun her around again, then pulled her ever closer. "I've dreamed of finding my one true love, yes."

She pushed against him as she glanced around. "You need to stop this, Phantom. The man in red could be watching us at this very moment."

"And what harm would that bring?"

"It could cause problems. You know that."

"No... What I know is, your father told me to whisk you off to the dance floor and keep you here as long as you allowed. Tell me, Princess." He leaned down. "Who could find fault with you obeying your devoted father's request? Certainly not me." He smiled softly. "Please... relax and dance with me, Lady Swan. Who knows what magic this night yet holds?"

"Why are you doing this?" she barely whispered.

"I'm not trying to hurt you, Princess. I honestly *am* trying to help you."

"How is *this* helping me? "

"Well, holding you in my arms has erased your desire to founder on Nectar, has it not?"

She blushed but didn't answer.

"I rescued you from that handsome man's unwanted advances."

"That *handsome man* is a King, and one of my father's trusted friends."

"He wasn't acting very *kingly* to me… more like the way you were describing Goblins earlier."

"He was only teasing me. He didn't mean a word of it."

"Well… *I* didn't like it."

"You were eavesdropping?"

"Yes, of course I was."

"Why?"

"To protect you."

"From a *King?*"

"From *all* other men, save me."

His answer made her butterflies return, but the feeling left her more nauseous than excited.

"But… what about my red Goblin? Will you *protect* me from him as well?"

He stiffened for a heartbeat, then relaxed and melted against her. "No… because *he* is your wish. And *my* wish is to see yours fulfilled."

Loli ran her fingers through his long raven hair before she even realized what she was doing. The Phantom shivered at her tender touch.

"We should stop," she quickly said.

When Loli tried to turn from him, the Phantom pulled her back and buried his face against her neck.

"Do not leave me, Princess. Please. Let me hold you just a little longer."

"But… afterwards… we will be able to go back to just being friends?"

"Do you want to?"

"…No. Yet, I am minus the choice."

"I will be exactly what you need me to be. Always. *Carpe noctem*, Milady. *Mutare fata.*"

She slowly relaxed within his possessive embrace. "Phantom… you melt me. If my father knew how badly I wished never to *stop* dancing with you, he would not have released me into your waiting arms. If he knew what I now feel… we would leave for the snow this very instant."

"Princess…" The Phantom gently squeezed her, then softly placed a tiny kiss on the side of her neck.

Loli froze completely.

"I wish to be your friend, yes," he whispered. "But I am far more interested in stealing your heart."

"Even if such a thing could lead to war?"

He tenderly kissed the side of her head and whispered directly into her ear, "Before this night is over, I wish you to fight for *me*."

Loli couldn't speak. She wished for that very same thing, but would never dare admit it aloud.

When the next song came to an end, they heard the muffled ring of Devlin's distant bell.

"Come, Milady." The Phantom led her toward the door. "If we stay here a moment longer, I fear a royal wrath will befall us. And, this time, I believe we *both* could use a bit of fresh air."

"This game is not a game," Devlin was saying as they stepped out into the cool air. "It is a quest… but not one for the faint of heart." He held up a long red ribbon. "There is a legend here at Castle Amhrán Oiche, a *special* kind of magic that dwells within these grounds. To my left, there beyond the southern tower…" He motioned as he spoke. "…there is an enchanted Wishing Tree. The only one of its kind, I am told."

Muffled chuckles and excited giggles spread throughout the gathered crowd.

"It is said that the ribbon of fate which binds our souls to one another…" He slid the silky fabric between his fingers. "…can become a *physical* thing, on but a single night of the year. *This* is that magical night. Come, my Lords and Ladies. If you have the courage to test your love… take a ribbon, write upon it your treasured desire, and tie it within the branches of the Wishing Tree. If your fate is truly linked with another, midnight this eve will reveal the truth of it. Tie this red symbol of your soul upon those magical branches, if the completer of your heart is present, the fateful toll when the hands of time point due

North will leave your ribbons irrecoverably entwined."

Before their host's warning words were even fully spoken, the Phantom was dragging Loli through the crowd and up to the silk-strewn table.

Devlin smiled. "Brave hearts, to be sure."

The Phantom picked up two ribbons and placed one in Loli's trembling hands. She glanced up at him, half panic-stricken.

He smiled. "What harm can it bring, Lady Swan? Your heart and will are already set upon your red Goblin, are they not?"

She didn't answer.

"Come. Let us tie our fates within the trees—see what *could* have been."

Theirs were the first two ribbons to lightly kiss the fresh cut blades of the manicured lawn, but not the last. Soon, that enormous old Wishing Tree looked as if it was shedding a hundred bloody tears. Silky red ribbons covered the tree's lower branches and hung all the way down to the dampening grass. When the gentle breeze caught them, it was as a dancing crimson waterfall.

"If the wind picks up, they're *sure* to become entangled. We should have tied them further apart… just to be sure."

"No, Lady Swan." The Phantom gently hugged her from behind. "I refuse to leave anything concerning us to chance. I want *assurance* regarding our hearts. If the night breeze is the chosen catalyst for our fate, then so be it. Whatever it takes to make you realize you should be mine… whatever it takes, Milady." He hugged her closely. "Come with me."

"Wh-where?"

"To the shadows." He took her hand. "Not far. There. Just beyond the torchlight."

"Phantom… I don't think—"

"Shhh," he whispered softly as they reached the far wall of the castle. "I only wish a tiny moment in private."

"We've had several of those, actually." She jumped slightly when her back touched the cold stones. "Many more *private moments* and people will begin to talk."

"I want them to talk, Princess." He looked down at her, tenderly caressing her cool cheek. "I want them to comment on what a perfect pair we make. If the other guests see us as a blooming couple… that would be marvelous indeed."

"Until my father caught wind of it."

"Ahh, but I *want* them to say it where your father can hear. I want him to see how perfectly we blend. And besides all that… your father is the very man who entrusted you to my care, is he not?"

"To a dance. Father entrusted you to dance with me."

"Yes, and to save you from those who would look at and treat you inappropriately. What better way to accomplish his noble goal, than to make it so no other man looks upon you… period?" He smiled. "I want them to see and *know* that you are taken… same as your father does."

"I'm pretty sure that's not the same thing my father was thinking."

"Can you be certain?"

"Pretty certain, yeah."

He chuckled. "Very well, then tell me what *you* were thinking, Lady Swan."

"Me? When?"

"When you tied your fate to that tree. Tell me. What was your wish?"

"You didn't read it?"

"I wanted to, but was terrified of that same thing. Did you read mine?"

She blushed. "…No."

"And why is that, Princess?"

"Same as you." She rested her head back against the wall. "I feared reading the bold truth of your heart, because then… this would no longer be a game."

"I am not playing, Milady."

"You know what I mean, Phantom. The masks, the absence of names, the *illusion* of accountability—or the lack thereof. These things give us courage we would not normally possess. If we were not enshrouded in these intricate secrecies, sweet promises and whispered vows of love would be much harder to come by."

Loli was shocked to suddenly feel the cool night air upon the whole of her face, soon followed by the warm, sensual sensation of the Phantom's nose encircling the tip of hers.

"Princess Swan… minus our masks, my words hold even more truth."

"You may have removed our masks, but this darkness yet keeps our secrets."

She felt his lips part into a smile against the corner of her mouth. "I am smitten by you, Milady. Wholly devoted to you." He gently placed her hand upon his chest. "The darkness cannot hide *this*."

The rapid rhythm of his racing heart seemed to almost keep time with her own. He lightly brushed the tip of his nose across her parted lips. Loli gasped.

"Phantom..." She clutched his cloak. "You tempt me beyond reason, Milord."

"Shall I tempt you further?" he whispered, tickling her closed eyelids with his sweet breath. "Tell me, Princess Swan. Have you ever been kissed?"

"...No." The breathy word came out trembling. "I have never been kissed."

He gently rested his forehead to hers. "Not even a tiny touching of the lips? —with a childhood crush, perhaps."

"...No. Never."

He sighed softly as he relaxed his weight against her. "You are my undoing, Princess. I am hopelessly changed. Never again will I be the man I was before this magical evening fell about me."

She ran her fingers into his silky black hair. "Your words speak my truth as well, Milord."

"As badly as I want to devour you where we stand... I will not steal your first kiss away in the darkness."

"But—" Her voice caught when she felt his nearing breath, then the gentle warmth of his lips as he tenderly kissed each fluttering eyelid. "...Phantom."

"My lovely Princess, I will not steal your first kiss here. I wish to take it from you as we stand before everyone you know and love."

She took several deep breaths, still clutching to his cloak. "Lord Phantom... you will most definitely be the death of me. Speeding my heart up, and then cooling it off. Filling me with butterflies, then walking away. Causing my mind to slowly spin, then promising to help me find another. You are the light *and* the darkness, Milord."

He half chuckled as he replaced her gilded mask and took her hand, leading her back into the torchlight. "Yes, and that is only because I am determined to make your dreams come true. Whether you leave this Ball with me in tow, or on the arm of your fated Goblin... I wish you never to forget me."

"You can stop then, Milord. That wish has already been granted."

"Your father spoke to me a little while ago."

Loli turned to Isabell. "About what?"

"Just wondering when I would be able to come back for another visit."

"What did you tell him?"

"I told him as soon as you invited me back."

"You know you're always welcome, Izzy. You don't need an invitation."

"I know." The Elf woman smiled. "The Summer King was asking about you."

"Pffts. Did he try to get you to dance with him?"

"He did." Isabell chuckled. "He wanted to know how you were getting on with your gentleman friend."

"My gentleman friend?"

"The one your father sent you off with." Isabell turned to face her then. "Sooo… want to fill in that huge gap, Loli girl? When did your Goblin show up?"

"He didn't."

"Then—"

"The Summer King asked me to dance."

Isabell giggled. "He's such a flirt."

"He's just nice. That's all. Anyway, Father wasn't having *any* of it—blamed too much Spring Nectar, then shoved me towards the first guy who passed by."

"Which was?"

"That Phantom man you met earlier."

"…Oh."

"Father told the poor guy to dance with me just so the Summer King would stop teasing me."

"So… no *gentleman friend*?"

"Not the one *you* were thinking, no." Loli sighed. "I'm hungry, Iz. You want something?"

"I'm good." She motioned towards a large table. "The pineapple is delicious."

Loli immediately headed that way. She was perusing the fresh fruit selection when someone grabbed her from behind—quickly squeezed both sides of her waist at once. She let out a high-pitched squeak and the Phantom chuckled. Then she began to choke on the cherry now stuck in her throat. He hurriedly spun her around to face him, eyes widening in panic.

"Are you alright?"

She coughed up the offending little fruit and took a deep breath, before slapping the worried man on the shoulder.

"Why did you do that?" She lowered her voice and glanced around at the gawking strangers. "Will you not be satisfied until you've scared the life right out of me, or all out killed me proper?"

He furrowed his brow as he gently tucked a loose curl back behind her ear. "Forgive me, Mistress Swan. I would never intentionally do you ill. I wished to play with you. That's all."

She half rolled her eyes. "I have already admitted the havoc you so easily wreak within me. Armed with such volatile knowledge, you should play nicer next time."

"As long as you promise there *is* a next time."

When he winked and smiled, Loli *did* roll her eyes then.

"I told you I was promised already. There'll be no more playing about between us. I can't handle it."

"Have you found him then? —your crimson-clad Goblin mate."

"No." She glanced back around the room. "If I'm lucky, he won't show."

"If *I'm* lucky, he won't show."

Loli sighed and pushed past the teasing Phantom man. "I wonder when the next game starts? Maybe he's been running about in the hedge garden all this time."

"Want to go see?"

"No," she answered, quicker than she meant to.

The Phantom chuckled.

"Where have you been all this time?" She glanced sideways at him. "It's been nearly an hour since we tied our wishes to that tree. What have you been up to?"

"It has only been about *half* that long, and I wasn't *up to* anything. I've just been milling about. Why?" He smiled with only one corner of his mouth. "Did you miss me?"

"Hardly." She snorted. "Pffts… Milling about. Is that what you call it these days? —groping strangers in dark corners."

"Mmm... Your jealousy is arousing."

"My what? How dare you—"

"Tell me, lovely lady." He leaned down closer, still smiling. "Are you jealous?"

"No, of course not."

"Is that so?"

"Yes, it is."

"Yet, you seemed flustered... agitated. Thinking about me caressing another woman, in the dark, pushed back in a corner—"

"Stop it," she hissed quietly, then slapped him again. "Now you're just being ridiculous."

"Am I?" His teasing smile softened. "I think you are trying too hard to resist me, little Swan. Counting the moments since last we met, getting flustered when I tease you, blushing when—"

"Pardon me, beautiful Swan."

Loli jumped and turned toward the bowing stranger now addressing her. When the man raised his head, she realized he was dressed as a regal golden lion.

"Will you grace me with this dance, lovely lady?"

She blushed brightly, thankful her mask covered the biggest part of her cheeks.

"She is spoken for." The Phantom stepped between them. "Your valiant request is denied."

When the lion man bowed again and walked away, Loli pinched the Phantom on the back of the arm.

"Ouch. What did you do *that* for?"

"I can speak for myself. Thank you very much."

"If you can, then why didn't you?"

"I didn't get the chance."

"What? Did you need more time to giggle and ogle him?"

"I didn't giggle, and I *definitely* didn't ogle him."

"Looked like it from where *I* was standing."

"Then perhaps you should stand somewhere else."

"Very well." He moved to her side and gently touched the small of her back. "Better now?"

"Not even close," she half grumbled.

"*This* way, perhaps men will think twice before approaching you."

She squirmed away from his protective touch. "If they request, I know how to deny. I've got this, Phantom."

"Yes. I've heard you say that before."

"Besides, what would my Goblin say if he saw you rubbing all over me? —here... in the middle of a well-lit ballroom."

"I was hardly *rubbing*," he mumbled. "So... we are back to this? You freely admit the crimson stranger is truly *your* Goblin."

"No. Th-that's not what I meant."

"It's what you said."

"I only meant that... Ugh! You *know* what my insides are going through. *That* is the only thing I have freely admitted to you." She swallowed hard and turned away. "Spare me. Please. Go... harass some other poor harmless soul."

Loli heard him chuckle as she stomped off, then felt his sudden embrace as he swept her out the door and back out into the night.

"What are you doing?"

She pushed him away, but the Phantom pulled her back to him.

"I am only trying to keep you safe from harm," he whispered, close to her ear. "Ensure you remain unmolested until your Goblin arrives."

"I'm not so sure that's what you're doing at all."

A bell rang out as Devlin Kilmartin stepped out onto the patio. "Players now gather for the ribbon hunt."

"Ribbons?" someone grumbled. "Didn't we only just play with ribbons?"

"Not like this, you didn't." Devlin smiled. "For this game... there are hundreds of green ribbons tied within the hedges, but only two are attached to keys. The couple who finds the matching room keys will win a night here at Castle Amhrán Oiche, and a private boat tour with the dawn."

Guests began to whisper and giggle.

"Yet... there is a slight twist, I fear."

A hush fell across the lawn as all eyes turned to their half-smiling host.

"This game will be played... in the dark."

With his words, the many torches throughout the maze suddenly were snuffed out.

"You will need your partner more than ever, my friends. Feel your way through the maze. Search every nook and cranny. Remember, you must emerge from the other side with *two* keys." His smile widened. "Ready? Begin."

The excited guests began to race towards the hedge maze. Loli was staring after them when she felt the tug on her hand.

"Come on, sweet Swan." The Phantom smiled softly. "Spending this time... with you... within a darkened, leafy labyrinth... That prize is as good as ours, Princess. I will do *whatever* it takes to ensure my night with you never ends."

"You are ripping my heart out in pieces," she half whispered, her tiny hand trembling in his. "I don't think I can bear another moment of it."

The Phantom stopped teasing then, his smile slowly fading.

"But... Princess... I only wanted to—"

"And you think I don't want the same thing?" Hot tears burned in her eyes. "How can you do it?"

"Do what?"

"Play at nothing more than friends one moment, then whisper to my heart the next."

"I was only trying to make you smile." He lowered his head. "I thought you *wanted* to be friends."

She didn't answer.

"As far as whispering to your heart... I have tried to control myself. Believe me. But when I look into your lovely eyes..." He met her watery gaze then. "...reason abandons me, Princess."

Loli held his sorrowful lavender gaze for several long heartbeats, then sighed and turned back towards the castle.

"I will find him, Lady Swan. If it's the last thing I do... I will see that you have your Goblin."

She didn't answer him, only let the door slowly close between them.

The night was fast coming to a close. Loli was excited, and saddened. She'd spent the last hour with Isabell and then with her father and his royal friends... trying to work up the courage to ask him to meet her Phantom, or simply to withdraw his promise of her hand to the Goblin. She could muster the strength for neither. Now, she was just biding her time, hiding out until she would be called to gift their gracious hosts with deserved payment—another magical extension to their already abnormally long mortal lives. Because of an ancient Fae debt earned through Devlin and Elsbeth's help and devotion to their kind, extended youth and beauty were granted the loving couple and their only son. Loli determined she would keep to herself until the event's end, bestow the priceless blessing on their hosts, and then hurry back to her room and the bounty of Spring Nectar awaiting her there.

"Not much longer now." She glanced towards the elaborate clock. "If I can hold out only a *few* more minutes—"

Her words ceased when a flash of crimson caught her eye.

"No… This can't… this can't *possibly* be happening right now."

"*What* are you doing?"

Loli squeaked and nearly jumped out from her hiding place behind the large marble pillar. She turned to find her Phantom smiling down at her.

"Did I surprise you? Again?"

"You made me half jump out of my skin! Again!"

She flicked his arm, the Phantom only chuckled.

"I finally found your Goblin, Milady." He leaned down. "Far wall… a little to the right… standing beside that ridiculous-looking Centaur."

"I know where he is. I spotted him just a moment ago. Why do you think I'm hiding here?"

"Ah ha! So you *are* hiding from the man of your dreams. I thought we had already discussed this. Many times."

"I am *not* hiding. And… he isn't the man of my dreams."

The Phantom saw the obvious pain in her pale blue eyes and swallowed down the words he *truly* wanted to say. "But how do you know for sure if you haven't even gotten a good look at him? Come on." He gently touched her lower back. "Dance with me. I'll spin you over there beside him for a quick look-see."

"Not a chance." She brushed his hand away. "What if he sees me? Sees *us*?"

"Well it's not like he can tell who you are or anything."

"Take a look around, Phantom. Do you see any other white swans?"

"No," he said. "I can see *no* other women," he whispered, mostly to himself.

"If my father told me what *he* was wearing, don't you believe it would hold true that he divulged the same information concerning me, to the Goblin?"

"I *suppose* that would stand to reason, yes."

"So if you take me out there on the dance floor, he's *certain* to notice me. Then I'll *have* to dance with him."

"But isn't that the point of this whole evening? —getting to know your betrothed."

"But it was almost over. I was almost free. Ugh... I think I'm going to be sick." She began fanning herself. "It's suddenly so hot in here... I can't breathe."

"Come with me."

Before Loli even understood what was happening—and while the room was still spinning—the Phantom whisked her through the crowd and back out into the night.

"*Breathe*, little Swan. That's it. Take a good, deep breath. Feeling better?"

She nodded as she filled her lungs once more, then leaned back against the cool stone wall.

"Are you sure, Maiden?" He gently cupped her forehead, then touched her pale cheeks. "You're not going to faint on me, are you?"

"I just might." She sucked in another full breath. "My heart is racing right out of my chest."

"Shhh... Calm down, Milady." He smiled softly. "The thought of gently swaying in that Goblin's arms set your mind to reeling, didn't it?"

"Stop it." She chewed on her bottom lip. "Why are you suddenly so happy about this? Quit teasing me, Phantom. Can you not see I am in distress?"

He moved closer. "I can see your rare beauty shines brightest by moonlight."

"W-what?" She swallowed hard. "Please, Phantom. Don't do this to me. Not now."

He smiled. "The gentle glow of your soft skin." He barely touched the side of her neck, carefully painting a tingling path down to her collarbone. "You are pure perfection, Milady."

"Have you gone mad?" She gently pushed against him. "The red-dressed man is just through this door. Stop playing, I beg you."

Yet, he didn't, only continued to gently caress her bared flesh.

"Phantom, have you been sampling the Spring Nectar?"

"Not a drop, lovely Swan. As tempting as that bubbly golden libation is, I refrained—wanted to stay stone sober so I could keep an eye on you."

"Still? Even though the man I have been waiting for has finally arrived?"

"Umm hmm." He leaned closer. "I had to make certain no filthy Goblin snatched you away from me."

"From *you?*"

He smiled. "From my honorable protection, yes."

"But that's all over now. Gratitude, Phantom, but I fear I must release you from your assumed task, noble as it is."

"And what if I do not wish to be released?"

When he smiled that time, Loli's heart suddenly sped back up... but in a good way.

"Tell me true, Phantom. Is all of this glorious hair actually yours? Not part of your mysterious disguise, or anything?"

"It is all mine, Princess," he barely whispered.

"It is stunning." She gently twisted a long raven lock around her finger. "It puts me in mind of a starless summer night."

"And your angelic tresses... your lovely hair *is* the stars, Milady. We blend well—opposite, yet perfectly matched." He tenderly ran the backs of his fingers down her soft cheek. "You remind me of the snow... pure and pristine."

When he bent down towards her, Loli's breath came faster and faster, her chest heaving with the effort. Yet, the kiss she was expecting didn't reach her trembling lips, but the feel of his sharp nose lightly gliding up the side of her cheek nearly made her swoon.

"So lovely," he whispered, close to her ear. "Would that I was the man your father chose for you." He pulled back slightly. "Would you have hidden from *me*, little Swan?"

She shook her head. "No," she barely managed to say. "I would seek you out in earnest. I wish to gaze into those magical lavender eyes in the waking dawn. Even by firelight—hidden beneath that pale mask... they are breathtaking."

His smile widened. "You are enchanting when you tease, and even more so when you're honest." He stepped back and offered her his hand. "The time has come, Lady Swan. Do you have the strength to face your future now?"

"No." She clutched the edges of his dark cloak. "No, Phantom. I do not wish to be parted from you just yet."

"But the evening is nearing its end, lovely lady. Only a few songs are left to be played. Will you defy your father's wishes? Will you accept my previous vow?"

When she didn't answer, the Phantom tipped her chin up and whispered, "*Carpe noctem*, my love. *Mutare fata.*"

When his lips barely brushed against hers, Loli gasped and pulled him closer.

"Come, Milady. Your destiny awaits."

Knowing she should not, Loli snatched a goblet from a passing tray… and discarded the empty container onto the next table as she passed. She squeezed tight to the Phantom's hand as he guided her across the crowded dance floor and right up to the crimson-clad stranger.

She swallowed hard and looked to the mysterious man she *truly* wanted to be with, and then to the Goblin her fate was now tied to.

Loli took a deep breath and cleared her throat, drawing the crimson stranger's unwanted attention.

When the man turned her way—still laughing from his current conversation with an Elf Lord—the hesitant Princess curtsied politely and tried to smile.

"Milord."

The man's eyes widened. "Loli!"

Before she even knew what was happening, swirls of red fabric had engulfed her. She was lifted into the air and then embraced in a tight bear hug. Loli gasped for breath when the man finally plopped her back down to her feet.

"Where have you been hiding all night? I've looked *everywhere* for you."

"I wasn't hiding, Milord. Just… building up courage, I suppose."

"Courage?" The man laughed loudly. "Courage for what?"

When she tilted her head to the side, the crimson man laughed again.

"Come now, Loli. It hasn't been *that* long, has it?"

The stranger removed his mask then.

"Bryn... Bryndle?" Her eyes widened with the realization. "Bryndle!" She tore off her mask and jumped into his arms. "When did you get back? Father didn't tell me you were coming to the Ball."

"Did he not tell you to seek out a man dressed all in red?"

"Yes, but... I thought he was talking about a Goblin."

"A Goblin?" Bryndle laughed again. "Is Father still trying to marry you off to that horde? How long has he threatened you with that?"

"My whole life, feels like."

Bryndle finally released her only when the Winter King approached.

"Father." His son bowed. "Seems your teasing has caused my little sister some undue stress this evening."

"I wasn't teasing." The King turned toward Loli. "Have you not enjoyed yourself this evening, dear one?"

"I have, Father, yes."

"And still... you are wavering where my wishes are concerned?"

"I'm..." She bit her lip and swallowed hard. "I fear I may be smitten, Father."

"I see..." The King furrowed his noble brow. "Will you yet defy me in this, dear daughter?"

Loli took a deep breath and lowered her head. "No, Father. Your will, my wings... always."

"Well met, my child. Well met." He smiled. "I am glad you have finally accepted your destiny, little one. After closely watching your actions this evening, I felt safe in going forward with the proceedings. With your gentle heart ever on my mind... I accepted your dowry and your betrothed now awaits."

At his words, Loli quickly looked up at her father. He motioned with a nod towards the dance floor. When she slowly turned, her Phantom was standing in the very center of that large room. He removed his haunting mask and regally bowed toward her. Loli's heart seized with her first glimpse of the unmasked man's handsome face. She smiled. Then, she quickly scanned the room.

"But... where's my Goblin?"

"Awaiting you on the dance floor," her brother whispered against the back of her head, then gave her a little push.

She focused back on her Phantom as she took a couple hesitant steps forward. He finally raised his head and smiled. Her knees nearly buckled.

"Hello, Princess Loli. I am Argoth LeRain." He bowed again. "First born Prince of the Great Goblin King… at your service."

When her feet suddenly froze to the floor, Argoth swooped in and protectively wrapped his arm around her tiny waist.

"Are you well, Princess?" he whispered softly. "Are you going to faint?"

Tears burned the backs of her eyes then. Loli bit her bottom lip and silently shook her head.

"Are you certain?"

She smiled and nodded.

"Then… may I have this dance, Milady?"

When the music started up he pulled her close, swaying and steadying her at the same time.

"Does my scent turn your stomach, Milady? Do I carry the foul stench of the rancid bogs?"

"You smell like wild honeysuckles." She giggled. "It makes my head swim."

"In a *good* way?"

She nodded. "In an *extremely* good way."

"I'm glad to hear it." He leaned down and whispered, "Because you'll be smelling me for an *extremely* long time."

She blushed brightly. Argoth spun her around, and she melted against him.

"Did you know it was me the whole time?"

"I did."

"Did Izzy know you were you?"

"Who's Izzy?"

"The Elf, in peacock clothing."

"Ahh, yes." He smiled. "No. I don't know Izzy, only that she is your friend. If she knew who I was, I haven't a clue."

A second song started up, but Loli didn't notice.

"I was so excited for this evening, I arrived early."

Loli furrowed her brow. "You did?"

Argoth nodded. "I watched as you gracefully glided down those majestic stairs on your father's noble arm. You took my breath away, Princess. I knew you were to be donned as a white swan, yes. Still… your beauty caught me off guard. Your beauty, *and* your sharp tongue."

She blushed again.

"I liked it," he whispered softly, tickling her ear. "I liked it *too* much."

"If you knew it was me, why didn't you tell me who *you* were? That doesn't seem very fair now, does it?"

"I was going to tell you… until you spoke true your heart concerning Goblins."

"Oh… yeah." Her cheeks flamed. "Sorry about that."

"No apologies necessary. Once I knew how you truly felt, I determined it would be best if you got to know me *before* I was unmasked. I wanted you to love *me*, Loli. I hate to think how our hearts would have progressed, had I simply been pushed upon you. Our fathers were bent on using us to seal their alliance, it's true. Yet… I would *never* force you to be mine, Princess. A loveless marriage can do much more harm than good, in the long run."

"Did you know it was my brother who'd be dressed all in red?"

"I did not. That was quite puzzling indeed." He furrowed his dark brows. "I will admit… that particular bit had me rather upset most of the evening. Had your father changed his mind? Had I missed his royal messenger because I left early for the Ball? Something was definitely amiss, yet I could not simply approach the King and demand answers of him. Not here. Not like this. I vowed to determine who this *cockscomb* suitor actually was. I mean… your father had arranged our meeting and he *knew* I was to be dressed as a Phantom. The whole *Red Goblin* spin had me teetering from anger to madness to the rawest form of jealousy imaginable. I couldn't fathom *why* your noble father would have betrayed me. I *had* to solve the mystery… while keeping you ever close to my side."

"What did you do when you found out the truth of it? —that Bryndle was my red-clad Goblin."

"I came to get you straight away." He smiled. "I swept you back out into the night and pressed you up against the wall."

"Stop it." She playfully pinched him. "You did no such thing."

"Didn't I?" He gently brushed his nose across her cheek. "Didn't I press myself against you? Cause your breath to catch and quicken… make your lovely breasts heave against my chest?"

Loli gasped then, her pulse steadily rising.

"You are my undoing, Faerie Princess." He tightened his embrace. "Why do you think I whisked you back into this ballroom and straight up to your waiting brother?"

She tightly gripped his firm shoulders, but couldn't possibly speak.

"I had to have you in my arms, Loli. I had to be holding you—

feeling your heart beat wildly against me. Here. Now. I feared if we stayed outside a moment longer…"

When he didn't go on, it only made her pale cheeks flame all the brighter.

"And when you tried to tell your father the truth of your heart, *tried* to ask for me… that was it, Milady. I was wholly undone. Nothing will ever make me happier. You are mine now, Princess. Are you satisfied with your fate?"

She nodded. "I am beyond satisfied, yes… but you err."

"In what?"

"You are *mine*," she whispered. "*Carpe noctem*, beautiful Goblin."

When Argoth's lips gently met hers, Loli didn't even realize they'd stopped dancing. When his tender kiss deepened… even the crowd's thunderous cheers were completely washed away. Time stood still.

"…Loli."

She didn't hear her brother calling.

"Hey… Loli."

Still, she did not dare break their enchanted embrace. Only when her brother yanked one of her curls, did the love-drunk Faerie Princess turn toward him.

"Hmm? Yes? What is it?"

"Father wishes to know if you are satisfied." Bryndle inclined his head toward Argoth, then looked back to his sister. "Are you ready, Loli?"

"Ready for what?"

"Your Amalgamation."

"What? *Now?*"

Brindle nodded. "The dowry has been accepted. The treaty has been signed. If the two of you have no objections, the ceremony will commence forthwith."

Loli turned back to her Goblin Prince, wide-eyed.

Argoth smiled at her. "Our fathers are anxious for peace." He leaned down closer and whispered, "I am anxious as well, my love." He met the Faerie Prince's noble gaze. "We are ready, Your Highness. We have no objections, and wish to be joined as soon as possible."

"Very good." Bryndle smiled. "The Summer King has asked to do the honors."

Argoth bowed towards the approaching monarch. "The honor would be ours, entirely."

The golden-haired Faerie King softly cleared his throat, then began his hauntingly beautiful song. Loli and Argoth faced each other, and when instructed, stepped toward and *through* the other.

The Summer King's song continued. "…Now turn… face one another… and join…"

He wove these words through the tune until the happy couple had blended their essence seven times—visibly marked by the raven lock of hair now framing the left side of Loli's face, and the starlight strands so obviously highlighting Argoth's high cheekbone.

"By my voice, my station, and the Holy Rite of Amalgamation… your souls have been eternally entwined. A creature can spend years trying to undo the song I have sung this day… only to find that they have entangled your hearts all the more. Go in peace, young ones. May you bless your houses with many noble heirs."

The ornate clock struck midnight just as the smiling couple kissed. Loli almost staggered when Argoth slowly released her. He pulled her against his chest and held her close.

"We have done well, Your Majesty," the Goblin King said as he stepped up beside Loli's father.

The Faerie King smiled. "Ever will our blood be as one."

When the Goblin King cleared his throat for the *second* time, Loli and Argoth finally turned towards him.

The King held out a key. "Your wedding gift… top room in the southern tower."

"Gratitude, Father." Argoth bowed before accepting. "You ready to go, Princess?" He placed the key in her dainty hands before sweeping her up in his arms and heading towards the gilded lift. "Shall we?"

Loli was still giggling when the elevator doors softly closed.

Warm sunlight and the sweet sound of birds chirping brought a smile to her lips. Loli stirred, then Argoth pulled her to him—spooning her there in the first rays of dawn.

"Good morning, Princess."

"Good morning, my love."

"For a heartbeat, I feared last night to be only a glorious dream."
She chuckled. "I've been pinching myself all night."

"Can I pinch you as well?" He lightly nibbled her shoulder. "Let's stay like this all day."

"Would that we could, but Bryndle will be here any minute."

"Nonsense. Your brother wouldn't dare disturb newlyweds during their first morning together."

"He would, and he will. We still have to bestow our Faerie gift upon the Kilmartins."

Argoth groaned and squeezed her tighter. Loli giggled.

"Don't worry. It won't take long. I'll have Moll round us up some breakfast and be back here before you can even miss me."

"Too late." He kissed the back of her head. "I already miss you."

A knock came at the door then. "You ready, Sis?"

Loli giggled. "Told you."

Argoth groaned again.

"Give me five minutes, Bryn."

"I'll wait right here."

"Of course you will," she grumbled under her breath as she reluctantly slid out from under the covers and grabbed her robe.

Argoth smiled at her. "Did you grow ever more beautiful as you slept? Tell me, Loli. Do Faeries always glow as they slumber?"

She winked at him. "*You're* the reason I'm glowing, my love. You and only you." She glanced out the window then. "Oh… The Wishing Tree." She quickly looked back to Argoth. "We forgot to check our ribbons."

"And what mere wishes could ever hold up before what we now share between us?" He stood and hugged her to him. "It is as the Summer King said… we are irrecoverably entwined, lovely Princess."

"Wow… Your eyes really *are* breathtaking in the daylight. Just like… sparkling gemstones."

Argoth smiled. "And *yours* put that shimmering water down there to shame. Tell me true, Loli." He gently twirled her single raven lock around his slim finger. "Are you a Faerie… or an angel in Fae clothing?"

"I was just thinking that exact same thing. You are the angel who listened to me wish upon a star every single night, aren't you? You fell from the heavens just to sate my heart's desire."

The Goblin Prince moaned as he pulled her against him and

kissed her deeply. Loli was lost—blissfully lost in his possessive embrace. She melted to his will, returned his worshiping caress. They no longer heard the birds chirping, the gentle waves cast off by the boats below… or the ever-growing pounding of her brother's fist upon their door. *Theirs* would be a love story for the ages.

Sabrina's Curse

Leanne Tyler
RTS '17

Leanne Tyler

Sabrina Gilchrist sat in the sunlight, but not for the warmth. Long ago, she'd resigned herself to the truth of her lot in life — never to feel the warmth of sunlight on her face again. Even in her home parlor, she wore a veil to cover the hideous disfigurement of her face.

A fire burned low in the hearth to ward off the chill of the March afternoon and allowed her to tat in comfort. A lady's profession which provided well for her and her father, yet she longed to have the adventures like those of her friend, Lydia. The village matrons didn't whisper behind their fans in Lydia's presence, and children didn't shriek in horror and run from her.

Sabrina stared out the window and wondered what it would be like to walk down the lane to the village, or to attend a social. Not that people were cruel to her. Everyone in the village knew all too well the cause of her disfigurement and pitied her for it. However, their pity did not extend to afternoon teas in their homes.

A quick knock interrupted her daydreaming, and Lydia Arms came rushing in. "Sabrina! Oh Sabrina. Look what your maid asked me to bring you. It arrived by messenger riding in an elaborate coach only moments ago. My carriage passed it as I was coming toward your house."

Me? Sabrina's breath caught in her throat and she put her tatting aside. Who'd be sending *her* such an invitation? Where was she being invited? Would her father even permit her to go?

With more questions forming than her mind could process at once, she joined Lydia at the window so they could look at this wondrous piece of stationary together.

"Surely this is a mistake," Sabrina finally uttered after swallowing several times just to form the words.

"It's no mistake, my darling friend. The envelope is addressed to you and you alone. Here, you do the honor of opening it."

Sabrina swallowed again, slowly took the crisp vellum paper with her trembling fingers, and held it for a moment, admiring the fine script of her name before looking up at her friend. "I-I can't."

"Of course you can. Don't be a silly goose." Lydia's eyes danced with mirth.

Taking a breath for courage, Sabrina slipped her finger underneath the edge of the vellum and broke the wax seal embossed with the ornate Kilmartin crest. She gasped, her knees grew weak, and she swooned.

Lydia rushed forward and took the invitation from her. "You are cordially invited by Devlin and Elsbeth Kilmartin to Castle Amhrán Oiche for their annual masquerade ball on the evening of March seventeen at seven o'clock in the evening." Lydia paused for a moment and looked at her with excitement. "Oh Sabrina! Do you know what this means?"

Weakly, she nodded, still not understanding how she had been selected to attend such a ball or why they'd even want her on the guest list. But it did not matter.

Lydia kept prattling on, but Sabrina only caught the tail end of her friend's words. "Not just anyone gets an invitation to attend the ball at Castle Amhrán Oiche. I'm so envious. You might even meet the Kilmartins' son. No one in the village knows what he looks like, or how old he is, but if he takes after his father, he must be quite handsome. Oh just imagine, Sabrina, what if you were to dance with him, and he fell in love with you? I'd give anything to be a firefly on the wall that night."

Years of pity had taught Sabrina to be more practical than her fanciful friend. "Lydia, you're a dear, but the curse laid upon me has quite sealed my fate. No gentleman could gaze upon my face and fall in love."

Lydia smiled and placed both hands gently on the sides of Sabrina's veiled face. "It's a masquerade ball, my dear. Everyone will be wearing costumes and masks. It's the perfect time for you to venture out. No one will see your face. I will create an exquisite costume for you. A beautiful harem girl with mysterious eyes."

"A mysterious harem girl?" The thought intrigued her. "But where will we get the materials to make the costume? Is there even enough time?"

"Of course there's time. I'll make the time. And as for materials, don't you still have that trunk of your mother's party clothes in the attic? Perhaps there will be something there I can use."

Sabrina shook her head. "No. We can't. You remember how father reacted when he found us playing with the clothes as children."

"Yes, but this is different. I'll take those clothes and turn them into something new. Besides, it's been so many years now, I'm certain he has forgotten what is in that trunk. And if he gets angry, I'll take the blame. He is so accustomed to being angry with me for any mischief we get into that he won't hold this against you."

They made their way to the attic, and Sabrina opened up the shuttered windows to let light in and they began their task. After searching among the many trunks, they finally found the perfect gown to alter into a costume.

Lydia squealed with glee as she took out a rich blue and green ensemble with an elaborate jeweled belt. They carefully packed the rest of the costumes back inside and went to Sabrina's room.

"First, you must try this on so I can see how well it fits." Lydia instructed.

Sabrina did and her friend took measurements before taking the dress and leaving for her home where she could work with her own supplies. But she promised to return the next day with a completed costume.

Excited, but afraid her father would not agree to the plan, Sabrina went back to the parlor and her tatting, trying to pretend nothing out of the ordinary had happened that day.

By the time Lydia returned the following afternoon, Sabrina had finished the handkerchief and was working on a special one for the hosts of the party. After she calmed enough to thoroughly read the invitation, she discovered the ball was also the Kilmartins' anniversary. Inspired by a dream, she'd sketched the Kilmartin crest and was tatting it into the design of the handkerchief when Lydia arrived carrying a large box.

"Let's see if this fits you."

"You want me to change in here?"

"I don't feel like climbing all those stairs to your bedroom carrying this box." Lydia set the box down and went to pull the drapes closed so no one would see in through the large picture window.

"Also, close your eyes."

"Why?"

"Because I want to see the expression on your face when you see yourself in the outfit for the first time."

"But how will I dress?"

"I'll dress you. It will be fun."

"All right." Sabrina undressed down to her underpinnings, closed her eyes. To her surprise, Lydia removed Sabrina's corset and laced her into a smaller one. She guided Sabrina's arms into what felt like sheer sleeves. Her petticoat was removed as well as her pantaloons, replaced with what felt like several layers of sheer silk that cuffed around her bare ankles.

"Don't open your eyes yet," Lydia instructed. "I'm going to fix your hair and put on the veil. I want you to see it all as one complete picture."

Sabrina sighed and kept her eyes shut tight, wondering what the costume must look like. She knew it was not a very warm garment for her stomach and feet were chilled. Surely there were shoes and warm stockings? The Spring Equinox hadn't arrived yet, and the temperature rarely rose above forty degrees.

Once Lydia had fastened the veil in place she stepped away. "Now you may open your eyes."

Sabrina opened her eyes as her friend pulled back the curtains and let the afternoon sunlight enter the room. She looked down at her waist and saw the elaborate jeweled belt hanging across her hips. The sheer material on her legs was split down the sides, exposing part of her bare legs, and secured into jeweled cuffs at her ankles. Her stomach was cold because it too was bare and what she originally mistook for a small corset looked more like a fitted piece of material and a short, sheer-sleeved bolero jacket.

The only modest part of the costume was the veiled mask that hid her identity. What had Lydia been thinking? There was no way she could venture out in public in such a scandalous costume.

Yet she liked the way it made her feel. She twirled around and swayed her hips back and forth, as she imagined a belly dancer would, and laughed at how free she felt.

Lydia laughed as well and they embraced for a moment, but when they pulled apart, Sabrina sobered. "What shall I tell my father?"

She had no more than uttered the question when the parlor door opened and startled them both.

"What about your father?" Lord Gilchrist asked, stopping short in the doorway. His eyes widened, as he slowly looked his daughter up and down. "What are you wearing, Sabrina? Cover yourself at once."

Mortified, she grabbed a blanket from the nearby bench and wrapped herself in it.

"It's a costume, Lord Gilchrist." Lydia quickly explained. "She's been invited to the Kilmartins' masquerade ball. I fashioned this for her. No one will ever suspect who she is while she's there."

His frown deepened and he shook his finger at Lydia. "I should have known you had a hand in this, Lydia Arms. But I will not allow my daughter to go to any party dressed like a strumpet."

Lydia rushed forward. "I can make her a matching cloak. Add a sheer, translucent material to cover her more but it will still give the appearance of seeing her skin. She will be a mysterious harem girl. The veil will conceal her identity. It will allow her to have a wonderful adventure."

He went to the fireplace to warm himself. "The Kilmartin affair, you say? My, my, this is an honor. Why am I only now hearing about this?" He clasped his hands behind his back and turned to face them.

"I only received the invitation yesterday," Sabrina explained.

"And she may never receive another invitation should she turn this one down," Lydia added.

"I do not like for Sabrina to go outside the village for her own protection. And now you say you want to go to a *party*?"

"Father, it is a masquerade ball. No one will see my face, and I am certain the Kilmartins will properly protect their guests."

Her father's eyes went dark and to the past. "Your mother thought the same about all the parties she attended, and you paid a dear price for her carelessness."

"Please, Father. No one will ever know it is me."

Lord Gilchrist was silent for a long moment. "I do not like it, but I cannot deprive you from this one night of fun. The guest list is different every year. As Lydia said, it is rare that the same person from the village is invited more than once in their lifetime. But sending you off to a party alone, unchaperoned..." He walked over to the window, staring out into the field for several moments before he turned back to them. "Mark my words, Lydia Arms. If Sabrina comes back harmed, I will hold you personally responsible. Do you understand me?"

Lydia swallowed and nodded. "I do."

"Very well. You have my blessing."

Sabrina squealed, clapped her hands together, and bounced on the balls of her feet.

An Arabian sultan? Stefan Kilmartin stared in dismay at the costume his valet had placed on the bed. His mother's idea complete with a jeweled turban, pointed-toe slippers, and flowing silk pants. *Mother, I think you've lost your mind.*

He donned his costume for the evening's masquerade ball, not sure why his mother had insisted he dress like an Arabian sultan. But he had to admit he liked the freedom the costume provided. The silk fabric molded to his slender hips and thighs, and then flowed loosely to the cuffs at his ankles. The sharp cut of the green, beaded and embroidered Sherwani jacket etched in black fit him like a glove—he couldn't recall another garment that had felt so natural to wear. His only saving grace was the mask he'd be wearing to hide his identity from the villagers who were invited every year. But it was one night. One night out of every year to celebrate his parents' anniversary, so he would wear the ridiculous outfit to please his mother. There was nothing he wouldn't do for her.

The curled-up toes of his shoes bounced as he headed down the winding staircase, turned at the east landing and crossed to the balcony bridge that overlooked the ballroom. A few early arrivals had already begun filling the marbled entryway waiting to be announced. A quick glance to the opposite landing, and he spotted his parents making their way down the stairs from the west wing.

He joined them for the receiving line. "You look wonderful, Mother," he said in greeting, amazed at how beautiful she always looked on these occasions. Her youth and vigor belied her true age thanks to the Faeries.

"Thank you, darling." She kissed him on the cheek. "You look handsome tonight. Maybe you will meet a beautiful harem girl."

"Don't start, Mother," he warned, good-naturedly. "Let's not make tonight about my finding a wife. It is about you and father celebrating another glorious year together."

"But I want you to be happy, Stefan. To know the joy that your father and I share together. It is high time that you gave us grandchildren. We really want to move on with our lives, but until you marry, we cannot."

"Elsbeth, you heard our son. Let tonight be about us and not him. Even if I, too, would like him to finally settle down, but we must be patient. I have faith that Stefan will know when the time is right, or rather when he meets the right one." Devlin wrapped his arm around his wife and pulled her close.

"It isn't that I don't want to marry, but I know very well that the *right* woman must be my bride. She must be kind of heart, gentle in spirit, and as beautiful on the outside as within. Alas, I have yet to meet her. And until I do…"

"I know." Elsbeth smiled and patted her son on the cheek. "It is my wish every year that this ball will bring the perfect maiden to our abode and you will meet her. Please don't discredit any of our guests this evening. You have lived among the magical so long, I fear you may have become a bit jaded."

Stefan gave in to her. "All right, mother. I will keep an open mind."

"That is all we can ask, son." Devlin smiled as the castle door opened and several more guests were escorted to the top of the stairs.

The butler announced the first guest. "From the Far East, Samurai and Geisha."

For nearly an hour he stood with his parents greeting their masked guests one by one, before his mother sighed and turned to him. "Well, did any of the young ladies catch your eye?"

"I fear not."

"The night is young, dear." Elsbeth took her husband's hand. "It's time for your father and me to have the first dance. Try to relax and enjoy yourself."

While he knew who some of the guests were under their masks, part of the fun was trying to guess who lurked beneath the costume. Perhaps a few of his friends had snuck in past the receiving line. However, he was certain his childhood friend Bryndle, the Fairy Prince, hadn't arrived yet. He wandered over to one of the many refreshment tables stationed around the spacious ballroom and selected a glass of spring nectar. Turning back toward the dance floor, he spotted the most enchanting creature on the balcony.

Mesmerized, he watched a footman take her cloak, revealing her next to nothing costume. It was the bluest fabric he'd ever seen complimented by a striking green, and he was certain he'd only seen that color combination one other time in his life. The Azorean sea. He'd fallen in love with the beauty of the water and land when he'd sailed to the coast of Ponta Delgada in Portugal. Who was this enchanting creature who moved with the grace of the sea? The question plagued him as he watched her slowly descend the stairs to the landing where he'd only moments ago stood in the receiving line.

As the young lady paused for a moment, he saw her costume more clearly and noticed she was dressed as his counterpart. A harem girl to tempt his heart. For a moment, he thought to dismiss the girl from his mind, but then the candlelight from the many chandeliers in the room shown on her eyes, and he was drawn to her like no one before. It didn't matter that he couldn't see her face for the opaque veil covered all but her blue eyes. His heart skipped a beat, and in a trancelike state he crossed through the center of the floor with disregard to the couples currently dancing the céili and causing them to separate out of time to the music, and went half-way up the steps to greet the lady.

He bowed over her hand, took her fingers in his, and gently kissed her hand. "Welcome to Castle Amhrán Oiche. Please say you will save a waltz on your dance card for me?"

Being late to the ball wasn't how she'd wanted to begin this evening, but a broken carriage wheel forced her to walk the last quarter of a mile to the castle. The journey had been easier for her and the footman because the dirigibles lighted the path. And despite the cold, the fur-lined cloak and slippers Lydia had fashioned kept her warm, or she'd have surely frozen.

Heart racing, Sabrina stopped on the landing to catch her breath. With the ball already begun, there was no butler to announce her, but she found a footman who delivered her gift to the designated table. From her vantage point, she stood mesmerized by the colorful costumes, the lively music from some sort of brass contraption, and what seemed like a thousand fairy lights. Yet nothing compared to the striking gentleman standing before her.

He stood well above her petite frame, and while he'd used the silken cloth of his turban to cross his face from his temple to his chin, the part of his face she saw was perfect. And she was certain the face hidden beneath the fabric, unlike her hidden features, was not disfigured.

Still dazed, it took her a moment to realize he'd asked her for a dance. Heat rose in her face, and she fumbled over her answer. "I've never... I d-don't know how."

"Perhaps, then, you will allow me to escort you to the refreshments?"

She took his proffered arm, and he led her down the stairs to the edge of the dance floor. Laughing couples swirled close, and she found herself laughing with them and swaying to the music. Lydia had been right. The harem costume with the veil for a mask was the perfect choice for her. Tonight she was no longer the scarred village girl, but a beautiful harem girl and as such it made her feel bold. She pushed aside all her timid instincts that came from living with a disfigured face, and she willed herself to have fun.

"You have beautiful eyes," the gentleman said. "Especially when they sparkle under the fairy lights." He stopped to let a group of dancers pass. "Have we met before?"

Unable to find her voice, she shook her head. She was certain she'd never seen this man before in town. For if she had, she'd never be able to forget the chiseled cleft in his chin or the deep blue of his eyes.

"What's your name?" he asked.

"Is it important?" Her words surprised her, and she tensed, but soon relaxed as a smile crossed his face.

"No. I suppose not. After all, this is a masquerade ball. It would spoil the mystery if we learned our companions' identities."

She returned his smile even though he couldn't see it, glad he didn't press her further. Taking a breath, she quickly came up with a question of her own to change the subject.

"Have you been to the masquerade before?" Too late, she recalled what Lydia and her father had said, that in their memory, no villager was ever invited more than once.

"As a matter of fact, I have. But tonight is different. It's like it's my first time because I'm with you."

His words were sweet, but she would not be swayed easily by his flattery. If he had been here before, then he was not from her village. That little detail piqued her curiosity, and she yearned to know more about him. What made him so special that the Kilmartins had invited him again?

The song ended, and the huge brass contraption that provided the music gave a wheeze and started another tune, this one a slower tempo. She watched the couples dip and sway in syncopation, and she wondered what the scene must look like to those standing around the balcony watching them.

"Would you like to give dancing a try, now?" He slipped his arm around her waist. "All you need do is hold on to me."

She slid into his arms, and he twirled her onto the dance floor. As she danced, she noticed the different costumes. Except for their masks, some wore what one normally did for a ball while others' costumes were more fantastical. There was a feathered swan talking to a peacock and in a corner, one woman's gown looked like a tree. Sabrina marveled at their choices of costumes and their imaginations. And she couldn't help wondering if perhaps they too had something to hide and had chosen their attire accordingly.

The thought that others like her could be at the party tonight excited her. She had always enjoyed watching people when she went into town. She would try to imagine what they might be like because she didn't dare risk speaking to them. For the most part, the village folk always shied away from her and her veil as if they might catch her curse. If it wasn't for her father and Lydia, she would live a very lonely life.

"Is something wrong?" her partner asked when the song ended and there was a brief break from dancing. "You've become very quiet."

"No. I'm having a lovely time. I have never been to a masquerade ball and I'm finding my surroundings overwhelming. The Castle is so beautiful, and the guests with their somewhat strange costumes have piqued my interest."

"I understand. I, too, found it fascinating my first time. Come, let's have some refreshment." He extended his arm and led her across the room to a table laid out with punch, pastries, meat pies and cheeses.

He poured two cups of punch and handed one to her.

"I'd like to continue our acquaintance, if you do not mind. I know the polite thing would be to allow you to mingle with the guests, but I am feeling greedy, and I want to keep you all to myself for a little longer. Do you mind?"

He had a way with flattery. But how could she find his attempt to monopolize her time rude when he was asking her permission to do so? What could it hurt?

"I would like that very much," she said. "And since you have been here before, I suspect you must know the Castle well. Can you show me more of it?"

"The living area is off limits to guests, but I will be happy to take you up the stairs to the bridged balcony so you can appreciate the architecture of the view better." He led her along one wall toward the stairs, stopping when they came to a curtained area. "There are hidden alcoves for privacy along the main floor here if you should find you need a place to sit for a moment's rest."

"Thank you." He was a good listener and a charmer, and wondered if all men possessed such qualities. Or, if only so when trying to impress a lady?

They finally reached a staircase that led up to the balcony when a hideous little creature of a man wearing a rumpled brown coat with green velvet lapels and tweed brown pants jumped out at them. His fuzzy shock of orange hair and beard, wide wrinkled forehead and bushy orange eyebrows were nothing compared to his large, red, bulbous nose so covered in warts that Sabrina yelped in fright and hid behind her partner.

"Finn, what are you doing?" her sultan demanded. "Trying to scare the ladies?"

"A lady? Where's a lady?" The little man cackled. "All I see is a harem girl and an uppity whelp trying to be a sultan."

Sabrina peeked around the sultan's shoulder at the creature he'd referred to as Finn. "Who are you?"

"Who am I?" the little creature repeated in mock amusement. "I am a leprechaun. Lord Finn Finnegan at your service." With that he bowed before her.

"He isn't a lord of anything. Don't pay him any mind. His claim to fame is being mischievous." Her partner wrapped a protective arm around her waist and brought her back around to stand beside him. "After what you did last time, Finn, I'm surprised you were even invited back this year."

"Oh, that. A misfortune of events. Elsbeth forgave me and said the ball wouldn't be the same if I didn't attend."

"I don't think so."

"Don't you believe me, Stefan?" The little man winked at him.

"Fine. Now please move out of our way so we can pass. The lady would like to see the balcony."

"Of course. Toot-a-loo." Finn stepped away and wiggled his stubby, wrinkled fingers in a wave.

"Strange fellow," Sabrina said, keeping herself pressed firmly against Stefan's side. "And dressed as a leprechaun. He certainly plays his part well."

He grunted and shook his head. "If you only knew."

"Is your name really Stefan?"

"Yes. So much for being mysterious."

"All good things must come to an end sometime. I'm Sabrina, and I am very pleased to have met you."

"Sabrina." He stopped halfway up the stone stairs, turning to face her. "What a lovely name for a beautiful girl."

Disbelief left her breathless at him calling her beautiful. Only her father had ever said so, but that was a father's love speaking. It took all of her willpower not to correct Stefan. What would it hurt for him to believe that she was as he wanted her to be? After all, would she ever see him again after tonight?

"I was named after a water nymph in my mother's favorite poem."

"I am quite fond of poetry. Don't tell me the poem. Let me guess." Stefan began walking up the narrow stairs again and she followed. He looked back over his shoulder at her. "I don't believe it was Edmund Spenser who wrote it, but one of his contemporaries."

"I don't know the title or the poet's name," she confessed. "My mother died when I was very young and my father doesn't like to talk about her. Sad memories and all."

"That's too bad, but you really should know the poem and the poet. Come, once we see the balcony, I'll take you to the library and show you the author. I'm certain the Kilmartins will have the book of poetry."

"But I thought you said the living quarters are off limits."

"The library isn't in the living quarters."

From the balcony, they looked down into the ballroom, watching the people dance. She spotted Finn Finnegan near one of the refreshment tables, and it looked like he was pouring something in the punch bowl from a tiny flask.

"Oh," she gasped.

"What?" Stefan asked.

"I saw Finn Finnegan put something in the punch bowl there." She pointed to where Finn was still standing. The little man saw her and winked at her before he vanished from sight. "Where did he go? He was there one second and gone the next."

"He probably slipped underneath the tablecloth."

A hearty laugh sounded from behind them and they turned to find Finn leaning against a tapestry hanging on the stone wall, arms crossed over his chest just as happy as you please. "Miss me?"

How did he get to them so quickly? There must be a secret passageway, she decided.

"Hardly, Finn." Stefan glared at him. "What did you put in the punch bowl?"

"Oh, just a wee dash of Irish spirits to add to the merry making going on down there. Nothing more."

"That had better be all you were up to, Finnegan, or I'll personally see that you are removed from this ball by the seat of your pants. Is that clear?"

"My, my, someone is letting his costume go to his head. You aren't the head of the clan, pup, so don't go acting like it." And with that the leprechaun disappeared again. *Definitely, a secret passage.*

Sabrina saw the way Stefan's jaw twitched and his hands balled into fists. "Don't let him upset you so. Let's go to the library now and look for that poem."

Stefan knew he shouldn't let Finn get the better of him. After all, that was what the little man wanted. It was part of his mischief. But Stefan also knew what happened last year when Finn put something in one of the punch bowls, and he did not want to see any of the guests sickened this year.

"I know you're concerned about what Finn put in the punch bowl, as am I, because putting Irish spirits in the wrong one could lead to pandemonium."

"What do you mean?" Sabrina asked. "Surely a little whiskey in the punch is a cause for concern? Why, my father adds a nip to his coffee every now and again."

How could he tell her that mixing Irish spirits with vampire elixir can send a sated vampire on the hunt for blood? Or, that Irish spirits in a human punch bowl could cause a mortal to become drunk after just one sip. Thankfully, the Fae, accustomed to the heady spring Nectar, weren't affected, but if the shapeshifters took even a small sip of it, they might start turning at a frenzied rate.

"Irish spirits are…more than whiskey."

"I see." Her voice was breathy, and he could tell by the confusion in her eyes that she didn't understand what he meant, but the way she held his hand told him she trusted him.

Stefan would have to hope Finn heeded his warning, and he pushed all thoughts of the leprechaun out of his mind as he led Sabrina into the library. The room was dimly lit when they entered, but he lit a candle from a torch on the wall and used it to light a few more candles to add the necessary light for reading.

"Have a seat on the chaise, and I'll see if I can find the whole poem for you. It is a shame you don't know more about where your name came from. Do I dare assume you know very little about your mother as well?"

She nodded. "Aye, I was a lass of four when she died in a carriage accident, so I vaguely recall what she looked like."

"And your father?"

"She was alone in the carriage. Coming home from a party. She enjoyed parties and such. The excitement. The beautiful gowns." A sad expression crossed Sabrina's face, but quickly turned into a smile. "In fact, my costume was repurposed from one of her gowns."

"Did you make it yourself?" he inquired, running his finger along the leather spines of the books filling the poetry section of the library. Both his parents loved poetry, and he was certain he knew exactly the poem, but for some reason the name would not come to him. He found it extraordinary, because he never had trouble remembering poems or their authors before, and he was certain it had everything to do with Sabrina.

"No, my friend Lydia is the seamstress. I am good at needlepoint as well, but I enjoy tatting."

"I heard tatting is the newest trend."

"You have?" Her tone told him she found that amusing.

"Yes. I do listen when talking with the fairer sex. In fact, my mother's lady's maid is forever going on about needle work and embroidery. She's an incessant talker, that one."

Her soft giggle stopped his search and he looked over his shoulder to find her leaning against the arched back of the chaise with her knees pulled to her chest and her arms wrapped around them.

"Are you chilled?"

"A little. For a castle this place isn't as drafty as I would have imagined, far warmer than my father's manor."

"We've... uh." He caught himself before he revealed his true identity and went in search of a shawl or something to drape over her. He found one on his mother's reading chair and brought it to her. "Here, see if this won't help. I'm surprised you haven't frozen to death in that costume."

"It isn't so bad. Lydia made me a fur lined cloak, and my slippers are fur lined as well, though you would never realize it by looking at them. But the sheer fabric gives little warmth despite the many layers and the flesh tone fabric doesn't give much warmth either. As long as we were dancing, I was warm, but now that we've come upstairs and I'm sitting..."

"I understand." He tucked the shawl around her tiny figure, breathing in the sweet scent he'd been unable to pinpoint when they were dancing among the other guests. But now that they were alone, its headiness had him sitting on the chaise and staring into her eyes.

She lowered her gaze and her lashes fluttered. "Do you have to stare so, Stefan? You're making me uncomfortable."

"Why? You have such expressive, warm eyes. You're so beautiful."

"My eyes, perhaps. But how do you know I am not hideous behind my veil?"

"You can't be." He reached for her hand and held it in his, rubbing it with his other. "The skin of your hands is so soft, and they are dainty, fitting into mine like we were meant to hold hands throughout the ages. Don't you feel it, Sabrina? Don't you feel as if we were destined to meet here tonight?"

She shook her head and pulled her hand away. "I think we are becoming friends, but that is all, Stefan. Did you find the poem?"

"Not yet. But I'll keep looking." He wanted to protest, but he didn't want to push. He couldn't quite explain it, but he was almost certain that Sabrina could be more than a friend, that she could be the woman he had been searching for his whole life. Leaving the chaise, he returned to the bookshelves and found the volume he'd been looking for.

"Shall I read to you?"

"Yes, please."

He returned to the chaise, sitting far enough away so they weren't touching, but close enough that if he wanted to reach for her hand he could. He'd seen the poem performed several times over the years in the play, *Comus: A Masque*. But as he read the passage, it was as though he were hearing the poem for the first time just like Sabrina. He glanced into her face and was startled to see tears glistening in her eyes, especially when he came to the water nymph.

> *"Sabrina fair*
> *Listen where thou art sitting*
> *Under the glassie, cool, translucent wave,*
> *In twisted braids of Lillies knitting*
> *The loose train of thy amber-dropping hair,*
> *Listen for dear honours sake,*
> *Goddess of the silver lake,*
> *Listen and save."*

He read another short passage and noticed she'd sat up, wrapped her arms around her bent legs once more, and rested her chin on her knees.

> *"Sabrina rises, attended by water-Nymphes, and sings.*
> *By the rushy-fringed bank,*
> *Where grows the Willow and the Osier dank,*
> *My sliding Chariot stayes,*
> *Thick set with Agat and the azurn sheen*
> *Of Turk is blew, and Emrauld green*
> *That in the channel strayes,*
> *Whilst from off the waters fleet*
> *Thus I set my printless feet*
> *O're the Cowslips Velvet head,*
> *That bends not as I tread,*
> *Gentle swain at thy request*
> *I am here."*

She wiped the moisture from her eyes and sighed. "It's beautiful." She leaned back against the chaise once more and softly applauded.

"What is it called?" she asked. "Who wrote it?"

"The poem is *Sabrina Fair, and it is from a* John Milton play entitled, *Comus: The Masque*."

"I find it very strange that it was my mother's favorite poem. The verse is so disturbing when the lady is captured, but so pleasing when the savior comes along and frees her."

"Sabrina Fair, in her turquoise and emerald green, just like you, here tonight."

She looked away, removed the shawl, and stood. "I'm no savior, Stefan. Far from it. Some may see me as the Necromancer."

Her words puzzled him. "I doubt that."

"It's true. The people in the village—" She stopped, and her eyes widened as if the words shocked her. A low cry escaped her, and she fled.

He left the book lying on the chaise and went after her, but she was nowhere he could see. The balcony, and the steps they'd taken up to this level, were crowded with guests, preventing her escape from the landing. He searched all the possible locations he could imagine she might have gone before coming to the curtained alcove upstairs. The space really wasn't an alcove at all, but the entrance to the Derrick's pneumatic lift. The tinkerer's latest addition to the castle, and thanks to Finn's mischievous pranks, the contraption didn't always work correctly.

Left with no other choice, he entered in the lift, and swoosh, he arrived in an alcove on the side of the main hall. He pushed back the curtains and stepped out in time to see his harem girl talking with the leprechaun. Perhaps she hadn't found the elevator after all. She didn't look rattled, but amused at what the fellow was saying. He started to move toward them, but the music ceased and a bell rang. The evening games were about to begin, and his mother expected him to fulfill his obligations as a host. Never before had he minded his part in the festivities, but tonight was different. Tonight all he wanted to do was spend it with his harem girl, his Sabrina Fair, his savior from spending his life alone. The woman he was certain he'd been searching for all of his life.

His mother approached the center of the dance floor and the guests attentively waited for her to speak.

"We have prepared some extra special entertainment for you throughout this evening. For the more adventurous among you, there will be games within the hedge maze out back. For those of you who choose to remain indoors, a schedule has been prepared for the various events available to you as well." She motioned toward him and the end of the ballroom where several small round tables were set up for games. "My husband will be seeing to the more *spirited* among you, while Stefan and I will do our best to keep the rest of you on your excited little toes."

A collective chuckle caused their host to pause and smile.

"Now…for those of you willing to brace the chill, Devlin awaits you through *that* door. For my inside guests, we will resume once the crowds have cleared."

When she finished speaking, the music once again began to play softly as guests moved about the ballroom. Stefan knew he should join his mother to begin the inside games, but he had to find Sabrina before Finn caused more trouble.

"Stefan. Stefan." He heard his mother call and he made eye contact with her, but shook his head before slipping among the crowd. He hoped she'd understand. He had to find Sabrina.

It seemed to take forever, searching among the many guests who had chosen to stay indoors for this part of the evening festivities before he finally found his harem girl. To his dismay when he touched her arm and the girl turned around, it wasn't blue eyes that met him, but green. He blinked and did a double take, realizing the lady in front of him wasn't dressed as a harem girl at all, but a tree. "I beg your pardon. I thought you were someone else."

"No harm done," the lady replied.

Feeling dazed and confused, Stefan continued his way through the crowd of people until he once again saw a maiden dressed as a harem girl. But he was more cautious in his approach this time. He looked the girl over and noticed her costume was similar, but instead of green and blue it was light pink and rose. What was going on? Was this some kind of trick to keep him and Sabrina apart?

He blinked again and the woman he'd been certain was wearing a harem costume was actually in a medieval gown and she was not a maiden but a matron.

Certain that some kind of tomfoolery was going on, he looked for the leprechaun, but Finn was nowhere in sight. And neither was Sabrina.

He continued around the dance floor in his search until he came upon a beautiful young woman he was certain wore a Faerie gown of lavender. Her wings sparkled in the candlelight and there was also a glittering glow about her cheeks. She smiled at him and motioned him to her.

"I know the one you seek, but is she your true love?" the Faerie asked.

"I don't know, but I am willing to find out."

"There are two harem girls here tonight, but you must choose the right one to have happiness. Beauty indeed is more precious than gold." And with a flutter of her wings, the Faerie vanished before his eyes.

Stefan found the fairy's words odd, but he knew the Fae sometimes possessed the gift of sight. However, it didn't explain why she felt the need to... what? Warn him? It didn't matter. He needed to find Sabrina. He kept moving through the crowd looking for his harem girl. When at last he found her, she was sipping punch by one of the human refreshment tables. Her costume looked bluer than he recalled, but then it could be the candlelight causing the change.

"There you are. I have been searching everywhere for you."

"You have?" The girl turned and he was met with warm brown eyes concealed by a mask and not a veil.

"You aren't Sabrina."

"No, I'm not," she said with a smile. "Too bad for her that I've found you."

"Yes, too bad, indeed. Have you been here all evening? I thought I had met all the guests who arrived tonight."

"Not long. I was detained when I first arrived by a wee little man. He greeted me and asked if I would walk in with him. Said something about not wanting to draw attention to himself by entering alone. We were able to enter unnoticed, and we parted company."

Stefan nodded. He had no doubt the little man this young woman spoke of was Finnegan. "I'm sure he's around somewhere. I wouldn't worry about it. Interesting choice of costume."

"Yes, isn't it? I received it with the invitation. I thought it quite an odd costume to wear to a party in the winter, but now that I see we somewhat match, I'm very glad I wore it instead of coming up with a costume of my own."

Were the Fae playing games with him? The girl was pleasant

enough, and though not quite as playful as Sabrina, he couldn't discount the fairy's heeding.

"Would you care to dance?" he asked, offering her his hand.

She placed hers in his and dipped her head. "I'd love to."

As a new song began he swept her out onto the dance floor, and they waltzed. In contrast to Sabrina, the lady was light on her feet, possessed an air of confidence, and had a pretty smile. But he imagined Sabrina had one too, if only he could see all of her face.

"What's your name?" the young woman asked.

"Is it important?" he replied, remembering what his harem girl had said when he'd asked her the same question earlier.

"I suppose not. Masquerade balls are supposed to be mysterious."

A feeling a déjà vu swept over him, and he longed to find Sabrina. Where could she have gone?

"You seem distracted."

"I'm sorry. I am. I really must find the girl I was searching for and make sure she is unscathed. We were touring the balcony area when she left me in haste, and I want to make sure I didn't upset her. I do apologize, but if you will please excuse me, I will try to find you again before the night is over to finish our dance."

She stepped back and curtsied. "I will be awaiting your return."

"Thank you." Stefan hurried away, but wondered if he was leaving the wrong girl. The Faerie's words repeated in his head. *Only one can bring you happiness.*

He made another round of the dance floor and even passed by the gaming area, being sure to avoid his mother, before he finally found Sabrina. She sat on a bench alone, on the far side of the entrance stairwell, and seemed perfectly content as she sipped what looked to be warmed cider from a crystal mug. When she saw him, she lowered her veil back down to cover her mouth.

"There you are," he said, sitting down beside her. "Why did you run off? Why did you say others would find you the Necromancer?"

"Because…" Sabrina's answer was stalled by his mother's arrival. Surprise that the hostess would appear before them was evident in the girl's eyes.

"Pardon, but I do not mean to interrupt. I'm Elsbeth Kilmartin. It's a pleasure to have you here. A harem girl and a sultan. How fitting that you found each other tonight. I hope you both are enjoying the evening?"

Sabrina nodded, getting to her feet. She immediately curtsied. "It is a lovely party, and I'm honored to have been invited."

"You are most welcome, my dear. Please do not let me keep you from taking part in the festivities or refreshments." And as quickly as she'd appeared, his mother left them alone.

"She's beautiful. Did you notice how smooth her skin looked? I hope I am as beautiful when I am her age."

Stefan smiled. "I have never heard of a Necromancer being beautiful before. You can't be both, Sabrina. So which is it?"

She looked startled. "You don't understand."

"No I don't, so why don't you enlighten me."

"I can't. Not tonight. Not ever. So don't ask me. Please, can't we go back to having a good time with one another? Can't we be content to be mysterious strangers?"

Stefan sighed in resignation and nodded. "Yes. We can."

Everything was right between them again, or so it seemed until Finn Finnegan pranced up to them as the music changed for another reel. He tapped Stefan on his arm and cleared his throat.

"The lady has promised me a dance."

"Go away, Finn," Stefan ordered.

"But she has put me on her dance card. "

Sabrina let out a gasp. "I did no such thing."

Finn cackled. "Better check your card."

Sabrina pulled the card free from the cuff of her sheer bolero jacket, and growled when she read Finn's name.

Not liking what was happening, Stefan motioned to two of the footman, and they lifted Finn by the arms. Infuriated, the little man began squawking gibberish in his Leprechaun tongue as they carried him from the dance floor and out of the castle.

Stefan went back to Sabrina's side. "I'm sorry. This is all my fault. I should have known better than to agitate him. I didn't want him anywhere near you. If we only have tonight, I want to make the most of it."

"And I you, but what's happened? Where's your mask?"

Shocked gasps could be heard throughout the ballroom as for just a moment the attendees' masks disappeared.

Stunned, Sabrina found that she was staring into her sultan's ruggedly handsome face, and his Black Irish good looks astounded her. Her body heated. Her palms were sweaty, her knees went weak, and she found it hard to swallow. But all too soon his mask returned and with it a jolt like a splash of cold water washed over her. If his mask had vanished, what about her veil? While she'd been mesmerized by his face, had he been repulsed by hers?

Trembling with fear, she dared looked into his blue eyes once more. She hadn't known what to expect, but what she saw left her paralyzed like a scared rabbit for a moment. He was looking at her with concern, yet understanding, and what she'd always assumed was pity from the villagers. She could stand anything but pity, especially from him.

A guttural cry escaped her throat, and she pulled free of him. Quickly scanning the ballroom, she wondered if others besides Stefan had seen her face during the brief moment when everyone's masks had disappeared. Unwilling to stay to find out, she hurried away from him once again, but this time in search of safety away from prying eyes. How, oh how, had this happened?

Seeing a draped alcove ahead, she hurried into it and was surprised she wasn't alone. A low burning candle lit the small space, and a woman wearing a beautifully beaded teal dress was reclined on a long bench with her eyes closed. At Sabrina's entrance, she bolted upright suggesting she'd been resting and not sleeping. Maybe she was trying to recover from a headache? Perhaps, like Sabrina, she was in need of privacy?

"Oh, I beg your pardon," Sabrina said quickly. "I didn't mean to disturb you."

"No dear, please come in and sit. I can tell that you are upset." The woman patted the bench beside her. "Let your heart calm down. It is why I sought refuge here. I don't mind sharing the space at all."

Sabrina wanted to bolt, but she didn't want to be rude.

"My name is Andromeda," the woman said softly. "Do you need to share something?"

Sabrina thought it odd that this woman was talking to her, yet was looking towards the curtain. Was she blind? Clearly this woman was in need of more assistance than she. "I'm sorry. Should I go?"

"No." The woman turned her face toward Sabrina. "I know you've just been distressed. Can you be strong enough to hear a truth that would affect the rest of your life?" She gave her a small smile with a hopeful look in her eyes.

Confusion set Sabrina's thoughts reeling. "Strong? I don't understand? What could you possibly tell me that would affect my life? I don't know you. I'm certain I have never seen you before in the village, so how could you possibly have something to share with me?" The words tumbled from Sabrina like a waterfall in her dismayed state. Had the woman witnessed her veil falling away? Had she seen her face?

"I'm sure you've sensed something strange here this evening. As if many people tonight harbor secrets."

Sabrina nodded, even though she didn't quite understand the lady's meaning.

"I am one of those people," Andromeda continued. "I can see and hear spirits. Some of them are here tonight. They have heartache or unfinished business regarding the living they desperately need to satisfy before moving on."

"What could any of your spirits have to say to me?"

"More than you might think."

Unsure whether to stay or go, Sabrina perched on the edge of the bench, prepared to make a quick exit if necessary. She swallowed. "How do you know this person wishes to speak to me? There are so many guests here tonight. Couldn't you be mistaken?"

The woman looked to the curtain again and nodded as if in agreement. "You're Sabrina Gilchrist, are you not?"

Jumping up, she inched away from Andromeda. "Uh…um…how could you possibly know that? No one knows who I am here. No one is supposed to know because of my costume."

"Your mother has known you since you were a wee lass. No costume could disguise who you are to her."

Sabrina willed her body to flee this nonsense, but her legs and limbs wouldn't move. Was she under a spell? What the woman was saying couldn't be true. No one, not even her father, had called her a wee lass since her mother had died.

She gasped. "My mother?"

"She begs you to please listen. She's never had an opportunity to tell you what you should know, what you deserve to know. That pain has kept her here in this world all through your life. And because you are here tonight, in this magical castle, she can now speak to you if you will only listen. She's afraid she will never have this opportunity again."

Sabrina shook her head. She didn't want to believe what she was hearing. She'd missed having a mother, but her memories of her mother visiting the nursery or playing with her were very few. All she really knew about her mother were things her father would say in anger. How she liked to attend parties, travel to London and Paris for shopping adventures. She'd watched her father suffer for years because of her mother's death, and it angered her. Her father was all she had in this world besides Lydia, and how dare this spirit of a mother come to her now to share anything with her?

A flood of emotions boiled up inside her, and she balled her hands into tight fists by her side. "Why should I listen to you or her? It's because of her I have been forever scarred. It's why I must wear a veil whenever I go out in public so I do not scare the village children. It's why I live a very quiet and lonely life." Tears came to her eyes as she spoke and she blinked them away, trying to clear her vision. "It is why I may never know the happiness of a true love…a true love like I may have met tonight."

Andromeda's face showed empathy for her. "I understand your pain. I too have resorted to a cabin in the woods and a quiet life. All of the spirits clamoring for my help, sometimes it is just too overwhelming. It's especially hard in large gatherings like this."

She looked over to the curtains again. She tilted her head as if listening to a voice or instructions.

Heart still colliding against her ribs, Sabrina waited. At last the older woman spoke.

"Sabrina, if it were me, I would want to know your mother's true story. Wouldn't the truth be better to deal with than rumors?" She paused a moment and looked to the curtain. "I will not force anyone if they do not wish to hear, regardless of your need." She said as if defending a child. "I am sorry, but it is her choice."

Sabrina closed her eyes and took in a cleansing breath. What could her mother possibly say to her that would make a difference now? It wouldn't change the fact that she was dead. And it certainly wouldn't take away the scar on her face.

She'd never met anyone with Andromeda's gift, and she was certain it was not an easy one to possess. Having the woman pass along what her mother wanted to share wasn't an everyday occurrence, and she wondered if she passed up this chance, would she regret it for the rest of her life?

"If you wish, I will repeat back what she is saying to you, so you can hear her words and feelings instead of my summarizing it. In this case, she needs you to hear from her heart. I'm not just relaying where to find something, or a fact like where her heirloom earrings are hidden."

In that moment, Sabrina felt an ache in her heart that she didn't know had been buried for years, and she made the decision to listen. She hesitantly nodded her head in assent.

With this, Andromeda continued, "I will repeat what she says word for word as I can." She took her hand and graciously put it over Sabrina's as a gesture of comfort, and support.

"I'm sorry. A thousand times sorry for my past transgressions. I have spent the last two decades regretting my careless ways. But my darling girl, I've been with you all this time. It has been my contrition that I never leave your side. If I could take away the damage done, I would. I cannot change the past, but I ask for your forgiveness, because if I had not gained the reputation I did, this never would have happened to you. I know you're hurt, because I have hurt for you ever since Avery marked you."

Sabrina heard her mother's words coming through Andromeda. It had to be true. How else would this woman know the details, or who had disfigured her all those years ago. The memory, still too painful to bear, crashed all around her. She closed her eyes remembering when she opened the front door, and Avery had been so kind until she caressed Sabrina's cheek, leaving her marked.

"How can I forgive you?" Sabrina found herself looking to the curtain.

"I know what I'm asking is difficult, but perhaps if you knew the truth of what transpired that evening—what really happened at the party where I was falsely accused of stealing my best friend's husband, and why I was fleeing the party with haste. I had had a little too much to drink when he found me in the library alone. I was bored and regretting coming to the party, and due to the wine, my head was muddled. Robbie smelled of beech wood and lemongrass, the same as your father. He was tall and had the same coloring as your father, so in the dim lighting of the library and in my foggy state, it was easy to forget that there was no way your father would have come to the party late. Their voices when speaking low sound so much alike. He took advantage of that fact and had me in a very compromising position when he kissed me. But that is where the similarity ended. I knew immediately he wasn't my husband, and I tried to get free, but he trapped me, pinned me down on the sofa and tried to force himself on me."

"Oh, Mother," Sabrina whispered as a crushing tightness spread through her chest, and her trembling fingers gripped the silken fabric of her costume.

"I was fighting him off when Avery came searching for him, but in the dark she mistook what she saw as the two of us making love. My dress was torn, and the pins holding my hair in place were falling out. I was a disheveled mess as I ran from the manor to the safety of my carriage. Many of the guests saw me flee, so I know the rumor mill had much fodder that night, but I didn't care. My only thought was to get home to you and your father, and to never go to another party again without him."

Silence filled the air within the alcove and was thick with remorse. Even without psychic powers, Sabrina felt it. She wanted to cry for her mother and the story she told, but all she could think about was her poor father and how he'd suffered because of that night. The tightness in her chest wouldn't go away.

"I never made it home that night." Andromeda's words softened, and she began to weep. Sabrina leaned over toward the woman and rested her head on her shoulder. In return the woman wrapped an arm around her.

After pausing a moment, Andromeda took a jagged breath and continued. "My carriage driver was racing back to our village when he lost control of the horses, sending us over the rocky edge of the mountain into the shore of Galway Bay below. My greatest regret is the time I wasted, my girl. I should have valued being your mother instead of being consumed with parties. Please forgive me. Please forgive a silly young woman her folly. Please tell your father I was never unfaithful to him, even though I am sure he has long ago resigned himself to the false accusation I was."

"It's all right, mother. I forgive you." Sabrina looked into the stranger's face and she imagined it was her mother's face she saw. "Father never remarried. He's stayed alone, caring only for me all these years."

"I wish he finds happiness again one day. I wish it for both of you." Andromeda laid a hand on her cheek. "Please, Sabrina, remove your veil, so I may see all of you, one last time before I go. Now that I have your forgiveness, I can move on. Thank you, my darling, for granting me this favor."

"Go? I don't want you to go." Sabrina sat back. "Not now, not after I know what really happened to you. Please, say you will stay. There is so much about you I want to know."

Andromeda removed a handkerchief and wiped her tears. "My time is drawing nigh. Please, remove your veil so I can see you as you are, my child."

Taking a deep breath, Sabrina unpinned the veil and let the sheer material hang loose. She swept it back, stood, and stepped into the ring of light cast by the wall sconces.

"You are beautiful Sabrina, despite the scar. Remember that. Your beauty comes from within. It is what Stefan saw when he saw you. Trust in him. Trust in yourself. You shall find happiness. You shall."

Andromeda stopped speaking.

"Is it over? Is she gone?" Sabrina asked, turning away to refasten the veil in place.

Andromeda nodded. "Thank you for listening to her. I hate to see those tormented think they have no hope."

"I'm the one who should be thanking you, Andromeda. You have helped me more than you know. You have given me something of my mother I never would have had if you were not who you are. Thank you for coming tonight. Thank you, oh so much." Sabrina hugged her tight before she left the alcove.

Stefan wandered in what seemed like circles searching every alcove, nook and possible hiding spot in the ballroom more than once. He even went back up to the library to see if Sabrina had returned there to get away from him, but she was nowhere to be found. Finally, he returned downstairs and ran into the second harem girl with warm brown eyes.

"You're back. Did you have any luck?" she asked.

"Yes I did, but then…she ran off again."

"Rude, don't you think?"

No, he didn't.

"I believe she was frightened when everyone's masks vanished."

"It was an odd few moments, but no harm was done. Don't you agree? I certainly wasn't frightened by it."

"Maybe you weren't, but I understand why Sabrina fled from me. I just hope she returns." Stefan scanned the area once more before he settled his gaze on his new companion. "Care to finish our dance?"

"I thought you'd never ask."

He held out his hand and led her to the dance floor. And even though he listened to what she said and carried on his half of the conversation, his mind was still on finding Sabrina and learning what had happened to cause the scar on her face.

Several dances later, a gentleman tapped him on the shoulder, requesting he step aside, and he obliged after promising his partner they'd dance again later.

Keeping an eye out for Sabrina, Stefan went to the gaming tables to see if his mother had spotted her before he dared venture outside to see if she might have gone out to the hedge maze games.

"What's wrong, Stefan?" His mother's words startled him, and he turned to face her. "Why so grim a look upon your face when you were so happy when I left you an hour ago?"

"I can't find Sabrina. Have you seen her?" He again scanned the masked crowd for her veiled face.

"Sabrina? Is that her name? What a lovely one, and isn't she just as lovely? So dainty and petite. Is she a mythical creature come to our castle, or one of the villagers from the bay area?"

"Yes, she is lovely. No, she isn't a mythical creature. She comes from the village."

His mother nodded. "What have you learned during your time together about her and her family? I know you have spent your time with her since she arrived. I haven't been spying, but every time I've seen you, she was by your side."

"I can't explain it, Mother. I know I shouldn't monopolize her time here, but I fear I am smitten."

"Oh, that's wonderful, Stefan. You know, all your father and I long for is you find the same happiness we have shared together."

He took in a deep breath. "But there is one problem, Mother. A Faerie appeared to me earlier and told me there are two harem girls here this evening, and only one will bring me happiness. The only differences are one wears a mask and the other wears a veil. Sabrina has blue eyes, and the other brown."

"I see. But you are searching for Sabrina. Is she the one you have chosen?"

He shrugged. "She is the one I long to find."

"Longing is good."

"Is it? When the masks vanished earlier and she saw my face, it frightened her away."

"Frightened her? Did she find your looks objectionable?"

He shook his head. "No, she ran away because she realized I saw her face. She came here tonight as a harem girl because she could wear a veil as her mask and no one would question it. Mother, something horrible has happened to her face. It is scarred and disfigured on the right side."

His mother tenderly touched his cheek. "Tell me, son. Does the scarring change the way you feel about her?"

"No, not in the least. In fact, it explains why she sees herself as evil because she perceives that others do. But she is not evil."

"Then you must find her and make her see she isn't. The night is still young. Go search for her and let your feelings known. The Faeries will give their blessing at dawn, and if you have found your happiness then, we shall all celebrate with the blessing."

The blessing.

Stefan knew that the Fae always bestowed it on his parents, but one year, when he had been sick all winter and no potions or elixirs helped, they'd given the blessing to him, and his health had been restored. Since that time he'd not been sick another day in his life.

"Would a blessing go to Sabrina if she desired the Faes' healing?"

"That is not for us to decide, Stefan, but the Fae. However, if you discover she wishes to change her appearance, there is the hedge maze game. One wish goes to the couple that reaches the center first. But Stefan, are you sure she desires this, or do you?"

His mother's questions surprised him, but it made him question his own thinking. Sabrina had refused to see herself as beautiful, and she'd likened herself to a Necromancer, but did that mean she'd want the disfigurement gone? He had no way of knowing, and if he proposed this to her, then she might think he wanted her to change the way she looked for him—that he didn't accept her the way she is—but it wasn't true.

"I would want it only if she desires, because I want her to be happy. She deserves to be happy. She lost her mother when she was a child to a horrible accident. Yet, she is not bitter. In fact, I believe she has to be the kindest soul I've met other than my nanny. And the most sheltered. Finnegan frightened her when she first saw him."

"Finn Finnegan is here tonight?" His mother looked alarmed. "How dare he show his face at my party again after what he did last time? How did he even get in here without an invitation?"

"I knew it. I knew that leprechaun was up to no good." Stefan balled his fists at his side and recalled what the brown eyed girl had said about the little man wanting to walk into the castle together. Clever move for a leprechaun.

"Don't worry, mother. He has been removed from the premises, and I will make sure the guards know to be on the lookout for him in case he should try to sneak back inside."

"Thank you, Stefan. Now run along and find your harem girl. I need to make my rounds among the guests again."

After leaving the alcove, Sabrina paused to allow her racing heart to slow. She couldn't wait to tell her father what she'd learned about her mother this evening. Hopefully, he wouldn't think her mad and try to lock her away in an asylum. She'd take the risk if the news brought him any comfort after all these years.

Content with her decision, she was jolted back to reality when she spotted Stefan dancing with another harem girl. A sharp pain quickly replaced her joy. The two were deep in conversation, and it was clear he'd forgotten all about her. How could he after the way he'd professed he wanted to spend his evening with her and her alone?

A dancing couple bumped into her, startling her from her frozen state.

"Beg your pardon," the man said.

"No harm," Sabrina managed to say, even though her throat constricted in protest. A pain unlike any she had ever felt before washed over her, and she quickly stepped off the dance floor, afraid she might burst into tears and draw unwanted attention.

He's only a stranger.
You only just met.
It was true, but somewhere between their meeting and her

running to the alcove, something more had taken shape within her heart. Could she be falling in love with him? Was that why she felt so crushed to see him with another?

Oh, if only Lydia had been a firefly on the wall tonight, they could have talked this over. Lydia had been to parties and had more experience in matters of the heart. But Sabrina never had a coming out, nor a suitor. She wished Lydia was here now to offer advice.

Spotting a refreshment table close by, she decided to get something to drink. The punch reminded her of Stefan, and her heart began to ache anew at the thought of him. A tear formed and she brushed it away quickly, but not before one of the nearby guests noticed. The woman gave her a kind look and came over.

"Is everything all right, my dear?" the matron asked.

"Yes. Really. I-I'm fine," she said, despite her voice cracking.

She heard Lydia's voice in her head. *Don't be a silly goose, Sabrina. You're there to have fun, not cry in your punch.*

She discarded her empty cup and hurried toward the gaming tables while avoiding making eye contact with any of the guests, afraid they might have seen her when the masks disappeared.

But at the edge of the gaming area she came to an abrupt stop when she once again saw Stefan. He wasn't with the other harem girl anymore, but was speaking with their hostess. The woman touched his cheek in a motherly way, and it startled Sabrina. Why would the hostess do that to one of her guests...unless Stefan wasn't one of the guests...but her son?

Sabrina's mind raced, remembering things he had said or did since they met and it made perfect sense. How else would he have known where the library was, or that the book of poetry he searched for would be found there? He'd even had the leprechaun removed from the ball. Someone who was a guest wouldn't overstep their bounds in such a fashion.

But if he were the Kilmartins' son, then why hadn't he just told her the truth, especially once she'd learned his name? Why keep his true identity a secret?

Confused and feeling betrayed, she found the side door and slipped outside putting distance between her and the castle. The night air was bone chilling, and she wished she'd thought to retrieve her cloak before making her exit. If she went back inside, then she might come face to face with Stefan, and she wasn't ready to do that just yet.

"Sabrina is it?"

Surprised to hear her name, she turned and found herself face to face with Elsbeth Kilmartin. When had the woman left Stefan's side and come outdoors? "Y-yes."

"Stefan has been searching for you."

"I'm sure he'll find me eventually. I just needed a breath of fresh air."

"I'm sure he will." The woman smiled. "Be careful of the leprechaun, dear. Stefan told me of Finn's earlier mischief tonight, and I'd hate to see you the victim of another of his tricks."

Finn? The leprechaun? "Beggin' your pardon, Mrs. Kilmartin, are you saying the dreadful little man dressed as a leprechaun caused the masks to disappear?"

"Please, call me Elsbeth. Finn is not dressed as a leprechaun, m'dear. He is a leprechaun. And yes, he is the cause of the masks disappearing." The woman shuddered. "I hate to think of what might have happened if a certain vampire had been in the vicinity of the shapeshifters."

Sabrina started to laugh at the absurd notion, but remembered Andromeda's earlier words and now understood what she meant by sensing something strange and people having secrets.

Is Stefan even human?

Mrs. Kilmartin smoothed her gown. "I know you have many questions, and I assure you my son will answer all of them soon. Please, do not remain out of doors too long, or you will catch a chill."

Elsbeth walked away, leaving Sabrina shivering. She ran her hands up and down her arms and tried to imagine she sat in front of a blazing fire as she walked toward a crowd of guests gathered near a fountain. She couldn't see why they were standing there, but she'd gladly join in if it meant she'd get warmed from the body heat.

But before she reached them, she heard her name being called again. She wasn't surprised at all to have been found.

"Sabrina, what are you doing outside without your cloak?" Stefan asked. He caught up to her and wrapped a fur-lined cloak around her shoulders.

"How did you know I needed it?"

He grinned. "Mother told me."

"I knew it!" The triumph she felt made her forget her anger with him for the moment. "What I mean is I'm glad you brought my cloak.

Who's saving whom now?"

He took her chilled hands in his own to warm them. "I'm sorry Finnegan's prank frightened you away earlier."

"You couldn't have stopped him."

"Yes I could have. If I hadn't had him tossed out the way I did, then he wouldn't have spewed forth that leprechaun gibberish. I can't explain it, but he's brought out the worst in me where he is concerned tonight. And I fear it has hurt you in the process."

"I wasn't hurt. But I had my greatest fear about tonight come true, Stefan. I came here because I could hide behind my veil. No one was to know what was underneath it." She paused and took a breath daring herself to finish what she needed to say. "The way you looked at me without my veil is the way the villagers do, the villagers who pity me for my disfigurement."

"I'm sorry if I hurt you, it wasn't my intention. I never imagined your veil hid your face for a reason. If you saw anything, it was my surprise."

She pulled her hands away. "I have no right to claim your companionship when there is another waiting for you inside. Someone who is whole. For that reason, I give you your leave to be with her. Thank you for sharing your time with me this evening. I will remember your kindness."

Without giving him a chance to respond, she turned and headed down a pebbled path away from the crowd she'd been going toward before he found her.

"Sabrina, wait. You don't understand. There is no one else. No one but you."

She heard his words, but she knew what she'd seen inside. Him dancing with the other harem girl. How could she believe him when she'd seen it for herself? And the fact that he was Stefan Kilmartin and he'd hidden his true identity from her proved he could easily be deceptive.

But you were being just as deceptive with your veil, Sabrina.

Again Lydia's voice echoed in her head, and she wanted to scream at the accusing tone she heard. Why was she hearing her friend's voice? Lydia had made the costume with the veil to hide the truth from the world so no one would discover Sabrina's face was scarred and hideous. She was the beast in children's nightmares. She scared little children away in the village if the wind blew her veil away.

A chilling breeze blew across the water near the moor of the castle, and Sabrina pulled the hood up on her head and the cloak more securely around her. But she wouldn't cry even if her heart was breaking. She'd been so close to finding true love—if that was even possible in one evening with a stranger.

"Hello, Dearie." Finn Finnegan jumped out of the shadows and landed on the pebble path in front of her.

She screamed and stepped away from him. But when she saw it was the leprechaun, she ground her teeth. "Go away, nasty little man."

"Tsk. Tsk. I see someone's surliness has rubbed off on you. Where is your protector? Why are you out here all alone? Doesn't he know anything could happen to you in the dark?"

"I am fully capable of taking care of myself, thank you very much."

"Ho oh! Feisty aren't we?" Finnegan bounced on his feet. "But I wouldn't be a gentleman if I left you unescorted. Come, let's turn back and go investigate one of the outside games. There's a wishing tree on the property, and I hear if you write your heart's desire on a ribbon and hang it from the branches, your wish might be granted by morning."

A wishing tree? "I am not in the mood for another of your tricks."

"I swear on the grave of me blessed mother, 'tis true."

Sabrina's interest was piqued. "Tell me more about this tree. Can anyone make a wish upon it?"

"Yes. But wishes are only granted on this night."

"Can you show me this tree?"

"I'd be happy to," the leprechaun said sweeping his arm out in front of him for her to walk past.

He kept up with her stride which surprised her, and they were soon on the far side of the castle where the wishing tree stood. To Sabrina it looked like an ordinary tree.

"Are you certain this tree is magical?"

"Everything around this castle is enchanted, even the ground under your feet. The Faeries blessed it many, many years ago. I have tried to figure it out, but I cannot discover why the Kilmartins are so special that the Fae would do it."

Sabrina didn't understand what the little man was prattling on about as she walked around the tree inspecting it under the moonlight. She stepped toward the tree and attempted to touch it, but the leprechaun ran forward and stopped her.

"Don't. Whatever you do, don't you dare touch it, or you shall die!"

"But you said one would need to hang the ribbon on a branch. How else are you going to hang them unless you climb the tree?"

"Yes. Yes, I did, but it isn't time for the receiving yet."

Confused, she furrowed her brow. "I don't understand. How will we know when the time is right?"

"Devlin Kilmartin will announce it. In fact, look, there he is now gathering the crowd around him."

Sabrina turned and saw the crowd had moved closer to where she stood. Stefan walked with them, and her heart sank when she saw the other harem girl walking close to him. If there was no one else as he claimed, then how did he explain her presence?

She took a deep breath and tried not to draw conclusions, but it was difficult when the fact was right before her eyes.

"Finn, should we draw closer to them?" she asked, but he didn't answer. She turned around looking for him, but it was as if he had vanished.

Confused, she took a few steps closer so she could hear what Devlin had to say about the ribbons he held in his hands. Maybe he did know when the time was right to hang their wishes on the tree. Renewed excitement began to bubble within her chest with each step she took up the small incline to where the group stood.

"This game is not a game," Devlin was saying. "It is a quest... but not one for the faint of heart." He held up a long red ribbon. "There is a legend here at Castle Amhrán Oiche, of a special kind of magic that dwells within these grounds. To my left, there beyond the southern tower..." He motioned as he spoke. "...there is an enchanted Wishing Tree. The only one of its kind, I am told."

Muffled chuckles and excited giggles spread throughout the gathered crowd. Afraid she'd miss what was being said, Sabrina inched closer, moving through the people until she stood in the front row and could hear and see their host easier.

"It is said the ribbon of fate which binds our souls to one another..." Devlin slid the silky fabric between his fingers. "...can become a physical thing, on but a single night of the year, this is the magical night. If you have the courage to test your love... take a ribbon, write upon it your treasured desire, and tie it within the branches of the Wishing Tree. If your fate is truly linked with another, midnight this eve will reveal the truth of it. Tie this red symbol of your soul upon those magical branches, if the completer of your heart is present, the fateful toll when the hands of time point due North will leave your ribbons irreversibly entwined."

Love? The wishing tree was about finding your true love.

That wasn't what Finnegan had led her to believe. He'd gotten her hopes up that she could make a wish, any wish, and have it granted tonight. She'd been on the verge of wishing for the impossible. She should have known it was a silly wish. Nothing could undo the damage of Avery's caress upon her face.

Stefan watched as the crowd thinned out, as couple after couple raced toward the tree with their ribbons to make their wishes.

Devlin smiled. "Brave hearts, to be sure."

Stefan wanted to be among the throng hanging his ribbon with Sabrina's in the tree, but it didn't look like that was going to happen tonight. Instead of joining the others, Sabrina stood alone, a cloaked figure looking down to the ground. It broke his heart watching her.

A tap on his shoulder caused him to turn and the brown-eyed harem girl reached out her hand to him.

"Stefan, shall we tempt fate?"

She'd found him moments before his father had beckoned the crowd to follow him toward the tree, confessing her name and that she'd discovered Stefan's identity from one of the guests.

"No thank you, Valerie. I know my fate. It was written long before tonight and no ribbon I shall write upon could change it."

She nodded and looked toward where Sabrina stood. "Is she your Sabrina?"

"Yes."

"She's a lucky girl."

"No, I'm the lucky one. If she'll have me."

The girl smiled and ran toward the tree, vanishing into the dark night. Turning his attention back to Sabrina, he slowly approached, hearing the soft muffled sounds of crying. Unable to stop himself, he wrapped his arms around her and pulled her close. She stiffened for a moment then relaxed, turning around and hiding her face against his chest. He didn't say a word. He just held her until she stopped crying. He handed her his handkerchief and watched as she dabbed at her eyes and skillfully slipped the cloth under her veil to wipe her nose.

"Why won't you leave me be, Stefan?" she asked without looking at him.

"If that is what you really want, I will do so, Sabrina. But first, tell me what made you cry?"

She removed the hood of her cloak. "You'll laugh if I tell you."

"Never."

She swallowed and sniffed. "Finnegan told me about the wishing tree. He said any wish could be granted, but it isn't true, is it? I-I was going to write my heart's desire on a ribbon."

"You still can." He took hold of her shoulders and stepped back to look at her. "There's still time."

"But Devlin said it was for lovers, not removing a curse."

Her words were clear as to what her heart's desire was tonight, and even though he wished it had been about him, he knew what she needed. "No, the tree won't do that for you, but there is a hedge maze race, and the Faeries have promised to grant the winning couple wish. If we win then you may use that wish for whatever it is you were going to wish for at the tree."

"You'd allow me to use the wish for myself?"

"I will."

"Thank you, Stefan. I don't know what to say. It is very kind of you."

Heart in his throat, he asked the one thing he feared she'd refuse. "Say you will go down to the wishing tree and place a ribbon there with me to see if we are fated to be together. In all my years attending this ball, I have never wanted to do so, but tonight I do."

Her eyes widened. "Why me? Why not the other harem girl here tonight? I saw you dancing with her inside. I also saw her standing with you in the crowd."

"So, that is what you meant earlier when you said there was another I should be with. Don't you get it, Sabrina? I don't want to be with anyone else here tonight. Only you."

She shook her head. "I find it hard to believe."

"Why? Because of your scar?"

"Because you haven't been truthful with me."

Her statement surprised him. He couldn't imagine what would make her think that. "When have I not?"

"From the time I entered the castle. When I first asked you how you knew so much about it. Once I learned your name was Stefan, why didn't you tell me you lived here? Why didn't you tell me you are Devlin and Elsbeth's son? Are you ashamed of it?"

Ashamed?

"Never!" He reached up, removed his mask, and held it in his hand for her to see. "Tonight is the only night of every year when I can be me because I wear this mask. I am free to move among the guests and enjoy the night. And since I am a Kilmartin, hiding behind a mask makes it easier for others to get to know me for who I am without liking me for what they think I can provide them. I stand to inherit this castle one day, to carry on what my parents have started. It is a burden I will gladly bear. Do you hold this against me, Sabrina?"

"I understand. It is like me, coming here tonight because for one night I could be free in my costume."

"Exactly." He put his mask back on. "So will you go down to the tree with me?"

She pushed back her cloak and reached for his hand, slipping her fingers in between his. "What if the ribbons don't entwine?"

"What if they do?"

Sabrina's heart skipped a beat at his response to her question. Indeed, what if their ribbons did entwine? Was she willing to risk her heart? Who was she kidding? Stefan already had it.

"Sabrina, will you?"

She bit her bottom lip, but did not speak. She looked at him and over to where his father stood by the table with the few remaining ribbons.

Without saying a word, she tightened her hold on his hand and led him over to the ribbons. She dropped his hand and reached for a ribbon and a quill to write her wish.

Stefan reached for his own quill and ribbon. Then they raced off to hang their ribbons.

Soon, the enormous Wishing Tree looked as if it was shedding a hundred bloody tears. Silky red ribbons covered the tree's lower branches and hung down to the dampening grass. When the gentle breeze caught them, it looked like a dancing crimson waterfall.

"Did we tie them too far apart?" Sabrina questioned as they stood and watched the ribbons dance.

"If it is meant to be it will happen." Stefan slipped her hand into his and led her over to meet his father. "Sabrina, this is my father, Devlin Kilmartin."

"Nice to meet you, Sir," she dipped in a curtsy.

"Nice to meet you, Sabrina. Have you taken part in the hedge maze games yet?"

"No, not yet."

"But we will before dawn."

"Excellent. The next one should begin in fifteen minutes. Then I'm going inside for some warm cider. Care to join me?"

"That sounds lovely. I'd like that, if Stefan is inclined as well."

"A trip indoors to warm up sounds good."

"Then it's settled. Come with me to the hedge maze." Devil said, leading the way." The fun and games are about to once again begin."

Stefan led Sabrina over to a fountain where they waited until the other guests gathered for the next game.

"This is the race to the center game. Unlike the other scavenger hunt games, couples will enter the maze in a staggered fashion. Whichever couple reaches the center first will find a fire pit and a torch to light fireworks, signaling the race has been won. The winning couple will be granted one wish. Those who have tied your ribbons to the wishing tree may decide to take the next step."

Chuckles and murmurings went up from the group, but Devlin held up his hand to quieten them. "Now who will be our first couple to attempt the next game?

Sabrina squeezed his hand. "This is us."

"Are you ready?"

She nodded.

"We will." Stefan called simultaneously with another man.

"Well...well. I believe we have a tie. We shall flip a coin to see who goes first. Please come forward gentlemen," Devlin called. He pulled out a large coin from his pocket and held it up for all to see. "One side is a Faerie and the other side is plain. The Faerie will be heads and the other tails. Gentlemen, which will you call?"

"Heads," Stefan called while the other man called tails.

Devlin flipped the coin into the air, but before it reached the ground, Finn Finnegan leaped out of nowhere and caught it. The leprechaun landed in the fountain, scooped water into his hands, and splashed it into Stefan's eyes.

Stefan removed his mask and wiped the stinging water away. His vision was blurry, but he could make out the shape of the leprechaun.

"Tails it is!" Finnegan sang, holding the coin up for all to see. He jumped up on the edge of the fountain and danced a little jig while continuing to hold the coin above his head. "Tails it is. Stefan loses. Stefan loses his precious sight."

The world went black. At first, Stefan thought the dirigibles overhead had floated too far away, or that the clouds had moved in front of the moon blocking its light. He found himself blinking several times.

"Sabrina." He reached out a hand trying to find her and then her hands clasped his. "Sabrina, I can't see."

"Stefan, what is wrong?" Devlin asked coming to him.

"Father, something is wrong with my eyes. My sight is gone."

Gasps and cries echoed among the guests. Then he heard his father's whisper instructing someone to go get his mother. Crunching footsteps retreating on the pebbled path followed.

"Stefan, are you sure you can't see?" Sabrina asked.

He sensed movement in front of his face, but he didn't see it. A cold sweat broke out on his forehead. He felt ill, and he thought he would lose the contents of his stomach if he didn't sit down soon. "Yes. I'm blind. Take me away from the crowd, to a bench. I need to sit."

"All right. Just lean on me. Let's take it slow."

"Where's Finnegan? Where's that lecherous leprechaun?"

"Uh – gone, it seems. He did this to you. Why?"

Stefan missed his footing and almost fell, but a strong body caught him.

"Lean on me son, just a little further. Now turn slightly. That's it. Now you can sit." His father helped him do it. "I must see to the game, get the focus off of this tragedy and back on the fun and games. But we will take care of this. Mark my words the leprechaun will pay."

Stefan took several slow breaths and waited for the queasiness to pass.

"I'm sorry for the delay folks, what has happened should not interrupt your fun. We will start the race to the center game with the winner of the coin toss. Is there another couple who will be joining in this game?"

"Sabrina, I promised you the wish if we won the race, and now I can't keep my word. I know that hedge maze like the back of my hand. We were certain to win."

"You do?"

"Yes."

"Then would you say you could find your way through it blindfolded?"

Her question surprised him, but he was certain he could. He slowly rose to his feet. "Yes. Yes, I can."

"Then I'll be your eyes. Together we can do it."

"Is there another couple?" Devlin asked.

"We're ready!" Stefan called.

"Are you sure?" Devlin touched his arm.

"Yes I made a promise and I aim to keep it."

Sabrina took a deep breath at the threshold of the maze with Stefan by her side and waited for his father to give the signal to begin. She wasn't sure how they were supposed to catch up with the first couple, or pass them by. She'd never been in a hedge maze before, but Stefan kept whispering that he knew every turn so she should relax. How could she relax? If they didn't reach the center first, then she'd not get her wish. She'd miss out on another chance to get her heart's desire. The thought made her feel guilty with Stefan standing beside her blind.

"When we enter turn to your left," Stefan said.

"Left. Got it." Sabrina wrapped her arm around his waist, and he wrapped his around her shoulders.

"On the count of three." Devlin held up his arm. "One. Two. Three."

She took a step into the maze and Stefan did as well. So far so good. They pivoted left and hurried down the small pathway to the first corner. "We need to turn right, Stefan."

"Got it. If my memory serves me this is a straight shoot down to the next turn, which is right, then immediately back left. Let's pick up the pace a little if we can here. This is the easy part."

"Are you sure? I don't want either of us to trip and fall on a protruding root from the hedge. The lighting here is dim and the path is hard to see." Her breathing became labored as they walked as fast as prudently possible. "Watch it—there is a root on your right."

Stefan caught his right foot on the root and stumbled a little, but she held him the best she could so he didn't fall and take her down with him.

"Are you okay?" he asked.

"Yes, but I'm getting hot. I need to take my cloak off. Its weight is keeping me from going faster."

"Okay, in the next turn, we'll go right all the way down to the first wall of hedge. Then right again. There should be a stone bench there where we can leave it. You're doing well, Sabrina."

"So are you."

They hurried as fast as they could through the next turn so when they stopped for her to remove her cloak it wouldn't detain them long. It was another right then back left until they came into the first clearing when they had to decide which direction to go from there.

"Which way?" she asked before describing what she saw.

"Veer left, then veer back right. Don't go down the other paths, they are dead ends. Sh-h-h, listen." Stefan slowed. "You can hear the groans of our opponents who have taken the wrong turns."

She did and remembered that three other couples had gone into the maze before them. But she couldn't be sure how many were lost in the wrong paths. Light showered down on them and she glanced up, seeing several dirigible balloons floating overhead again, shining their lights.

"All right. Let's keep going before we lose the light from above. The path is clear ahead of us. Where do we go from here?"

"At the next turn go left, then left again, veering left before there should be a straight shoot. Tell me if you see it. If not, then we may need to back track."

Backtrack? No, they didn't have time to backtrack. She silently prayed they were going in the right direction, and she listened closely for any chatter from the other couples ahead of them. Were there any couples following behind them? Or were they the last ones to enter the maze?

Finally, they reached the end of the shoot. "Okay, we're going back right. It looks like there is another turn ahead, so left now?" She directed him and they took another left before a sharp right.

"There's a bench up ahead, Stefan. Do you need to sit and rest for a moment?" she asked.

"No, but it sounds like you might from your labored breathing. I'm sorry, Sabrina. I know the burden of supporting my weight is taxing on you. If I could make it any other way…"

She sat down, removed her shoe and rubbed the bottom of her foot. Somehow a tiny shard of pebble had gotten inside and was poking her flesh. As quickly as she could, she replaced her shoe and got back up to begin their journey once more.

"I believe it's this way!" a voice came from the other side of the hedge.

Stefan grinned. "Tell me what you see now?"

"We have a decision to make. We can either go left or veer right."

"Left." He reached for her arm and urged her to begin moving again. "If I am correct we are at the back of the maze, and we are now headed toward the front. The voice you heard calling is from someone who went right and is now lost in the many twists and turns of the interior. The only way out for them is to come back to this spot, but it is very tricky because by the time they reach this point again they will be so turned around they may take the wrong turn and find themselves right back to the starting point."

She listened to him talk as they hurried down the path. "Okay, do we need to turn right?"

"Yes, then another left?"

She nodded, but caught herself. "Watch your step. There's a hole in the path."

"Hobbits knob."

"What?"

"Hobbits knob. It's a long story from my childhood. I'll have to tell you about it some other time. Right now we need to veer right again, and at the opening of the hedge, go left."

"Are you sure?" Her gut told her if they were supposed to be going to the front of the maze then they shouldn't be going left, but right.

"We have to make one more turn to the back of the maze now before we go to the front."

She started to protest but heard voices coming closer. "Okay, let's go."

A few more left hairpin turns and they were heading back to the right.

"Remember the first right then left when we started?" Stefan said. "We're about to come upon one similar, except this one has a twist. You have the option to go right or back to the left. Stay left, and we'll be in the home stretch."

Sabrina listened to him, but as they approached the turn she saw what looked like a glowing light up ahead. She was so certain what she saw was light from the fire pit that she steered Stefan toward it instead of veering back left. They went until the bend turned them right and came upon a hedge wall.

"Oh no." She stopped short and Stefan stumbled forward, but caught himself before he fell.

"Why'd you stop?" he asked.

"We need to turn around."

"Turn around? I don't understand. We should be near the center."

"And we will be. We just need to go back a little piece where I veered off your directions."

"Why'd you do that? Did you not trust me?"

He was right. She hadn't. "I'm sorry. I-I thought I saw the glow of the flames coming from the fire pit. But I was wrong."

He had a frown on his face. "Okay. Let's go back to where you need to turn. I promise if you go right and straight down to where it turns right again that you will truly see the flames there."

She turned him in the correct direction and wrapped her arm around him and they hurried back toward the turn. As they did, she saw a couple coming around the bend, less than twenty yards away. "Oh no!"

"What now?"

"A couple has caught up to us. Do you think you can run if you hold onto me tight?"

"Yes. I can run, you just lead the way."

She took a deep breath. "Here we go, fast walking then run. The path looks clear."

Her heart began beating faster than it had through the maze so far, and she felt Stefan tense against her side. They had to reach the center first. If they lost after coming all this way because of her going against his directions she'd never forgive herself.

"Turning right in three strides," she called.

In unison they turned and thankfully the path was clear. No roots or holes to make them fall.

"Another right in two strides."

As soon as they made the right, she saw the fire pit and the flames. And all too soon they were slowing down. Stefan was panting so hard he fell to his knees. Sabrina wanted to join him, but she had one more task to perform. She rushed forward and grabbed the torch, stuck it into the fire pit, and lighted the fireworks. Then she tossed the torch into the pit and moved away to a safe distance.

The stench of sulfur filled the air as the fireworks shot up into the night sky and burst into showers of twinkling light overhead. Thankfully the dirigibles had moved away again or there could have been chaos.

"We did it Stefan. We reached the center of the maze." Sabrina fell down beside him and hugged him.

His hands came up to her face and he worked until he got the pin that held her veil in place loose. "Can I kiss you?"

She nodded, unable to speak, but he must have felt her movement in response because slipped his hand behind her neck and pulled her forward as he leaned in to brush his lips against hers.

It was a gentle brushing that lasted only a second. Then there was a second and a third until she felt herself yearning for more. Her heart raced, her body warmed, as a delicious feeling flowed inside and pooled between her legs. Whatever was Stefan doing to her?

"I love you, Sabrina." His whispered words warmed her mouth and her face as he began to brush kisses along her cheek, down to her neck.

She never knew her neck could be so sensitive, but heaven help her, each kiss, each nibble sent shivers down her spine and the warmth between her legs pulsed with every heartbeat.

She tilted her head back, giving him access to more of her and his kisses trailed to her ear and the sensitive little spot behind it. A moan escaped her lips.

Somewhere close by she heard the sound of someone clearing their throat several times, each one getting louder until Stefan must have heard it too, for he stopped kissing her.

"I don't think we are alone any longer." His hot breath seared her sensitive flesh.

She looked to their left and saw Devlin as well as two other couples watching them in fascination. Her cheeks flamed and she looked away. "It's your father and a few others."

A chuckle rumbled from Stefan's chest. "See what I mean, I have no privacy."

She laughed as well and repined her veil before she got to her feet. Stefan stood and wrapped his arm around her waist. This time if felt more as a protective gesture than out of necessity.

"I believe we have a winning couple in more ways than one," Devlin said. And the couples behind him applauded. "Follow me through a secret doorway in the hedge and we shall return to collect your prize."

"Did you know about the doorway?" Sabrina whispered.

"No. It must be new, or the Faeries created it for tonight," Stefan said. "I'll send a guard back into the maze to collect your cloak."

"Thank you. I'd forgotten about it in all the excitement."

"You don't sound as happy about our winning as I thought you would be. You will get your wish."

"I know, but if I make the wish…" She swallowed unable to finish her thought. "We're entering the door in the hedge, you'll need to duck down so your head doesn't get poked by the low-hanging hornbeam branches."

He did as she suggested, and when they stepped away from the maze, Elsbeth was there to greet them. She was crying as she pulled Stefan into her arms.

"I'm fine, Mother. There is no need to fret."

"The leprechaun has gone too far this time," Elsbeth said.

"Has anyone been able to find him?" Sabrina asked.

"Not yet," Devlin supplied. "But the guards are searching."

"It won't do any good to look. He's gone into hiding, vanished out of sight." Stefan frowned. "He knows what he's doing."

"But we need him to undo whatever spell he has placed on you so you can regain your vision. It's the only way." Elsbeth kissed Stefan on his cheek before she turned her attention on Sabrina. "I hear congratulations are in order. You are the winners of the race to the center. And as such you have been granted one wish from the Faeries. Please consider this wish carefully before asking it. Suzette will grant it."

A shimmering girl in white with pink sparkles in her blonde hair came forth from the crowd, and her gossamer wings appeared. She glowed with a bright light around her and hovered off the ground. "Which of you will be asking the wish?"

"I will," Sabrina said. "I would like for you to restore Stefan's sight. Undo what the leprechaun has done. He doesn't deserve to live the rest of his life in darkness."

"No. Sabrina no." Stefan stumbled toward her. "This is your wish. You should use it for yourself."

She touched his cheek tenderly. "I am using it for myself, Stefan. I'd rather you to see me as I am, wearing this veil, than to never see me again."

"Very well," Suzette said. "It is granted."

As soon as the Faerie spoke the words, Stefan regained his sight, and the first thing he saw was Sabrina's beautiful blue eyes. He pulled her to him, crushing her against his body. "Thank you. Thank you for sacrificing this for me. You didn't have to do that."

"I would do anything for the one I love," she whispered.

"And do you love me?"

"You know I do, Stefan. I think you've had my heart since we met on the steps in the ballroom tonight."

He smiled. "Then may I ask one question of you, my Sabrina Fair, my savior?"

"You may."

He knelt before her in front of his mother and his father and all the guests who had been partaking of the outside games. "Will you agree to spend the rest of your life with me, to be my friend, my lover, my soul mate? Sabrina, will you be my wife?"

She swallowed and tears formed in her eyes, causing her to blink several times. "Yes. Yes, I will marry you, Stefan Kilmartin."

He leaped up and pulled her into his arms. He pushed her veil aside and kissed her. But the kiss was not a gentle brushing of his lips, it was a deeper one that caused her to gasp when his tongue parted her lips and began to explore the sweet depths of her. She wrapped her arms around him and melted against his chest.

When they broke apart, fireworks were bursting into the night sky and everyone erupted in applause. He searched the crowd and saw his parents, standing together with their arms around each other and they were smiling at him.

"Now that you've said yes, are you sure you are ready to take on my way of life, living here in this magical castle with me?"

She laughed. "Now, you ask me. I think I'm up for the challenge. As long as you keep Finnegan away. The last thing we need is for him causing mischief for our children."

"Children? We're having children already?"

"Someday."

"Someday sounds good, Sabrina Fair. Shall I send for your father so we can be wed tonight?"

She sighed and nodded. "That would be perfect. And my ⌐ ' Lydia, she should come as well."

"Consider it done."

Happy with their fate. They walked back to the castle to have warmed cider with his parents, not needing to find out their fate from the wishing tree.

Andromeda's Gift

I hope you enjoy the stories!

Felita Daniels

Felita Daniels

In a matter of seconds, she had entered a different world. One moment, she was guiding her horse-drawn carriage down the dirt road, enjoying bird song and the shade from the forest's oaks and maples. The next, she turned the curve and the scene before her looked amazing. The forest opened, and she gazed upon the bridge and front architecture of the stately Castle Amhrán Oiche.

She had, of course, visited Elsbeth and Devlin at their splendid home before. This masquerade gala was the social event of the year. Like a beautiful woman who could not go unnoticed in everyday wear, when dressed in her finest, she took your breath away. Flowers and candles floated in the fountain as its jewelry. Greenery decorated the doors and windows. Somehow delicate lighting sparkled through the manicured shrubs, as if sequins sewn to magnificent gown fabric. No doubt magic of the Fairies had something to do with this.

Just as in nature, some birds blended into the forest and others were as peacocks showing off with color or ornamentation. The carriages ranged the gamut. Some were modest, such as hers, and others shone like works of art- evidence of wealth and station. Many of those in attendance came not only to enjoy the music, food and dancing, but alliances formed at a gathering such as this. Some hoped to find love in such a mysterious costumed atmosphere. She knew many attending tonight kept secrets, just as she did.

Some guests arrived by sea, and vessels approached the docks for unloading. Graceful dirigibles loomed above, and Andromeda was struck by the contradictory manner that something so large could move with such grace. Surely dignitaries and military officers occupied the aircrafts. She knew not of titles and rank in that industry, and tried her best to avoid anyone who had served in battle as they posed a significant worry for her. The average person may have one or two ghosts attached to them, but military leaders? They could have a whole platoon of spirits attached to them. Her heart raced at the thought. She could not realize their deportment until she was too close for safety. If they were loyal to their leader and felt they could not desert him, she was safe enough. If the officer had been careless with their lives, and they were angry and wished to visit bad tidings or try to warn off others from following their thoughtless or incompetent superior, the sheer number of them was a danger to her.

She trembled at the thought of the occasion she had learned of this perilous situation. Realization of the repercussions and possible results had caused her to run to her solitude of her home in the woods. It had been five women, and they didn't mean Andromeda harm, but their anguish and horror of what had happened to them, their emotions pouring out to Andromeda, over-took her, and she fainted with what could only be described as an overload of the burden. She feared she could not hide her revulsion of the man that caused their pain and ran from the dining room. The other dinner guests must have thought her ready for an asylum.

But Elsbeth followed after her. It was a blessing from the gods this well-bred woman recognized the incident was no mere histrionics of a woman vying for attention. She was kind and not surprised at all a person could see someone who wasn't there. Through sobs, Andromeda explained what this despicable monster had done to the poor girls.

She remembered her pleading to this kind woman she had just met. "Their families probably assume they had run off. How can I help them? I have no proof a sane person would accept. He is of social prominence, and I am an orphan with no merits. My invitations to such dinners had been a courtesy and appreciation of my manners and ability to carry friendly conversations."

The fine lady gave Andromeda her handkerchief. "Dear one, we tonight have become the best of friends. What merit I have, I share with you. But let us keep this secret between us tonight. You will come home with my husband and I now for your safety. I agree it may be hard even for me to look him in the eye. If he suspects anything, you might be in danger."

Elsbeth held Andromeda's hands in comfort. "Do not concern yourself. I know of other sorts of monsters. Together, we will see the man in the dining room gets exactly what is warranted for his sins."

That night, a bond formed between the two women. Andromeda valued their friendship more than words could express. Which is exactly why she mustered up all her strength to attend tonight's anniversary celebration. Andromeda shook off thoughts of their meeting occasion as she shook the reins to the horses to continue their journey.

The psychic reminded herself this was an evening of fun, gaiety and happy unions. Her only concern was the number of guests with attached spirits also in attendance. She could mitigate the discomfort by steeling herself off to alcoves, or even escaping to her dressing room. Retreat and respite constituted her plan for coping.

Her horse knew the way, as she frequently visited to help friends and acquaintances of the Kilmartin's with their spiritual needs. It had turned into a very complimentary arrangement, and the Kilmartins had provided her with a small plot of land and a cottage not far from the estate. Many of their circle were more than happy to compensate Andromeda for her services. Some profusely so. She was sure there would be some in attendance this evening who she had helped in the past. Though with the costumes, it might be hard to identify them.

She finally reached the front of the house, and, a young man arrived by her side just in time to offer a hand as she descended "My host and hostess are happy to see you have arrived safely, please allow me assist you." He summoned a footman to handle her luggage.

A slight chill in the March wind made her pull her favorite cloak tight. The thick purple velvet, its color like the deep hues of an eggplant, with its black silk lining kept her warm. With the hood pulled up, she sometimes felt invisible and indeed, she saw it as protection and never left home without it. Silly of her to think it so. It could do nothing, wound nothing, nor defend her against a sword or bullet. Yet, it provided her greatest comfort.

Once in her room, she was happy to see her usual maid, Shannon, just inside the door.

A smile crossed the servant's face as she saw Andromeda. "And a good evenin' to ya, Miss Andromeda. I've readied the room so you can wash the dust off and take a wee bit of rest."

Andromeda removed her cloak and gloves and eased into a chair. "I am equally happy to see you are well. And your kin, how does life treat them?"

"Oh, thank ye miss for such concern over one as lowly as me." She opened the trunk and began the task of unpacking. "They are well, and I can't complain of wanting for a thing." A small gasp escaped her. "Oh, Miss! The gown is beautiful beyond words."

"Thank you for your praises. It is one of the only good things about the solitude of my home. With no one to carry on a conversation with, share memories, or cook and care for, I have all the time in the world to sew. It was somewhat of a relief to have something to occupy my time." She fingered the multitude of small pearls and sea shells she had sewn onto the dress.

"May I be so bold as to ask where you procured the beautiful fabric?"

Andromeda gave her a soft smile. "Shannon, I consider you my friend, not just a maid. I am not royalty, only a friend of the Kilmartin's. You may always speak freely with me."

She continued, "One of the people Devlin sent to me a few months back was a sea captain, and his route took him to the orient often. They must have told him I would be in need of finery for this night. He brought a trunk full of silks and wondrous fabrics. There were boxes of stones, pearls, sequins and all manner of decorative notions and findings. In his gratitude, he instructed me to select anything I desired from the selection. When I saw these gentle little sea shells they called to me in a way I could not resist. The spectacular teal color reminds me of the blue-green of the ocean. I've never seen it in flowers or greenery. I felt it would evoke the sea and a mermaid's home."

"My, the gentlemen will not be able to resist you. You will mesmerize them just as a mermaid calls to sailors."

"From your lips to God's ears," she said sadly. "I fear I will never find companionship and love- my lot may be born an orphan and die an orphan, with no family or attachments."

"I beg you are a walking mystery. Mercy, I know not why you have not bewitched a man thus far. You have too kind of heart to think this way."

Andromeda laughed, "Well, I have attended these parties for five years now. I have witnessed many romances blossom on every instance. I am always the bridesmaid as they say. Keep in mind, I have no dowry or family name to influence any matches."

As the maiden assisted her in dressing she proclaimed "I will stay in this very room, vigilant and praying for you. This will be the occasion you meet your soulmate. My Mistress instructs me to meet your every need this evening." As she nodded her head up and down in assertion "And you shall have it, every ounce of anything I have."

"Thank you my dear, sweet friend. But do not find yourself

embarrassed if it does not come to pass." She absently looked around the room. "I must find my invitation for the announcement at the top of the stairs."

"Here it is mi-lady, and do not forget to participate in the Enchanted Wishing Tree."

"I will follow your instructions. After all, I should do my part to match your efforts on my behalf." Andromeda went to the desk and used the quill to write the word Mermaid on the back of the scripted invitation. "There. I am ready!" With a happy attitude, she kissed the maid on the cheek, put on her mask and went out the door of her temporary sanctuary.

As Andromeda made her way down the hall and focused on the task at hand instead of the forthcoming barrage to her senses. She told herself to keep taking one step in front of the other to get to the ballroom entrance, gripping the invitation as if she might draw strength from it.

When she arrived to the procession area, she was relieved to find the entryway to the ballroom was filled with happy emotions.

The couple in front moved closer to their turn. Two gentlemen escorted the woman dressed as a butterfly. The first, a ghost, who, judging by his finery, was a gentleman of standing while alive, and the second, her flesh and bone companion for the evening dressed as a pirate. The lack of compatible costumes made Andromeda curious about the pair.

As the tall male took the step, he handed their cards to the butler. "Butterfly, accompanied by Pirate," he announced.

The three completed the steps and approached the receiving line. At her turn, she stepped forward and followed suit.

"Mermaid."

The moment of silence and curious stares embarrassed her, but soon enough their attention returned to their conversations. When she reached the bottom of the stairs she overheard Devlin and Elsbeth warmly greeting Butterfly.

"Ah, this costume suits you wonderfully." Devlin gave a wink to the woman. "I am sure your garden draws many a butterfly, and you have enjoyed watching them flirt with your beautiful flowers."

The masked woman smiled "Thank you so much for the invitation this year. It is good to venture out of the house. So many things remind me, you see."

"Yes, yes dear." Elsbeth clasped the woman's hand. "But there are happier days ahead. We can't forget, but you know he would have wanted you to be happy."

The ghost by her side watched the butterfly's face intently through the discussion. He bowed to the host and hostess with respect, however, the Pirate seemed a little impatient with the formalities and took a step closer to indicate Butterfly should move on along.

The woman ignored her escort and continued speaking to the Kilmartins. "Congratulations on your happy union, and may there be too many to count in the future." She then complied with her escort and moved on into the ballroom.

Pirate shook hands with the hosts. "I look forward to this evening. I have heard many kind words regarding your galas."

At his departure Andromeda approached the two, and Elsbeth broke protocol and gave Andromeda a warm embrace. "I am so glad you came."

Devlin added "You look perfectly brilliant tonight!"

"Thank you, I wish to add my blessings to you in your anniversary. I too hope these galas never end. No one deserves contentment more than the two of you. Both of you are precious to me beyond expression."

Elsbeth leaned in to whisper in her ear. "I don't think the Pirate is a good match for Duchess Ravenwood. Might you visit with them sometime during the evening and give me your impression of him? He's the Duke of Landry, there are rumors he may propose to her soon. She has passed the year of mourning."

"Of course. I am happy to offer any assistance and counsel I can."

The beauty of the ballroom took her breath away. The lighting, the decorations, the gowns and attire of the other attendees. She'd never heard such wonderful music and was first drawn to see the orchestra. The musicians held their instruments with care and the sounds produced from the mechanical instruments made her heart pound. She always considered the music of the rustling leaves and birdsong a blessing, but this music was so bold and robust. The emotion the melodies conveyed couldn't be described. Tears came to her eyes as she realized she probably missed many other things by her voluntary solitude.

A tear escaped, and she reached up and brushed it away. She turned and made her way across the room, and again the sounds and voices competed for her attention. In addition to the sounds of the living laughing, drinking and talking, others echoed through the crowd. They were frustrated, some angry, some sad, all trying to reach those they were tied to. Some cried or moaned from their discomfort and sorrow. She knew as the night edged on, the living would get noisier as they enjoyed the Spring Nectar, warm cider, and other wines and beverages through the evening. Maybe their drunk singing and boisterous conversations could drown out the voices of the others. She could only hope.

She decided to check in on the Duchess straight away. She made her way over to a small cluster of women carrying on an animated conversation with the lady. She tentatively walked over to join their tête-à-tête. Andromeda assessed the Duchess to be in her late forties.

"I just don't know what I would have done if Duke Landry hadn't spoken to me that day!"

A younger woman dressed in an Egyptian Goddess costume replied. "You were so forlorn after your Duke passed, I was so worried about you" She emphasized the worried with dramatic flair.

The next woman nodded in agreement. "We didn't know what to do for you. Anytime we even mentioned getting you to come out of the manor to visit or attend an event, you broke into tears saying you couldn't bear it without your Duke by your side."

Andromeda wasn't one hundred percent sure, but thought the woman was supposed to be some type of forest creature. A rabbit, maybe?

"I know, I know." He was the love of my life, and I just couldn't imagine my world without him."

The Duchess noticed Andromeda and graciously changed the subject, "Well, hello dear, come, come let us admire your beautiful gown!"

"Thank you ever so much, I'm flattered. With so many gorgeous gowns and creative costumes here tonight, it's hard to imagine one outshining another. I supposed we're all like stars in the night sky."

They all nodded in polite agreement. "I'm Duchess Ravenwood." She laughed and offered a hand to Andromeda. "We aren't even attempting to keep our identities a secret."

Andromeda curtsied and took her hand in greeting. "I am pleased to make your acquaintance. I am Andromeda Granville, a family friend of the Kilmartin's."

Duchess Ravenwood, ever gracious, turned to the woman on her right, "This is Lady Melody and my other dear friend Lady Wren is to her left. Isn't her costume so imaginative?"

Lady Wren shrugged. "I wanted to be warm during the outside games. What better way than soft, fluffy fur."

"Yes, very clever. I am sure there will be many a lady coveting the warmth of your costume later this evening."

"I'm hoping a handsome gentleman might want to rub my lucky foot hoping for warmth, too."

They all laughed in agreement. Duchess Ravenwood's face brightened. "And here is my escort."

By the looks on her friends' faces, they didn't seem as happy to see him.

She turned her attention to the man joining their little group. The Pirate was tall and handsome, a little younger than the Duchess, but not scandalously so. To her surprise the spirit she had seen by the Duchess side was following behind the Pirate with an angry look. In the next moment, he hauled up his leg and attempted to kick the Pirate in the ass.

A giggle escaped Andromeda's throat before she could catch it. The Pirate looked to her momentarily, but dismissed her. As the man maneuvered himself to the Duchesses side, he acknowledged the others "Lady Melody, Lady Wren he nodded, "You both look wonderful, as usual."

Andromeda no longer listened to his honey laden drivel. The real Duke walked over to her with intent of purpose. He stood next to her and bowed.

"Fair lady, I perceive you saw my actions. Feel quite certain I am a friend, and I wish not to cause you distress. Forgive my ungentlemanly behavior. I am greatly frustrated by my impotence in my ability to protect my love from this scoundrel. He may have a title, but he is no gentleman."

She graciously interrupted the ongoing living conversation, "I feel I would like to take a short stroll and introduce myself to more guests, please continue your fun. Maybe we will run into each other again later in the evening."

The Duke ghost looked crestfallen.

The women in the cluster all assented and resumed their discussion of the evening's dance card arrangements. The psychic looked at the Duke and tilted her head toward the curtained alcove.

"Oh, yes, yes!" and he hurried after her.

She had closed the curtain and sat down.

"You look drained miss, forgive me. My wife's happiness is paramount to me. I am not just a jealous man who is trying to break up a union. She is my world, and I know it will come to pass that she marries again."

"What do you wish of me?

"I know her heart. She does not trust she could have such fortune to find another love of her life. She thinks if it is a societal obligation, it does not matter who it is. She is just settling for the first man who has come along."

"And what do you think?"

"I have seen him sneak away and corner maids for their affections. I worry even though they may never share a bed, and she doesn't expect passion from him, he will still hurt her heart. He will not offer her even companionship. He will not behave as a gentleman in his business dealings, and will embarrass her. She will remain lonely. Happiness will escape from her grasp."

"What qualities and requirements do you seek in an acceptable suitor?"

He placed his hands in a prayerful position, "Only this, that the suitor respects her, is a friend to her, and relieves her loneliness for the rest of her days. If a passion between them grows, I pledge I will not be jealous, but at peace if he keeps her warm until the day she can rejoin me."

"I know all too well, loneliness can be a cruel prison. I will do my best to help in any way I can. There may be a day I tell you it is better for her if you move on to the next world. Would you comply?"

With a resigned look he assented. "Yes, I wonder on occasion if she senses me. She has never said anything aloud for me to know for certain. Sometimes she gets a sad look on her face when I have been sitting close to her for a while."

"I believe ties to a loved one are strong enough to be felt despite our physical existence. Though for most, it's just a feeling they don't understand, and they discount it as simply being in a mood."

"I have nothing to offer you for your assistance." He shook his head. "That's the devil of my situation. I was a man who could get things done, pay my debts, and give love, honor, and protection to my wife. Now, I have nothing to give, no power to move even a piece of straw."

"Do not concern yourself. Frankly, I have done nothing yet, nor can I promise results. But I have a new purpose in view and hope to offer you some peace. Go now, let me rest a moment, and I will come up with a plan."

He bowed to her and quietly walked through the curtain into the grand ball area. Her head started to swim with all the voices she heard. Was it worse this year than last? It didn't seem as if there were significantly more guests in attendance.

Somewhere, a child pleaded with his parents. "Too much crying. Mommy, please stop crying. Daddy, why won't you play with me?"

Her eyes flooded with tears. The poor child did not understand he was dead. How could a child cope with the thought of his mother no longer wanting to hold him, or their father not wanting to play catch? She rubbed her temples and vowed to try her best to seek out this ghost child later.

She should find Elsbeth now and let her know what the Duke had shared and question her knowledge of a family from the area who had lost a toddler or young boy. Surely with the Kilmartin's standing, Elsbeth would know who had lost a child and could introduce her to the family.

Tentatively, she peered out the curtain. Couples swirled around the dance floor, and others stood in polite group conversations. Some paired off in private dialogs that seemed seductive in nature. A Knight whispered in an Angel's ear. On one side of the room, a Mummy had just told a joke and the whole group of guests around him laughed heartily. A Swan conversed with a Phantom. Andromeda thought their body language seemed particularly promising.

Andromeda decided she could do with a cool drink, and glanced around at the multitude of refreshment tables. All of them had glorious choices, and the serving dishes, platters, and candelabras all added to the sense of indulgence. As in years past, so many choices graced the tables, even if only a few of the choices appealed to her. She poured herself a drink.

The crystal tumbler she held with both her hands contained a cool cider that felt like satin on her throat. She carried the cider to a bench placed against the wall. Maybe being farthest away from the dance floor would give her some small amount of relief.

So many happily danced to the wonderful music, and she longed for the prospect of having a gentleman hold her close in the guise of a dance. These were the times she wondered if her gift was really a curse. She was happy she could use her powers to heal and help others, but why must the price be such torment? How could she protect herself from the avalanche of emotions and pain of some and the evil of others?

She was so lost in thought she hadn't noticed the woman who approached her. The ghost, obviously hesitant, stopped a good six feet in front of Andromeda. "May I speak with you concerning a matter dear to my heart?"

"I could not deny your gracious inquiry." She responded and indicated the seat next to her.

"With no one to properly introduce us, I shall venture first to inform you I am Countess Rachel Murdoch. Our property is to the East of the Castle Amhrán Oiche."

"I am Andromeda, a personal acquaintance of the Kilmartins. Undoubtedly you have ascertained I have the ability of being able to see and hear ghosts."

She smiled in response "Yes. It is a blessing to me that I may possibly do some good through you."

"You are still tethered to this world due to some unfinished business?"

"I am apprehensive for my son. You see, my husband, the Earl, was a kind, honorable man. He was good to our friends and servants to a fault. He passed a few years ago and left me and my son in precarious financial status. Then I found myself ill and I, too, have unwillingly abandoned my son before our finances could be improved and his marriage arranged."

It seemed to Andromeda everyone was looking for lovers and soulmates for their loved ones tonight. Who was her advocate? A sad sigh escaped her. She then remembered Shannon.

Rachel didn't know how to interpret her sigh. "Please do not misjudge me. I am not simply asking for money for my son." Rachel wrung her hands and continued. "He is a gentle, wonderful man. He is not overly attractive, nor is he homely. He would offer in return loyalty, caring, sensitivity, and kindness. I had hoped to make a favorable match for him, financially and in affection."

"There is much magic here tonight, and many miraculous unions are made at these annual events. Even so, a marriage of true sensitivities cannot always be arranged." As Andromeda saw the pleading in Rachel's eyes, she relented "I will see what I can do. I have a possibility in mind."

Relief flooded Rachel's features. "I am forever indebted to you. May grace and blessings be bestowed on you and your attempts. I will leave you to your beverage and keep my fingers crossed. That is my son just there, in the blacksmith costume. He is Thomas Murdoch, Earl of Dunbrody."

Following to where the ghost indicated, Andromeda saw a tall, strong looking young man. He listened to a conversation between a gentleman in a Monk costume and another in a Jester wardrobe. The Blacksmith costume suited him, and it surprised her that his physique didn't garner more interest from the ladies. He had a strength of back and muscles in his arms. Indeed, you might think he was an actual blacksmith who hammered and lifted metal all day.

The Countess rose, curtsied and moved to a place where she could observe her son and be away from the commotion of the dance floor.

Andromeda made her way to a nearby waiter and placed her empty glass on his tray.

"Would you like me to retrieve a refill for you milady?"

"No, thank you, I should begin mingling again."

"As you wish." He bowed and added "My mistress asked if I were to see you, to inform you she appreciates your helping her guests and sharing so generously of your gift. She is aware it does not come without cost."

A woman in a Medusa costume passed by, and the blue, otherworldly glow stunned Andromeda for a moment. The waiter saw her facial expression, and followed her line of sight.

She took a breath and recovered herself, "My apologies. Even after years of attending, I can still be a bit astounded by the strange natures of some of the guest." Andromeda shook her head as if to rid herself of the sight.

The waiter attempted to relieve her anxiety. "I will talk of nothing to distress you, but there are many here tonight that are of a spirited nature. Perhaps you witnessed such?"

"You deserve praise for attempting to comfort me. Do convey to Elsbeth I am happy to help others when I can." She nodded a thank you and she began her noble task by approaching the small group where the blacksmith stood.

They made an opening in their cluster. "Do we know you?" the monk asked.

"I am unaware if you and I are acquainted, good Lord. I have been told the identity of the Blacksmith by a mutual acquaintance. Though I will keep his secret," she said with merriment in her voice.

The Blacksmith looked surprised. "Do I know you?"

"May we have a moment or two in private?"

The Earl bowed. "I am at your service, milady. Where would you feel comfortable talking?"

Andromeda smiled. Countess Rachel was not wrong. He emanated kind-heartedness and an air of tenderness. There was no rough, daring, sweep you off your feet sense to this gentleman.

She led him away from the group. "It is of a delicate situation of which I care to discuss with you. I have been told you are of a kind disposition."

"I endeavor to be so. Please continue."

"I have an acquaintance, a lovely woman who has lost her husband not a year since, and she loved him dearly. Though she has many friends, they cannot find words to comfort her."

"Why would words from me, a stranger, offer any more relief?"

She explained, "I wondered if sharing the loss your father and then your mother..." She paused a moment. "Knowing she was not going through this alone might offer some easing of pain? Would you be willing to be introduced to her?"

"I see the logic to your approach and the awkwardness of it also. I cannot walk up and discuss such an intimate matter on first encounter." He scratched his head and added "I am willing to attempt the undertaking. Lead the way to this unhappy woman."

"You should be aware; she puts on a brave face. She pretends a suitor is appropriate for her, when every friend who cares for her knows he is unacceptable. He is too involved in his own needs to notice her pain and loneliness."

"How dreadful."

"I share your opinion. Though, it is not your problem to solve. I felt you should be aware of it. She looked around the ballroom and found Duchess Ravenwood. "Ah, there they are. It is a happy event that the suitor, he's dressed as a Pirate by the by, isn't by her side."

The Blacksmith offered his arm graciously and upon her acceptance they made their way over to the Duchess.

"The beautiful Mermaid has returned!" the Duchess remarked.

"I have brought a dear friend of mine to you. I was telling Earl Murdock of my meeting you and your lady friends. Maybe you all still have a spot open on your dance cards for him?"

Lady Wren was the first to pull hers out and offer it to him. As the Duchess lent her card she asked, "Are you relation to the late Earl Luke Murdock?"

"Why yes, he was my father. Were you acquainted?"

"My husband spoke of him. The Duke was very impressed with his character, and we were both sorry to hear of his passing."

He was intelligent enough to take advantage of her expressed sympathy. "Thank you. We were further saddened when my mother passed not nine months after."

"Oh," she put her hand to her heart. "I had not heard this heartbreaking news. My apologies."

"You have been experiencing grief of your own Duchess. My condolences to you also. Having gone through bereavement myself, I can share that some days, I could barely comprehend if I had eaten dinner or not." He paused a moment, dipped his head ever so slightly and added "Shall we change the subject to more happy thoughts in honor of the celebration tonight?"

"Yes, let's share memories of younger and happier days if necessary," she agreed.

Andromeda listened to their exchange while searching the ballroom for Elsbeth. She wished to find out about the boy before her nerves were overly burdened.

A ringing bell quieted the ballroom, and Andromeda turned toward the sound to find her friend in the center of the dance floor.

"We have prepared some extra special entertainment for you throughout this evening. For the more adventurous among you, there will be games within the hedge maze out back. For those of you who choose to remain indoors, a schedule has been prepared for the various events available to you as well." She motioned toward the end of the ballroom where several small round tables were set up for games. "My husband will be seeing to the more *spirited* among you, while Stefan and I will do our best to keep the rest of you on your excited little toes."

A collective chuckle caused their host to pause and smile.

"Now…for those of you willing to brace the chill, Devlin awaits you through *that* door. For my inside guests, we will resume once the crowds have cleared."

The Blacksmith smiled and asked the women "Would you all care to join me in a game? The men in the room will wonder what spell I have cast to enchant you all to be seated with me."

The women seemed enthusiastic at the prospect and Andromeda disentangled her arm from the Earl's. "Excuse me, I need to speak with Elsbeth. I've been trying to locate her unsuccessfully, and I'm afraid I'll lose her again amongst all the guests." She slipped off in Elsbeth's direction as the others moved toward the games.

As Andromeda crossed the space between her and Elsbeth others moved all at once. Some heading to the tables, some outdoors to the maze, and some switched dance partners. The voices and emotions washed over Andromeda like an avalanche, and the room seemed to swirl about her.

Elsbeth came to her rescue and guided her into a draped alcove. After pulling the curtains shut, she lit a candle and sat down next to her. "Are you calmer now?"

"I feel I've been tossed in wind and wave, but it is subsiding. I needed to ask you something."

"Pray, ask anything of me."

"Do you know of a family that has been visited by death of a child?"

The woman's demeanor changed and sympathy took over her face. "Our neighboring Baron and Baroness Ramsey. They lost a son, and it has devastated them as a family. Such a thing is expected, but most can get to a place after a time," she paused. "The father experienced misery early in life, because his mother had run off."

She reflected a moment and continued. "I believe he was around four or five when she left. His father was temperamental, and blamed the child, or at least took it upon himself to say cruel things. He told him his mother didn't love him or she would have taken him with her."

Eventually his father passed. When the grown young man met his wife, things began looking up for him. When their son was born, he swore to be a kind and caring father, the opposite of his own. I thought he had his happy ending. "

Elsbeth sighed. "Tragedy struck when the boy got sick. They brought in every doctor they could, to no benefit."

"Thank you for the information, it may be important. Do you know what costumes they are wearing?"

"Yes they are both dressed as gypsies. They look like a sad lot, lurking around the edges of the party. Do you need me to find them for you?"

"No, I think I would like to rest for a few moments, maybe close my eyes for a spell."

"Take as long as you need. Don't attempt to find the Ramsey's until you are fully recovered."

She returned a weak smile. "I will gladly obey your instructions." She reclined over the long bench and shut her eyes.

No more than ten minutes passed when Andromeda was startled by the sound of the curtains being disturbed. At the realization someone else had entered the alcove she sat up and saw a young woman dressed in a harem girl costume, obviously distraught.

"Oh, I beg your pardon," the girl said quickly. "I didn't mean to disturb you."

"No dear, please come in and sit. I can tell you are upset." Andromeda patted the bench beside her. "Let your heart calm down. It is why I sought refuge here. I don't mind sharing the space at all."

The young woman looked hesitant, unsure of what course of action to take.

Andromeda also saw the lady who had accompanied the younger woman. "My name is Andromeda," she said softly to the ghost. "Do you need to share something?"

The harem girl asked "I'm sorry. Should I go?"

This was always a difficulty. Trying to converse with a spirit when the live person thought you were talking to them. Then there were the occasions when both were speaking at once. What a hindrance.

"No." Andromeda turned to the young woman. "I know you've just been distressed. Can you be strong enough to hear a truth that would affect the rest of your life?" She gave the harem girl a small smile.

"Strong? I don't understand? What could you possibly tell me that would affect my life? I don't know you. I'm certain I have never seen you before in the village, so how could you possibly have something to share with me?"

"I'm sure you've sensed something strange here this evening. As if many people tonight harbor secrets."

The confused girl nodded, acknowledging the truth in her words.

"I am one of those people," Andromeda continued. "I can see and hear spirits. Some of them are here tonight. They have heartache or unfinished business regarding the living that they desperately need to satisfy before moving on."

"What could any of your spirits have to say to me?"

"More than you might think."

"How do you know this person wishes to speak to me? There are so many guests here tonight. Couldn't you be mistaken?"

Andromeda listened to the lady and nodded as if in agreement. "You're Sabrina Gilchrist, are you not?"

Jumping up, the girl inched away. "Uh…um…how could you possibly know that? No one knows who I am here. No one is supposed to know because of my costume."

"Your mother has known you since you were a wee lass. No costume could disguise who you are to her."

She gasped. "My mother?"

"She begs you to please listen. She's never had an opportunity to tell you what you should know, what you deserve to know. That pain has kept her here in this world all through your life. And because you are here tonight, in this magical castle, she can now speak to you if you will only listen. She's afraid she will never have this opportunity again."

The young lady shook her head.

"Why should I listen to you or her? It's because of her I have been forever scarred. It's why I must wear a veil whenever I go out in public so I do not scare the village children. It's why I live a very quiet and lonely life." Tears came to her eyes as she spoke and she blinked them away, trying to clear her vision. "It is why I may never know the happiness of a true love…a true love like I may have met tonight."

Andromeda felt empathy for her. "I understand your pain. I too have resorted to a cabin in the woods and a quiet life. All of the spirits clamoring for my help, sometimes it is just too overwhelming. It's especially hard in large gatherings like this.

"Sabrina, if it were me, I would want to know your mother's true story. Wouldn't the truth be better to deal with than rumors?"

The girl's mother reached out a hand, as if she might caress the child's face. "I simply must, must tell her."

"I will not force anyone if they do not wish to hear, regardless of your need." Andromeda felt she was defending a child. "I am sorry, but it is her choice."

Andromeda turned to Sabrina. "If you wish I will repeat back what she is saying to you, so you can hear her words and feelings instead of my summarizing it. In this case, she needs you to hear from her heart. I'm not just relaying where to find something or a fact like where her heirloom earrings are hidden."

The young lady looked distressed, but nodded her consent.

"I will repeat what she says word for word as I can." She took her hand and graciously put it over Sabrina's as if saying 'we're in this together' and to give her strength.

"I'm sorry. A thousand times sorry for my past transgressions. I have spent the last two decades regretting my careless ways. But my darling girl, I've been with you all this time. It has been my contrition that I never leave your side. If I could take away the damage done, I would. I cannot change the past, but I ask for your forgiveness, because if I had not gained the reputation I did, this never would have happened to you. I know you're hurt, because I have hurt for you ever since Avery marked you."

"How can I forgive you?" Sabrina found herself looking to the curtain.

"I know what I'm asking is difficult, but perhaps if you knew the truth of what transpired that evening—what really happened at the party where I was falsely accused of stealing my best friend's husband, and why I was fleeing the party with haste. I had had a little too much to drink when he found me in the library alone. I was bored and regretting coming to the party, and due to the wine, my head was muddled. Robbie smelled of beech wood and lemongrass, the same as your father. He was tall and had the same coloring as your father, so in the dim lighting of the library and in my foggy state, it was easy to forget that there was no way your father would have come to the party late. Their voices when speaking low sound so much alike. He took advantage of that fact and had me in a very compromising position when he kissed me. But that is where the similarity ended. I knew immediately he wasn't my husband, and I tried to get free, but he trapped me, pinned me down on the sofa and tried to force himself on me."

"Oh, Mother," Sabrina whispered.

"I was fighting him off when Avery came searching for him, but in the dark she mistook what she saw as the two of us making love. My dress was torn, and the pins holding my hair in place were falling out. I was a disheveled mess as I ran from the manor to the safety of my carriage. Many of the guests saw me flee, so I know the rumor mill had much fodder that night, but I didn't care. My only thought was to get home to you and your father, and to never go to another party again without him.

"I never made it home that night." Tears flowed and Andromeda couldn't continue.

After pausing a moment, Andromeda took a jagged breath and continued. "My carriage driver was racing back to our village when he lost control of the horses, sending us over the rocky edge of the mountain into the shore of Galway Bay below. My greatest regret is the time I wasted, my girl. I should have valued being your mother instead of being consumed with parties. Please forgive me. Please forgive a silly young woman her folly. Please tell your father I was never unfaithful to him, even though I am sure he has long ago resigned himself to the false accusation I was."

"It's all right, mother. I forgive you. Father never remarried. He's stayed alone, caring only for me all these years."

"I wish one day he'd find happiness again. I wish that for both of you." Andromeda laid a hand on her cheek. "Please, Sabrina, remove your veil so I may see all of you, one last time before I go. Now that I have your forgiveness I can move on. Thank you, my darling, for granting me this favor."

"Go? I don't want you to go." Sabrina sat back. "Not now, not after I know what really happened to you. Please, say you will stay. There is so much about you I want to know."

Andromeda removed a handkerchief and wiped her tears. "My time is drawing nigh. Please, remove your veil so I can see you as you are, my child."

Taking a deep breath, Sabrina unpinned the veil from the side of her face, letting the sheer material hang loose. She swept it back and stood, stepping in the candlelight of the wall sconces.

"You are beautiful Sabrina, despite your scar. Remember that. Your beauty comes from within, that is what Stefan saw when he saw you. Trust in him. Trust in yourself. You shall find happiness. You shall."

Andromeda stopped speaking.

"Is it over? Is she gone?" Sabrina asked, turning away to refasten the veil in place.

Andromeda nodded. "Thank you for listening to her. I hate to see the tormented think they have no hope."

"I'm the one who should be thanking you, Andromeda. You have helped me more than you know. You have given me something of my mother I never would have had if you were not who you are. Thank you for coming tonight. Thank you, oh so much."

Sabrina hugged her tight before she left the alcove.

Alone again, Andromeda closed her eyes and took a breath. Then she heard him again.

"Daddy, Daddy, did you hear that woman. There are games! Let's play one, please, please. Do you think they have dominoes?"

She could not abandon this poor child. He must be somewhere near. She understood him clearly even though he didn't raise his voice or throw a tantrum. He was only pleading. In her mind's eye, she imagined him pulling on the father's jacket.

She stepped out of the alcove and looked left and right. Remembering what Elsbeth had said, they were probably not going to be on the dance floor, but watching from the edge. There were chairs lining the walls, but also clusters of guests talking amongst themselves. She spotted the pair of gypsies standing apart from the others that were enjoying themselves. They did indeed look like they were just going through the motions of attending the party. They held hands, but that was the extent of any affection between them. The wife watched the dancers. The husband's eyes looked unfocused, and the wrinkles on his brow indicated an unhappy mood. And running all around them was a ghost child wearing pajamas. Three times clockwise. Then he stopped, playing like he was dizzy. Then he ran three times around them counterclockwise. He couldn't have been more than five or six years old.

She made her way over to the family. "Dear gypsies, I have been told the Kilmartins have a wonderful library. Can you direct me, I should like to visit it."

The woman, pointed to their right and in a soft voice "I believe it is just there through the second doorway."

With a thank you Andromeda made her way to the doorway. As she approached she wiggled her finger to the boy indicating she wanted him to come with her. His eyes lit up and he came running towards her.

"What's a lie barry?" he asked. "What is your name?"

As they crossed the threshold, she replied, "Why, it's a place where people keep books. I bet your mother has read books to you before?"

"Oh yes, I enjoy it a lot. Expecially the ones with pirates." Then he looked sad. "She hasn't read me a book in a long time."

"I almost forgot, my name is Andromeda. What is your name?"

"I am Elliot Ramsey" with a puffed out chest. "Will you be my friend?"

"Certainly, I would be honored. You know one of the things friends do is help each other with problems. Do you agree?" She walked over to a couch and sat down.

He came over and had to take a bit of a run to jump up to sit beside her. "Do you have a problem? I will help you." He said earnestly.

"I knew you were the best to have as a friend." She smiled at him. "I want to help your mother and father. They seem very sad."

"I dinna know what I've done wrong." He hung his head. "I've told them I'm sorry for anything I've done bad, but they won't speak to me."

"Oh, Elliot, you have not done anything wrong. I have a secret, but since we are friends I can tell you my secret."

"Pirates have secrets, passwords and maps sometimes. Is it like that?"

"Sort of, I will tell you, but you should not tell others about my secret. You promise?"

"Cross my heart, hope to die, stick a needle in my eye."

She laughed. "I can see invisible people. Ever since I was a little girl. Back then people just thought I had an imaginary friend I talked to, because they couldn't hear the invisible person talking back to me."

"I've seen girls talk to their dolls. They don't talk back either."

"That is true. Do you remember getting sick?"

"Yes, I didn't feel good at all, and I had to stay in bed all the time. Mother would only feed me broth. Yuck."

"Well, what you don't know is when you stopped being sick, you turned invisible. Your dear mother and father can't see you."

"What craziness. You don't know what you are talking about."

"Elliot, I would not lie to you. You are a very dear friend to me. This is why your mother cries, and your father is unhappy as well. They are missing you. They don't know where you are. They can't hear you when you speak to them." She looked at him in earnest.

The young boy thought of this a moment and asked "Is that why the woman in the dark place cries too? She can't see me? I thought it was because she might be afraid of the dark."

"Tell me of this woman and the dark place," she encouraged. "Perhaps I can help."

"Oh, I wish you could. I don't really like the dark place. Sometimes I find myself there, but I don't remember how. I can see the lights of our home and have to walk all the way back to my room."

"What does she say or do? What does she look like?"

"She never says anything. She just cries and cries." He shook his head as if perplexed. "She wears a purble furry dress. She has yellow hair like Father's."

"Tell me, does the dark place have big stones in rows. Some may stick up in the air and some lay on the ground?"

"Yes," his eyes got wide "You are good guesser. I bet you win a lot at games!"

She patted his hand. "Let us see if we can solve the mystery of the lady in the dark place. She may be able to help us with your parents, too."

"Is there a way she can make me stop being inbisible?"

"No, sweetheart," she said sadly. "But if I am still a good guesser, she will help your papa's sadness, and she can then be your friend and keep you company until your mother and father turn invisible too." She paused a moment. "You see, you will all be together again someday, but there's no way to tell how many nights it will take until this happens."

"Mother and Father are going to turn inbisible?" he asked incredulously.

"Someday yes, and then you can all see and hear each other. It will be in a happy place. It will be bright and cheery."

"Good." He confessed to her. "I don't really like the dark. Do you think less of me? When I got sick, Papa said I was his brave boy, but I don't know if he was just being Papa."

"Come, I believe you to be brave too. You made a new friend today. You received startling news about being invisible, and you accepted it as a champion." She stood, "You no longer get cold, but I think I will need my cloak at the dark place. We must get the key to the cemetery from your father also."

He slid off the couch and looked about the room for a moment. "They really have a lot of books."

She smiled at him, "Yes, isn't it wonderful. One can never have too many books. I think I could spend the rest of my life in this one room if they would bring me food!"

"You are silly. You would have to take baths too."

"Well, yes. I would get stinky." She wrinkled her nose and pinched it with two fingers. They both laughed.

"Remember, I won't be talking to you much outside where others can hear me. They would think me crazy and lock me up. But notice when I speak to your mother and father. They haven't been ignoring you at all. Look around the room you will see other invisible people and how they are trying to get their loved ones to see and hear them, too."

She found the couple had not moved. "Baron and Baroness Ramsey, thank you so much for the directions. It is a wonderful library."

The Baroness gave a polite smile and agreed. The Baron sulked and looked away as if bored with the conversation. Andromeda glanced to see how the boy was doing. He was looking at the whole room. He had his hands upon his hips in evaluation of what his eyes were finally noticing about what had been happening around him.

"My condolences to you both regarding Elliot. He is such a delightful child."

Baron Ramsey turned his attention to her. "You were acquainted with our son? Do we know you?"

"I beg your patience as I explain. I daresay living next door as you do, you cannot be unaware of the Kilmartin's spirited friends. There are many here tonight who are extraordinary in some way. I am one of those people."

"What has that to do with us?" he blustered. The Baroness seemed to shrink a little.

"I can see and hear ghosts who have not passed on, and I have spoken with Elliot this evening."

"What type of trick are you running? I will give you no money. How dare you put my wife through such torment. You are lower than a snake." Hatred and anger mixed with spit seethed from his teeth.

Elliott returned to Andromeda's side upon hearing his father's raised voice. "I do not request money. I simply desire to ease your pain and help him move on. You see he has thought you both angry at him because you weren't speaking to him."

The Baroness's hand went to her mouth as a gasp escaped. She settled to the chair behind her in shock. "No, I would never!"

Elliott went over to her and put his hand on her knee. "Don't cry mommy, please don't cry."

"He has his hand on your knee and is pleading for you not to cry." She turned to the Barron. I know this is fantastical. He has told me his favorite books are the ones with pirates."

"What boy doesn't like pirates" he accused.

She looked to Elliott, and quietly said "You know we talked of passwords and secrets before, is there something you have shared with your papa no one else would know? Some way I can prove to him I am speaking with you? Take time to respond to me, I know it may be difficult to think of something."

The young boy's face scrunched in concentration. "Once a long time ago when I was really little, like four, I couldn't sleep. We ate cake we found in the kitchen and had milk. The next morning the cook was screaming angry. The cake was for the church. Papa thought it was just for our dinner and said we had to keep it secret, or the cook would burn our dinner and make us eat it in punishment. He would give extra money to the church that Sunday to make it up so we would not carry guilt. He said we had to keep this secret, even from Mother."

Andromeda relayed Elliot's story, and the Baron sank into a chair behind him.

"Would you like me to gesture for a waiter to bring some cider or spring nectar? You both have had such a shock."

He looked to his wife, "Yes, I feel a drink would do her wonders." He himself stood and waived a waiter over, and in a surprisingly pleasant tone made his request of the servant.

"What do you require of me now? You have earned my trust."

"Only the key to your family cemetery. The dark of it is unpleasant for him, but he is repeatedly pulled there. I must see why there is an entanglement to the place for him."

The waiter returned with drinks, and Andromeda gestured to her left. "Perhaps we should go to the library where you can await my return with news."

She accompanied them. The parents settled on the couch. "I don't know how long we will be. I do not wish for you to be anxious of the outcome. Elliot may go to the happy light place from there. Is there anything you want to tell him now in case we are met with success?"

The Baroness asked "Where is he? I wish to tell him something."

Andromeda pointed to a spot between the man and woman. "He is standing right here."

The mother leaned down to the height of where his head would be. "Son, I have missed you so and love you. I would never have ignored you if I had known you were still here. I swear I would have read you books and talked to you all day long until my throat was hoarse."

She looked to her husband.

"Elliott, I too miss you more than the air I breathe. I am sorry I was mad at your friend at first. I am ever so proud of you for making a friend who could let us know of this magical thing. If she suggests you do something or go somewhere, I think you should. We want you to be in the happy place."

Andromeda listened to Elliot's reply and relayed it to his parents. "He says he doesn't want his mother to cry anymore, or for you to be upset. He wants you both to be happy until you turn invisible and you can be together as a family again." She winked as she said invisible. "That's how I explained it to him."

They both smiled and nodded their heads in agreement. The father pulled a set of keys out of his pocket and handed them to Andromeda. "I don't know why, but knowing this somehow makes me feel better."

"It should keep you both on your toes knowing he's watching over you both." She shook her finger back and forth as if scolding. "No more crying and sulking." She smiled as the mother crossed her heart so her son could see. "I will return and report back of events."

"Come on Elliott, let's get my cloak from my room and check out the dark place. We will solve this problem together."

Christenson sat on a tombstone and pouted. The Ramsey's cemetery was on the edge of their property in such a way that it was actually closer to the Castle Amhrán Oiche. He supposed he should be grateful. Certainly, much more activity took place there. If he only had the Ramsey's home for entertainment, he surely would have attempted to put himself out of his misery in some way before now. If he could curse himself for his own rashness, he certainly would. Twenty years of being bound to this place seemed like a lifetime. Duller than dull and the added misery of listening to the woman cry. Would she never stop? At first he truly felt guilty over it. As the years yawned on, he became so sick of the crying, he became sullen and angry. Not angry at her, but at himself for the words which had so easily tumbled out of his mouth before he had thought out the possible consequences.

Tonight was evidently one of the Kilmartin's annual bashes. Ships, carriages and dirigibles had deposited guests all day, and all manner of creatures and spirits intermingled with the royalty and normal folk. Lights glowed, and he enjoyed the orchestra's music traveled on the wind. Even though there was a chill in the air, party goers moved in and out of the castle. The Kilmartins always had some fun with their maze. Every year he saw costumed individuals put ribbons on a tree as if decorating it. He wondered what that was all about.

The doors opened from the West wing, and a woman emerged wearing a dark hooded cloak. Her steps indicated a purpose and not a simple stroll in the night air. Mercy, she was heading this way with a toddler child in tow. Now, this was curious.

As he watched her approach, he realized she spoke to the ghost child. She could see him! Ah, this woman had some powers. Maybe there was an opportunity here to be had. He must keep his wits about him. "Yes, Yes, come closer dear lady," he whispered to himself.

"Now, you have to keep calm and behave," she explained to the boy. "I have to become friends with her to discover her story. If she cries, there is certainly something which brings her grief, and it may be hard for her to discuss the reasons with a stranger."

"But please get her to stop crying" he insisted.

"Darling, it is hard to get someone to stop crying while they are upset. They have to let it out sometimes. It's like your jumping around and tugging at our clothes trying to get our attention. You can't stop yourself when you think no one is listening to you."

"I'm sorry, I am not usually unruly. I was a good boy before." His bottom lip trembled.

She smiled at him. "I am sure you were. Your parents' grief is a testimony to how much they love you. Let us endeavor to relieve this lady of her sadness, too."

"Do you think we can?"

"I will try my best." She paused at the arrival to the gate and withdrew the key from her pocket. She inserted it and swung the gate open. The creaking of the metal shrieked through the cemetery.

"Oh my," she exclaimed. "It's enough to wake the dead."

"Indeed" Christenson announced. He hopped off the tombstone and gave her a low bow.

She jumped back a step, took a moment to recover, and curtsied. "Sir, we did not mean to disturb you."

"How could a creature as beautiful as you disturb any rational person?"

Embarrassment heated her cheeks. As her normal behavior was to stay on the fringes of gatherings, she was not accustomed to flattery. "Everyone has their own need for privacy and solitude. I do not mean to disrupt your repose."

"I welcome your presence. Tell me what takes you away from the festivities and brings you to this place of death."

"Dear sir, we are seeking a woman who is bound to this place. The boy is sad for her. He tells me she wears a purple velvet dress and cries."

"Yes, I know of the ghost you speak of. Incessantly she mourns." He eyed her curiously. "What is your business with her? Is she a family member?"

"The poor dear is no relation of mine, although I have my suspicions of her lineage." Andromeda tilted her head towards the boy. "I would make effort to ascertain certain facts and her disposition before introducing her to others. I do not want to cause harm in any disclosure that would serve no purpose but to cause sorrow."

"Milady you are so gracious and circumspect. It is very wise of you to understand repercussions of some types of knowledge."

Christenson nodded in understanding and put his finger on his lips to indicate he would keep hush.

"I am not without experience in these types of situations. Certainly, I can still be surprised. I am well aware there are a multitude of circumstances and obstacles to spirits influencing and communicating with the living."

"May I please offer my humble assistance in your noble task?" He bowed again, straightened, and gave her an incredibly charming grin.

Andromeda considered his kind offer, and wondered if anyone had ever been able to decline his charm. What was he doing here? She noticed a faint purple glow to him. Why was she seeing colors on individuals tonight? No time to worry over such things now. She must get back on task.

He offered his hand. "My sincere apologies, I should have introduced myself straight away." He hesitated a moment. "You may call me Fredric. May I have the ladies name and hand?"

She offered her hand. "My name is Andromeda."

He placed a light kiss on her hand, and she was shocked to realize she felt it. Truly, she had never had this sensation before with a ghost. To be fair, she had never had such a sensation with a human either. Was this part of the magic of the castle grounds? No, she was no longer on the Kilmartin's property.

The boy started jumping up and down. "Where is the lady?"

Christenson kneeled to the boy's level. "Let's just see if we can locate her, shall we?" He started to lead the way to the left. "She sometimes sits in the mausoleum. Maybe we will be lucky and find her there now."

"Yes, yes. I want to be lucky." Elliot clamored and followed the spirit.

They stopped at the open doorway of The Ramsey mausoleum. Elliott squinted. "It looks really dark in there. Do we have to go in?"

"We don't want to invade her in her thoughts. Let us invite her out here in the radiance of the moon where we can see each other," Andromeda suggested to the boy.

"How wise and considerate you are. I admire you more and more," Fredric commented.

"Ma'am," she called. "My name is Andromeda. I am here with little master Ramsey and Fredric, and I would like to speak with you. Would you grace us with your presence in the moonlight? I would like to hear your story."

There was a moment of quiet. It seemed the only sound was the frogs croaking. Then a rustle and the woman emerged. She looked momentarily at Fredric and a fearful, questioning look crossed her face.

Andromeda pleaded, "Do not be alarmed. We mean you no harm. Little Master Ramsey wishes to bring you relief from your sorrow. Why do you come to his grave and cry? Can we do anything to help you find peace and go to the next world?"

A look of frustration crossed her face. A tear trailed down her cheek as she looked to the boy. The woman gestured for Andromeda to follow her a step or two away from the boy. As they turned their backs from the two, the woman pulled the scarf away from her neck.

Andromeda's heart melted. A horrid wound gaped from where the woman's throat had been slit on the side, and ghostly blood dripped onto a necklace.

"May I see your locket? If you cannot speak, I may find answers in the portraits?"

The woman's eyes filled with hope, and she quickly reached around, undid the clasp, and showed the locket to Andromeda. In the woman's delicate hands, the family jewelry opened to show a man's portrait, presumably her husband, and another of a young child. It did not surprise her that the face was the mirror image of the boy not three feet away.

Both the son and grandson carried the same shaped nose and chin of the poor dear woman. "I wish I could take this to show your grown son. I don't know if he will believe me, that you didn't run away without him. It is a lie he has been fed his whole life."

The mother attempted to place the locket in her hands, but it fell through them to land on the ground. Andromeda attempted to pick it up, but it was impossible. "Please replace your necklace, it is a precious reminder of your love. I don't wish to deprive you of its comfort if it serves no purpose to surrender it."

The woman did so, but was clearly disappointed. She replaced the scarf at the same time and turned back toward her grandson.

"I am glad you have stopped crying." He kicked at the dirt. "I was worried for you."

She walked over and gently caressed his cheek.

And as a child will do, he abruptly brightened. "We can leave this dark place, now?"

Andromeda answered, "Dear, it is not a simple as that I'm afraid. She may still need to let someone know something."

Grandmother Ramsey's ghost took a few steps and pointed towards the mausoleum entrance. But she avoided getting too close to Fredric. Andromeda, curious about the lady's avoidance of him, took a step back. Could he possibly be her killer?

Frederic recoiled seeing the Grandmother's desire to have Andromeda enter the tomb. He pleaded with the ghost. "Please, I beg of you. It is too much to ask of her. No. No."

Seeing Frederic was clearly distressed and concerned for her in some way, she felt him less a danger. "What, is there something in there to help our dire situation? What do you know of it?"

"I, I," he stammered.

"Do not deceive me. Are you the one who used a knife on her?" she demanded.

"No, but I was here when it happened, and I witnessed the atrocious event. It happened so quickly I could not step in and put a stop to it. In my horror upon seeing it, I vowed I would not abandon her."

"This is why you are here in this cemetery? Not because of a love of anyone here, but of a vow you gave?" Elsbeth had said the mother disappeared some twenty years before. Fredric had kept his word to this woman for two decades. What honor and patience he had.

"Yes, but I must also confess to you. I am not a ghost such as she." He pointed to the woman. "This is possibly the reason for her avoidance. She doesn't understand why I am here and the changes she has seen in me over time."

"I have grown weaker with each passing year, and my physical appearance deteriorates to the point I look a ghost." His head hung in embarrassment.

Andromeda looked to the woman for her reaction to what had been said. She too looked ashamed, but she cautiously still gestured to the doorway.

"I wouldn't go in there if I were you," the boy chimed in. "I bet there's a ton of spiders and it's dark." He shuddered.

She took a step, and Fredric moved to block her way. "No, it's where her jealous husband took her body after."

Andromeda stopped and looked to the woman, "Is that what you want me to discover? You can cross over even before we properly have you buried." She said encouragingly. "I have seen it before."

The distressed mother shook her head.

"So, there is more to be found?" She squared her shoulders. "Then I will venture to discover what it is."

The man stepped to her side. "I will accompany you. I should not be able to catch you, should you faint. But I will not leave you alone to face it."

"I will accept your offer. Thank you, sir." Other than Elsbeth, no one else had ever offered or attempted to protect her. She was touched by his proposal.

Upon entering, she discovered the tomb wasn't entirely pitch black. Moonlight found its way through a circular stained glass window on the back wall and projected a colored replica of the artist's work on the floor. A large bench, constructed much like a window seat in a library, sat under the window. She was certain this would be the hiding place. She lifted the seat and a musty smell announced itself. Yes, there was the skeleton of the lady. But Andromeda saw something else there. A suitcase with the family crest upon it.

"I regret I cannot pull it out for you. A lady should not have to do such a thing. There is no way to get it out without disturbing the bones. Please leave it. Do not distress yourself."

"It is my belief it will prove to a son that he was loved by his mother. It is paramount he knows he has been lied to. No wonder his father treated him so. The child's sorrow was a daily reminder and accusation of his own guilt."

She half closed her eyes as she reached in for the handle of the case. She gave it a tug and it came up part way, but as the body was placed in afterwards, part of the dry bones caused an obstacle. She took a deep breath and yanked. She had thought to hold her breath and was happy she did.

Fredric evidently hadn't and started coughing and waving his hand back and forth in an effort to find fresh air. "Come, let's leave this place."

"Gratefully so."

Outside the mausoleum, Andromeda addressed the woman "I am sorry dear lady, I cannot stomach to remove your necklace from the bones. When we arrange for your burial and proper funeral it will find its way to the family's hands."

She turned to Elliott "I would like to introduce you to your papa's mother. You see, your grandmother turned invisible before you were even born. She is going to be alright now and so are you. You and she can go to the happy place together. When you get there she will be made whole and will be able to talk, and you can keep each other company. She can tell you stories about your Father when he was a little boy. "

Elliot looked at the quiet woman "Do you know how to play dominoes?" he politely asked. "I can teach you if you don't."

Andromeda looked at the grandmother. She was nodding her head up and down to let him know she did, in fact, know how to play that game. She reached her hand out to the boy, and he offered his to her. In the moment their hands joined, they disappeared from sight.

The harsh noise of the gate shattered the silence, and Andromeda jumped at the abrupt sound. "The wind must have pushed the gate to. I need to get this case back to Baron Ramsey."

She turned to Fredric, "Would you like to come in and enjoy the music?"

"I would be honored to escort such a beautiful lady. Are there any places left on your dance card?"

They traced their way back to the gate, and Andromeda gave it a push, but it didn't budge.

Fredrick's eyebrows furrowed. "Perhaps the key fell out when it hit and it threw the lock. Feel around the ground just under—"

A cackle of laughter interrupted him. "Ha, Ha, look what I have. You like talking to ghosts so much, why don't you just live with them, too." Finn Finnegan waved the key in his hand and pranced around.

"Finn, I have never treated you unkindly. Please unlock the gate. The Ramseys will not take kindly to your stealing their keys."

He stopped for a moment, put his hand to his chin as if he were considering it. "Ah, hum, No!" and he ran away.

Fredric turned to her "You know this imp?"

"He seems to be getting worse every year. I once thought his pranks harmless and mischievous, but he's gotten meaner with them." She looked at the tall gate. "I really don't think I can climb over it in my dress. I don't even know if I could in riding pants."

"I may have a solution. I wouldn't hazard to mention it, but I've seen you venture into a cemetery at night, talk to a woman with a slit throat, and pull a suitcase out from under a skeleton."

"You say such charming things," she said sarcastically and laughed.

"There is a break in the fencing at the back of the cemetery. The brush is so overgrown I dare say the property manager doesn't even know it needs repair. We may be able to escape through."

"Lead the way," she announced gaily. The thought crossed her mind she was in a predicament, but oddly didn't mind. She had laughed at Frederic's comment, and she truly enjoyed his company.

She followed him to the back of the cemetery where vines and shrubs grew together to look like a solid wall.

Frederick pointed to an area "Here, I think it is through here."

"Are you coming with me?"

"I should very much like to. I hope I shall be able to follow." He looked very unsure of himself.

"Well, stay close. I won't be able to part the obstacles for myself and keep a hole behind me too." She lifted the suitcase to push it through clearing a way for herself. This would at least keep any thorns from scratching her face. It was cumbersome work. The branches and vines represented years of growth. The living fence was probably two feet thick. At one point she felt the rusted iron of the manmade fencing and felt for the break in it to pass through. The bushes on the other side of the fence proved less of a hindrance.

When she emerged, her first action was to turn to see if Fredric was behind her. In the distance, she heard the sound of applause and cheering, and the night sky lit up with fireworks just as Fredric emerged with a smile on his face.

"You certainly know how to make an entrance."

"I feel like exploding too, I am free! Though I am certain the applause and fireworks are more for something happening over at the Kilmartin's castle and not my humble freedom." He teased.

"Maybe, but let's enjoy their light on our walk back to the castle."

He took a step ahead of her and to her surprise nonchalantly took her hand as if it were the most natural thing in the world. She had never felt such a sensation. Was this what the other women described as butterflies in their stomachs? Here she was trotting along, dusty suitcase in one hand, and a man's hand engulfing her other. His hand glowed purple, as the rest of him, and she noticed the purple light seemed to be creeping up her arm also.

"Will you honor me with a dance, please tell me your dance card is not full?" he begged politely.

"It is not full, but I must deliver this case and its meaning. I beg you to solve the conundrum of how should we will be able to dance when others cannot see you?"

"I found the enigmatic lady you sought and rescued you from a locked cemetery, I will solve this mystery also. Leave your worries to me dear lady. Indeed, it would be my honor to remove all your fears."

"Speaking of fears, I should confess to you. Sometimes I have difficulties in large gatherings such as this. So many people, spirits and voices. I may not be able to endure being on the dance floor with them. I shouldn't want you to believe my distress is due to you being my dance partner."

"Leave it to me dear Andromeda." He smiled at her.

She truly hoped he could keep his promise. What a joy it would be to dance on the floor as any other woman does. They came upon the terrace door and she steeled herself for the onslaught of voices and emotions that would hit her upon entrance to the grand ballroom.

She walked a few steps into the room and surprisingly felt calm and at peace. What was this? She looked around, everything seemed to be as it had before. People drank, danced and played games. She spotted the Duchess and her companions still at a game table. Their body language and demeanor indicated to Andromeda things were amicable, but there didn't seem to be any passion ignited there.

"Maybe this suitcase will bring the Ramseys happiness," she said almost half to herself as to Fredric. "I left them in the library, across on the other side."

"Let us complete your mission so I can have a dance." With her hand still in his, he led her across the room.

The click of the door brought the Ramseys to their feet, and Baron Ramsey moved close to inspect the case as Andromeda placed it upon the library table

"That's the family emblem. Is Elliott here?" What has happened?"

The mother pleaded, hands clasped in prayer, "Is Elliott happy, now?"

Andromeda nodded to the woman. "I offer the most wonderful news on Elliott's account. But there is a certain amount of sorrow in the telling of it. Are you both prepared?"

The mother clung to the father and he put his arm around her. "We will bear it together." He looked into his wife's eyes. She nodded in ascent.

"I do not wish to be overly theatrical, but there is a family secret that must be revealed for tonight's events to make sense. Why was Elliott being pulled to the cemetery, why was the woman was crying at his grave." She pointed to the table" Do you have the courage to open the case?"

The father took a step toward the table. He paused, but opened it nonetheless with the Baroness looking over his shoulder. Inside, two stacks of clothing lay neatly side by side. A wooden, toy soldier guarded the boy's clothes on the right.

Barron Ramsey picked up the soldier with tears flowing down his face. "I wondered what had happened to Jaime. Father said I had been careless and lost him. I looked everywhere for him. He was my favorite toy."

"If you both would like to sit, I will attempt to convey the sad story. There is another spirit here with me who was a witness to the events of that miserable night."

The husband and wife sat down, so close to each other they touched from shoulder to hip. The Baroness' manner indicated she understood what a difference this secret would make to her husband's soul.

She looked to Fredric and listened as he recounted that night. She then shared with them, "Fredric, he is the spirit I am talking too, had been to see your father on a matter of business. He passed your mother in the hallway before being admitted to your father's study. She smiled at him politely as she passed to go outdoors."

The look on Andromeda's face turned sympathetic as she spoke to Fredric. "Of course, it is not your fault. He obviously had an unbalanced mind."

She turned back to the Ramsey's, "During the meeting, Fredric, in conversation, complemented your father on the beauty of his wife. With this, he flew into a rage. He began shouting and ranting she hadn't gone to the cemetery to visit her departed mother, but to meet him so they could run away together."

"Your father punched Fredric and ran out the doors of the library into the evening. Fredric could only follow not knowing what was to occur. Clearly the man needed to be calmed. Your father came upon your mother in the cemetery. She held you bundled in blankets with a suitcase by her side. Fredric was straggling behind and saw your father slap her with such force that you flew out of her arms. Fredric went to you to see if you were injured. Upon picking you up unharmed, he turned to watch your father," she paused. "I am sorry but there is no way to spare you this."

"He slit her throat." She pointed to the left side of her neck. "I believe the knife also severed the vocal cords on that side, as she has moaned and cried these past twenty years, but cannot speak."

Upon hearing this Baroness Ramsey let out a sob.

Andromeda waited a moment for the shock to pass, and continued to recount Fredric's story. "Fredric was so aghast, he vowed he would not leave your mother's side until she found peace. He felt so guilty his words had caused this awful chain of events."

"He watched as your father hid the suitcase and your mother's body in the family mausoleum's window bench." The room was quiet except for sniffles and breathing. Baroness's handkerchief was tear soaked.

Softly Andromeda began. "Your mother cried over Elliott's grave because she did not get to meet her grandson, and her grief kept pulling him there. She couldn't leave this world because she feared for you in your father's care. When he passed, she still knew how much pain you carried over the lies you had been told.

"Upon my assurance you would know the truth, she felt contented to move on to the next world. I explained to Elliott she was his grandmother and they could keep each other company." She added cheerfully. "He was happy to learn she knew how to play dominoes."

Both father and mother laughed. The Baroness looked to her husband "Let us go home. There's so much to accept and understand. I wish to watch the fire quietly for a while before we retire. We have a funeral to plan, and I want to do her justice."

The husband rose, "Andromeda, I have no words appropriate to convey our gratitude. If ever you should want for anything that is within our grasp, do not hesitate to inquire of it. We, well I especially, cannot fully fathom how my life has changed with this information. How I have felt about my mother, myself, and my father." He took hold of his wife's arm, picked up the case and began to leave.

"A moment?" Andromeda asked. "If you have no need for your

mask the rest of the evening, could you leave it?" The ghost who is here has need of it."

The Baron turned with a surprised look, "Surely." He took it off and laid it on the library table as they departed.

Fredric touched the mask. "I have put my mind to this puzzle, and I believe I have a solution. I would ask to borrow your cloak dear lady, add his mask, and I should have form enough to dance with you this evening."

"I have never seen a ghost be able to hold items other than what they wore in death."

"You have so much to keep track of in other's lives and deaths. I should gently remind you I am no ghost. Let us see if this will work as I expect."

He walked over to the arm of the couch where she had laid her velvet shelter. To her surprise, he was able to lift it and swing it around his shoulders with flair. "Now, the mask."

Before her was a form that could pass in the ballroom in front of others. A fellow dancer would need to be very close to notice anything false. Still, she found herself a wee bit nervous.

"Come." He held out a hand to her. "We will give it a try. If you are in distress, tell me. We will escape back to the library, and I will hum a tune to dance by. Trust me, you don't want to be put through such a barbarism as my musical talents."

He brought such cheer and levity to her. She couldn't remember laughing in someone's company as much as she did when she was with him. She decided to trust this gentleman, and she placed her hand in his. They departed the library, and he led her straight to the middle of the dance floor.

She could not fathom it, but the voices were not overwhelming her. What magic of the evening was this?

"Will my fair lady place her hand on my shoulder and allow me to place mine on your waist?"

She blushed, but complied. As she did so, all the spirit voices silenced. Astonished she asked in a hushed voice "Are you a sorcerer?"

"No, my dearest, it is not sorcery that holds up the cloak. Let us dance a moment in silence so you can enjoy the music. I will explain more when we are off the dance floor."

He held her gently, as if she were might be blown away by a puff of wind. He twirled her and sashayed her in time with the music, and joy filled her heart. She closed her eyes and wished the music would never end, and they could go on like this forever. She wondered at the odd sensation she felt where his hands touched her. It was like the warmth of a fire in the hearth.

A bit of vine tickled her hand, and she found it and a flower had found a home in the velvet of the cloak. "Look, a flower has escaped from the cemetery just as we have."

He plucked it from the fabric. "May I adorn your hair with the flower?"

"My charming sir, I would be delighted." As he placed it in her hair the music stopped. They lost physical contact when they relaxed their dancing posture. The voices returned full force. A little cry of anguish escaped her lips.

Fredric took her hand. "Let me lead you off the dance floor and to a chair to relax a moment."

Once seated, he leaned in to softly speak to her without being overheard. "I thank you profusely for the energy you have shared with me this evening in our dance. It has replenished me greatly. I would not prevail upon you any longer. I will dance with others for my continued recovery." He hesitated a moment as if debating with himself and added. "I would very much like to spend more time with you, just to be with you and enjoy your company. I do not know if you consider me worthy, but I must inquire, or I would never forgive myself."

Confused by his strange words, she looked at him "Share my energy? Of what do you speak? I do not understand."

He pulled back with a look of surprise. "Let me choose my words carefully, as your comprehension seems to be lacking. Did your mother or father not instruct you on the sharing of your energy powers?"

"Energy powers? What do you speak of? I have no powers. Only that I can see and hear ghosts has set me apart from others."

"Is that what your parents told you?" He shook his head in disappointment. "How could they not realize what calamity would befall you as your powers strengthened?"

"I am an orphan," she answered.

"What could I say to soothe your heart? I wonder you have managed on your own to this point with no guidance." His eyes filled, but the tears did not escape.

She begged of him, "If you care at all for me, please inform me of what you know that I do not. I have endured such sorrow, I have had to take myself to a cabin in the woods for the solitude. I would surely throw myself off a cliff if I had to endure the voices at full force day after day, week after week."

"I do profess affection for you, yet I do not know how to reveal the truth I suspect. I wish to never cause you distress. I give you my oath, my hesitation is only due to my worry I cannot help you properly. I already failed to protect the baroness by my rash comments." He hung his head.

Andromeda placed her other hand on top of his, and with her hands on both sides of his, she spoke gently, but firmly. "You have seen I do not panic as other women sometimes do. I am aware of the guilt you carry in the Ramsey family circumstances, and I will not hold you accountable for my situation. But surely you have human enough senses to see my burden can be perilous at times and brings me personal sadness. A simple thing such as attending a party for friends," she waived her top hand to encompass the ball room. "Makes me worry and fret. How will I cope? What if I should have to flea early from the event?"

He straightened. "I beg of you to remember all I wish to share, I offer to assist you." He looked in her eyes for courage.

She shook her head. "I trust you. I've trusted you all evening long."

"You seem to believe the spirits and ghosts you see are showing themselves to you, imposing their voices on you. I believe you are the one calling to them. Your energy emanates out in all directions and draws them to you. You haven't been taught to harness it. Maybe subconsciously when you are solving a particular spirit's dilemma, you have learned to direct it."

Could it be? "The cacophony of voices does seem to drift to quiet when I am speaking with one certain spirit."

"I am now embarrassed and ashamed of our dance. I beg for your forgiveness; I was unaware you did not freely give me your energy. "

Andromeda quickly assured him. "No, do not spend a second with those thoughts. There is nothing to forgive. It was the most wonderful time of my life. The beauty of the music, the feeling of being held by someone." She averted her eyes at the last admission. "But why did it quiet the voices?"

He smiled softly. "Because I siphoned off your rampant energy to heal myself. It is why I wouldn't allow myself an additional dance with you, even if societal etiquette were relaxed with tonight's drinking and celebrations. I wouldn't normally need so much energy to replenish myself, but I was in the cemetery for twenty years. I will still need to be in contact with others through the evening, those will be little nibbles here and there. Shaking a hand, a dance, even petting a dog, nothing that would harm anyone. By the end of the evening, I dare say, I will be on my way to recovery."

"I should be eager to meet your normal self. Go now, I have much to think about. I need to check on my last undertaking of the night in the Duchesses situation. You asked me earlier about spending more time with me. I should like it very much if you found me again later to share a goodbye before I leave. Converse like normal people?"

He stood and bowed. "I should like that greatly. Will you be all right when I let go of your hand?" He kissed the back of her hand as he released it.

She felt a tingle and smiled brightly. "Yes, I believe I will. I am heading toward one of my spirits straight away."

"Very good, I bid you farewell for the time being. When do you plan to depart? We could meet at the fountain, and I can return your cloak."

"Shall we rendezvous at a few minutes past midnight?"

"How mysterious and dramatic, yes it will be a fine remembrance of our evening."

She watched her treasured cloak and its occupant pass into the cluster of guests. With a determined breath, she went in the opposite direction to the table where the Duchess and the Blacksmith still played cards with the other two ladies.

The spirit of Countess Rachel Murdock was at her son's side. He was dealing out another set of cards. Rachel shook her head sadly from side to side when she saw Andromeda approach.

"Are you having fun?" Andromeda asked when she approached the table.

"Yes, we are grateful you introduced us to this gentle soul, he has been a great companion," answered Lady Wren.

The Duchess looked up and a bright smile lit her face "My dear, is that a moonflower in your hair?"

Andromeda unconsciously lifted her hand to touch the flower, "I suppose. I don't really know. I got it from the Ramsey's cemetery."

She smiled at their inquiring looks "It's a long story involving Leprechaun Finn." She waived her hand as if it was trivial.

The young Blacksmith rose from his chair and came to her side to inspect it closer. "Yes, it is." He turned to the Duchess. "I have some of these on my grounds."

"You do?" She expressed excitedly. "I have wanted some of those for my garden. Is it true the blooms only open in the evening?"

"Truly, they do. Most opposite of other flowers that open with sunlight. It is where they get their name. I would be most happy to share some starts with you." He returned to his chair.

"If you wish to save seeds from season to season, would a paper envelope be appropriate, or do they need a sealed jar?"

He answered "an envelope is best for them. My lady, do you have an interest in gardens beyond enjoying them?"

Lady Wren and Lady Melody rolled their eyes in good humor. "There's our cue to excuse ourselves to complete the obligations of our dance cards."

As they rose, Andromeda took it upon herself to take one of the seats. She noticed the Duchesses' Duke had found his way over and sat down to complete the table.

"She loves her garden," he said with kindness. "Spends countless hours puttering around." He looked to the duchess in astonishment "Even in the winter months, she makes maps and shopping lists for the catalogues and markets."

The Duchess blushed with the ladies' departure. "Yes, I know I should let the gardeners complete their duties, but I really enjoy it."

Nodding in agreement the Blacksmith offered, "I know exactly what you mean. It is how I work out frustrations and get my exercise and constitution. Nothing like shoveling compost to sweep out the cobwebs."

They both laughed, and he continued. "I have seriously thought should I come to dire consequences and had to sell off our property, it is the one occupation I could find myself happy at and be able to earn a living with."

"Oh surely, your circumstances are not so dreadful." she expressed in dismay.

"Time will tell, but in the meantime, may I invite you to come see my garden? If there is anything you would like a start or seedling of, I would be most honored to gift it to you."

"What a wonderful invitation. I can think of nothing I would rather do than enjoy discovering your design and selection of plants. I would be remiss if I didn't return the offer and extend the same invitation to you. My dahlias and camellias are spectacular in their coloring."

"I also have an herb garden. Do you have an interest in those in addition to flowers?"

They continued chattering happily about their plants, and began using the playing cards to show the placement of flowerbeds and hedges in their gardens.

The Duke and Countess Rachel had broad grins on their faces, and the Duke addressed Andromeda "Thank you countless times over. My dear love has at the least a true friend who shares her ardent love of gardening. She won't be lonely."

The Countess chimed in. "Even if a romantic passion does not kindle, she would have the connections to find him a master gardener position on an estate. Seeing him content, it is all a mother can ask for."

The Pirate sauntered over, and upon seeing their animated discussion, tried to insinuate himself into their conversation. "Dearest Duchess, why don't we share a dance." He offered his arm.

She waived him away. "You have been collecting many dance card spots tonight, feel free to fulfill those obligations to the young ladies. I am content, no, beyond satisfied." she smiled at the Blacksmith and continued, "conversing with Earl Murdoch about our shared pastime."

The Duke smirked at the Pirate "There's my darling. Her spark is back. Off with you." He dismissed the scoundrel. He turned to Andromeda "The Enchanted Wishing Tree is upon us. The Countess and I could know it safe to move on by the chimes of midnight. Do you think you could encourage them to complete a ribbon?"

She thought for a moment and spoke to the gardeners. "I have a question for the two of you. Have you heard of the Enchanted Wishing Tree?" They looked up from their cards as she continued. "I wonder what type of tree it is? Do you know the legend behind its magic?"

The Duchess replied "I was already matched with my Duke, and had no need to investigate it." She looked to the Blacksmith.

He ventured "I admit, I never made study of it either. Would you like to give it a go? We can observe the leaves and bark and see if we can identify the specimen. Between the two of us, I wager we can discover its lineage and origin of the legends even if we must consult books in the library afterwards. Let us participate fully?" He rose and offered an arm to each of the ladies.

They all happily went outdoors and gathered around with the others.

"This game is not a game," Devlin was saying. "It is a quest... but not one for the faint of heart." He held up a long red ribbon. "There is a legend here at Castle Amhrán Oiche, of a *special* kind of magic that dwells within these grounds. To my left, there beyond the southern tower..." He motioned as he spoke. "...there is an enchanted Wishing Tree. The only one of its kind, I am told."

Andromeda had heard the speech before in years past. She had never been hopeful enough to place her name on a ribbon. Shannon had bid her to do so this year. The friend and housemaid had put her prayers forth for Andromeda, the least she could do was write her name on a ribbon.

"It is said the ribbon of fate which binds our souls to one another..." Devlin slid the silky fabric between his fingers. "...can become a *physical* thing, on but a single night of the year. *This* is that magical night. Come, my Lords and Ladies. If you have the courage to test your love... take a ribbon, write upon it your treasured desire, and tie it within the branches of the Wishing Tree. If your fate is truly linked with another, midnight this eve will reveal the truth of it. Tie this red symbol of your soul upon those magical branches, if the completer of your heart is present, the fateful toll when the hands of time point due North will leave your ribbons irreversibly entwined."

She thought for a moment of what to write. "Someone to love, who will love me back" were the words she penned. As she hung the ribbon, she found herself looking around at the others gathered around the tree. Some seemed to already be paired off, placing their ribbons near each other as if to influence the outcome. Others looked as lonely and forlorn as she felt at the beginning of the evening, then she realized she felt some hope for her life with her newfound knowledge from Fredric. She looked around to see if he were placing a ribbon also, but it was dark, even with the lanterns, and many people surrounded the tree. The crowd made it impossible to find him.

Now she realized Shannon had her believing in fairy tales. For goodness sake, she had just met Fredric, and she was not a foolish young girl to indulge such thoughts. Andromeda smiled as she looked back to the tree and saw the Earl and Duchess shaking their heads in conspiracy. He held the lantern and she felt the bark, inspecting it. Andromeda had no need to wait for midnight to know the ending to their story. They would be happy as peas in a pod, a honey bee and a flower, or any other gardening cliché there was.

She began her walk back to the castle and shivered a little without her velvet cloak. The oddest question skittered across her mind. Were any sugar plums on the food tables? She realized she had been so busy with all her spirit problem solving and matchmaking she had not eaten anything all evening.

She had lots to think about regarding her 'energy' as Fredric had called it. She didn't seem to be energetic. With every step toward the castle, she began to feel more and more tired from the evening's excitement and drama.

Once inside, as she approached the first table, she noticed all the people partaking of the refreshments had a low red glow about them. Then she recognized one of them. A man wearing a black suit sporting a fashionable cane she had met previously at a dinner party thrown by the Kilmartins. Yes, his companion, Claire, stood next to him wearing a red dress. She had taken them for ghosts that evening, confused when others could see them and speak with them.

Later, she'd asked Devlin about them in private, and he'd replied "That's curious. Well, maybe not. You see they are vampires. Together, they determined because the vampires were undead, she perceived them as ghosts.

Realization struck her that all those with a red glow tonight must be vampires, and the food and drink at this particular table was appealing to them. She was like Elliott taking in observations and drawing the appropriate conclusions she had not made before. So the different colors she saw must indicate a different type of spirit or being.

She found a table that carried the most wonderful cheeses and meats, and pastries and desserts made her mouth plead to sample every one. Despite her desire for the puddings in little edible pastry cups, she delicately selected an assortment of savories which offered more sustenance for the ride home. If she had room afterward, she would try two or three of the sweets.

The little alcove provided her with a quiet spot to enjoy her food. It occurred to her that in years past a lot seemed to happen between midnight and dawn, and she should make her way to her room and prepare for her journey home. And her appointment at the fountain.

When she opened the door to her room Shannon jumped up from the chair happy to see her. "How was it Miss, did you meet anyone?"

"As a matter of fact, I did have a dance with someone. It was perfectly lovely, but do not get your hopes up."

The maid squinted at Andromeda. "Did you put your name on a ribbon? Please, tell me you did?"

"Yes, Yes. But I did not see him there." She placed the last of her items in her portmanteau. "Can you have the footman load my carriage? I wish to leave just after midnight. He is to return my cloak at the fountain, and then I am off to home."

"Oh, my lady," Shannon gasped. "A farewell kiss by the candlelit water of the fountain. How romantic."

Panic filled Andromeda. "Do you think it? Shannon, you must help me. I am truly desperate. I have never kissed a man. Tell me how to do it. What did your mother instruct you?"

The maid laughed light heartedly. "M'lady, mothers don't tell you what to do with a man, they tell you what *not* to do with a man. No more than three dances an evening with the same man, ladies will gossip. Don't believe them when they say they won't tell a soul, those are the ones that brag to their mates. Never, never, never lift your petticoats before you are married."

Compassion showed on Shannon's face. "Does a flower need to be instructed on how to bloom?"

Andromeda sunk into the chair. "I dare not think of it."

"I did not mean to cause you such alarm," Shannon answered. "It is a happy thing to be kissed by one you admire. Or do you not wish his attentions?" I will escort you to avoid such awkwardness if you wish."

"I find I am hopeful and happy in his presence. I just am so unsure, and wary such happiness could come into my life." She rose and retrieved her present for the Kilmartins. "I shall write to you upon my return home to share with you what transpires. However, I fear you may be too optimistic, and I have worried for nothing."

"I shall continue my prayers and anxiously await your letter." Shannon handed the Kilmartin's gift to Andromeda and whisked her friend out the door. She crossed her fingers tightly on her behalf.

The tablecloth she had fashioned for the Kilmartin's library table had the family crest carefully embroidered at the center, adorned with delicate pearls from the sea captain's chest. As she placed it on the gift table with the others, she was aware something was happening in the main ballroom. She saw the Faerie dressed as a swan and the Phantom at the center of attention. There was to be an Amalgamation tonight!

As everyone else gathered to witness the event, she carefully made her way out to the fountain. The footman would have her carriage waiting, and she did not want to miss Fredric before she left.

She turned through the doorway, and her pace quickened as she approached the fountain. He stood there waiting for her. Thoughts competed for her to decide what to do next. Should she speak first, what should she say that was clever or appropriate? She had never been so fickle in her thoughts before.

Fredric took both her hands in his. "I admit to you freely the time has passed slower this evening in anticipation of this moment, and with more agony than the whole of my years in the cemetery."

Relief filled her heart. "I, too, must confess to a certain anticipation of our meeting."

He removed the cloak. "May I return your cloak to your shoulders to keep you warm?"

She turned and allowed him to adorn her with it, and when she turned back around they were so close together she worried he would hear her heart pounding.

"I wish I could kiss you, darling Andromeda. In this moment, it is all that I desire with all of my being. But my heart says it would not be fair to you. As I told you before, I only wish to behave towards you as a gentleman. I must confess my faults to you."

She realized she sought only to have him kiss her. "Please sir, I would welcome a kiss." She leaned in to him.

"Bold as ever." He smiled down into her eyes. "Remember, I have been absent from the world for so long. I may have nothing to offer you. I must see my banker and determine what has happened to my land and accounts."

She scoffed lightly "I am an orphan remember, no family name or dowry. I match your status and raise you an uncontrolled energy for this poker hand."

He laughed, but his voice carried a serious tone. "You do not know the worst of it. I have lied to you."

She pulled away. "What lie?"

"I did not tell you my true name."

"Of what consequence is your name? Why would you lie about such a thing?"

"I am a demon, and when a person knows your real name they can have a power over you. When you first came upon me, I did not know if you would be friend or foe. But I wish for you to have that power. I want only for you to trust me and believe I would do anything in my power to protect you. My name is Christenson." He reached for her hand. "Please forgive me."

"Christenson," she repeated in a whisper.

"It sounds like music upon your lips." He caressed the edges of her lips, and she felt a tingling down to her toes. She also noticed his hand flashed for a moment, no longer the aura of a ghost, but that of a normal person.

"I can see the logic of your hesitancy. It is difficult to tell someone you are a different. I have met many exceptional creatures through my association with Devlin and Elsbeth. I confess there was a moment when Grandmother Ramsey seemed afraid of you, I wondered if you had been her killer."

"I hate you thought me capable of such an act." He caressed her hair. "I seem to not be able to keep my hands off of your beauty" his eyes pleaded.

"It was only for a moment. I have been happy and thankful for meeting you ever since. Even now, I am grateful I go home with the thought there is someone in the world that cares for me beyond Shannon, Devlin and Elsbeth. I have been so lonely."

"Truly, have I brought you any amount of happiness? I would cherish the thought to my dying day to know if I have."

"You have brought me hope in my circumstances of my spirit relationships with your honesty, joy in the dance we shared, and helped me in solving problems caused by Finn. When I look back over the evening, I wonder if there isn't a couple better suited for each other."

"Dare I ask permission?"

"Though I am apprehensive, I would like nothing more than to go home with a kiss to remember you by."

He leaned down and granted her wish. It began as tenderly as if he were afraid of breaking her. She was timid for a heartbeat, then wrapped her arms around his neck and let him know she welcomed all he would offer to her. A spark of energy traveled through them, and he stepped away from her. In the candle light, she saw him as whole as any other normal human waltzing in the castle.

"Did I hurt you?"

A laugh erupted joyously from him. "No, no, my dear one. It was just our own sort of fireworks."

She looked to the ground. "I was worried I would not know how to kiss properly."

He wrapped his arms around her shoulders and pulled her to his chest. "Sweetheart, there has never been a kiss ever in the course of history as wonderful as ours. We will find our way," he comforted her. "I thought I might require a longer period of healing to get back to myself, and to see the banker and return to court you. You have sped that course of action up rapidly."

"Court me?" She looked up at him.

"Yes, I will consider Devlin and Elsbeth your guardians and arrange for supervised time to share conversations with you. You must tell me who this Shannon is also. She is important to you?"

"Oh yes, you will wish to thank her also. She was in my dressing room all night praying I might find a suitor."

"Well, well. Yes, she will deserve our gratitude. Let me escort you to your carriage. You may return home and dream of me. I have much to do to establish myself for you."

On her way home she wondered if the sea captain may have further need of her services. She could request some white satin of him and more pearls. Yes, she would need a great deal of pearls.

Bryndle's Choice

Mallory Kane

The first-born child, and only son, of the Winter Faerie King stepped into the gloriously appointed bedchamber and dismissed the servant who led him to the room, despite the servant's polite but insistent protests.

"Fear not." He'd waved away the elderly man's worries. "I assure you, the king is expecting me."

One grizzled brow twitched, but there were no more protests on the servant's part. He backed away, his thin, stooped shoulders bowed. "As you wish, Sir."

Once the servant had disappeared at the end of the hall, Bryn squared his shoulders, ignoring the faint tickle as his wings rustled beneath his leather coat, then turned the latch and stepped into the Winter King's bedchamber without knocking.

The king stood at the window, gazing out onto the beautiful grounds of the castle and gave no indication of hearing the door open. Or, he knew who entered his chamber. Bryn reminded himself that the King had summoned his son.

"Your Majesty."

The King turned slowly and looked at Bryn. Bryn bowed his head, enough that an onlooker would believe he was giving obeisance to the King. His gaze, however, never wavered from his father's.

"Bryndle," the King said quietly. "I was…" he gestured toward the open window, "…thinking about your mother."

"Indeed?" Bryn said shortly. "Yet, you so rarely thought about her while she was alive."

The King stiffened and took a sharp breath to retort, but instead, he sighed, as if the very act of breathing in had tired him. "No mind. I am glad you're here. How was your journey?"

"Pleasant, Sire. How kind of you to expend a servant in order to summon me."

"Expend? He died?"

"No." Bryn shook his head, perversely happy to have worried his father. "But he is now stuck in those godforsaken Borderlands, with no means to earn his way home except to hire out as a soldier."

The King looked pained, but managed to turn the fault back to Bryn. "You should have brought him with you."

Bryn laughed. "Seriously? I gave him what I had, then had to hire out my services as a chariot guard just to get inside our border. I nearly died traversing the tundra. Once the weather became more temperate, I caught small animals and ate non-poisonous plants to keep myself alive. Then, in a port city somewhere a few hundred miles away from the Kilmartin's castle, I bought passage on a transport by pawning my ring."

"Your *ring?* Your mother designed that ring. It's made of pure Nasprosium."

"I am aware. Hopefully the captain of the ship is not Fae. By the way, I told him you would buy the ring back. His ship will be in port for another week."

The King frowned at him as he rang a bell on the beautifully carved desk near the window. The elderly servant appeared immediately. The King scribbled on a sheet of paper, folded it, melted sealing wax onto it, and sealed it with his ring. "Send one of my knights to deliver this to the captain of the—"

"Green Dragon," Bryn supplied.

"Immediately," the King finished. Once the servant had left, he glared at Bryn. "How in seven hells did you manage to end up penniless?"

"Really?" Bryn shot back. "You *are* aware there is a *war* raging on your northernmost border, are you not?" He felt the rage building, the rage he'd nursed for three years. "You sent me out there with no training. No understanding. No concept of what the world was like. I learned, of course. I learned there are people who have no servants they can treat like so many dogs, eager to do their bidding. I learned there are women who have no idea if their husbands are dead or alive, or if they will ever return, who are feeding their children by begging from those whose husbands or fathers or sons have *happened* to return without a life-altering injury or disease. I learned there were children— *children*—fighting and dying."

"And what? You gave away all your money? That was supposed to sustain you. You cannot be responsible for the entire country."

"I am the son of the King of the entire country! Of course I am re—" Bryn stopped, unable to force his words through the red haze clouding his mind.

"No, Bryndle. I sent you on your journey so you could see what the real world, if you will, is like. You cannot fix the entire world. What you must learn is that all that you saw, while it is sad and awful and regrettable, it *is* life. You learned in three years what you never learned in all your childhood, because back then you were more interested in books and maps than in animals and bugs. You never learned about the circle of life, as most children do."

"You sent me out to *learn about life*, and yet now you complain. I didn't save coin from the money you gave me?"

"Bryndle, you persist in misunderstanding me. Why don't you ponder on it for a while." He stood and came around the desk. For a moment he stood still, looking Bryn up and down. "You look good," he said finally. "Better than good. You are a man now."

The king sighed and his mouth turned up into a small smile. "It's been so long. That's what I was thinking..." he stopped. "But again, no mind. We have quite a lot to discuss. Have you been to your chambers yet?"

Aware of the amount of dust and grime in his hair and clothes, Bryn grimaced. "No, your Majesty. I came straight here. I think the hall servant thought I was a robber." He smiled, already half-regretting the bit of levity.

Despite his moment of rage just now, he found it harder to maintain his anger and distance from his father than it had been before he'd left. He'd taken the time to study his father while the king was assessing him.

To his surprise, his father had visibly aged in the three years he'd been gone. The King was still a handsome man, his back still straight, but the lines in his face had deepened, his hair streaked with gray, and blue veins trailed the man's hands.

"You will find a costume in your chamber, and you will wear it to the masquerade tonight."

And his anger returned. "A costume? What am I? Ten years old? Is this why you declared I should come here first? I do not want to play dress-up or waste time on silly games. If this is all you wanted, I'll take my leave now. Where is Loli? I will see her before I depart."

"Your sister is not available now."

"Not available?" Bryn had not expected that his father would actually refuse to let him see Loli. A spear of resentment stabbed his chest. "She is here, isn't she?"

"Sit!" The King snapped.

Bryn started to protest, but the look in his father's blue eyes reminded him that there were times, even now, that it was the better part of valor to do what the King commanded. He sat.

"I have allowed you to be disrespectful toward me, because you just arrived and you look as though you have not eaten, slept or bathed for the entire time you were gone. However, *now* you will listen to me." The King stood in front of him—above him. "I have planned your visit as a special surprise for Loli. She will become betrothed during the Masquerade Ball this night. No! You stay quiet. She and Argoth LeRain will be introduced, and their betrothal announced toward the end of the festivities."

"Argoth—The Goblin King's son?" Bryn started to rise, but his father put out a hand, so he sank back into the chair. "Are you senile? My sweet sister's soul will be crushed by those vile creatures."

The Winter King propped his fists on his hips and glared at Bryn. "Think before you speak, boy. If you hope to ever rule the Winter Lands, you cannot be so shortsighted. Just moments ago, you spoke as if you'd learned tolerance and acceptance of those unlike yourself. You must have fought alongside many different folk. Did you learn nothing? Tell me. Have you not fought alongside the Goblins against the Dokarq?"

"Of course. They are magnificently brave and strong, but those attributes do not change the fact that they are coarse and rough and unfit for my delicate sister."

The King laughed. "Apparently three years has been too long for you to be away from Loli."

"What do you mean? Three years is not so long."

"Yes, it is, for a young woman. She was eighteen when you left. Now she's twenty-one, a young woman. She can handle the household finances, the domestic schedules and the duties of hostess for a royal a meeting or an informal get-together. And not only that—"

"So, you've now got Loli under your thumb, as you once had my mother." Bryn stood, making the most of the two inches height he had over his father.

The King did not move, but his muscles tensed, and his pupils narrowed to pinpricks. "Do not speak of your mother—"

"Gone and forgotten? Is that the lesson I was supposed to learn?

Bryn took a step back, his bristly cheeks feeling warm. Embarrassed by his lack of control in the face of his father's chiding for Bryn's baseless prejudice against the Goblins, and his unwillingness to accept that his sister had grown up while he was gone. Bryn stomped over to the door.

"Where are you going?" his father asked shortly.

"I need a bath," Bryn said. "Possibly two. I've three years grime and dust to wash off before the festivities begin. Plus, I have no idea how long it will take to don the *costume* you have designated for me to wear." He grimaced to himself, then bowed. "May I be excused?" he asked quietly.

"One more thing. And this is an order from your King. You *will* wear the costume I have provided for you, and you *will* remain masked throughout the evening. Your task is to avoid Loli at all costs. She will be wearing an exquisite swan costume with a swan feather mask. You cannot mistake her. Do not approach her and avoid her if she tries to approach you. Toward the end of the night, prior to the Wishing Tree Ceremony, I plan for Loli's betrothed, LeRain, to bring her into your presence, where you will reveal your identity, and Loli will have both her newly betrothed and her brother. It will be a glorious evening for her."

A glorious evening indeed, for Loli.

"Sire, I am tired," he said, not disguising the resentment in his voice. "I wish to bathe and dine, *see my sister,* and then sleep for at least a fortnight. I do not want to be the butt of a ridiculous joke with the punch line of sending my sister into bondage to a Goblin."

The King's face turned red and his lips thinned. "Do not forget to whom you are speaking, boy. And mind, after the festivities, I want to hear all about what you saw and heard and learned as you traveled the Borderlands."

Bryn seethed, but he tried to speak evenly. "I am perfectly aware of who you are, Your Majesty. I am pleased to do the King's bidding. May I be excused?"

The King turned away and waved his hand. "Please."

Two hours later, despite his soul-deep weariness, Bryn felt better than he had in months. He was finally clean—really deeply soap and scrub-brush clean. He was dressed, not in stiff leathers and heavy armor that made his wings ache with the restriction, but in soft woven linen and velvet. He wriggled his shoulders to adjust his wings, then lifted the rather gaudy red mask to his face. It covered the upper half of his face and dipped down his right cheek past the corner of his lip to his chin. He knew the pinnacle of the Kilmartin's anniversary celebration each year was always the famous Masquerade ball. Not that he'd ever participated. He and his friends had usually spent the evening in a juvenile contest to see who could sneak into the ballroom to sip the spring nectar and spiked punches the most times without being caught.

Four years ago, he'd discovered something sweeter than the spring nectar. At the last Masquerade Ball he'd attend before being sent on his extended exploration of The Winter King's lands and gotten himself involved in the war against the Dokarq, Bryn had his first taste of love, so besotted with Isabell, the daughter of the first knight to the Vale Elf King, that he'd followed her around all evening instead of pursuing mischief with his friends. But Isabell had ignored him, and Loli had made fun of him.

Bryn shook his head as he walked out of his room and down the hallway toward the back stairs. He didn't like to think about that long ago humiliation at the hands of Loli and Isabell. Stopping at the women's hall, which intersected the men's hall in the middle of the guest wing of the castle, he considered striding down that hall and knocking on every door until he found his sister, but stronger than his brave urgency was the glower of the servant who guarded the women's wing.

He nodded to the man, whom he recognized from past years at the Kilmartin's yearly masquerade festivities, and continued toward the stairs. The back stairs, as he knew from his explorations as a teenager, opened into a narrow service hall behind the row of alcoves on the north side of the ballroom. No servant had shown up at his door with food and drink for him after his bath. He was starving and longed for a sip of spring nectar, the world renowned wine rumored to be produced by magical grapes that grew in the Summer King's vineyards. The last time he'd tasted it, the sweet wine had been given to him by a masked woman he had not known. He'd suspected she was at least a decade older than he, and before he'd tasted more than that one sip, she'd been grabbed by the arm and pulled away to dance with a man dressed in hunter green with a mask that was swirled in colors of the forest.

Bryn slipped through a door into the service hall and chose a door that opened into one of the velvet-draped ballroom alcoves. He sat on a gilded bench and straightened his mask, pulling his too-long hair back and anchoring it with the silk ribbon he'd found in his elaborately appointed bedchamber. He took a couple of deep breaths to center himself and prepare for the long, dreaded evening ahead.

What better way to spend his first evening back among his family and friends than dragging his tired body around in a silly red costume and deliberately avoiding his sister, whom he hadn't laid eyes on in three years. Standing, he stepped out of the alcove, intent on filling a plate—and a glass—and heading back to the alcove to appease his appetite.

In the three years since he'd left the Winter King's castle, he'd had bad food, mediocre food and no food. Again, as he had forgotten many things during those long years, he'd forgotten just how wonderful fresh, perfectly prepared food tasted. He couldn't remember when he'd had boiled hen eggs or aged goat cheese or the succulent meat from a boar that had been pampered all its life as opposed to being hunted and chased, while scrabbling for every meal.

He stepped up to a servant who proffered a tray of glasses filled with Spring Nectar. Bryn grabbed a glass and the bottle, which was displayed on the heavy tray to let guests know what they were being offered. Although the servant yelled at him to bring the bottle back, he headed toward his private alcove. But when he ducked through the curtains, he discovered that his haven had been invaded—by a peacock, it appeared. And a delicate scent filled the air. Bryn took a long breath. It was faint, but he was pretty sure it was the scent of gardenias.

"Excuse me, dear sir, but this alcove is taken," the peacock said in a low voice.

Bryn studied the woman. She was dressed in a gown of blue and green and purple fabric that flowed over and under and in and out through the skirt until it was impossible to know where one color stopped and the next started. The satiny material shimmered almost as if it were alive. Bryn had seen places, peoples and things in the past three years that he'd hardly believed were real, but he had never seen such a rich array of colors as he was looking at now. As the material of the skirt flowed downward from the high waist of the gown, so did peacock feathers flow upward, until they culminated just above the points of the woman's breasts.

From the milky white flesh above the tips of the peacock feathers up her chest and shoulders to her neck and the undercurve of her chin, she was bare. Her chest, neck, shoulders and upper arms were bare of any decoration. She wore gloves of the most transparent gauzy silk he'd ever seen. Not even his wings were as fine. But the crowning glory of her costume was her mask. It was made entirely of peacock feather eyes. Each one was placed such that it drew the eye upward to where the mask curled up and around the woman's head. And just below her eyes, tiny new feathers had been placed, one frond at a time, over the nose of the mask so that it jutted out just slightly, not unlike a peacock's beak.

"Did you hear me?" The woman spoke softly, almost in a whisper. "This space is taken."

Bryn cleared his throat, hoping that his voice would not sound as raspy with intense longing as he felt. "So I see," he managed. He swallowed. "Are you expecting your cock, lovely peahen?"

The woman's head jerked up. "What did you say?"

Bryn smiled knowing only half of his upturned lips would be visible. "You did not mishear me, I am certain."

"You—I've nev—! You—! I should call my father. You are a vile creature!"

It didn't escape Bryn's notice that the woman used the same epithet for him as he'd used for a Goblin just a couple of hours ago in his father's chamber. "Truly I am not, sweet bird. I am merely unable to think because of your beauty." And that was no lie.

He could see a pink flame spreading from her neck down to the curve where the plump flesh of her bosom began. She apparently knew it because she spread her palm and fingers over her chest. "Hardly," she said, then harrumphed.

"I actually was here in this particular alcove before you, sweet bird. I came in through the back stairs and claimed it prior to helping myself to some food. If you require proof, those are my gloves right there." He indicated the pair of fine red kid gloves lying where he'd left them on the bench. Then he sat on the bench, his knees a mere fraction of an inch from the drape of her skirts, and took a long sip of Spring Nectar before starting to peel an egg.

"Is that smoked boar I smell?" the woman asked.

"It is," Bryn said. "You should go peruse the tables. There is a king's ransom in delicious tidbits out there. Take a look at this." He held up the peeled egg and turned it so it glistened in the lamplight.

"Oh," she breathed, lifting her hand to her mouth. "I do apologize, sir, but I have eaten nothing this day. It took hours to get me into this dress and all that time, the only thing I've had was a small glass of Spring Nectar with a friend." Her fingers slid to her temple. The gesture was a bit lost, since her forehead was covered in peacock feathers. Nevertheless, Bryn got the message.

"How can I be of assistance to you, sweet bird?"

She turned her gaze to his and he caught a glimpse of eyes that rivaled her peacock feathers for emerald beauty. "A few sips of water would benefit me greatly."

"I have a bottle of Spring Nectar right here."

"No, no. That will just make me more faint. Water, please sir."

Bryn stood and set his plate down on the bench and his glass of wine on the floor. "I shall return as soon as possible," he said. He saw a servant across the room wielding a tray of goblets that were dripping with condensation. He made his way through masked dancers. "Water?" he asked the servant.

"Yes, sir." The servant bowed his head.

Bryn grabbed two goblets and headed back to the alcove. When he entered, the alcove was empty, save for his plate and the glass and bottle of wine. He frowned at the plate. The thick, succulent slices of meat were gone. He glanced at the bench. As were his gloves. He shook his head and chuckled dryly.

Bryn's smile faded. He really didn't feel much like laughing, although he did think the woman's trick was pretty funny. He was too tired and, to be truthful, too intrigued by the woman to laugh it off as a moment of flirtation between two strangers. Despite his best efforts to the contrary, he was enchanted with the little peahen, certainly a misnomer, considering she was dressed in peacock feathers, and appeared to be as haughty and arrogant as a peacock could ever be.

He quickly downed the remainder of the food on his plate, mostly vegetables and fruits, not nearly as filling or satisfying as the slabs of boar he had been anticipating, then stepped back into the ballroom.

He felt a bit out of his element. Here he was dressed as gallantly and expensively as anyone at the ball, but to his surprise and dismay, the linen and velvet no longer were luxurious and soothing against his skin and wings. The velvet was clingy and hot. He realized he missed the leathers he had worn constantly during the past three years—had worn, worn out, repaired and worn some more. His pants and boots and tunic were stained and rubbed to a sheen until they were as soft, if not softer, than this velvet. His boots had fitted him well when he started on his journey, but the longer he'd worn them, the more comfortable they'd become.

When had he stopped resenting his father for sending him on what he'd considered a fool's errand, and begun to feel as though he were doing something real and purposeful? Maybe when he'd met his Elven friend Stellan and allowed himself be persuaded to ride beside him to the borderlands to fight the Dokarq.

Bryn glanced around at the guests. He'd once been the best of all his friends at recognizing the magical creatures hiding behind their masks and differentiating them from those of the mortal realm. But right now he couldn't even recognize his own kind—the other Faeries. Within a few seconds, he found himself searching the crowd for a peacock feather mask and billowing, jewel-colored skirts.

"Pardon, handsome crimson knight. May I have this dance?"

Bryn started, then turned to see a tall, slender young woman in a silky green and brown gown with a mask made of beautifully shaped leaves sewn together. "I um—" he started. She smiled. "Please. We are perfectly matched, in height, dress and hopefully, expectations of what this night might hold."

Was she not only asking him to dance, but also to—? Had mores changed that much since he'd been gone? Or was it just because he was older, a man now, in height, build and temperament? "I beg milady's pardon, but I seem to have misplaced my evening's companion."

Her lips parted into a little O. "You're rejecting me? What kind of rude lout are you? Do you have any idea who I am?"

Bryn sketched a little bow, irritated now. "No, I do not. And, if I may point out, you do not know who I am either. Now, please excuse me. I must find my evening's companion." He turned on his heel and walked away.

Just as he was about to take a turn around the ballroom, looking for the lovely peacock who had escaped with his food, Devlin Kilmartin stepped up to him and proffered his hand. Bryn took it, unsure whether to reveal his identity.

"Prince Bryndle," Devlin said softly. "What a pleasure to see you. You must have grown four inches since last I saw you, what? Three years ago?"

"Mister Kilmartin, the pleasure is mine."

"Please Your Highness, call me Devlin. You are a man now."

"Thank you sir. This is a wonderful celebration. The largest ever, it appears. I assume the Winter King unmasked me to you?"

"Of course. How have you been? No injuries, no accidents while you were exploring the farthest reaches of your father's vast kingdom, I pray."

"None that will keep me from dancing," Bryn answered. *Watching a beloved friend die leaves no outward scar.*

"Wonderful, wonderful. I'll be directing the guests into the maze very soon. Would you prefer to watch with the dignitaries? You must be tired, since I understand you just arrived. Too, you are no mischievous boy any longer, and you're the star guest of the Masquerade. You can be the mysterious Crimson prince, an unknown but obviously important person. Everyone will be talking about you before the evening is over."

That was the last thing Bryn wanted. He'd bowed to his father's wishes, but he didn't have to agree to be Kilmartin's conversation piece. Besides, he had an agenda of his own now. "Thank you. It sounds tempting. However, the King wishes me to avoid Loli until the end of the evening. He has a plan, although he did not share it all with me."

"Very well." Devlin clapped Bryn on the shoulder. "It's wonderful to see you. I'll keep your identity and your whereabouts secret from all, so that the Winter Faerie King's plan is not foiled."

"May I ask one question of you? Who is the green-eyed beauty dressed as a peacock."

"Smitten already?" Devlin smiled. "The guests are masked for a reason, you know."

"I certainly understand that," Bryn said. He groped for an excuse to demand her name. "It's just that she seems to be feeling a bit under the weather. I thought I'd keep an eye on her."

"I'm sure she's fine. I saw her a moment ago and it appears that she and her lovely friend have caught the eye of many of the young men here tonight, and some not so young." Devlin winked conspiratorially.

"I see. I do need to speak to her, however. I believe she walked away with my gloves."

Devlin's masked head nodded. "Your gloves," he repeated. "Would you like me to summon her for you? Wait here."

"Um, Mister Kilmartin? Perhaps it would be better if I waited for her in one of the alcoves?"

Devlin's eyes sparkled. "I'll have her come to you anywhere you wish—if she will do it. As we all know, one can never make a woman do something if she is not agreeable. Am I right? Do you wish to use the same alcove you were in earlier?"

Bryn stared at him, aghast. "You know about that? How—?"

"It's a magical night," the host of the Masquerade replied as he headed toward the doors to the patio.

Bryn went through the thick drapes to the alcove where he had found *and lost* the little bird earlier. He paced back and forth. What had he gotten himself into? He'd thought surely Devlin Kilmartin would tell him who she was, since he knew who Bryn was. But of course, his father's wishes and the carefully planned anonymity of the Masquerade were working against him. For an instant, Bryn considered fleeing, as the peahen had earlier.

That might have been an option, had he spent the last three years as a prince living in his father's opulent, kingly domain. But he was different now. He'd seen life and death in the raw in the harsh, remote borderlands of the Winterland. He'd build a snow cave in the shadow of a mountain to keep from dying, lost in the middle of a blizzard. He'd killed and eaten rabbits and foxes and even rodents raw to keep from starving. And he'd met some of the bravest men and strongest women he ever hoped to meet.

The King had not told him what lay beyond the beautiful and temperate coastal region of Winter Land. His friend Stellan, a Frost Elf, had. On the northernmost border of Winter Land were the

Borderlands, where the cold was so severe that the ground never thawed. Stellan had shown him a map he kept rolled up in his saddlebags. Bryn had recognized it. Two similar, but larger, maps hung on the wall opposite his father's desk in his private study. To his embarrassment, he'd had to admit to Stellan that although the maps were of the northern and southern parts of the Winter realm, he'd never paid any attention to them. Stellan had not commented.

There were clans of nomadic Dokarq who wandered in that desolate, frozen land, searching for food and a place to settle. At the place where the Winter Faerie realm met the Frost Elven realm at the border with the uninhabitable northern land, the Elves had waged a decades long war with the Dokarq to protect their land from invasion. It had been difficult for Bryn to understand why the Frost Elves were so intent on keeping any and all Dokarq from squatting on their land, until Stellan had pointed out to him that while the map showed only the northernmost portion of the Winter Faerie realm, it showed the entirety of the Frost Elven realm, a slender branch of a country which was completely surrounded. Winter Land was on the Western border, the Dokarq on the Elves' north and east, to the South was the Goblin realm.

"We do well in the cold," Stellan had told him, "but if we are not diligent, the Dokarq could eventually run us out of our homeland. I fear it is a never-ending war. We lose scores if not hundreds of fighters each year, and our population, especially of strong and virile young men and women, is dwindling fast."

Bryn had asked him why they were so cut off from other Elves. Stellan had pointed to the eastern border. "Once, we and the Marsh Elves shared the eastern border, but they were defeated along with the Goblins in a long-ago massacre that destroyed Goblin lands quite far to the south.

"Elves and Faeries get along well together. I will talk with my father about sending more troops. We should be concerned about invasions from these Dokarq as well."

Stellan had been grateful. Bryn stopped pacing and rubbed his eyes. He had fought alongside the Frost Elf prince for four months. The two together were unstoppable, and they had quickly become best friends. Bryn had talked about his hatred and resentment for his father, whom he was sure had forced his mother into an early grave with his overbearing stubbornness and neglect. Stellan had talked about his fiancée, to whom he'd become betrothed at the Masquerade Ball the year he and Isabell were eighteen. He'd gone to the military the next year, just before his nineteenth birthday.

The drapes rustled as the beautiful peacock entered the small alcove. "You," she said. "I should have realized. Devlin told me that a mysterious stranger wished to speak with me. I suppose you want your gloves back?"

He laughed when he saw his red kid gloves on her small hands. Their fingers were hanging limply. He waved a hand. "Please, keep them if they are comfortable and warm. I would be devastated if your fingers suffered the cold."

"*Devastated?* You seem to have a proclivity toward excessive drama. Besides, these are worthless to me. They are larger than my boots. It's unfortunate that you were cursed with such gigantic, obviously clumsy hands." She took off the gloves and dropped them on the bench.

"I can assure you, milady, these capable hands are *just* the perfect size." He held them up for inspection.

"For what?" she asked, then immediately, the pretty flame spread over her bare shoulders and the plump flesh at the apex of her gown. "Never mind. You are arrogant and apparently interested in only one thing. You should be dressed as a rooster."

He laughed. "Haughty words from a woman wearing peacock feathers all over her head. Tell me who you are, my sweet, gaudy bird?"

Her head tilted, rustling the feathers on her mask. "I will reveal myself if you will do the same."

"I cannot," he said. "I made a promise to keep my identity secret until the end of the evening."

"We all made that promise. That is the promise of the Masquerade. But since this must obviously be your first foray into such an elegant scene, let me assure you, not everyone keeps that promise. I don't think it was meant to be kept. All through the castle and all over the grounds young men and women are revealing their identity to each other and wondering if they will be one of the couples whose lives are entwined by the magic of the Wishing Tree."

Bryn knew the legend. It was said that the ribbon of fate that bound two souls together could become a physical thing on this one magical night, the night of the Masquerade. It took merely the courage to write your treasured desire upon a ribbon. "Of course," he said.

"The legend says if your future is truly bound to another, the ribbons will intertwine at the stroke of midnight and no force can ever disentangle them. Regrettably, my promise," he replied, "is not the simple game of the Masquerade. I have pledged to a higher power than our esteemed hosts, not to reveal my true identity to anyone until the end of the evening when the presentations begin."

His companion did not speak. She seemed lost in thought.

"But you, my flirtatious bird, you sound as though you know all the details of what transpires here at the Masquerade Ball from experience."

She stiffened, then turned away. "I do," she said. "I did."

"So you are married?" he said evenly, disappointed in spite of himself. He was fascinated with the pretty peacock he'd happened upon in the quiet alcove. It would not take many more minutes in her presence to become more than fascinated. But now that would never be.

"No," she said, "not married."

"Then betrothed."

She turned to look at him. After a moment, she nodded. "Yes. I was betrothed, three years ago tonight."

Only days after his father sent him off on his exploration journey, three years ago. "I see. Three years is a long time for a betrothal. Where is your fiancé tonight?" Bryn asked.

She lifted her chin. "He is away."

Something in her voice, in the tilt of her chin, struck at his heart. She sounded like the women he'd met who lived near the battlegrounds of the Borderlands, with children at their skirt tails and babies in their arms. They would say things like, *He's been gone nigh two years*. Or, *nay, my husband went off to fight—been more than a year now*, or *it's just me and my girl now. My man died fighting the Dokarq.*

"He is fighting in the Borderlands, isn't he?" He did not want to hear the answer, but he felt compelled to ask.

Her head jerked, as if she'd been startled. "Who are you to ask all these questions? You remind me more and more of my Nana's rooster." She lifted her chin, then touched a fingertip to her eyebrow. "Now, if you would please take yourself to another side of the *barnyard*, I need to compose myself. I am supposed to be meeting a friend."

"I can fetch you another glass of water," Bryn said.

"No." Her voice sounded strained. "No. I am fine. Thank you."

He stepped through the curtains into the ballroom, then remembered his gloves. Turning back, he rapped quickly on the alcove wall, then pulled the curtain aside enough to slip inside. "Excuse me, sweet bird, my gloves...."

The young woman was sitting on the bench, her mask beside her, and her face buried in her gloved hands. Her golden brown hair was coming loose from its bun and tendrils were falling down around her bent shoulders. When she heard him she looked up.

Bryn took one look. "Izzy—?" he breathed.

She gasped and turned her face away. "No! Go away."

It was Isabell. His sister's friend and the subject of his teenaged crush. *No wonder he'd been fascinated by her.* He must have known, on some deep level who she was. "I mean, are you all right?"

Isabell shielded her face with one hand and grabbed her mask with the other. "Please, sir. Leave. And please forget that you saw me unmasked."

"I cannot, milady. I can neither leave you here, in distress, nor forget who you are. I beg your pardon, but--," he shrugged as he struggled to come up with a believable reason why he would instantly know her without revealing his own identity. "You are the daughter of the Vale Elf King's First Knight, you must know that anyone would recognize your lovely countenance."

Her head tilted slightly and he knew that she had accepted his explanation. He breathed a sigh of relief. But then, she turned to look at him. It was the face that had traveled with him these past three years. Her flawless Elven skin and those clear, sparkling eyes shining from beneath her mask, made his mouth go dry and his chest tighten.

Nothing had hurt him more than to hear Stellan talk about his lovely betrothed, Isabell, the daughter of the Vale Elf's first knight, until that awful day when he'd held his dying friend in his arms.

"Please sir. Now you have the advantage," she said. "You know me, and in this gaudy, feathered costume you can hardly forget me, but who are you, Sir Rooster, dressed so brilliantly that there is no human nor Fae who would fail to notice you, yet so mysterious and coy?"

Bryn swallowed. He was a prince and a warrior, and he did not like to lie. But he had given his father his word that he would remain masked and unnamed until the end of the ball, so he told a partial truth. "I am a warrior," he said. "Not unlike your affianced."

The burden Stellan had unwittingly placed upon his shoulders felt heavier than it ever had. Could he—should he, tell Isabell what he knew? It was a burden he had carried for months. A burden he had prayed would be taken from him. But the gods obviously had not answered his prayers.

Because here he was, in the presence of Isabell, daughter of the First Knight of the Vale Elf King, and fiancée of Stellan, the Frost King's son. What wry twist of fate had sent them to the same alcove on this fated evening? She was the first person, besides his father, that he had seen tonight, and now it was his duty to give her the most heartbreaking news she would receive in her lifetime.

A lump grew in Bryn's throat. "Milady Isabell, it must be fate that brought us here, to meet in this alcove, and fate that caused you to remove your mask. Since I now know who you are, I regret that I have news for you." He took one knee, and bowed his head, as a carrier would who was bringing bad news to a royal.

He heard her breath catch, then she sighed. "Do not cause yourself distress, Sir Rooster. I know. I have known for the entire time."

"You—know?" Bryn lifted his head. "But what? You cannot possibly know what news I have for you."

"I do. I know about my betrothed. I know that he perished."

"But that's impossible. There was no one to bring a message. It took me the better part of a year to make my way back."

Izzy smiled sadly and touched a finger to the corner of one eye, where a teardrop was gathering. "When two people are chosen by the Wishing Tree and their ribbons are irrevocably entwined, there grows a bond between them. As the two straight, innocent ribbons join and meld into one, beautiful strand that no ordinary hand can ever undo, so do the two souls." While she spoke, her fingers were busy with two slender, satiny ribbons on her many colored skirt. She had entwined and knotted them until they looked permanently tangled.

Bryn watched her fingers as they illustrated her words. *Two souls,* she had said. Isabell and Stellan, joined together for eternity. He tried to ignore the pain in his heart and concentrate on Isabell. Whether she really had known before now, Bryn couldn't know for sure. But he knew that everything that had happened to him—his friend's death, his summons from the Winter King and his chance meeting with Isabell in this small alcove, had happened for a reason. So that here and now, he could deliver the most devastating news that a woman could receive.

If this was the most that he could ever give her, and if the only bond that could bind her to him was that both of them had loved and lost Stellan, then so be it. Still on one knee, he said, "Milady Isabell, Prince Stellan, son of the Frost King, died valiantly in battle, and as I reached him and held him, he said with his last breath—"

"Don't grieve for me Bella," Isabell whispered.

Bryn was taken aback. "You heard him?"

She shrugged and the sad smile touched her lips again. "It's what he said to me the morning after the masquerade ball. He said he had to go fight the Dokarq, to keep them from overrunning his father's border, and that he would send for me as soon as he could. Then he held me and told me—" she stopped to swallow, "—if he did not return, that I was not to grieve for him. He had a gift, above and beyond the magic of the Wishing Tree. Stellan could transcend time. Not many elves have that talent any longer. He told me he could not look ahead, but that he had to go into a very dangerous place and that he would be there for a long time. His greatest wish for me was that I live and love and laugh."

Bryn closed his eyes as his father's voice echoed in his ears from across the years. *Princes don't cry, Bryndle. Crying is for princesses.*

Bryn stood. "I regret that—"

But Isabell continued talking. "Two years ago this very night, I excused myself from the festivities and went upstairs to bed. At some point before dawn, I awoke and realized I'd been dreaming of Stellan. I dreamed he stood beside my bed and held out his arms for me. He said, *don't grieve for me Bella. Embrace the happiness to come.* By the time I threw myself out of bed and reached him, he was gone."

Bryn took a long, steadying breath. "That was the day he died," he said softly. "I remember thinking it was probably Masquerade time. I only knew Stellan for a few months, but I speak the honest truth when I say that I have never known a better man."

Isabell nodded. "Thank you for that, and for telling me. Perhaps it was meant for you to see me without my mask." She stood and put the mask on, then shook out the flowing layers of green and purple and blue and gold that made up her skirt. "Now I am late in meeting my friend. She is waiting for me." She looked at Bryndle, her eyes still sparkling, even through the eyeholes of the mask. "Sir Rooster, you and I may have shared a small destiny here, but there is a larger destiny awaiting you. You and my friend are fated to meet before dawn."

"Your friend?" he said, his voice high with anxiety. "Who is your friend?" But he knew who and what Isabell was talking about, but he was a little surprised that she knew. Loli must have shared her secret about the Red Prince. Obviously, the two young women had built the presence of a mysterious, red-clad man into a vast romantic game.

"I must tell her," Isabell said. "She is reticent to meet you of course, but I will let her know that you have arrived and she should be looking for you." She lifted her head and studied his face, what she could see of it. Then she reached for his hand. "I know! Better yet, come with me. We'll surprise her. I am late to meet her, so she will be impatient with me. It will be fun. Come on."

He looked down at her small, slender hand with its elegantly shaped nails, so different from his own. His hands were much larger than hers. And brown, from the months and months of exposure to the sun, not to mention calloused and rough. "No," he said gruffly.

Izzy's hand jerked a bit.

"I apologize for my tone. It's just that—" he bent his head and sketched a bow. "Please understand, I beg you. I have been given my orders by the Winter King himself, not to approach the princess until tonight, before the Wishing Tree Ceremony."

"What? Why? That makes no sense. You must have misunderstood. What is the Masquerade Ball for if not to bring together two people who are destined to live in happiness, ever after." Isabell let go of his hand and slid her arm into the curve of his and pressed close. She looked up at him. "Oh my, you really are very large and very, um, hardy. I have never been so close to a—" she stopped, as if searching for a word, then shook her head slightly, causing the peacock feathers to rustle. "Never mind. Let's go."

The feel of her body against his, even through the layers of clothing they both wore, sent a pulse of longing through him. His silly crush from years ago had not faded, not one jot. Not even after he knew that she was betrothed to Stellan. He felt his face heat up and thanked the gods that his mask was in place. He pushed those feelings back where they belonged, in the deepest recesses of his heart and with staunch determination, turned his mind to something perhaps easier to manage. He would love to put a stop to the ridiculous charade that the King had dreamed up. How dare the man dictate at what moment he was allowed to see his sister for the first time in at least three years.

He was the Winter Faerie King. That's how he dared.

Bryn grudgingly admitted to himself that it was probably a good idea to keep his identity a secret from Isabell. If he brought her in on his father's ruse, she might accidentally or purposely reveal who he was to Loli.

To her, Bryndle was merely her friend's skinny, odd older brother, considered a bookworm even among friends his own age. He'd much preferred pouring over the maps and historical tomes in his father's study than tumbling on the ground playing games or sneaking out to ride the untamed horses with his friends.

"Milady," he said, thinking quickly. "I dare not go against the Winter King's wishes. It could mean my life." *That* was a gross exaggeration and unfair to his father, who was notoriously generous and kind to his servants. Still, at this moment, it served Bryn's purpose and apparently worked, because Isabell gasped and let go of his arm.

"No!" she exclaimed. "Loli's father would never do such a thing— would he?"

Bryn tightened his throat muscles, going for a fearful tone. "Begging your pardon, Milady, but I dare not risk it. Please do not, for a poor warrior's life's sake, mention me to Lo—to your friend."

"Sir Rooster, it is I who must beg *your* pardon. I regret that my silly idea could cause you harm or mean your death." She started to curtsy, then caught herself. Bryn smiled to himself. Princesses didn't curtsy to mere soldiers. "Now I must leave. I truly am ridiculously late to meet Loli."

"Loli!" Isabell grabbed her hand and pulled her off to the side. "Where did you get to? I was worried sick."

"When? What are you talking about?"

"I told you to wait right outside the door. When I came back, you were nowhere to be found. You had me on the verge of tears."

"I'm sorry, Iz. I guess I was a little tipsier than I thought."

"Ugh… My stomach's hurting just thinking about what your father would have done, had I told him." Thoughts of the Winter King's reaction to Loli's behavior weren't the only thing that had her stomach in knots. What of his reaction to her behavior with the man dressed in red?

"Told him what, Izzy? I did what you said—waited."

"You did no such thing."

"Yes. I did. Then this man asked me to go for a stroll down by the water. So, I went. And I'm glad I did, Iz. It really helped to clear my head."

"What?" Isabell grabbed her shoulders and squeezed. "You went off alone with some stranger?"

"I—"

"Did he molest you? Did he try anything?" She glanced around the hall. "Where's your father? He should be aware of this."

"No, Izzy. Calm down. The man was a complete gentleman. Trust me. He even worried that my arms might get cold—didn't have a clue I was a Winter Fae."

"Did he touch you, Loli?"

"Only to tighten my cloak. That's all."

Isabell sighed heavily and leaned back against the wall. "Thank the stars." She looked back to her friend and narrowed her gaze. "Never. Do. That. Again."

"Okay, Iz."

"Promise."

"I promise. I promise."

The relieved Elf sighed again.

"Hey... While you were searching for me, did you come across the man all dressed in red?"

"Your Goblin date?" Isabell gulped. "Oh, there was a couple with black and red patches on their costumes."

"No. No. Completely red—head to toe."

"I know, Loli, but I haven't seen anyone like that."

The frustrated Princess sighed and rubbed her forehead.

"Still anxious about your Goblin, huh?"

"He isn't *my* Goblin."

How she wished it were so. "Well, you know what I mean. The Goblin's the one in red, right?"

"I don't know of anyone else Father would possibly think to mention to me—intentionally describe." She frowned and looked away. "It *must* be the Goblin."

"Hey... Loli..." Isabell gently touched her arm. "I know this whole thing is hard right now, but it'll get easier. Promise. Meeting new people is always nerve-racking, *especially* if that person is a potential suitor." She smiled softly. "Why not give the poor man the benefit of the doubt? Tell me. Do you truly plan on defying your father in this?"

"No."

"Then why make things harder for yourself and for the red-dressed stranger as well? If you already know you'll eventually give in, quit being so difficult. Besides, if you are rude to the man and hurt his feelings as soon as you meet… that'll just end up creating another huge obstacle you'll have to overcome. There'll be plenty enough challenges as it is. New relationships are like that."

"I know you're right, Izzy, and I'm trying to sort it all out. Believe me."

Bryn was still smiling, wondering what Isabell, the pretty elf, would think if she knew that the tall, *hardy* soldier she'd failed to curtsy to was in fact the Heir to the Winter King's throne. When he pushed aside the curtain to the alcove to enter the ballroom, a tinkling glass bell rang out and interrupted his thoughts. Their hostess, Elsbeth Kilmartin stood in the middle of the ballroom holding a sparkling crystal bell. She rang the glass bell and patiently waited until her guests fell silent.

"We have prepared some extra special entertainment for you throughout this evening." The elegant woman smiled. "For the more adventurous among you, there will be games within the hedge maze out back. For those of you who choose to remain indoors, a schedule has been prepared for the various events available to you as well." She motioned towards her son and the table he was standing next to. "My husband will be seeing to the more *spirited* among you, while Stefan and I do our best to keep the rest of you on your excited little toes."

"As those of you who have been here before are aware, we have prepared some extra special entertainment for you throughout this evening." Elsbeth smiled. "For the more adventurous among you, there will be games within the hedge maze out back. For those of you who choose to remain indoors, a schedule has been prepared for the various events available to you as well." She gestured toward her son, who was standing next to one of the food tables. "My husband will be seeing to the more *spirited* ones, while Stefan and I will do our best to keep the rest of you on your excited little toes."

The ballroom erupted in laughter and applause. Elsbeth continued her instructions as more than half of the crowd followed Devlin outside into the maze. Bryn stood still. He was aching to see his little sister, and if he knew her mischievous mind, and he did, she would be in the maze. When they were little, she'd begged him constantly to play hide and seek or scavenger hunts with her. Meeting her and Isabell in the maze, it would spell disaster to his father's plan for their reunion at the dawn presentation of gifts.

Elsbeth's indoor games involved dancing, dice and cards, magic shows and puppet theaters, none of which interested Bryn. The realization that the man he now was bore no resemblance to the boy he'd been three years before had become more and more obvious on each leg of his journey home. When he pawned his ring for passage and boarded the ship for the final two hundred miles, he declined the captain's offer of his own quarters to his highness, the Heir to the Winter Land Realm, and chose to bunk with the crew and take a shift right along with them.

He walked past the overburdened tables, past the masked dancers, left the laughter and chatter behind as he went outside. The air was pleasantly cool on the patio. The entire area was dimly lit, a combination of the moon's light and the torches lining the walkways and koi ponds. The maze was beautiful, thick and lush, but the entryway was shadowed. Glancing longingly at the vast expanse of coastline and the moon's light glinting off the water, Bryn sighed and decided that although he'd rather spend the evening and night there, his vow to his father would have him prancing about, being mysterious and draped in crimson, avoiding his sister, whom he was aching to see, and her beautiful Elf friend Isabell. Isabell, whose sweet gardenia scent lingered in his nostrils and whose pale startled expression and brilliant green stare had burrowed its way into his man's heart tonight more than in all the times he'd met her when he was a boy.

He stepped into the maze and within a few steps, was confronted with his first impossible choice, to continue ahead or turn right. He chose the right turn, as he figured most entrants would, therefore his headstrong sister Loli would have gone straight ahead, pulling Isabell along with her. He met various couples and individuals as he strode along the corridors made of high, precisely cut holly. Almost all were masked, but many of the couples seemed to know each other very well, he observed. Others, couples, groups and singles, seemed engrossed in the game, which didn't take Bryn long to realize was an amusing, and apparently fairly easy, scavenger hunt. Easy for him, he thought, because he'd spent his childhood in constant contests to figure out the clues faster than Loli.

He heard two spirited voices. One voice was louder, and her words were slurred, plus it sounded as though her mouth were full of something. He stopped, his heart skipping a beat. It was Loli. He strained his ears. The thick brush of the maze and the width of the corridors made it difficult to hear very well, and his sister sounded as though she were tipsy and stuffing food into her mouth.

"What's wrong, sis?" he muttered to himself. She had always eaten when she was distraught or unsure about something, in other words— unable to control it. Then he heard a musical, lilting voice that made his pulse sound so loudly in his own ears that he was half-afraid the girls might hear it. Deliberately calming himself, he listened.

"I've got two more items to go, a purple coin and a…call to dinner, whatever that means."

"A vell," Loli said, her mouth still full. "It means a bell." She said something Bryn couldn't understand, then, "buh the furfle coin id about twenty faces from the entrance."

Isabell giggled, her name identifying the sound. Her laugh was truly like a bell to Bryn. "Are you giving up?"

"There is no fuzzy ball," Loli responded, her voice clearer now. Apparently she'd swallowed the mouthful of food, finally. "I've searched high and low and everywhere else in-between. This cheese is probably better than the grand prize, anyway. Go on. Grab your coin and find that bell. *One* of us needs to be the winner."

Bryn looked both ways. He was quite a distance from both the right and the left intersections, which meant if Isabell turned his way, he'd be trapped. At least Loli wouldn't be with her. He had to choose a direction. He'd heard a slight rustle from the right, so he chose to go left. *The odds favored no one.*

Then, as he was listening to see if he could hear the rustle of her peacock feathers, something odd happened. He felt a sudden cool breeze on his face—his whole face. His hand immediately went to his forehead. His mask was gone. Blinking, he looked at the ground, but before he could decide it had not fallen off, he heard gasps and screams and shouts from all over the maze.

Behind him, he heard quick, short footsteps. A child? He lifted a hand to his face, to repel recognition if he did run into someone who might know him. A screechy sound, more like an ungreased wheel than anything else, came from the direction of the footsteps. Bryn dared a look. It was no child, that was for sure. It was a wizened little man in dark clothes that almost blended into the deep green shadows of the maze. He skipped toward Bryn, his yellowed teeth shining from his face in what Bryn could only describe as a mischievous, if not downright evil, grin.

"That'll show 'em," he muttered as he passed Bryn as if he were not even there. Bryn turned to watch him skitter away, but right in the middle of the skitter, the man disappeared and Bryn's mask returned.

He walked a few steps in the direction the leprechaun had disappeared, just in case he'd merely blended in with the maze, but no. He was gone. Too late, he heard the rustle of feathers behind him.

"I thought I wouldn't see you until dawn," the familiar voice said.

Bryn whirled. It was Isabell. Before he could say a word, she continued, her voice strained with irritation—or distress?

"Why would you take such a risk, when you just told me the King would kill you if you ran into Loli? You must know she's right here." She pointed left. "Just on the other side of the maze!"

Bryn used the only defense he could think of. "Maybe I came to the maze looking for you, fair peahen with aspirations to be a peacock."

He saw the lovely pink flame ignite the bare skin between her dress and her mask. It was what he'd been hoping for. Maybe it would lead her away from the subject of his sister.

Her hand fluttered to her chest, then down to clasp her other hand in front of her waist, like a proper lady. "I could be a peacock," she murmured.

"Pardon, milady. I didn't quite catch that."

"I said, I could be a peacock." This, quite a bit louder. "I'm tough enough. My father taught me to shoot with a bow and arrow when I was quite young."

Bryn was captivated by her. She was tough. He knew that. He'd watched Loli and Izzy try to keep up with the boys during those rare times when the two friends got to visit together. Izzy had always done a much better job than Loli. Although they were best friends, Izzy had always liked the outdoors more than Loli had.

He stepped closer, wanting to refill his nostrils with her scent and wondered if the heat from the blush on her chest and neck would reach him should he stand close enough. "But, are you tough enough for a rooster?"

Her head tilted up, and below her mask he saw her soft, full lips. They were parted, as if waiting for him. He'd never seen lips so beautiful. Bryn was experienced, to an extent. He'd had experiences, but not as many as his cronies, during the past three years. He'd spent a lot of his evenings being the butt of jokes because he indulged much less often than they did. But then, he'd not only been a pampered prince, he'd been taught by his father to respect women, so it had taken him a long time to accept the concept of a one-night only intimacy. He never quite adopted the attitude of *for tomorrow we die,* although he'd witnessed the truth of it many times.

But here and now, looking at Isabell's lips, he thought he might accept anything she offered.

He bent his head and she did not turn away. He met her gaze. In it was a deep green glow. It could have been wide-eyed anticipation or wide-eyed fear. If he stopped now, he would never know which, but if he continued, he might be crossing a line he could not even see.

He bit back what he wanted to say, which was *Izzy?* And instead, settled for "Milady?"

Izzy blinked and turned her head, delicately clearing her throat. But no mind, he'd been closer to her than he'd ever been, and if that was all he could glean from her presence, then so be it. It could be enough. It had to be.

"Um," she said, sounding as though she were collecting her thoughts. "I don't know where Loli has gone, if she even has managed to lift her head up from that bench she was reclining on and eating cheese, but if she has moved, she is heading for the end. She will probably get the prize."

"Not *probably,*" Bryn said, smiling.

"What do you mean?"

"What? Oh." Bryn was still staring at Izzy's mouth, half-hidden under her mask now that she was no longer so close. What had he said? Then he remembered. "It, um, sounds like she's almost got all the clues. Is anyone else so close?" He spoke quickly, hoping to cover for his near gaffe.

"No, you're absolutely right. Loli, much like her older brother, does love to win."

Bryn could barely force his mouth to form the question he knew he had to ask. "Her older brother?"

"Mm-hmm. He's two years older than we are. The Winter King sent him off on some on some quest up in the North country, maybe even in the Borderlands. Loli misses him very much. She adores him and it's been so long ..."

Bryn waited, but she didn't continue. "You were saying?"

She looked at him. "Oh. No. It was nothing. I was just thinking about Bryndle. He's no warrior." Then her hand flew to her mouth. "Oh no. I should not be talking about the heir to the Winter Land Throne, especially when he is in such a dangerous place and might not ever come back."

Then he knew. She was thinking of her betrothed. Talking about the Borderlands had taken her mind off the festivities and made her sad for her dear Stellan, whom she would never see again. He reached toward her, but did not actually touch her. After all, she was the daughter of the First Knight of the Vale Elf King and believed him to be naught but a warrior. "I beg your pardon," he said. "I did not mean to bring up sad memories."

She shook her head absently. "Do not apologize," she said. "As I told you, I've known a very long time that Stellan was no longer alive. And I fear I did not thank you sufficiently for telling me you were there at his passing. I am very grateful that you could ease him into death and forward. I had so feared that he'd died alone."

"Rest assured, dear Isabell, I was with him. He was my best friend and the bravest being, bar none, I have ever known. He loved you so dearly."

She turned to look at him and he saw tears in the eyes behind the mask. "But now I'm sad for another reason. I'm afraid for Loli. What if Bryndle never comes back, like my Stellan never has. I've never dared to speak of it to her, afraid it would destroy her, but I am so worried for her."

"The princess Loli is a dear friend of yours, isn't she?" Bryn asked gently.

"The dearest. I wish I could see her more often. She keeps me from being maudlin or sad. She is always smiling and excited about something. I'm happier when she's around."

Bryn nodded. He was thankful that the two young women had

each other, and a little pleased that maybe their friendship meant he might have a chance to see Isabell on occasion. That would make *his* heart glad.

Isabell continued speaking. "Do you recall ever meeting Prince Bryndle? He was tall, not as tall as you of course, and thin."

"No." It wasn't strictly a lie. He had never met himself, having always known himself. He almost chuckled at that, but Isabell's crestfallen face took the amusement away.

"Of course not. I'm sure the Borderlands are a huge and awful place. I'm amazed you met Stellan. Oh how did he—how did you or anyone—stand it, being out there alone in that bitter place?"

"Some people, like your Stellan, and Prince Bryndle, have family and lovers at home. You might be surprised at how comforting and even warming it can be to remember loved ones and friends during dark and stormy nights, or while staring into a brave little fire. There is no one so alone as a warrior with no one waiting for him at home." He bit his lip. He wasn't sure why he'd said that. He had his father, his friends and of course Loli. Still, he knew that he was lying to himself about not knowing how alone one could feel huddling by a meager fire in a shallow cave.

Once he'd met Stellan, whom he'd loved as his own brother, and listened to him talk about Isabell and the life he'd wanted to build for the two of them, a new and painful emptiness had been gouged into his heart. A loneliness that was deeper and sharper than the loss of his mother. This was a hunger for something never known before, but something his soul knew was missing.

"Sir Rooster, as arrogant as you are, I would not wish you to be alone beside a dwindling fire in an ice-covered world."

"You are too kind," Bryn said wryly.

"Yes, I am. And now I must excuse myself. I am expected elsewhere."

"By many a suitable suitor, I'm sure."

Isabell laughed and ran down the maze in the opposite direction, lifting her peacock-colored skirts. At one point she turned around, looking as though she were floating on air. To Bryn's shock, she blew him a kiss, then turned back around and soon disappeared around a corner.

He turned away to carefully make his way to the entrance of the maze, considering that Isabell was absolutely correct that Loli would have headed directly toward the maze's exit on the other side to claim her victory in the scavenger hunt. He had not gone a foot when he saw something white and gauzy on the ground, near the flickering light from a torch above him. He bent to pick it up. It was Isabell's glove. He held it to his nose to catch a whiff of her sweet scent, then started to put it in his pocket.

"Sir Rooster!"

He whirled. Isabell was trotting back toward him, the scarves of her skirt flowing around her. "Dear peahen, I believe this is yours." He held out the small, translucent glove.

"Thank you. Sir Rooster, I must ask you something."

He sketched a bow. "Anything, milady. Anything you wish shall become my command."

"When you first saw me unmasked in the alcove, you said something."

Bryn frowned to himself. What was she talking about? "I believe I said something along the lines of *are you all right.*"

The peacock mask turned from side to side. "No. Before that."

He looked at her blankly.

"I believe you said, *Izzy.*"

He felt his face drain of color. "Is he?" he tried. "Why would I say *is he?* Maybe I thought someone was bothering you. But then I saw there was no one in the alcove but you and me."

She was still shaking her head. "No. Not '*Is he,*' you arrogant man. You said *Izzy.*"

He didn't speak. He stood there, still as death, waiting to see where she was going with this. Maybe he could convince her that Izzy was Stellan's pet name for her, but he knew it was not. Stellan had called her Bella.

Isabell stepped up closer to him and punched him in the chest with her forefinger. "You said *Izzy.* Why?"

"I truly have no idea what you're talking about, milady. You must be thinking of someone else."

"I am not. *And,* lest you continue to think this is all in my head—"

"I never said that—"

She waved a palm at him. "Just now, I saw you bent over picking up my glove, with the torchlight on your hair. *Your hair.*"

"What?"

"You heard me. Now unmask yourself, *warrior.*"

From beyond the hedge, he heard someone speak, then laugh. "You must lower your voice, milady. People will believe I am assaulting you. You are screeching rather loudly."

"Screeching? *Screeching?* You will hear screeching, if you don't take that mask off right this minute." To her credit, she had lowered her voice a bit.

A man's voice called out, a woman giggled and Bryn heard footsteps behind them. "Not here," Bryn whispered. "Let us go somewhere quiet and uncrowded and I swear I will reveal myself to you, dear peahen."

"And stop calling me that. You know what my name is, and I shall soon know yours."

He took her arm and led her back toward the entrance to the maze. As soon as they exited, he saw Devlin coming their way. Instead of acknowledging their host, Bryn risked a supreme rudeness by turning away as if he hadn't seen his host and escorted Isabell down the side of the tall green shrubbery and around it toward the water. As they stepped off the patio, he waylaid a waiter passing by and grabbed a large bottle of water.

"Why are you taking me this way? I'm not sure..." she strained against his hold on her forearm.

Bryn let go of her and glanced behind to be sure no one was in earshot. "You asked me who I am. No, you *demanded* to know who I am. I am not at liberty to say, nor can I reveal myself among the crowd for very real fear of defying my—the Winter King. So come with me or don't. It is your decision. But this is the only way you will get your way, little peahen. You told me you're tough. But are you tough enough to trust this masked stranger?"

Isabell stared at him for a long time, then turned and strode toward the beach. This was no prim and proper young lady in a beautiful multicolored gown. No. She turned into the tomboy who would periodically leave Loli behind to try to keep up with him and his buddies. He smiled at the memories as he watched her wrench her skirts up as far as she could, considering their abundance, and trudge through the grass until she finally stopped to take off her shoes before stepping into the sand.

Bryn followed, still smiling. She was a good one, he thought. He hoped his ruse would not make her too angry at him, although it was difficult to imagine her more angry than she was right now. He took off his fine kid boots and left them beside her small green-dyed shoes, then stepped onto the little beach.

Isabell had trounced about halfway across the narrow stretch of beach and plopped herself down on the sand, not caring whether she ruined the dress or the mask, which she took off and set beside her.

When he reached her, she glanced sidelong at his bare feet. He lowered himself next to her.

"I wish I had something to drink," she said. "I'm so thirsty I can hardly talk."

Bryn produced the bottle of water. "Here."

She looked at the water, then at him. "How--?"

"What? I don't have glasses, milady. You will have to make do with the bottle."

"That is not a problem." She grabbed it from him with a huff and turned it up. He watched her throat move as she drank. After a few seconds he laughed. "Hey, save some for me."

She held the bottle out to him and gave him a stubborn stare. "Please. Have all you want, but you can't drink out of the bottle with that mask on. If you want water, you will have to unmask yourself."

He let her keep the water for the moment. "What did you think you saw when I bent down to retrieve your glove earlier?"

She looked at him then away, trying to remember, or unsure of her answer. "I—it was—your hair. I saw your hair. I have only known one person in my life who had hair the color of gold on fire."

"Really?" he said, sounding surprised. "Because I have known many." His mother, his grandparents, and several cousins from their side of the family who had visited from time to time. Loli had taken after their fair-haired father, the Winter King.

"Yes, really." Her answer was short and a bit hesitant. Was he making her unsure of herself? And was he glad about that or not?"

"Reddish hair is not that uncommon. You truly must be a sheltered young thing to have ventured no further than to know only one person with hair that color."

"I've traveled plenty. I've traveled to Winter Land. I've traveled—here."

"A world traveler indeed, peahen."

"Oh shut up."

He laughed.

Isabell didn't speak again and so he did not either. He looked up at the stars. The moon and the lights from the castle and grounds masked the twinkling of many of them, but the comforting sight of several constellations that he knew made him feel more as if he were home, or at least closer to home than he'd been in what seemed like a lifetime.

"During the dark nights in the Borderlands, the sky was filled with so many stars that they lit the night like a million fireflies twinkling in a meadow."

Isabell looked up. "Why are there not that many here?"

"Oh there are. They are all out there, each one as bright to its own world as the sun is to ours."

She lowered her gaze from the heavens to his masked face. "To its own world? What do you mean?"

"The sun is a star, just like the ones that twinkle above us. And our sun is a very small   star, compared to many of those."

"Tell me more."

He glanced at her, but she had turned her attention back to the sky.

"The sun is quite far away, but the nearest star is thousands of times further away. The whole sky full of stars that you see here tonight is but one group, called a galaxy, and we are on the edge of that galaxy."

She stood and brushed off her skirts.

Bryn stood too. "Milady?"

She turned to him. "How do you know all that, warrior?"

Suddenly, his mouth was dry. "I—I have been fortunate in the people I have met in my travels. I have learned things from many of them."

"*Sir Rooster*," Isabell said and stepped up close to him. "Take off your mask, or I will march back up to the patio and let everyone—and I mean *everyone*, know who you are."

Bryn stared at Isabell. Her emerald eyes were flashing as hot and bright as the sun. Her pretty mouth was set stubbornly and she had propped her fists on her hips.

"You know?"

"Take it off," she said, her voice low, yet shaking with fury.

Bryn looked around them. There was no one near. Voices and laughter, vying with the music from the ballroom, drifted toward them. He took off his mask and tossed it down on the sand beside hers. The breeze felt cool on his heated face. With his eyes cast downward, he waited for Isabell's reaction.

"Bryndle," she said, her voice still shaky. "I knew it. I knew it was you. There was something familiar about you, even that first moment when you walked in on me in the alcove. I felt as though I had known you all my life." She searched his face, and as she did, she shook her head. "How can it be you? You're familiar and yet so different. Oh, but it's so good to see you."

She held out her arms, and with only an instant of hesitation, he took a step toward her. Isabell hugged him tightly. At first, Bryn hugged her back, feeling as though he were truly being welcomed home for the first time since he'd arrived. The King did not hug— never had, and he hadn't seen his sister, nor anyone else, who knew who he was. He'd traveled here as a stranger, returning to a world where he no longer really belonged, and he'd remained a stranger in this world, no matter how elegantly he was dressed, until this moment.

"It's good to see you, Izzy. It's been a long time."

He felt her nod against his chest, and he bent his head and drew in the fragrance of her hair. And everything changed.

No longer was he Bryndle, the bookworm older brother who merely tolerated his little sister and her friend. Nor was he Bryndle, the adolescent who had a boy's crush on a girl. He was a man, a warrior and a prince, and the stirrings he now felt had nothing to do with crushes or children. Nor were they welcome to him.

Yes, he wanted Isabell. He might even love her. But he'd accepted long ago, as he'd watched her betrothed take his last breath, that his would always be an unrequited love. He was a friend to her and nothing more.

Right. If only he could convince his body of that. The tension building inside him would soon manifest itself physically if he couldn't contain it.

"Izzy?"

She leaned back in his arms and looked up at him. "You've changed, Bryn," she said softly. "A lot. No wonder I had trouble recognizing you. Last time I saw you, you were a skinny boy who would rather read and study than ride or play." Her hands rested on his velvet-covered biceps. She squeezed lightly. "Now you're—you're a man." Then, as if she'd just realized what she'd said, she stepped backward, away from him.

He made sure she was steady on her feet, then let go and met her gaze. He felt like a fraud. Actually he was a fraud. He'd allowed his father to manipulate him yet again, in order to set up a *glorious* prank for his sister. "Izzy, I didn't mean to deceive."

For a moment, she studied the ground. When she lifted her head, her expression was ironic. "You didn't mean to deceive? You didn't—? Come on Bryn, at least have the courtesy to be honest with me now. What exactly was the point of hiding behind this elaborate costume and making yourself the mysterious man of the hour at the Masquerade Ball? I don't know if you realize it, but your father told Loli that she would meet her betrothed, a mysterious man dressed all in red, before the end of the ball."

"No," Bryn said quickly. "That's not what Father—the King— said. He told me to avoid my sister until the last possible second prior to the Wishing Tree Ceremony. Then she would be brought to me by her betrothed, who is the son of the Goblin King, and I would reveal my identity for a glorious reunion and an unforgettable evening for her."

"Oh dear," Isabell said, her hand going to her mouth. "Your father has created quite a mess."

"A mess? Hmm." Bryn shook his head. "I'm not surprised, but what do you mean?"

"Loli said her father told her that she would meet a man dressed all in crimson before the end of the ball and that she should make every effort to speak with him, because he was anxious to meet her and have a dance with her. She thinks this *devil in red*, as she calls him, is her betrothed."

"Of course. That sounds like something my father would do. Although I have no idea why. This could end badly for my sister. What if she doesn't allow the magic of the evening to unite her with her betrothed because she believes that the man in crimson is her destiny? This is a cruel joke by my father. I have heard of his jokes in the past, but now he is making his beloved daughter the victim, and using me— her brother—to perpetrate the ruse. I cannot, I will not be a part of it."

"Wait, Bryn," Isabell said. "Let's think about this a moment. Loli is terrified of being betrothed to a goblin."

"Right. Well, I'm not exactly delighted about it either. The Goblins are rough and coarse, and my sweet sister's optimism and joy for life could be crushed by such a mate."

"I met Argoth LeRain a couple of years ago here at the Masquerade. I did not realize he was the phantom who has been wooing Loli all evening, but now that I know, I can see it." Isabell clapped her hands together. "Oh, Loli is going to be so surprised when she finds out."

"Wait. Now suddenly you're happy that my father has done this?"

Isabell shrugged. "Not exactly happy, because my poor friend is so confused right now. But I believe your father has created the perfect way for Loli to fall in love with her intended before she has any idea what is happening. Then when she realizes who you are and who he is, it will be too late. She will already be head over heels in love with him."

Bryn stared at her. "Um...what?" He rubbed his temple. "I have absolutely no idea of what you just said."

She waved a hand. "You are male. Don't even try to understand it. Just trust me. If we can keep you away from Loli until the presentation of gifts, your sister, not the Kilmartins, will be the richest person here. She will have her husband and her brother."

"As well as the most faithful and true friend a person could ever have," Bryn added.

She smiled shyly. The pretty pink flame that started at the top of her bodice and bloomed upward to color her neck and cheeks made her the most beautiful thing Bryn had ever seen. His fingers twitched to touch her and he felt the tension rising in him again. He wanted to lay her down on the sand and make love to her, with the ocean's waves drowning out their cries of ecstasy and the millions of stars above lighting their way.

But of course Bryn did nothing of the sort. All he could do was stand, frozen, staring at the pink, creamy perfection of Isabell's skin and hope that his face didn't reflect how he felt inside. Because if Isabell ever found out how he felt about her, he would—he didn't actually know what he would do, but what he did know was that she would never find out. Ever.

"Bryn?"

He looked from the curve of her breasts up to her face. "Right. What? I mean, yes?"

"What are you thinking?"

Bryn had faced Dokarqs that were twice his size, ice storms so long and cold that he was afraid that every time he went to sleep he would never wake again, and passages so treacherous he never even expected to live to see the other side. But he had never faced anything as completely terrifying as the expectant look on Isabell's face as she waited for him to answer her question.

"I'm not really thinking of anything, Izzy. Why?"

"I don't know. It seemed to me that for a moment there, you were going to do something...unexpected."

"Something unexpected? Such as what?"

Isabell was looking at him thoughtfully. "Bryn?"

"Hmm?"

"When we were children, you know, before, and we played while all the grownups had their Masquerade Ball, did you ever notice me?"

Bryn swallowed and turned away. He hoped he looked casual, but he felt stiff as a board. He hooked a thumb into the waistband of his pants, then took it out. "Why? What do you mean? Of course I noticed you. We played together."

"Yes, I know. We did, some. But I don't mean just regular noticing, like you guys did when you'd get annoyed because I was following you, or because I wanted you to help me get on my horse so I could—you know—follow you."

"I'm not sure what you mean."

"I mean, I noticed you. You liked playing outside with the other boys, but you liked being inside too. I'd see you on the boys' hall reading or studying maps. And I know you sneaked outside at night and caught things in bottles. That's right. I saw you with your bottles."

"You spied on me?"

"No. No." She paused and chewed on a fingernail for a couple of seconds. "No. Sometimes I'd see you chasing fireflies or the giant ghost moth that flies around near the windows of the castle after dark."

"I never caught one."

"I think a ghost moth could have carried you away if you'd caught onto it." Isabell studied the fingernail she'd been chewing. "Not now though." She shivered.

"You're cold," Bryn said. "Here. Let me give you my coat." He unbuttoned the velvet coat and took it off, then laid it across Isabell's bare shoulders. He smoothed the velvet over the curve of her shoulders and down her arms. For some reason he couldn't stop.

After a moment that could have been an aeon, Isabell reached across and put her hand on top of his where it rested near her elbow. "Bryn, why are you here?"

"I told you. My father sent a message, summoning me home in time for the ball. He dispatched the messenger immediately after last year's ball. Even so, I barely made it in time."

"I don't mean here." She threw her arm out in a wide gesture that encompassed the ocean, the Kilmartin's castle and all the surrounding areas. "I mean here."

"You asked me to reveal my identity, and I did not want to disobey my father."

She made a sound that could have been a growl, had it come from a wild dog. "Please Bryn, don't turn back into the boy who never looked up from his maps or his insect collection." She turned around and lifted her head until she was looking directly into his eyes.

What he saw there, he dared not name. Dared not even believe. Did Isabell, the pretty friend of his sister, want him? "Isabell…" he said in a warning voice. "What are you saying?"

She closed her eyes briefly, then opened them again. The pretty flush began to rise until it painted her cheeks like the blush on a peach.

He swallowed drily and sketched a quick, stiff bow. "As a prince and an honorable man—"

Isabell's hands came up, palms out. "Stop! I have to tell you I have encountered nothing in my entire existence so frustrating as an *honorable* man."

Bryn had no idea what to make of her or what she was saying. "What are you saying? Any man worth his salt must be honorable. I have been nothing but protective and proper toward you, even before I knew who you were. Then once I found out you were Lady Isabell, my sister's dearest friend and my friend's betrothed, I have treated you like—"

"Like a baby bird or a—a—something so fragile I might break if you touched me." With another soft growl, Isabell stood on her tiptoes and kissed Bryn on the corner of his mouth.

"Izzy!" He gasped, and not entirely from surprise. At the touch of her lips on his, the tension and the fire smoldering inside him caught and flared. He did his best to tamp it back down. "What are you doing?"

She didn't answer. She just looked at him, still teetering on her bare toes, so he caught her waist to steady her. Isabell seized the opportunity and wrapped her arms around his neck. He bent his head and gave her back the tentative kiss she'd given him.

She pressed closer and her mouth opened slightly under his. Bryn pulled her to him and kissed her, no tentative kiss this time. This time his was a lover's kiss. A kiss that was years overdue, and, were he to have enough brain left to form the thought, totally worth the wait.

Isabell gave him back kiss for kiss, and when he took the kiss deeper, tasting and probing her mouth with his tongue, she moaned with pleasure. He felt the sound more than heard it. It rumbled up from her throat to her tongue and lips. It was a sensation like none he'd ever felt. The encounters he'd had on his journey had been quick and purposeful, a casual night's enjoyment and a relief from tension, in more ways than one.

This was not casual. This was as far from casual as the Borderlands were far from the Kilmartin's magical castle. He finally held in his arms the one person he'd always known could make his dreams come true. Her face, as much as his sister's and yes, even his father's, had sustained him through the dark, frozen nights and the long, blood-stained days of battle.

Then he'd met Stellan, her betrothed, and he'd vowed to bring her his final words.

Stellan.

Bryn froze. Mere seconds after he had bragged that he was an honorable man, he was kissing and caressing his slain friend's betrothed as if he were her lover. In his mind, he was. He had carried her sweet face in his memory for three long years to soothe his battle-weary heart. But that did not mean that he had any right to touch her outside of his dreams.

"Isabell," he panted. "I beg your pardon."

He stepped backward.

"What's the matter?" Isabell's hair was coming loose and dipping down over her shoulder. Her eyes held a soft glow and her lips were parted. She slid her hands up to his neck and lifted her head for another kiss.

"This is wrong, Izzy. You know as well as I do. We are not alone here. There is a third person standing between us."

Isabell's brows furrowed. "You're talking about Stellan." Her fingers tightened on the back of his neck. "Listen to me. Look at me."

Bryn didn't want to meet her gaze. When he looked into her eyes, he lost all sense of reason or honor. Until he'd seen her without the peacock mask this evening, he hadn't known how much he loved her.

"Look at me," she commanded.

He did. Her eyes were bright with unshed tears. "I told you that I knew when Stellan died, more than two years ago. He not only spoke his dying words to you, there in the frozen Borderlands, he spoke them to me also."

Bryn's gaze wavered.

"Bryn, listen to me. Stellan knew." She blinked and a tear slid down her cheek. "He knew you loved me."

An arrow of pain tore through his heart. "No," he said, horrified. "No. Why would you say that? I swear to you I never—"

"Shh," she whispered, pressing two fingers to his lips. "Listen to me. He knew because he knew you and loved you, just like you loved him. Do you remember what he said as you held him?"

He nodded. "Of course," he whispered raggedly. "He said, *don't grieve for me. Embrace the happiness to come.*"

"He was talking to you."

"But you told me he appeared to you at that moment."

"He did. Don't you see? Remember what I told you? That some of the Elven have the gift of walking outside of time. It's rare, but Stellan had it. He spoke to both of us that night." She slid her hands down until they were resting over his heart. "Open your heart, Bryn. I believe you love me, but I need to hear it from you."

For a moment, Bryn didn't speak. He held Isabell close and stared out over the inky water, his mind in the past, holding Stellan as he took his last breaths. A breeze stirred and sent cool air across his hot face. Then, as if carried by the breeze, he thought he heard a voice speaking.

Embrace the happiness.

Bryn smiled and ran his finger along Isabell's jawline until it was under her chin, then he lifted her head and touched his lips to hers. "I vow to embrace happiness, milady, if you feel the same way."

Isabell smiled. "I vow to embrace happiness, Your Highness."

"Look yonder," Bryn murmured, nodding toward the east. "The maze is dark. Devlin must be starting a new game. Shall we play?"

"I have no wish to do anything that involves more than two people, Sir Rooster," Isabell said, "but speaking of games, I need to check in with Loli. She has been enjoying a flirtation with a mysterious man dressed as a phantom all evening, while agonizing over the prospect of meeting the *demon in red,* as she calls you."

"Right. And I need to speak to my father about this whole business. Since I still must hide from my sister, shall we meet in our alcove, say in an hour?"

Isabell smiled at him. "We cannot meet later unless we go our separate ways now."

Bryn raised an eyebrow. "What do you mean?"

"You must let me go."

He nuzzled the side of her neck. "Must I?"

"Sir Rooster, unhand me!" she giggled.

"Does the dear peahen squawk?"

"I'll squawk if you don't let go."

They parted, laughing.

Isabell decided to go with Bryn to speak to his father. The two of them put on their masks and shoes, Bryn grabbed his coat, and they made their way up the hill from the beach, keeping to the shadows. There was a lightness in Bryn's heart that he could never remember feeling before. As they walked, he tried to explain to Isabell about his relationship, or lack thereof, with his father. "We lost our mother when I was fourteen and Loli was twelve. I found it harder than Loli to get over her death. I've blamed my father all this time. Accused him of terrible deeds regarding his treatment of my mother, and I still blamed him when I started out on my journey, but now…."

Isabell took his hand in hers.

"I feel I owe him an apology. Perhaps several apologies. I wasted a lot of time blaming him, for my mother's death and not realizing how hurt and saddened he was at losing the love of his life." As Bryn talked, he led Isabell around the perimeter of the maze until they were behind the thick purple draped canopy where the dignitaries watched the festivities while enjoying an assortment of the finest of delicacies and libations offered to the rest of the guests.

Bryn stepped through one layer of draperies and tapped a servant on the shoulder. The man turned, looking Bryn up and down. "Yes?"

"Let the Winter King know that I wish to speak to him."

Another sweeping gaze, and the servant said, "And you are—?"

"His son." It both surprised and embarrassed Bryn that he had slipped so easily back into the haughty voice of a prince talking to a servant. "If you please," he added, but the servant, wide-eyed, had already bolted toward the King.

The King finished a glass of something, set it on the servant's tray and whispered to his companion. Bryn was pretty sure the other man was the Summer Faerie King.

"Bryndle?" the King called softly.

Bryn placed his hand on the small of Isabell's back and they stepped out from behind the purple canopy. "Father."

"Yes?" the King asked impatiently, then noticed Isabell. He sent a questioning look toward Bryn, then bowed his head in her direction. "Isabell. How are you? It's a pleasure to see you. Bryndle, this is the second time I've excused myself within twenty minutes. The Summer King will think I can't hold my liquor for a moment."

"Father, I—" suddenly, Bryn had no idea what to say. "It would have been nice if you'd let me know all the twists and turns of your prank."

"Twists and turns? Prank? What are you talking about?"

"Don't you know by now how confused Loli is?"

"You haven't spoken with her have you?"

"No, Sire. I have followed your instructions to the letter." *Mostly* to the letter, he amended to himself, since the King had told him not to interact with anyone.

"Actually, if you'd followed my instructions to the letter, I do not think Isabell would be here with you." He waved his hand as if dismissing that issue. "How do you know Loli is confused? And what's she confused about?"

Isabell took a step forward. "Pardon, Sire, but I told His Highness about Loli being confused. She and I have spoken at length about her confusion and fear of the *demon in red*, as she calls him."

"Fear?"

"Apparently, Loli is under the impression that the Red Prince is to be her betrothed," Bryn said.

"What?" The King turned back to Isabell. "Surely she doesn't think such a thing, does she?"

"I'm afraid so, Sire. She has built up the mystery of the man dressed all in red until she believes he is a hideous Goblin who at the end of the night will whisk her away to be his reluctant bride."

"But, that's ridiculous. The Goblin King's son is wooing her even as we speak. I have already, barring any severe objection by my dear Loli, accepted her dowry."

Of course he had, Bryn thought. And knowing Loli, she would do anything for her father, even become betrothed to someone she didn't love.

When he looked at the King, he was staring into space. "How could she have misinterpreted—"

"Sire? I have kept myself hidden all this time. Do you wish that I reveal myself earlier than you had previously planned?"

His father looked from him to Isabell, then back again. He shook his head, slowly and thoughtfully. "No. I will speak to Loli. I want to gauge her feelings for her phantom suitor. Then I will speak to her betrothed, Argoth LeRain. We will play out the surprise for her."

Bryn started to speak but his father continued. "I think I will have LeRain bring her to you at the appropriate time. She will have her betrothed by her side and her brother right there in front of her. It will be glorious. Can you continue to remain out of her sight until then?"

"As you wish, Sire. Izzy should find Loli so that Loli doesn't think her friend has abandoned her, and then Izzy and I can meet in one of the alcoves and spend a pleasant hour or two together as we wait."

"I should go ahead now, before Loli gets involved in another game," Isabell said. She squeezed Bryn's hand, then disappeared back through the draperies.

His father's clear blue eyes met his and he smiled. "You and Izzy? What is this? Are the two of you planning to tie red ribbons on the Wishing Tree tonight?"

Bryn lowered his gaze, but he couldn't keep a smile off his own face. "No, Father. Izzy and I do not need entwined ribbons to prove we belong together."

"You left here a boy and returned a man, my son. You accomplished what I had hoped and more on your journey to the Borderlands. I can't wait until we have a chance to talk and catch up." The King put out his hand. "I am proud of you, and I think you and Isabell are a perfect match. Marriage for love is risky, especially without the magic of the Wishing Tree, but it worked for me, and I know it will work for you and Isabell."

Bryn took his father's hand. "Father, I feel that I should—"

The King shook his head. "I'm so glad you're home, Bryndle."

"Me too, Father. Me too."

The King shook his son's hand then returned to the festivities. Bryn watched for a while from the shadows of the draperies, then slipped away and headed toward the servant's hall that led into the alcoves. He slipped into the one where he had met Isabell and sat on the gilded bench to wait for her.

"Sir Rooster? Hello? Sir Rooster."

Bryndle came awake to the sharp crow of a rooster, but didn't open his eyes. The sun shone bright and there was someone close to him. Very close. Without moving a muscle, he tried to decide what to do, preferably very quickly, before he felt the cold metal of a knife at his throat or the sharp double edge of a sword piercing his belly.

Then he heard the rooster again.

No. It wasn't a rooster. It was the word *rooster*.

"Sir Rooster?"

Something was tickling his nose. Was a Dokarq about to cut off his nose and string it on a leather cord around its neck? He'd seen one once, wearing a cord that held at least six noses. Sure that he was doomed, Bryn opened his eyes to find laughing green ones staring back at him.

"Sir Rooster, at last. You're a lazy rooster who cannot be awakened without a feather tickling his nose."

In answer, Bryn sneezed twice, then fished a handkerchief from his coat pocket. "Begging your pardon, milady." He wiped his nose then re-pocketed the handkerchief. By the time he'd sat up straight, Isabell was on his lap.

"Careful, milady, you might want to go easy on my trousers," he said, grinning. "They're velvet and you wouldn't want to brush them too harshly. Makes the pile stick up in odd places."

Isabell blushed and Bryn pulled her close so he could place his lips on each and every flaming inch of the flesh above her bodice. He trailed soft kisses over the curves and up to her delicate collarbone, where he nibbled his way along the bone and on up to the delicious column of her neck and chin, across her jawline and up to her ear. He made her moan deep in her throat when he lightly bit and suckled on her earlobe, then made her shiver when he blew warm breath in her ear. The fragile skin at her temple was no match for the rasp of his prickly beard, which could already be felt only a few hours after he'd shaved.

"Bryn, stop. As quiet and solitary as this alcove is, someone could walk in at any moment."

"Ask me if I care," he whispered, his lips accentuating each word across the fringe of her eyelashes.

"It's obvious you don't care. T'is I whose reputation will be ruined should someone peek in and see me sitting on the lap of the infamous and mysterious Sir Rooster."

"If anyone interrupts, I will split them in half with my sword," he vowed.

"What sword, Sir?" You have no scabbard, not even an empty one."

Bryn shifted. "And yet, I could show you a sword worthy of the bravest warrior, milady, if you would but yield."

Isabell clapped her hand over his mouth. "Shh! People could be listening. What has gotten hold of you that you are so funny and teasing and downright naughty all of a sudden?"

Bryn paused and looked at her pensively, his grin fading to a frown. "I don't know, milady. Could it be the mysterious *happiness* I have heard about in my travels? It apparently is shy and can be fleeting, much like butterflies darting here and there, trying out the various flowers to see which is sweetest."

"Ah," Isabell said, cupping his face in her small hands. "Happiness. Yes, I believe it may very well be the cause of your current state. It appears to be more potent than Spring Nectar."

"That it is, my lovely happiness-filled vessel. That it is. I must have more. Please allow me to drink." He kissed her, long and hard, pulling her head down and pushing his fingers through her beautiful dark brown hair.

Much later, Isabell lifted her head and smiled down at Bryn from her perch on his lap. "Oh that was delicious," she said.

"Mmm," was the only answer she got from Bryn. His eyes were half-closed and a sweet smile curved the edges of his mouth.

"I tell you what, my dear Sir Rooster. Why don't you relax here for a while, and I will come and get you when it is time for you to make your official appearance in front of Loli."

"Mmm-hmm," he said.

"Goodnight, sweet prince," she whispered, her lips against his cheek, then she stepped through the curtains of the alcove and onto the ballroom floor.

An hour later, Bryn was straightening his clothes and hair when Isabell peeked in. "Sir Rooster, time to crow."

He rolled his eyes at her. "As much as I cannot wait to see my sister, I dread this. I'm not sure how much more confusion and excitement she can take." He stood. "How do I look?"

Isabell kissed his cheek. "You look magnificent. Don't forget your mask."

He donned the mask and made sure it felt straight. "You know she is prone to headaches and moods, don't you?"

"Loli? Yes, but you're her brother. Have you not noticed that those headaches and moods come upon her when she is not getting her way?"

He sent her a narrow look. "Perhaps," he said. "So, let's do this."

Isabell hung back. "I'm going to go find Loli and talk to her for a bit. Then her Phantom and I will do our best to maneuver her toward the area of the ballroom where you will be waiting. Don't stray."

Bryn shook his head. "Don't worry, dear peahen. I'll be fine." He stepped out onto the ballroom floor and glanced around. People were still masked, but most of them seemed to be less steady and slower moving than they had been hours ago. Many masks were askew or beginning to look tattered and Bryn figured that people were not as unknown to each other as they had been at the beginning of the evening.

He stepped over to a table laden with fruit and picked up a piece of pineapple. It was delicious and reminded him of his hunger. He never had gotten any of that succulent boar that Isabell had stolen from him hours before. He eased toward the tables that held heavier fare and managed to eat some meat and cheese without completely unmasking himself. Then he grabbed a bottle of cold water to wash it down. Thinking how good something sweet would be, he started toward a dessert table, excusing himself to an Elf as he sidestepped him to reach for a square of cake.

A gasp echoed through the crowd, and it seemed as if the entire ballroom went completely quiet. Bryn saw his sister, Loli out of the corner of his eye dressed in a beautiful flowing white dress with a swan mask covering her face. She held onto the hand of a tall man dressed all in black. The Phantom.

The two of them glided across the dance floor as the dancers stopped to watch them. By this time everyone had heard the rumor of the red-clad warrior who might or might not be the betrothed of the lovely Swan Princess. And now, to their delight, the two were actually face to face, right in front of them. A path cleared between the swan and the red warrior.

The white, feathered mask turned toward him. Bryn cleared his throat and set down the bottle of water.

Loli turned her head to look at the Phantom, then back to him. He saw her take a deep breath. He took one too and turned full toward her.

She curtsied hesitantly and tried to smile. "Mi-milord."

He couldn't maintain the ruse any longer. He grinned and threw out his arms. "Loli!" he shouted. "Loli-pop!"

Loli was still bowed in her curtsy when he reached her. He grabbed her up and lifted her into the air, then down, and up again and down. "Loli!" he cried again. Now that he had seen her, now that he was holding her, he felt as though his heart were going to burst out of his chest with happiness.

He hugged his sister tightly, then set her back down on her feet. Remembering the ruse his father wanted to play, he cried, "Where have you been hiding all night? I've looked *everywhere* for you."

Loli's mask was a little crooked, but it was still on. Beneath it, he could see that she was shocked. She hadn't quite figured out the joke yet. "I wasn't hiding, Milord," she said, her voice quivering. "Just... building up courage, I suppose."

"Courage?" He laughed. "Courage for what?"

Then she tilted her head, and he knew she was beginning to figure it out. He smiled. "Come now, Loli. It hasn't been *that* long, has it?" He reached up and took off his mask and tossed it aside.

"Bryn... Bryndle?" Her eyes widened with the realization. "Bryndle!" She tore off her mask and jumped into his arms.

He staggered backward, but held onto her. Over her head he saw his father standing in the door to the ballroom with Isabell at his side. The King smiled in her direction.

"When did you get back?" Loli asked between kisses. She was kissing his face, his nose, his chin, his forehead. "Father didn't tell me you were coming to the ball."

"Did he not tell you to seek out a man dressed all in red?" Bryn teased, kissing her back and hugging her tightly before setting her on the floor. She stayed close to him, holding onto his arm as if he might disappear if she didn't hang on tight.

"Well, yes, but I thought he was talking about a Goblin."

"A Goblin?" Bryndle shook his head. "Is Father still trying to marry you off to one of their horde? How long has he threatened you with that?"

"My whole life, feels like."

Bryndle saw their father approaching. He straightened, and, feeling his stiffness, Loli let go of his arm and stood straight as well.

"Father." Bryndle bowed. "Seems your teasing has caused my little sister some undue stress this evening."

"As you already know, I wasn't teasing." The King turned toward Loli. "Have you not enjoyed yourself this evening, dear one?"

Loli tried to act like a princess, but she couldn't wipe the smile off her face. "I have, Father, yes."

"And still you waver where my wishes are concerned?"

"I'm…" She bit her lip and swallowed hard. "I fear I may be smitten, Father."

"I see." The King furrowed his noble brow. "Will you yet defy me in this, dear daughter?"

Loli took a deep breath and lowered her head. "No, Father. Your will, my wings… always."

Bryn winced. He knew the King had planned this surprise for Loli, but it was going on a little bit too long. *Father. Tell her the truth.*

"Well met, my child. Well met." He smiled. "I am glad you have finally accepted your destiny, little one. After closely watching your actions this evening, I felt safe in going forward with the proceedings. With your gentle heart ever on my mind… I accepted your dowry and your betrothed now awaits."

At his words, Loli quickly looked up at her father. Bryn leaned over and kissed her on the cheek and whispered, "Don't worry, Loli-pop."

The King motioned with a nod towards the dance floor. When Loli turned, her Phantom was standing in the very center of that large room. He removed his haunting mask and regally bowed toward her. Isabell had darted behind the Phantom to cross the room. She walked up to stand beside Bryn.

Loli stared at the Phantom's unmasked face, smiled, and then, she quickly scanned the room. "But... where's my Goblin?"

"Awaiting you on the dance floor," Bryn whispered against the back of her head, then gave her a little push.

Loli took a couple hesitant steps forward, then stopped. Argoth LeRain, the Son of the Goblin King, swooped in and protectively wrapped his arm around her tiny waist and whirled with her into a beautiful, flowing waltz.

Bryn watched them moving together as if they'd been lovers for years.

"She is so beautiful and so happy," Isabell murmured, slipping her hand into his.

"As are you, my lovely peahen. As are you." He took off Isabell's peacock feather mask and set it aside, then took her into his arms. "Let's see if I can remember how to dance a waltz, my lovely lady."

Argoth maneuvered himself and Loli around toward Bryn and Isabell as they began to dance. Loli looked at Bryn, then at Isabell, then back at her brother. "You two have some explaining to do," she called out as Argoth swept her around and danced back across the ballroom.

"How angry do you think she's going to be that we did not tell her anything?" Isabell asked.

"Angry as a red demon, I suspect," Bryn said. "But we'll just have to remind her it's a magical night."

Epilogue

"Dear friends and honoured guests." Elsbeth Kilmartin smiled at the small gathering. "As the dawn approaches, it is Devlin and I who are truly honoured by your presence and blessed by your generosity these many years."

The Winter King stepped forward, a glass of Spring Nectar raised in toast. "Well we remember the day a young, newly-wed couple gave freely of their essence to a dying Fae." The crowd cheered behind him. "The selfless act saved the life of my greatfather, and in turn, provided protection for the Fae from the creeping fever that threatened our existence."

Devlin took his wife's hand in his and brought it to his lips. "Milady's heart knows no bounds. It is one of the many reasons I fell in love with her."

"However," the King continued, "in doing so, it almost cost her the precious gift of her own life. Another five hundred years of the blessing could never repay the debt we owe."

One after another, magical folk came forward to recount the ways in which the Kilmartins had offered help, sanctuary, or simply friendship to them.

Once all the toasts had been raised, Elsbeth motioned for Stefan and Sabrina to join them. "It has been such a wonderful and exciting evening. It is not unusual for love to blossom on our anniversary celebration, but this year, we have been blessed to see our son find his heart's desire. It is our pleasure to announce Stefan and Sabrina were wed in a quiet ceremony this night."

Another round of cheers went up from the crowd.

Devlin motioned for quiet. "Please, we have one more announcement. Elsbeth and I have decided to forego the acceptance of the gifts, and ask that you bestow them on our son and his bride. They will continue the tradition of our name and remain a friend and guardian to all magical folk."

The crowd fell silent and allowed the Winter King to approach the couple. "I shall miss you, my friends. Yet, I understand the burden the long years have been on your mortal lives. May you relish your final years, and may you be blessed with hordes of mischievous grandchildren."

He then turned to Stefan. "Bring your bride forward."

They stepped reverently to Loli and Bryndle and bowed. "Our wings, your will." They recited the vow in unison.

Bryndle laid his hand over Stefan's heart, and Loli's hand rested over Sabrina's heart. "*O'rishe Mondùr Baleen...* Our favor sustain you until we meet again."

The blessing bestowed, the pixies fluttered their wings and showered the young couple with thousands of tiny lights as the remaining guests formed a procession to present their gifts.

Elsbeth took the opportunity to pull Devlin away from the festivities. "Let's walk on the grounds and let Stefan and Sabrina have their moment."

They made it as far as the Wishing Tree when the Winter King caught up to them. "Sneaking away, eh?"

Devlin gave a little laugh. "A couple should be able to spend some time alone on their anniversary, don't you think?"

"Of course." A contemplative look softened his features. "Have you given any thought to what you will do now?

"Yes," Devlin answered. "We will age and grow old, and go contentedly into the beyond knowing we have lived, and loved, to the fullest." He pointed to the eastern edge of the estate. "In the little manor house just over there."

The Winter King squinted into the dawn. "How much Spring Nectar have you imbibed? I see no manor house."

"Did you meet our recent houseguest, Lexie?" Elsbeth asked. "She is a remarkable woman. Designs houses. And she has painted such a vivid picture of the manor, we feel as if it is already our home."

"The lady not of our time? I did not have the pleasure of meeting her, no, but I noticed the... aura of lost years about her."

"Yes. Finn brought her here from the future." Elsbeth sighed. "You should hear the wonders she describes."

"Perhaps I shall seek her company on the morrow. Now, these old bones seek the comfort of my bed." He winked at them. "Something I daresay will afflict the two of you soon enough."

They watched him walk back to the manor house, and Devlin

hugged her close. "Do you fear the coming ailments and afflictions?"

"No. Not as long as you are by my side."

"Alw—" He started to answer, but a pair of ribbons on the Wishing Tree caught his attention. "Look, this pairing…"

Elsbeth left the warmth of his arms and inspected the tangled ribbons. One of them was only red half the way down, then turned black as coal to the end. The second one had a sliver of a brown stripe that started at the same point the first turned black.

"I've never seen this before. The Ghillie Dhu who planted this tree told me a black ribbon is an indication of a broken soul."

Clearly concerned, Devlin asked "To whom do they belong?"

She delicately looked to see the names on the ribbons. "Christenson and Andromeda," she choked.

"He will suffer horrific agony. Andromeda will suffer the pain and tragedy with him, but survive."

"Christenson?" He furrowed his brow. "I do not recall a Christenson on the guest list? Something impedes their love and they separate?"

"No, they are true soul mates. The ribbons are intertwined." Elsbeth stroked Andromeda's ribbon. "Poor dear girl, she stays by his side even through some dreadful catastrophe."

"Can we discover who this Christenson is and possibly avert this crisis?"

She looked at him with a sympathetic smile. "Always wanting to fix things and save the day." She took him by the arm and started the walk back to the castle. "The Wishing Tree only shows the truth. I remember the smile and happiness I saw on Andromeda's face while she danced with a cloaked figure. His back was to me, but it must have been this Christenson. I know nothing of him, but even if we were to find him, there would be naught we could do or say to keep them apart."

Devlin commented "Then we will endeavor to rejoice with her during the joyful times and not lose sight of her. When the trouble comes, we will not abandon her or this Christenson."

Elsbeth stopped walking and took his face in her hands. "My love, your heart and caring are why I fell in love with you." She kissed him. "I should need a day or two of not visiting with Andromeda for fear I will burst into tears."

Devin wrapped his arms around her. "Dear, we will find a way to help them."

They silently returned to the castle. The wind rose, and a lost mask rolled across the lawn, bumping and bouncing 'til it was stopped by the trunk of the Wishing Tree. The wind's strength increased and caused the leaves to rustle and the ribbons to flutter, but the silken strands held fast to their pairings, as if knowing a storm approached.